The
Witch Hill
Murder

The Witch Hill Murder

(A Superintendent Capricorn Mystery)

Pauline Glen Winslow

St. Martin's Press   New York

For Sheila and Lawrie, with love.

Library of Congress Cataloging in Publication Data

Winslow, Pauline Glen.
The Witch Hill murder.

I. Title.
PZ4.W78Wi3   [PR6073.I553]   823'.9'14   76-28068
                ISBN 0-312-88428-1

Prologue

NOAH HIGHTOWER

Year 1, A.S. (After Siderea)
Summer

The summer that Noah Hightower formed his Army of the Stars was very warm. June 30, the official Founding Day, was not only the hottest June 30 in England's history of weather recording but also the hottest day in the memory of the people of England. Daines Barington, a small market town, though surrounded by fields and meadow, suffered with the rest of the country. The slopes of neighbouring Witch Hill were oppressed by the sun that glared out of a glazed Wedgwood blue sky. The grass gave up its green, the mayweed drooped, the loosestrife curled on its stem. In the hedges the wild strawberries withered. Quiet hung over the somnolent countryside, cows and sheep drowsed and no birds sang. Only the great rooks wheeling overhead gave their rasping cry.

Positively the hottest place in the neighbourhood, and perhaps in the country, was the makeshift auditorium that had once been a cluster of greenhouses up at Witch Hill Manor, lately bought by Noah Hightower for himself and his disciples. The sun, high in the sky, poured through the glass panes onto the tightly-packed audience. Somehow about three hundred people had been crammed into the small space, squeezed on platforms, sharing chairs, lining the walls, and standing four and five deep in the doorway: people of all ages, races and conditions, all sticky with sweat, oblivious of their discomfort, their eyes bright and enormous, their attention consumed by the fantastic figure on the platform.

There looming over them was Hightower, looking larger than life size. He wore bush clothes like a white hunter complete with belt and revolver but hatless, and the sunlight blazed on his huge mane of red hair and lit it up into a conflagration as though that had been the sun's purpose, the reason and the meaning of the scorching afternoon.

Hightower laughed and roared, and his audience laughed and roared with him. He threw his arms wide apart as though he embraced them all, and roared again with a flash of leonine teeth.

'Man is celestial!'

'Man is celestial!' they echoed.

'*You* know,' he beamed on every one present, from the portly woman closest to him with the air and dignity of a classical matron, to a lean youth with hot brown eyes in the front row, over to the smallest child sitting on the furthest side of the doorway. 'You all know. But *everyone* must know. Everyone on the planet. They must all be cleansed. The rubbish of the ages must be cleaned from their minds.'

His audience roared with enthusiasm.

'We will begin here. Right here!'

He pounded his fist on the lectern until it quaked and shattered, to the delight of his watchers.

'This is what must happen to people's earthly minds!' he shouted, picking up the broken pieces and flourishing them widely.

'We can do it! We will start here in Daines Barington, and wake the town up! Smash its ideas! Clean it clean! And from Daines Barington, our earthly base, we will reach out over the planet.'

As he spoke of the town a faint flicker of worry touched the usually calm features of the dignified matron closest to him. She alone in the crowd was not caught up in the frenzy as Hightower swept on.

'Siderea saves!'

'Siderea saves!'

The audience screamed and roared. An old man laughed until his spectacles slid down his wet nose and crashed to the floor; he paid no heed to them, but only to the figure on the platform. A pregnant woman felt her child's first kick and screamed louder, trying to call for them both. A young girl in the front row wearing a thin white blouse so wet that the fabric clung to her breasts appeared to be half naked, but she was unaware of her state and the young men who sat on either side of her paid no attention either, but with all their energy yelled back at the speaker.

'Cleanse the planet! Cleanse the planet!'

'Man must be separated from his body!' The speaker's voice seemed equal in amplitude to that of his assembled crowd.

'Separated from his body.'

'Then man will know he is not a piece of meat! He will know himself to be a spirit! An immortal, all-powerful spirit of the stars!'

'Sidereal,' the pregnant woman called ecstatically, and felt her child move again, as if in affirmation.

'Sidereal,' muttered a little boy, about six years old, red-faced, intent.

'All you need to know is the Paths. And that's what you're here to learn! And I'll say this,' the speaker added, beaming, 'You are the goddamnedest best, brightest, smartest set of pupils and ensigns ever collected together on the face of this poor, old suffering earth!'

The audience applauded wildly.

'We are going to lead humanity out of the pit! We are going to take man from the mud of the millenia to the stars! And we are going to do it Right Now! No waiting for the Messiah! No hanging around for Gabriel's Horn! *Right Now!*'

The audience beat approval, stomping their feet rhythmically on the floor.

'That's it!' the speaker yelled. 'Did you make those feet touch the floor?'

'Yes,' the three hundred screamed as one.

'Good! Now You make those hands touch each other!'

They beat their hands, each one against his neighbours'.

'Fine! Did You make those hands do that?'

'YES!'

'GOOD!'

The sun was now directly behind the speaker and he blazed and seemed to expand.

'And now, the task is to move You around! You know all the Paths. For you, the aware people, Sidereans born, all You need is Path One.

'BE ON ALDEBERAN!'

'Now, did You do that?'

'Yes!' Each replied, without looking at his neighbour. 'Yes!'

'GOOD!'

'Now, for people who can't do that, but are in very good shape, Path Two.

'BE ON THE SUN.'

'Did You do that?'

'Yes, yes,' they chanted.

'Then, for the group slightly worse off, there is Path Three.

'BE ON THE MOON.'

'Did You do that?'

'Yes, yes.'

'And for the guy who can't even find his way down to Daines Barington,' the speaker chuckled. 'Well, there is Path Four. If he can't get there, let him pull it here.

'Take Daines Barington and stuff it into You!'

'Did You do that?'

'Yes!'

'Great!'

From the pasture came a lowing of cows, perhaps in response, perhaps in protest of the heat, or perhaps just in protest.

'And you will have all the Paths, all the way down, from the guy who can get to Aldeberan, to the poor bastard who can just get the idea there is such a thing as a pea. For everyone on the planet, there's a Sidereal Path. Forty-four Paths for the human race, that's not an earth race and never was! Forty-four Paths!'

'Forty-four Paths,' his watchers intoned.

'And that takes care of everyone! Everyone! Down to the lowest, meanest, rottenest son-of-a-bitch who ever lived. A Hitler! A Stalin! They can all be separated, cleansed!'

'Siderea saves!' moaned a girl in the front row, a heavy-set girl with stringy hair and eyes wildly rolling. Her lower lip drooped and she dribbled slightly.

The speaker, whose glance had fallen on her, looked away. He tilted his face up into the sun. For a moment his face relaxed into a look half-mischievous, half-bored, as if the assent of his worshippers was becoming dull.

'But suppose there was someone that none of the paths worked on?' he said softly. 'What then?'

For a moment the audience faltered, their shining eagerness halted by a break in the familiar pattern, clouded by a second of doubt.

The speaker laughed and roared, bathed in his red aureole, Lucifer transcendant.

'Well, there's always Path 45!'

'Forty-five?' The audience was hushed now, a little confused at the interjection of something new.

From his belt he drew a pistol and pointed it straight from the hip in the exaggerated stance of an actor in a Western film.

'We've got to get the bastard out of that body!'

He brandished the gun in a wild arc about his head.

'Path 45! If nothing else works, there's Path 45!'

The matronly woman stared up at him, her mouth open, her face a study in dismay.

Hightower threw his head back, looked at his startled followers and roared with laughter.

'Path 45!'

The sun gleamed on the arcing pistol, the audience got to their feet and roared in return.

'Path 45!'

'Avenging angels; righteous assassins,' the murmur was started, no one quite knew where, but it seemed to come from the vicinity of the loose-lipped girl in the front. It was like a spark in a field of dried-out hay, blazing.

'Path 45!'

'When all else fails, Path 45.'

'Path 45! Path 45!'

Book One

RICHARD BREWSTER

Year 3, A.S.
Spring

one

If it were not for the Sidereans, there would never have been a
Moo-Cow Milk Bar in Daines Barington. The people of the town ate
at home, or at the restored Tudor Roseacre House, known for its service and fine cooking, or they drove to the equivalent of Roseacre
House elsewhere. They did not require 'Quick Service, No Tipping,
Food To Take Out. Please Do Not Ask For Credit.' Nor would they
care for the interior, chromium and white plastic, already shabby
after a few months' use, ornamented by the head of a demented-
looking brown cow that hung over the counter.

But the Sidereans, who were not fed at the Manor, found it a
godsend. The food was bad but cheap and there they ate with each
other; only a few young people wandered in from the town. Since
Hightower had left the country two years before to build his mysterious Ark, tension had grown between Town and Manor. The Sidereans, although professionally calm, were by now uncomfortable in

9

the presence of the townspeople who had become openly hostile at the sight of a Siderean uniform.

The young counterman, a newcomer to Daines Barington who was saving his money, hoping one day to study Siderea, watched the group covertly. It was certainly a wild uniform: scarlet tights, purple leather boots and belts. Their short purple cloaks hung on the hooks by the door, topped by the silver helmets that he himself had seen light up in the dark. Hightower had put them in uniform when he left the country, people said. They added that he certainly did not want his followers to escape notice.

Except for the uniform they seemed ordinary enough, eating and drinking the same as earth people, he thought, amused at his little joke. Four of them sat at a corner table underneath a banner they had put up—he wasn't going to tell them not to!—'Siderea Saves!'

Three of them were young, but there was one middle-aged lady. She was tall and rather stout, very dignified, and wore a skirt instead of the tights and kept her cloak folded around her. All of them were decorated with striking flashes and emblems, a glittering gold braid 'S' a foot long, spread across the chest, gold or silver bars on the shoulder, a metallic 'NH' clasping the belts and the older lady's cloak. The counterman didn't know it, but he was looking at the highest officers of the Siderean organization. Only high officials could have been in the Moo-Cow at that time, for the meal they were eating, although indistinguishable from the dinner, was actually lunch. Students, non-coms and ensigns were not given time enough for lunch in town and had to make do with sandwiches and thermos bottles that they kept in the damp cloakrooms, believed to be converted outhouses, up at the Manor.

The four pushed their cups and plates aside and returned to studying the papers they had brought in with them. Whatever the papers contained was apparently not to their liking, as they had looked glumly at them before, and now the young man with the dark curly hair, not soothed by his meal, was furious. He smashed his fist on the table.

'That bastard Brewster,' he shouted. 'He's really done it to us.'

'Come now, Jed,' the middle-aged woman spoke calmly. 'As the law stands, he had to do what he did.'

'Hark at Portia the just. Always full of sweet reasonableness,' the young woman intervened. Thick set, with drab stringy hair, she had a strong and determined look and gazed on the lean and handsome

10

Jed with favour and then turned, with marked hostility, to Portia, who was regretting her Christian name perhaps for the thousandth time.

'But Noreen—' she tried to interject.

'You don't think it means anything that Brewster disallowed *our* plans but he okayed the extension of the Gosport Nursing Home and Merrydale College? "Merrydale for Merry Girls," ' she mimicked the school slogan and snorted. 'Plenty of space for those giggling idiots but——.'

'The nursing home and the school received planning permission because they weren't, originally, private residences,' Portia explained, once again. She pointed to the plans of the Witch Hill estate, unrolled before them on the not too clean table, resisting an urge to ask for a cloth to clean it up—it would be too much to expect the counterman to do it himself, she thought resignedly. He was too busy staring at them as he leaned against the tea urn, apparently holding it up. But if she did it herself, Noreen would mutter about compulsive cleanliness. Better to let it go. The young people were antagonistic enough already.

Her finger moved over the plans, showing the manor house itself with the land and all the outbuildings. 'You see, this is pasture and——.'

'Stow it!' Noreen said brutally and looked up at Jed for approbation, but he had sprung from his seat and was pacing about, too tense to sit, treading between the close-packed tables like an angry cat.

'He could have arranged permission if he wanted to,' Jed said bitterly. 'You know he's the law around here. And now look at that!'

They looked, perhaps for the fiftieth time, at the white notice. Portia, the first up, had found it on their main gate that morning. The day before, Jed and Noreen had conducted a demonstration at the Town Hall to agitate for a settlement of their request for planning permission, and had been confident of their success.

'We *showed* Brewster,' Noreen had exulted.

But the white notice had been wired onto the gate and the workmen that Jed had engaged to work upon the foundation of the new building (Why Wait? had been his watchword) had disappeared with all their tools and equipment.

'Notice,' was the heading and it looked at first glance innocuous enough. But a section of the local law was quoted, pointing out that the construction taking place on the north pasture of Witch Hill was

11

in contravention of the law and that anyone engaged in that work was liable to prosecution and imprisonment.

It had been a fine, sunny morning. The large hole in the ground, dug out at such expense, had gaped up at them. The piles of brick and stone ordered by Jed and paid for in cash—no one would give credit to Sidereans—loomed embarrassingly.

Jed was pacing about again, two hot red patches suffusing his cheeks. Portia watched him curiously, wondering about the intensity of his anger. Of course, Jed was hot-tempered. And this was a big blow. Hightower had made him Commander-in-Chief just before he left to go off and build what he called his Intergalactic Ark. Jed had seemed to her too young and inexperienced for the job, but it was Noah's decision. A surprising one, except for that other, wretched, business—but of course it had nothing to do with that. Very likely there was nothing to 'that' anyway. She put the thought out of her mind. Of course, Noah understood that young people could forge ahead, and not worry about possibilities and probabilities as older heads would do, and he had certainly been right there. Siderean growth had been phenomenal, though at the expense of the good will of the town.

And now Jed had failed in the one thing he had been directly commanded to do. Expand. EXPAND!!!!!! The word had come from Noah himself: they had already expanded to include more people than they could possibly accomodate, and he had ordered them to enlarge their premises by building an annex on the north pasture. He was right; it was inevitable; they had already converted every last hen house and pigsty on the property. And Noah himself had been friendly with Brewster and expected no trouble. If he heard that Jed had failed, he would have no compunction about reducing his Commander-in-Chief to private. That could happen, in Siderea, in five minutes. And Portia knew Jed well enough to know that her Commander-in-Chief, who had been a general at twenty-four, would never, ever, be willing to be a private, in the legions of heaven——or hell, for that matter. He looked now as if he were burning with fever.

'They knew we were going ahead, and they didn't say anything, those beasts,' Noreen blurted out, suddenly schoolgirlish.

'Those bastards,' the fourth member of the group, an apple-cheeked, flaxen-haired boy, echoed with a menacing bang of his fist.

12

His round blue eyes, like Noreen's small hazel ones, followed Jed worshipfully.

Portia sighed. It was true that Jed had applied, quite properly, for planning permission to make the necessary changes. Richard Brewster, in accordance with his duty as Town Clerk, had refused. Jed, in accordance with Siderea principle, had gone ahead anyway.

'How they dare!' he muttered.

Portia knew very well how they dared. The town had its laws and the power to enforce them. The wants of Siderea were as nothing to the Town Council. During the last two years the inhabitants of Daines Barington had come to wish that all of Hightower's followers would go away, preferably to the mysterious Ark outside the British Isles.

For the Sidereans were determined proselytizers, as they had to be in accordance with Noah's teaching, and of all the people in the world, Portia considered, the inhabitants of Daines Barington least wanted to be proselytized. Rich, orderly, secure, they considered that heaven was likely to fall short of their town, and their present neighbours to be better company than angels and archangels, who might not play bridge. It was a pity that Noah had picked such an area to be Siderea's earthly base. The Army of the Stars had found many great metaphysical reasons why he had done so, but Portia knew that price had been the main inducement. Witch Hill Manor had sold for a modest sum. And Noah, though he could make great fortunes, could also spend them, and at that time had been pinched for money. In those days, before Jed had arrived, Portia had kept the financial records.

'It's war!' Jed shouted.

'War!' echoed the apple-cheeked boy.

'Don't, Chris,' Portia said wearily. 'Must it be war? After all, Noah has said himself we're all celestial beings, even the people in this town. *He* got on all right with them when he was here.'

That's the best line to take, she thought; that's it.

'And you know I met Brewster: I spoke to him when we first came here, and he seemed a very decent sort,' she went on. 'He was going to give us the permit for the lunch room, before Noah decided we didn't need it.'

She looked sadly at her plate, as she was not fond of overdone hamburgers and chips. 'Brewster only signs the papers, it's the Town

Council that decides, not the Clerk.'

'Clerk,' Jed repeated sarcastically. 'Some Clerk. Look at that great house of his and his cars and his servants, and his sister, Miss High and Mighty of the town. Rolling in graft, he must be.'

The counterman looked up from the coffee urn, the place at the counter nearest the group, which he had been wiping over and over in desultory fashion with a dirty cloth all during the conversation.

'They says in town that the Brewsters 'as always been rich,' he interjected. 'They're real nobs, they are.'

Jed glared at him.

'This is a private conference, dammit,' he shouted. 'You listen in, you'll have our Assassins after you.'

Portia winced.

'Yes, I'll say it, Portia,' he rounded on her. 'We're a beachhead in enemy territory, and they might as well know we're here. And it's no use you looking like a shrinking violet, because we've had it out in Council. Noah authorized the Assassins, and that's that!'

It was useless to point out again that Path 45 and the Assassins was one of Hightower's jokes. The young Sidereans were ardent, they were faithful, but they none of them had much sense of humour and Noah had too much. He just had to tease his worshippers once in a while. Then no one was more surprised than he when he found he had been taken seriously. Portia had reminded him gloomily of Henry II and Thomas a Becket, but the idea had made him laugh prodigiously. Fortunately the Assassins, a group headed by Jed Frost himself, with Noreen as chief lieutenant, although much feared among Sidereans with rumour puffing the unlikely to the incredible, did very little outside the group. A few nasty anonymous letters, Portia knew, was the furthest they had ever gone.

'Have you seen what they said about us in last Sunday's papers?' she remarked, hoping to change the subject. 'Pictures, too.'

'Let's see,' Jed said shortly, looking quickly to see if he appeared.

'SIDEREANS DESTROYING QUIET MARKET TOWN,' the headlines screamed. A photograph showed Portia, cloaked and helmeted, apparently brandishing a staff at an old lady.

'What *were* you doing?' Jed asked, crossly.

Portia studied the picture.

'Pointing out the way to Woolworth's, I think.'

He pulled open The Views of the Globe. The centre fold showed young Sidereans, male and female, jumping about clad only in tights and boots.

'WITCH HILL MANOR, OLD HOME OF BATTLE OF BRITAIN HERO, NOW USED FOR ORGIES OF HIGHTOWER'S FOLLOWERS.'

In one corner, framed in black, was a photograph of an attractive young man in RAF uniform.

The story began:

'What do we do to Britain's Heroes and their Families? Ron Gaylord, holder of DFC, killed in 1940—and his family have to sell their ancestral home for taxes. Gaylord's father was killed on the Marne. A Gaylord died at Majuba Hill. Now who enjoys the benefits of their heroic sacrifice?'

An arrow pointed to the cavorting Sidereans.

'What on earth was that?' asked Portia, peering at the photographs.

'Friday night get-together,' Noreen made out, after some brainracking. 'That was the night we learned some South African folk dance. But how could they have got that picture?'

'Photographer in the bushes,' Jed said in disgust. 'What a sod. It even looks like an orgy.'

They laughed, gloomily. Hightower, as far as his followers were concerned, was strict on the subject of sex.

'We can't frighten the yokels,' he had said, beaming, before his departure. 'Cleansing the planet, that's the goal. Nothing must interfere. So—we play by their rules. No sex, unless you're married. And then,' he said firmly, 'only with the person you're married to. Get it? And as far as Daines Barington is concerned, better no socializing at all, and you'll stay out of trouble. Saving, not socializing, that's what we're here for! There'll be pains and penalties for backsliders.'

There were backsliders, but the pains and penalties were severe and the efforts to comply were strenuous.

Jed was still looking at the paper.

'You notice the way they make it seem our fault this dead guy's family got kicked out? Foreign usurpers, it says down at the bottom. And they were sold up in '41, Noah told me. He bought it from some Indian who took it and then couldn't stand the cold. I don't blame him—no damn heat in a great place like that. Brewster ought to be shot.'

'But Jed,' Portia remonstrated, 'Brewster doesn't control the London papers.'

'All those old farts are in cahoots,' he said gloomily. 'Well, we have to do *something*.'

'Perhaps we should wait a while and let it cool off,' Portia ventured. 'Right now everyone is upset. In the meantime we could partition the ballroom in the main block. I've looked it over, and it wouldn't be as big a job as we thought. And after a while the law might be changed. There's still a chance; Brewster told me himself. They were meeting on it yesterday when you had the demonstration.'

She spoke mildly, but her listeners caught the implied criticism. Portia had been opposed to the demonstration and had refused to join it. Three young faces now glared at her. Brewster's name had been on the letter rejecting their appeal and on the notice stopping the work. Five hundred Sidereans now considered Brewster to be the devil, though on a larger scale: for the devil was of this world, whereas they were of the stars. And Brewster was stopping their spread and development, their reach into the galaxy.

'He makes the devil look like a piker,' Jed proclaimed, his back turned to them, looking out of the windows at the calm and peaceful High Street as though he saw a vision of Super-Hell. Christopher jumped up to join him and scowled in support, and Noreen Stacy went over and glowered with both of them.

Portia felt uneasy. She knew Jed didn't want to lose his job: it had been a great honour when he got it, surprising many Sidereans, as he was not only young in years but junior as a follower of Hightower. Nevertheless he had got the appointment and now he was in danger of losing it. In the Army of the Stars any failure meant instant loss of rank. And, despite Jed's great fervour for the Cause, Portia sometimes suspected that if he were reduced to private he might desert entirely, at any rate for a while. He was that kind of young man. But just the same his present agitation was out of all proportion, and he was whipping up other Sidereans to a very unhealthy hate. Noreen, usually so hardheaded, would follow the handsome Jed at a whistle, and Christopher Venable, though a bright boy, at nineteen was very impressionable and could be worked on easily by Jed, whom he admired. She was sorry that young Christopher had been made a full colonel and so a senior Siderean, fourth in command. It would have been much better if the tall Texan, Garry Wyatt, had taken the post. He was quiet, level-headed, and experienced in command—he had served in the Vietnam war. How strange it must be, she thought parenthetically, to be, without a wound, a veteran of a war that was still going on. But Garry wanted to go home.

'You can't imagine this is personal with Mr Brewster,' she said. 'He's a busy, important man in London. He just does this work for the town because he lives here and—'

'Not personal!' Jed exploded. 'Portia, you're a fool.'

Yes, I am, she thought. To tell Jed he was not the centre of every universe could only cause disbelief.

'You know what Noah has said,' Noreen contributed. 'Anyone who isn't with us is against us. And they have to be got out of the way. They can't block our route to the stars!'

Noah said a lot of things, Portia thought grimly, but he went off and left other people to be responsible for them. She knew what Jed and Noreen were thinking of. It was in the minds of young Siderearns a lot more than was good for them. No good to explain that it all happened because it was so hot that day in the old greenhouse. It was hot, and they were all excited—she knew, she had been there; in fact, she, Noreen and Jed were the only ones left of the original group who had been there, for the rest it was all gossip and rumour—and Noah had been having a lovely time. Noah ate enthusiasm the way other people breathed air. It had mounted higher and higher, until it got to a pitch that could not be surpassed. And then suddenly, as he often did at such moments, Noah got bored. His disciples, he had confided to Portia on occasion, were a good lot but dull. Noah hated to be bored. On such occasions he would dream up anything, just for mischief. Like a little boy. Portia was a grandmother and knew all about little boys. She knew Noah to be a great visionary and a great man, but he was also a child. Still, she knew from hard experience that she couldn't argue with the young people. They would only consider her too old and stodgy. Rebellious for a moment, she felt like reminding them that she was not much older than Hightower himself. Then she laughed at herself for illogic, for she had just been thinking of him as a child. Perhaps the youngsters were closest to him after all.

Jed seemed to tune in on her thought.

'All right Portia, you're the eldest officer, and you're in charge of communications. Do you want to cable Noah we've failed in the most important thing he's asked us to do? D'you think he'll like that?'

'No, but we can wait and try again,' she said. 'We might win people round. A lot of other people would like to see the planning laws changed. But if the Assassins start making threats the town will get furious.'

'That lot of walking meat is panicked anyway,' Noreen pronounced. 'We've cured some of their idiots and healed some of their sick. You know how that sets them off. Wogs!''

'We've got to attack,' Jed shouted. 'Attack.'

'But it must be better to wait,' Portia protested again.

'Now you sound like a wog, Portia,' Noreen said incisively. 'What's the matter, are you afraid? *Wait! Perhaps it will work out!* Let the earth roll round and round and we'll all be dead. That's static thinking. If we don't expand, we're dying. It's the law of this universe!'

'Right on,' the others chanted. Portia sighed and sat back. It was one of Hightower's favourite speeches.

'Expand! Grow! And this minute!'

'This minute!'

'Waiting is dying!'

'Movement is life!'

'And I tell you,' Jed shouted, 'we'll act. Brewster has had his chance. I've offered him all the Paths. And he's refused. So you know what's left. The hell with the town! Let them wait! Life for us! Death for them! There's always Path 45!'

Oh, no, not that rubbish, Portia thought crossly. Oh, blast you, Noah, with your Wild West jokes and your big grin. Blast you for leaving the country and taking that girl and not Jed. Jed was just spouting off, of course, for the benefit of his admirers, but she hated that kind of talk.

'Siderea Saves,' she said grimly.

They paid their bills and took their helmets from the hooks. Portia struggled to balance hers over the chignon which she wore as a solution to the problem of what to do with her hair when she had no time to get it set. Feeling silly, she had to fasten the strap under her chin. Another one of Noah's jokes. How he would laugh to see her looking like this, and that young counterboy gawping as if they were a group of circus performers. Jed seemed to have quieted down but the red spots still burned high in his cheeks and his hot brown eyes glittered sullenly.

'Life for us,' Noreen cried exultantly, linking her arm with Jed's.

'Death for our enemies! Path 45!'

'Path 45,' Jed repeated, slowly.

'Path 45?' Portia looked around from the corner where she had been surreptitiously trying to adjust her cloak to a dignified level, thoroughly exasperated with the childish display.

But the only answer was the bang of the door. The others had already gone.

two

To outward appearance, the next day seemed to begin well at Brewster House. The sun shone warmly on the perfect Georgian mansion, set in its well-kept gardens, crowning a gentle slope with the road to the town before it and the river Baring glinting in a curve around.

Richard Brewster, first thing on waking, looked from his bedroom window over to his apple orchards. Yes, the sun had brought them to full bloom, mile upon mile of pink and white blossom holding a promise of splendid crops—the usually splendid crops, for the Brewster lands were the best in the county, a rich mixture of clay and sand, unlike what was left of the Manor lands to the west, good only for grazing. The Brewster ancestors had chosen well.

But today that thought did not give him the usual pleasure. The day before had been his birthday. He was fifty-five. His shaving glass reflected a well set up man with clear grey eyes and the glow of perfect health, but he hardly saw the reflection, as he moved about still in the shadow of his dream.

Last night he had gone to bed at the usual time, after the usual card party, with his usual guests. His stepsister's guests, rather. But the spring had troubled his sleep: an image, pink and white as his apple blossom, had flitted through it, now erotic, now chaste, an image of a lady who had not been a guest, and would not be.

Already, below his window, his stepsister Beatrice was busy in the garden. She was working in the steep escarpment that fell away from the drawing-room terrace. The escarpment was carefully planted with bushes and rambling roses that wound behind a chunky, primitive grey stone Madonna, which stood at the base line of the house, staring blindly towards the river.

Beatrice herself looked square and chunky. Her short, dark hair was cut like a man's, and her heavy tweed coat and skirt accented her dumpy figure. The very image of the settled spinster, Brewster thought with a sigh. His little stepsister was over forty. As he watched she was spreading a paste of some poisonous chemicals around the stems of her shrubs, destroying insects that might threaten her garden before they were born.

She looked up at him and smiled, and her rather heavy, sallow face flashed for a moment into attractiveness.

'We're going to have roses well into the autumn this year, Ricky,' she called. 'You'll see, it's a splendid year for the rose.'

Beatrice, it was said in the town, lived only for her stepbrother's approbation and pleasure. Now she had used his pet name, which she did rarely, prosaic and dignified as she was; Brewster tried to respond to her mood, but for some reason he found it hard to be interested. His love for the garden and house was almost as great as her own, but the shadow of his dream was still with him, dogging his steps to the dining room, where it hung over his chair and spoiled his appetite for his excellent breakfast.

As her mother had done before her, Beatrice served breakfast in the great dining room instead of the little breakfast parlour where the male Brewsters had eaten rather casually when the house was without a mistress. That morning the long double doors to the drawing room and the terrace were still open, left that way since the party of the night before. Each room was long and beautifully proportioned, two stories high. A picture gallery ran the length of the dining room wall; from its centre, a life-sized portrait of his dead stepmother dominated both rooms.

For the first time in his life, Brewster, watching Beatrice pour his coffee, her square hands with short, gardener's fingernails dealing practically if not gracefully with the delicate Cozzi china, felt that he and his sister were inadequate to their surroundings. So much beauty and elegance as a setting—for what?

Flower scents drifted in from the garden, daffodil, crocus, and the outlawed periwinkle that sprang up everywhere, disturbingly sweet, drawing him back to his dream.

'Beatrice, you've never called on Mrs Lavender, have you?' he said casually, nibbling on a piece of toast without tasting it.

'Lavender?' Beatrice wrinkled her forehead. 'I don't think we know . . .'

Brewster was certain she knew who Mrs Lavender was. A fierce chatelaine, Beatrice did her ordering in person and went into town at least twice a week. She could hardly have missed sight and mention of the beautiful, rich and well-dressed Mrs Lavender, who had charmed the whole town and had even affected that permanent celibate, the Rector. At last night's bridge table the Rector, Geoffrey Theale, Jasper Norris, the bank manager and Chauncey Hartle, the town lawyer, had spoken of her in very admiring terms when Beatrice had certainly been present.

'You've heard me speak of her,' he said shortly. 'The widow with the asthmatic young daughter. She bought the old Drew place.'

'A lovely house,' Beatrice said absently, with the air of a woman with more important things on her mind. She turned aside to give some instructions to the parlourmaid and sent a reprimand to the girls who were audibly running the vacuum cleaners. This was never permitted while Brewster was in the house, but for once, in a continuation of his odd mood, he felt no gratitude for the attention. Instead, as Beatrice poured his second cup of coffee, he had a sudden picture of another pair of hands: white, slender, pink-tipped, that hovered gracefully, in seeming inconsequence, but were, though dainty, just as practical. He could not help thinking how agreeable those hands would look performing the same office.

'She isn't anyone, is she?'

Brewster knew his sister was not denying Mrs Lavender's physical existence, but her social one, as he had known she would. In her view, Mrs Lavender did not exist as a person to be called on, however rich and well-dressed she might be or irreproachable her character. Mrs Lavender's parents were not distinguished and her late husband had made his money as a linendraper. Lavender shops were known in cities all over England and that, as far as Beatrice was concerned, was that. Useless to remark, Brewster knew, that nowadays a very small portion of the Brewster money came from their land and that the Brewster name was synonymous with commercial enterprise. Beatrice had all the social prejudice of her mother, the aristocratic Roman lady.

As if to emphasize her remarks Beatrice glanced up at the portrait

22

of the Roman lady herself. It was the people of Daines Barington who had called her the Roman lady. Mrs Brewster, though an old and honourable title, did not seem impressive enough for such an aristocrat, and the word Italian, to them, conjured up associations of ice cream and spaghetti. And so the Roman lady she had remained, although to the young Richard Brewster she had never been anything but Lucrezia. She smiled down from the canvas in a familiar pose, glancing over her shoulder, a mischievous, careless look, as if acknowledging a conspirator, or deluding a fool.

Brewster considered, not for the first time, how odd it was that Beatrice, inheriting so much from her mother physically, should look so entirely different. Both women were small, dark-haired, brown-eyed, thin-lipped, quick of speech. To add to the resemblance, each had a mole on her left cheek. Yet Beatrice, in contrast to the sparkling continental dragon-fly, was entirely the staid English spinster, and all without one drop of English blood, for her father, Lucrezia's first husband, had been another poor though aristocratic Roman.

Aristocracy, or the lack of it, was Beatrice's theme at the moment, as she commented on the gathering of the night before. Theale the Rector, Hartle the lawyer, both bachelors, and Dr Bailey, a widower, all of old county stock, were her preferred guests, in spite of Dr. Bailey's tendency, which she deplored, to be late or even absent from her table if the health of one of his patients demanded the sacrifice. She secretly felt such devotion to duty somewhat middle class. Yesterday Dr Bailey had sent a message that he might be late or not arrive at all, at the whim of an infant about to be born. So she had been forced to ask Jasper Norris. Against Norris was the fact that he was in business, although his business was banking; and he was a 'newcomer' to the county—his family had only been in residence about forty years. Also, he was married. In his favour, he was cousin to a lord. So Norris had been invited. His wife, of course, was ignored. Nor could Mrs Norris complain; bachelor evenings at Brewster House had become a tradition. Beatrice's invitations were never refused; her cook, her wine cellar and the service at her table were not to be matched in the experience of her guests, and the men enjoyed her occasional dry wit.

Norris, she was complaining, had put himself forward too much. Brewster recalled Norris had been very exercised about the Sidereans and the 'demonstration' they had made at the Council meeting that day, at which Norris and he had both been present. It had been an unproductive meeting, the first Brewster remembered. He had always run the Council—the Mayor's position was purely decorative—in a very efficient way. But the Sidereans certainly interfered with that.

After the yelling, screaming Army of the Stars had been cleared from the room, the meeting was still held up. It had been scheduled to discuss the new Town Planning scheme which he himself had promulgated. Daines Barington would remain residential in character, but some relief had to be afforded to the largest estates. Almost no one could keep them as single-family residences any more. Noah Hightower himself had been one of the chief advocates of the new law, as he wished to add to his buildings to bring in more followers.

'Our base for our route to the stars' his application said grandly, but it was filed with the others in 'Planning Permission 1, Cross Ref. Fee Simple.'

Unfortunately his followers, too eager, had brought the plan into disrepute. Although the townspeople wanted to help the other estate owners, they disliked the thought of encouraging more Sidereans. But Brewster himself thought the Sidereans would disappear one day as quickly as they had come and was not disposed to let their activities affect the running of the whole area.

He had gone to the meeting in good spirits, convinced he had enough votes to be successful. Then had come the demonstration, and afterwards it was found that the town engineer, who was supposed to have spoken in favour of the new plan, was absent. His daughter had just run off to join the Sidereans; his wife was in hysterics, and he, town engineer or not, had had to stay at her side. This situation, it transpired, was not uncommon, and the meeting had degenerated into a harangue against Hightower and his followers until Brewster had sensibly adjourned it.

Last night Norris had been in a choleric, table-thumping mood, insisting that the whole lot should be deported, grandly ignoring the fact that some of them, at least, were British.

'Why, why . . .' he had choked over the beef Wellington, 'they stopped my wife in the street the other day and told her to tell them her ruin! When she wouldn't answer one of them said she was sex-starved! Sex-starved!'

Brewster had not been able to look at Dr Bailey, who had arrived after all, too late for the soup, bragging about an eight-pound boy. Dr Bailey was a fine doctor, much loved in the town, but it was well known that he had a fault: Dr Bailey was a gossip. And from some hints that the doctor had dropped from time to time about the unfortunate state of Norris's health., Brewster deduced that the Sidereans had guessed correctly.

Beatrice was not interested in Mrs Norris's problems, nor in Norris's difficulties. He had had, she thought, far too much to say.

'For a newcomer,' she said, meaningfully.

'Really, Bee,' Brewster said in some exasperation, 'the Norrises have lived in Daines Barington nearly forty years. Norris has been coming to dinner here for seven.'

'And his wife is nobody,' she went on, 'no one at all.'

She had never called on Mrs Norris. Nor would she call on Mrs Lavender, Brewster knew, even when she had been there forty years.

'Lucrezia—' She always referred to her mother by her Christian name, as that lady had disliked any reference to her motherhood. In fact, she had been rather pleased if people took her daughter to be a mere niece or even a more distant relation. Beatrice brought her name up strongly now as an incantation that would end discussion.

'Lucrezia would have been astonished.'

Lucrezia would not have been astonished, because she would not have known any of the guests except for Geoffrey Theale. They were far too dull for Lucrezia. Back in the thirties, when she had first arrived, Theale wasn't yet a rector, or even a clergyman; he was merely the handsome, very young son of Sir Walter Theale, Bart, who had fallen in love with Lucrezia and written her some poems that were considered rather good.

He sighed. Lucrezia's snobbishness had been different from her daughter's. It had enlivened the stolid Brewsters, as she filled the house with a fine mixture of English and continental nobility, as well as the best brains and wits, enlarging their circle as she entertained on a scale unknown even at Witch Hill Manor since its great days, using the Brewster fortune to live as no Brewster had before. But Beatrice used her fastidiousness to diminish their acquaintance, snipping and pruning until it was almost gone. The war had come, Lucrezia and her husband had died, the nobility, the brains and wits had melted all away. Beatrice kept the house as a shrine to her dead mother and no women entered Brewster's life through her.

Rising, she rang the bell sharply for the table to be cleared, bade her brother good-bye and marched off towards the garden room. The subject of Mrs Lavender, obviously, was finished. Her calm assumption of his concurrence, her sturdy form, her heavy tread on the rug, her air of total confidence, stung him into speech.

'I should've thought you would be on Norris's side,' he called after her. 'A wild new religion upsetting the town.'

Beatrice glanced back over her shoulder, her hand on the door. She smiled, and for a moment he saw, disconcertingly, the ghost of Lucrezia.

'One heresy is much the same as another, isn't it?' she said sweetly, and left.

Got me there, Brewster thought, and had to laugh. Beatrice, of course, was a Catholic, something that he didn't think of often as she made no parade of it. Her quick malice reminded him of their youthful arguments when he, an adolescent boy, had been the protector of the small Italian girl, so quiet and awkward in Lucrezia's wake, thrown into an alien world, and yet as stubborn in her thoughts and ways as only a child can be. He was her friend, but 'Heretic!' she would say when she was angry, her eyes bright with scorn: a hissing kitten, he had called her, and his father observed that she had more anger than sense.

Smiling, he left by the garden way and paused for a moment outside the drawing room on the colonnade that ran the width of the house. Just below him the grey stone Madonna, the one purchase of his stepmother's that he had never liked, looked softer, more mellow in the warm sun.

There was a fresh, lilac-scented breeze. From the other side of the gardens came the blue glint of the river. Somewhere out of sight a linnet was singing a dreamy song that held a note of pleasant expectation, almost an exuberance, a promise of summer and unknown delights to come. Richard Brewster, looking over his land, felt a sudden rise of spirit, his exasperation with his sister quite gone. The linnet sang on, Beatrice was unimportant, the sun shone, the gardens glowed, the long reeds dipped into glittering water between the grassy banks. The whole of nature held a promise from which he, Richard Brewster, was not excluded.

In the town the ladies wore bright spring clothes and very pretty they looked, though one familiar figure was not among them. The nine forty-five pulled quietly out of the station on its way to London, the slow train, rarely taken by business men, useful if one wished to go up to town without causing comment. Brewster, who had had, through the years, various companions in London, had been quite a patron of the nine forty-five. Charming women, all of them, but none with whom he had wished to share his life in Daines Barrington, and he had kept the two existences separate. Lately he had been too busy, his life had been too full. But that was nothing to do with being fifty-five, he thought. Nothing at all.

He quickened his pace. He had to clear his mind to deal again with the problems of the new town plan. Certainly it should not be pushed aside merely because of the actions of a few foolish young people. It ought to have been dealt with long before, he knew that, but he had been away too much in the past year or two. Several old Brewster aunts and uncles had died childless and their properties had passed to him. The legacies had entailed a lot of business which most men would not have found unpleasant, but his acquisitions had left Brewster thoughtful and close to sadness. He had only one young male relation left, a son of a cousin and not a Brewster. A Londoner born and bred. The Brewsters of Daines Barington were dying out.

Almost at the gate of the Town Hall, he paused to admire the effect of the black beams against the plaster panels, the latter having been newly whitewashed. Daines Barington admired antiquity, but it also liked its buildings fresh and clean. Sunlight sparkled on the windows and seemed to be reflected in the spills of golden crocus that flowered in the neat beds by the gates, in window boxes and in any scrap of earth all the way down to the bank at one end of the street, where they might have been a gay heap of coin glinting through the gravel, and up to the church at the other, where the blossoms peeped more modestly among the sober graves. From the nearby fields the soprano call of young lambs sounded, and Brewster wondered, without quite realizing that he did, what small disturbance had upset the even tenor of their ways.

Hardly was the thought formed when he found himself suddenly accosted. His cool, dry hands were seized and held in a warm, moist, double grasp; a spearmint-smelling breath was over his face while a voice yelled, 'Siderea Saves!'

Brewster looked down on his attacker, who was, though he did not know it, Noreen Stacy. He saw a sturdy young woman encased in the scarlet Siderea tights, like a big German sausage, her large, pale eyes staring intently up into his own, staring so hard that it seemed the eyes might pop out on two stalks. Her bosom was heaving and she was yelling at him again from a distance of about six inches:

'Siderea Saves! Tell me your ruin! You can be saved today!'

He removed his hands from hers with dispatch, lifted his hat and said in his most matter-of-fact voice,

'Thank you, not today.'

Turning into the hall, he walked under the lovely four-centered arch, his eyes resting in the cool, filtered light. He remembered now that the Rector had been murmuring at dinner the night before somewhat disapprovingly about a lot of young women dressed in nothing but tights. It was not entirely disagreeable, Brewster considered. The Rector had to be professionally old-maidish about such things. Daines Barington was full of old maids and old bachelors.

The encounter, however, was not yet over. Noreen ran after him and grasped his hands again.

'Richard Brewster,' she said commandingly.

The Sidereans didn't believe in ordinary polite forms of address, he had noticed before. Nevertheless, they themselves had very imposing titles which they expected outsiders to observe. General seemed to be one of their lower ranks.

'Richard Brewster, did you pass the new Town Plan yesterday?'

Council business was made known to the public on the first Thursday after each meeting in the Daines Barington Record. Still, there was no reason not to tell the girl what she wanted to know. He had gathered, from the demonstration of the day before, that the Sidereans were very perturbed about the notice on their gates stopping the illegal construction. It had been purely a routine matter, of course, handled by the Department of Works, but there was no use explaining that. Probably it was no use trying to explain either that if they had (a) refrained from demonstrating, and (b) resisted the temptation to seduce the daughter of the town's engineer, his new law might have been passed yesterday and their troubles already would be over.

'The meeting was adjourned,' he said. 'Possibly for a month.'

The girl's rather heavy face darkened.

'You're holding us up,' she said bitterly. 'You're doing it on purpose, just to spite us.'

Brewster regarded her for a moment, wondering why she was so excited. Hightower himself had been entirely relaxed. Brewster had spoken to him about the new plan just before the Prophet went off to his Ark. Hightower had given his huge laugh, slapped Brewster on the back, and said he was happy to leave the matter in his hands. Further, he had offered Brewster a tankard of ginger beer, a drink of which the great man was very fond, and Brewster had had some difficulty in declining. He seemed to be having the same difficulty in

28

politely detaching himself from this limpet-like young woman.

'Madam, you are quite mistaken,' he said. 'I suggest you leave this matter in the hands of the Council. And now, if you will excuse me . . .'

'You miserable old fart,' she shouted after him. 'You rotten dried-up old maid in trousers!'

Her face was puckered like a disappointed baby's.

Brewster started, taken aback. No one had spoken so rudely to him, he reflected, since a drunken private had accosted him in low language after the victory at Alamein. And then the private had meant well; his remarks had been intended as comradely. Not even the prisoners, Rommel's men, had been that abusive. Of course, they had the language problem.

Noreen saw his flinch, and she blushed.

'Well, you'd better tell me your ruin and get saved,' she muttered. Her feet squirmed a little. She was not as tough a case as she liked to pretend, he realized, over his soreness at her remarks.

'There might not be that many chances. We must advance! We must go to the stars! We've got to find your Path! There's a path for everyone, even you!'

He turned and walked to the staircase.

'Thank you, I don't care for one.'

'Then there's a Path for that, too,' she shouted, the moment of shame evaporated.

Brewster's secretary, Miss Hartle, peered over the bannister, with her pale face and watery eyes looking like a startled rabbit.

'Watch out!' Noreen bellowed. 'You might not like it! Don't stand in our way! Siderea Saves!'

She banged the door so hard that a pane in the mullioned window on the left shattered, leaving shards and star points of glass in the entrance way. The porter rushed out of his cubby-hole by the stairs and Brewster instructed him calmly to take care of the damage. But he did not feel calm as he went up to his office. His heart was banging and he was furious that he should be so much affected by a silly, rude young woman. He could understand now why the townspeople were perturbed. This was not a standard of behaviour accepted in Daines Barington. It reminded him more of Cairo with its importunate beggars. But this girl had been demanding, not begging.

Old bachelor . . . She saw she had made a hit there. He remembered the shrewd guess about poor old Norris's potency. The star children claimed to have second sight, he'd heard. Old bachelor. He puckered his mouth. The word had a sour taste. He had never thought of himself as an old bachelor. Still, he was fifty-five. But fifty-five wasn't old.

He sat at his desk with a certain reluctance. His office, which was the office of the Town Clerk, one of the posts that he held, had not been refurbished by his father, John Brewster, when he had restored the Town Hall to its Elizabethan grandeur. It was a bare, masculine room with buff-colored walls and solid oak furniture, unornamented in any way and overlooking not the busy street but the yard of old Wilcox's farm, empty now except for a few hens moodily scratching at the dirt.

A pile of official papers awaited his attention. As he lifted the top one a flock of dust motes rose up and tickled his nose. He sneezed. Really, he must speak to Miss Hartle about that, he thought crossly, knowing very well that dust was not her province and should be attended to by the charwoman, and also that when Miss Hartle had the time she often furtively crept around the room with a feather duster.

She came in now with a file folder, stamped, tied, knotted, with a great air of finality about it.

'This is the Lavender file,' she remarked. 'We're quite finished with it. I'll take it over to the rates office. They'll be waiting to make the new assessment.'

Miss Hartle was perfectly right. The Lavender file was finished as far as he was concerned. The widowed Mrs Lavender had consulted him officially on her coming to Daines Barington a few months before. She had bought a fine Queen Anne house and was restoring and modernizing it with a maximum of taste and obviously no care about expense. In his official position, Brewster had to approve her architect's plans but he had no business except to applaud. Her taking over a property that was beginning to run down and making it once again what used to be called a gentleman's residence was a piece of good fortune for the town, and her arrival, Brewster thought, had been one of the most pleasant things that happened in a long time.

He had taken care of her applications promptly, and generally smoothed her way while, without consciously procrastinating, keeping aside a document or two that would make further meetings necessary. Miss Hartle had noticed that in his dealings with the Lavender file, Mr Brewster had ignored the very efficient Daines Barington post office. But now all business between them was finished. There was nothing to do but have the records filed in the appropriate place. It was a distinctly disagreeable thought.

Miss Hartle waited patiently, clutching the folder, which was brown, brown-taped, buff-labelled, dull. Brown and dull, nothing like the lady, but he was oddly reluctant to let it go.

'Put it on my desk, Miss Hartle,' he said shortly. 'I have a telephone call to make.'

And defiantly he dialed Mrs Lavender's number, without pretending to have to look it up, gave his name to her maid, and only when Mrs Lavender answered—how delightful she could make a simple 'Hullo' sound—only then did he realize, under Miss Hartle's pink, inquiring gaze, that he had nothing whatever to say.

'Oh, Mrs Lavender, Richard Brewster here,' he said. 'I'm sorry to bother you, but a question has come up about—about your assessment on the rates.'

Miss Hartle's eyes widened, and her thin sandy hair almost stood on end. She knew very well that no such thing could have occurred as yet, and that it was certainly not their business if it did.

'There will be an increase, but as this is a restored property of some historic value . . . Well, it's rather complicated to discuss on the telephone, and I thought perhaps if you were coming to do some shopping today . . .'

'Why, yes,' Mrs Lavender sounded slightly puzzled but agreeable. 'You know, I'm silly about things like rates, I don't understand them at all, but if you think I should come in—I *was* going to do some shopping.'

'Very good,' Brewster said firmly.

The only chair for visitors stood next to his desk. It displayed a patch of dust and a crack that had come suddenly from nowhere and which would certainly rip the delicate nylon stockings of a lady. Miss Hartle, he saw, wore sturdy lisle and probably hadn't noticed. She was still standing rooted in front of his desk and her mouth was open very slightly.

'Oh, Mrs Lavender,' he went on casually. 'My office is about to be spring-cleaned. Could I offer you some coffee in the Roseacre House?'

Mrs Lavender said that he could.

'See if you can do something with this mess,' he muttered, unfairly, to Miss Hartle, as he quickly left, feeling only slightly ashamed of himself.

31

The cobblestones in the street had just been washed down and gleamed invitingly outside the Town Hall. A lark sang overhead, two matrons twittered at a display of hats, and two Siderea girls, their cloaks off, were up on a ladder pasting something on a shop window, their little scarlet bottoms wobbling like the hindquarters of a pair of rabbits. A man would have to be very testy to object to that, Brewster thought, smiling. Old and testy . . . and he, Richard Brewster, certainly wasn't old.

A flock of sheep were being led through the street on the first stage of their journey to the slaughter-house if they but knew it. They clattered and baaed loudly enough but Brewster walked into the lead ram as if he were a blind man. He then collided with Wilcox the farmer and apologized to the sheep.

Wilcox, who knew him well, wondered if Mr Brewster was going a bit silly. Though he had never heard of any of the Brewsters going silly, far from it. Sharp they were and always had been. Still living well in their own house on their own land while the Gaylords, from the manor house, were gone and forgotten. He thought of Witch Hill in its great days, when Queen Mary had come to stay with a large royal party. Princess May she had been then.

He could remember as if it were yesterday, a fine spring morning and he a lad of seven toiling his way up the hill with a basket of eggs for the kitchen. The Royal standard was flying high and proud over the main block. And a footman had given him a mug made for the wedding celebration with a picture of Prince George and Princess May, and his mother had kept it all her life.

Well, the German wars had killed off the Gaylords, as they had killed Wilcox's brother and sons. The Manor was full of foreigners and the whole town was going daft, the farmer thought in disgust, as his progress was held up by a trio of young women holding up a banner that said:

'Siderea Saves!'

Saves what, he wondered, but he was not going to ask questions of young women with no skirts to their behinds, and he and his sheep went their way.

Roseacre House was hotel, restaurant, coffee shop, and tap room. The tap was old and masculine, a favourite meeting place for the men of the town, but the coffee shop was stained oak, copper pots and cretonne, the waitresses wore frilly aprons, and it was usually filled with women shoppers clucking to each other. Brewster always referred to the place as the Hennery.

Fortunately it was early for the shoppers and the place was half empty as he took a table by the door. He had been there only a short time, fussing with the waitress about the coffee and demanding and getting a plate of scones hot from the oven, when Mrs Lavender appeared and quietly took her place. She was not one of the lady cluckers, he thought with approval. Although she recognized some of the women present, she gave them only a nod and a smile, after her greeting to him.

To look at her was just as pleasant as to listen. Against the background of the dark settle she glowed with a most becoming radiance. She wore a coat and skirt of lilac-coloured tweed but there was an impression of something soft and fluttering, a scarf at her throat, a gleam of silk at her wrist, and he thought of garden-party frocks and butterflies. Mrs Lavender, he considered in a rush of sentiment, was a butterfly, a pink and white, very English butterfly. He thought of her in his apple orchards, and the thought was very good indeed.

Brewster did not know Superintendent Capricorn of Scotland Yard, who was an old friend of Mrs Lavender, but if he had heard Capricorn's description of her he would have agreed with enthusiasm.

'Rose Lavender is the only woman I've ever known,' the Superintendent often said, 'who is, at the same time, beautiful and very pretty. Some women are one, and some the other, bur Rose combines them both.'

It is true that the Superintendent also lovingly commented that the pretty Rose had a mind like an eiderdown, practical, comfortable, and no strain on anyone, but Brewster would not have accepted the implied criticism. She was decorative, soft-spoken, very much the lady, and that was quite enough. And if he thought of another woman, long since dead, whose brilliance had even surpassed her beauty, looking back over his troubled youth, he might have felt that it was all too much. Hardly necessary. Foreign, in fact, and Richard Brewster at fifty-five was feeling completely English, very much the country squire, very close to Daines Barington.

But for all Mrs Lavender's pleasant manner that morning, Brewster, finely attuned to her feelings in a way that would have surprised his stepsister, thought he detected a slight shadow over her normally sunny expression, a certain nervousness in the graceful movement of her hands.

33

'I hope I haven't troubled you about the rates,' he said guiltily.

'Oh, no, it isn't that,' she answered, 'I mean, I'm not worried about that. Whatever you decide, I'm sure is right.'

Brewster didn't bother to say that one of the few functions he did not perform was assessing the rates. He could always speak to the assessor if necessary. There was a possibility of an amelioration, he explained, as she had restored a landmark, and she thanked him prettily, but it was soon clear that she was not troubled about the assessment. As he had already known, Mrs Lavender was a rich woman and not averse to contributing to the town without any favours being granted. Yet her hands were plucking at her napkin and she seemed distressed.

'You are troubled, though,' Brewster said gently. 'Is it anything—anything I can help you with?'

She turned her blue gaze full on him.

'I shouldn't bother you,' she hesitated, 'But I had thought of asking . . . As a matter of fact, when you called I was on the point of ringing you up myself.'

Brewster's heart grew warm and expanded. The clatter of coffee cups and the soft babble of ladies' voices seemed to him the most agreeable of sounds and if anyone had asked his opinion at that moment he would have held that the despised Hennery was a most delightful meeting place.

'It's my daughter Linda,' she went on, 'So silly, but I am *quite* worried.'

Richard remembered that young Linda was asthmatic.

'The lungs no better?'

'Well,' she frowned a little, 'when we first came here they seemed to be. Dr Bailey is very good and the clean air helped. But then, you see,' her lashes fluttered as she sought his gaze again, 'after the first improvement, it remained the same. Better, but the attacks still came back at times. Dr Bailey told her to be patient, but you know that young people have no patience and now . . .'

She was twisting her napkin again; her slender, pretty hands, rosy-tipped, looked appealingly helpless.

'The child has met some of these odd people,' she said, perplexed. 'You know, "Siderea Saves"? They've persuaded her she can be cured by this Hightower's method, whoever he is. And now she won't see the doctor or follow his advice, and she's very excited, which is bad for her, you see.

'Mrs Norris tells me they're not at all well thought of and the Rector—' she blushed faintly, for no apparent reason—'The Rector, I know, doesn't approve.'

While nine-tenths of Brewster's mind was concerned with Mrs Lavender's problem, one tenth noted that of course Mrs Norris had called on her. And after Beatrice, Mrs Norris, he supposed, was the leading matron of the town. Norris *was* the cousin of Lord Arley, after all.

'I would rather she continued with Dr Bailey,' Mrs Lavender was saying. 'It's very worrying because these people seem to have quite bewitched her mind. I really don't know what to do. Dr Bailey says one can't do anything about them. But she must continue her treatment. And she isn't studying, either. I was hoping, if she improved, that she might go to that nice college for girls over in Merrydale. "Merrydale for merry girls," so pleasant.

'If only something could be done. That's why, you see . . .' Her hands rested in her lap, her lashes fluttered and widened. They were the exact shade of blue, he noticed with delight, of the periwinkle which was flowering now on every bank and shady place around Daines Barington and had crept into Beatrice's garden. It was as though Mrs Lavender had been fashioned in the very colours of the place. 'That's why I thought of you.'

Brewster gazed into those eyes until the ghost of his night's dream was laid to rest; the morning's impatience and irritation were fled away, and only a sense of chivalry and well-being remained.

'Something will be done,' he promised, his memory of the little scarlet bottoms wobbling like rabbits quite forgotten, his easy tolerance transformed to stern resolution by Mrs Lavender's plight. 'These people will be controlled, I assure you—Rose. They will cause you, and the town, no further trouble, rest easy about that. Our lives . . .' the plural form deepened his happiness and made it more intense. 'Our lives are not going to be disturbed by this nonsense. You won't have to hear of them any more.'

He reached out boldly and covered her fluttering right hand with his own, and she smiled up at him, accepting his embrace and his judgement. But for once Richard Brewster, prudent, intelligent, farseeing as all the Brewsters were, was wrong. For on the grassy slopes between Witch Hill and the manor house events were taking place that would tie Mrs Lavender to Siderea for some time to come.

35

three

In the pasture belonging to Witch Hill, a young man was watching the sky. It had looked like a clear and perfect day, but an old countryman, cutting through the fields, had pointed out a patch of darker colour drifting in slowly from the north, neither cloud nor smoke.

'Blight,' the countryman had said gloomily. 'Orchard blight.'

The young man, more familiar with the high, wide skies of Texas than the low-canopied orchard lands, stared curiously at the coppery drift.

'Blight in the sky; blight on the leaf. Blight eat the air; flies suck the leaves. London blight!'

The old man had snorted and gone his way.

Some kind of smog, the young man thought. He'd never heard of smog bringing orchard blight, but he supposed it could. He gazed down from the pasture to the orchards in the valley, where the rich green spread of leaf promised a splendid harvest. He hoped the old

36

man was wrong. But he remembered the old men about his father's ranch, their faces dark and leathery from the sun, unlike the withered crab-apple complexion of the Englishman yet the brand of old knowledge and long experience was the same, and the old men were usually right.

As he gazed eastward something light and bright caught his eye; a white dress fluttered against the green; a fair-haired girl was walking effortlessly up the steep incline as though untroubled by the force of gravity. She hesitated at the wooden fence that enclosed the pasture at that point, causing the road to take a wide curve round.

The young man smiled, watching the game, for everyone who came up that road paused at that spot. The staid and middle-aged walked prosaically around. The young jumped the fence and trespassed, braving the horses that grazed the field; the old, more slowly and creakingly, would often do the same, as the countryman had done, his remarks perhaps in payment for his trespass.

The girl flew over the fence in one graceful swing and walked across the field. His heart beat faster. Before he could see her face, from the form, the movement, the sleek bright hair, he knew it to be Linda Lavender, whom he had promised himself earnestly that he would not meet, and not try to know: Linda Lavender was a student from Daines Barington, a Siderean in embryo as it were, taboo to other Sidereans by order of Hightower himself.

He had tried not to think of her and he had thought the more. Now he withdrew into a clump of bushes on the far side of the field, unseen, and knew by the pounding in his chest that his efforts had been wasted. She must be all of seventeen, he warned himself, entranced as he had been when he first saw her in Daines Barington, struck by her milky complexion, her pale hair, her large and clear blue eyes, her soft voice, and her speech, clipped and neat as the English fields with their prim and tidy hedges. She was as different from the tall, tanned girls of Texas and the dark, full-fleshed Mexicans, as if she came from another time as well as from another place, a medieval maid.

Linda walked across the grass unseeing. Soon she must decide, and Linda was not fond of deciding. Rather she would postpone the evil, but that would not be possible. Her first studies were coming to an end and she must either become a Siderean, join the group and continue, or make an end, thank them for their help and leave.

She didn't want to leave. The Sidereans were young and exciting and she had been having fun. Her asthma had entirely gone away. She had never liked lessons, but in the Siderea school she had done well and received praise. But on the other hand, if she joined the Army of the Stars and took the oath and wore the uniform, her mother would be very upset indeed. Linda was rather embarrassed about it, but she was very fond of her mother and didn't want her to be upset.

It was only a year and a half since her father had died; Her mother had been very unhappy and had only lately recovered her spirits. Linda knew that, although other people considered Mrs Lavender placid. Her mother was brave and good-mannered, and would never intrude her grief. No, she didn't want her mother upset. Mother had been good about her not going to Merrydale College, but she would think joining Siderea too much.

Linda also knew that if her mother complained once Linda had taken the oath, the Sidereans would ask Linda to leave home. A Siderean could live at home as long as there was no talk against the group, but once a negative word was said, that was the end. The person might even be sent a Warning.

'Those who are not with us are against us. They must be cast out!'

It was a bit like the Old Testament, Linda thought irreverently, but on the other hand, there were so many young people, it was so much fun, and they did good for everybody.

Her white dress caught the light and the attention of the roan stallion idly grazing among his mares. He sniffed curiously. The figure was moving, whatever it was, and he took a few steps forward to observe. But the figure continued to move. He was a good way off and quickened his pace. His mares looked up and saw him moving and cantered up to join him. The white thing fluttered on, obstinately far away. He would not be outrun by his mares and began to gallop.

The noise of hooves broke in on Linda's musing. Looking up, startled, she saw a pack of horses thundering down on her. A town girl born and bred, she had never seen a horse except reined and bridled, its eyes covered, cowed and miserable in the middle of motor traffic on busy streets. These great whinnying, naked animals coming down on her at a great pace were something very, very different. With a start of terror, she began to run.

The stallion neighed joyfully. This looked like a little sport. He had really been rather bored. His mares neighed and galloped faster. The field was not very wide. Soon Linda was out of breath and she felt the familiar clutching squeeze in her chest. The pounding hooves were closer.

Before her was the fence with safety on the other side, but it was harder and harder to run with her chest squeezing into a small and suffocating box. She made a great effort and was almost there but her eyes closed and squeezed tight in pain and tears. Her hands reached out, groping forward, surely the fence was— Her foot kicked against a hummock; she tripped; gasped and fell. The horses were so close her choked breath bore their sharp and pungent odor. Her eyes opened and she looked back into the rolling eyes of the stallion. He was almost upon her. A thin scream came from somewhere and she hardly knew it was from her own pain-racked body.

The thunder of hooves filled her ears; she couldn't move an inch and she didn't know if she felt more fear or pain until she saw the steamy breath curling from under the stallion's nostrils and knew fear was greater. She collapsed and huddled low, her fingers scrabbling in the grass.

Suddenly she felt an arm round her waist; some tall, strong person was lifting her up and, blessedly, the thick white poles of the stile were behind her, and the noise of the horses faded away, replaced for a time by the drumming in her ears, as hope and breath came back and released her body.

Looking up weakly, she saw the smiling face of the tall Texan. His arms were still round her and she was leaning on him as hard as she could. Her heart was still pounding, and she could have sworn his was too, yet he looked amused and not frightened at all.

'They're tame, honey,' he grinned. 'They wouldn't hurt you, not in a million years.'

His slow, flat, American voice was awfully nice, she thought comfortably. It was lovely, not being eaten by horses. It was lovely, not having asthma and being able to breathe. Easy it was now, her breath coming in and out with only a little pain, getting less and less. She was still leaning on him. The bees hummed in the white clover, working away, and the world revolved slowly back to safety.

She knew who this American was. His name was Garry Wyatt and he was a Siderean, although he didn't wear the uniform but stuck to blue jeans and shirt and moccasins. She remembered hearing that he took care of Hightower's horses. It was funny, she thought, with the sun warm on her back, she had liked the look of him and wished he would ask to take her home from the Moo-Cow sometimes, although it was against the rules. And now here she was. He was sweating, very slightly. She liked his smell.

Pains and penalties, he was telling himself. For such an infringement of the rules, he could be put off course for six months. And he couldn't waste six months. Soon he would have to go home. His father needed him on the ranch. And there was no chance of not being found out. He'd better get back to the horses right now, even if this girl was like the Lily Maid of Astolat, only warmer. And very soft.

She looked up at him and smiled, her eyelids fluttering.

Linda was not a tall girl and Garry was well over six feet but as he bent to kiss her the distance was nothing. Nothing at all. They stood in the sun, embracing, in a kiss that lasted a long, long time. A mouse scuttled into a hollow. A starling rose from a branch at a sharp angle, gave them a long, hard and dubious glance, hovered over their shadow, then shot off, vanishing in the summer air.

Book Two

MERLE CAPRICORN
Year 3, A.S.
Summer

one

Even at Scotland Yard a warm summer day made itself felt. Superintendent Capricorn, soberly going through his correspondence at his desk, was not impervious to the warm sunlight at the window and an urge to be outdoors, out of London altogether, as well as other urges which he did not bother to examine.

The pile of letters in front of him consisted mostly of official inquiries and responses on Department business. There were a few grubby missives claiming to contain valuable tips, which he put aside to check for any usefulness. Two invitations from hostesses who didn't know him well enough to know his home address or the fact that he spent little time in social engagements seemed to complete the morning's post, when a small envelope of fine-quality paper slipped from the pile onto his blotter, a familiar-looking envelope addressed in a familiar light, skipping hand.

Rose Lavender. The Superintendent gazed at the letter, smiling without realizing it, the pleasure of the morning somehow crystallizing into the piece of paper before him. He had not heard from her for some time. But why had she written to him here, at the Yard?

He opened the letter swiftly. Rose, the pretty widow, had taken a sister's place in his life, and he had for her a brother's concern even when he recognized, amused, that the concern was not entirely brotherly. The letter was post-marked Daines Barington, where she had been living, he remembered, for about six months. A placid little market town, it seemed very suitable for the sheltered Rose and her invalid daughter.

'Dear Merle,' the letter began, in a script that seemed to fly over the page even more than usual.

'You will think I'm so silly, writing to you like this, in a flutter about something you will probably think nothing at all. And I had meant to write to you before, as I had some happy news. I don't know why it is, but when one is happy time seems so long, if you know what I mean, and then when one is worried, like now, it gets all sharp and short and I felt I ought to do something and so I thought of you, although I expect you're much too busy. And Richard has already told me Scotland Yard couldn't possibly do anything.

'Oh, dear, here I am at the end and I haven't got to the beginning, so I will have to start all over. I should have rung you up, perhaps, but I was rather ashamed to bother Scotland Yard in person and I am too fussed to find your private number that I know is put away somewhere but we really haven't got everything sorted out yet.

'Well, that was partly because of the happy part of my news. It may seem odd, only eighteen months after poor Sam's death—that's why we haven't made any announcements yet, I wouldn't want to upset any of the Lavenders, such dear people as they are—but the truth is when I first moved here I met the most charming man, Mr Richard Brewster of Daines Barington. He is the Town Clerk and he helped me about the restoring of my house with permits and things—so kind—a most dear man, Merle, a bachelor—and to get to the point, somehow or other we seem to have become engaged. Linda likes him, and we were planning to be married this month, in fact, next week—and I had thought this letter would just be an invitation to a wedding.

'But you see this dreadful thing is happening and Richard doesn't take any notice, but it is very worrying. And I think perhaps even Richard is worrying a little, because he told me yesterday that he wants to have it cleared up before the wedding—he doesn't want to have me involved in unpleasantness.

'Oh, dear, I keep forgetting you probably haven't any idea of what's going on, although you do have them in London but it wouldn't be the same. The Sidereans, you know. You must have seen them, they walk around in scarlet tights and purple wraps and have helmets that light up in the dark? And they think that everyone is ruined and must be saved?

'They have quite taken over Daines Barington, like a mass of gypsies, which is *quite* annoying, and the Health Department is upset about the overcrowding, but the worst thing is, they are planning to kill Richard. At least, they keep sending him letters saying so, anonymous, of course, but I'm quite sure . . . Hightower, their leader or prophet or whatever he is, has been gone a long time and they are running wild. And the Rector—another charming man, Merle, and *so* attentive, almost . . . but I'll tell you all these things when I see you—the Rector says that although most of their nonsense is play-acting he feels it *could* be dangerous. And I've been to the police here, and they are so kind, but they can't seem to do very much.

'It's not that they even *know* Richard—or they couldn't feel like that, he is such a *good* man but as Town Clerk he had to stop them building all over the manor land—it's against the law, I don't understand it, but it is—so he had to stop them. And so they think he is like Hitler, only worse, and there are just so many of them, and as I said, they make threats against his life. Richard just laughed at first, but it is dreadful because I am afraid they might mean it. Not that I've heard of them killing anyone else, but they are very serious people and Richard is the first one ever to have tried to stop them from doing anything.

'Oh, dear, what a rigmarole this all seems! But really, Merle, I had no idea what to do, and so I thought of you. I would love to see you but I know you are probably in the middle of an important case, but you perhaps could mention this to someone. Richard is very dear, Merle.

'Linda, who is getting to be a grown-up girl, and, oh, dear, interested in the Sidereans, sends you her best wishes—she's too young and too old to send love. But I send you mine, and congratulations for all the successes I read about your having—who would have imagined you a Scotland Yard superintendent, all those years ago in Chuffield? I do wonder what your father would have thought!'

The signature, Rose, was squeezed in a tiny corner at the bottom of the third page, almost an afterthought. Dear, silly Rose. Capricorn the man felt slightly dashed that the lovely widow was marrying again but Capricorn the detective immediately went to the files to see what he had about Noah Hightower and his Sidereans.

Like the Rector of Daines Barington—had Rose been hinting that he, too, was an admirer? Incorrigible Rose!—the Superintendent very much disliked anonymous letters. Mostly the work of harmless cranks, it was true, but sometimes not so harmless.

No criminal charges had ever been filed against Hightower or his group. Complaints had been made, but no arrests. From newspaper clippings Capricorn saw that several civil actions had been started. People complained of Siderea's predatory financial habits: large donations were expected from the spiritually saved, which they themselves did not mind, but their relatives did. The Views of the Globe reporter referred sarcastically to Hightower's much vaunted 'Cleansing' as being a simple cleaning out of his devotees' worldly goods and to his 'Paths' as being not ways to the stars but to his personal strong box believed to be in Tangiers.

In all of this there was no hint of violence. It was about three years since Hightower had started the Siderea movement. There were branches in London now and all over England, but he had kept Daines Barington as his headquarters. No one had complained of threats or coercion. Parents had grumbled, he recalled, that their children were blandished—some of them called Hightower the Pied Piper—but Sidereans seemed like peaceful souls. Their greeting was perhaps over-enthusiastic: he had seen them grasp the hands of perfect strangers and yell, 'Siderea Saves!' with the characteristic eyeballing stare.

He sat at his desk and thought, looking down at his pile of unanswered letters, hardly seeing them. Rose was fluffy, but she was no fool. If she had gone so far as to write to him, she was afraid. He remembered cases where threatening letters had preceded acts of dangerous violence, even murder where a mind, unbalanced, tipped over into real instead of imagined crime.

It should be handled by the local people, of course. Perhaps he would give the local Super a ring and see what was going on. Then he could talk to Rose.

Two sparrows flew by his window. In the old building by the river, birds would come and perch on the window sills on hot summer days, preening and quarrelling in the sun. Now not even a brash London sparrow could venture onto the austere modern block that housed New Scotland Yard. He thought of old and mellow places, cool and green, away from the heat and dirt of the city. He was due for a leave. And he and Sergeant Copper had just cleaned up the case they were working on. Perhaps he should take some time in the country before anything important broke. It would be good to visit Rose and relax. He smiled again in pleasant recollection.

The Vicarage of Chuffield, with Mr Raintree the Vicar and his wife and his daughter Rose, had been as much a home as he had ever known. Chuffield had been his happiest stop on the interminable tours with his father, the Great Capricornus, the Most Famous Escape Artist in the World, or with his aunts, the Magic Merlinos. The northern town had meant a homecoming. It was there, at the Vicarage, he had learned the delights of civilization.

Yes, he would certainly go and do what he could for Rose. He approached his Chief on the subject of a few days' leave, and found him interested in the subject of Daines Barington.

'The Chief Constable down there has been in touch with us on this Siderea business. The town is up in arms. They feel there must be a law against a foreign invasion like this and if there isn't there ought to be. Just between us, I think that's being looked into, not our pigeon of course.'

'Hightower,' Capricorn was trying to remember, 'came to us from Australia was it, or South Africa?'

'Wherever it was, I wish he'd stayed there,' the Chief said in disgust. 'He's off again, in any case. In his Ark, they say. Though he looks more like a pirate than a patriarch to me.'

'Where is the Ark?' Capricorn wondered.

The Chief shrugged.

'We don't know. Some of his people say he's on the seas, some of them say the Ark is a spacecraft. I can tell you he's nowhere in the British Isles or near any British territory. But he's left those damned followers dumped in our laps.'

'What are the complaints? Any of this threatening-letter business?'

'No,' the Chief frowned. 'That's new. Money. Breaking up marriages. Kids leaving home. But mostly it's that they bother people. Evangelists. The town wouldn't have cared if they kept to themselves up at the Manor. It's a great place, almost the size of Blenheim. I visited there,' he mentioned casually, 'when Prince Ranook was in possession.'

Capricorn refrained from smiling. The Chief's mild snobbery rather amused him, but the man's formidable capabilities insured Capricorn's complete respect.

'Anyway,' the Chief went on, 'they go down in droves and harry the good burghers. Brewster, you said,' he repeated thoughtfully. 'He's the big panjandrum down there. Cousin to Brewster in the F.O., too, and some relation to Venable in the Home Office.

'Well, if you want to go down unofficially it might be a good thing. See what's going on. P'raps something we could shoot along to another Department. Officially, we're not in, of course. No crime . . . unless the Chief Constable kills one of them in a fit of rage. I understand they told him *he* was badly in need of salvation.'

two

The next morning Capricorn drove in his own two-seater down through Surrey towards Daines Barington. It was surely not the thought of seeing Rose that made the day so fine, the bachelor Capricorn told himself firmly. He knew her far too well. A fat ewe, grazing behind a hedge at the roadside, looked up as his car ripped by, baaing indignantly, unimpressed by the power of his logic.

As he had left the traffic of the main road and turned East along the Baring valley, the Superintendent found his mind dwelling more and more on the Raintrees. Driving swiftly he saw the grey-blue water flashing through trees, behind banks, circling around hills, appearing and disappearing and appearing again like the anticipation and recollection that bubbled through his mind.

'You're cold, Merle,' his aunts always said, but his remembered friendship for the Raintrees still warmed his heart. Mrs Raintree had searched into the state of nourishment and clothing of the theatrical children that passed through Chuffield, and the Vicar had made sure that they went to school. And he had saved Capricorn from a life on the stage.

The young Merle had an aversion to theatrical life partly by disposition and partly since, at the age of twelve, he had seen his Aunt Tilly saw her husband in half in full view of a packed house. Her husband had been about to run off with a dancer on the same bill, and as the injured party she had the sympathy of the troupe. The police had accepted the story that the cutting wheel had slipped, as the troupe all swore husband and wife had been on the best of terms. Eventually, Aunt Tilly had gone to a pleasant home for the slightly dotty, where Capricorn still visited her from time to time and where she gave performances, thinking as much of her new audience as she had of the old. But as a young boy he had been sickened and horrified by the affair, and in contrast he had admired the neat, methodical, quiet men of the Force and longed to join their ranks.

He had been brought up to follow his father. The Great Capricornus had taught his son to escape from small enclosed places from the time he was three years old. He was intended for the great tradition. At five, Merlin Capricorn, as he was billed, could wriggle out of a sealed wooden crate with the aid of nothing but a small screw that was concealed in his mouth. In later life he decided his father had been too eager, for although by his teens his skills were highly developed, he also had a tendency to claustrophobia.

It was the Vicar who relieved his burden of guilt and taught him that a man did not have to follow his father's footsteps—or sealed packing cases, or whatever his line might be. The Vicar's own father, he had told Capricorn, had been a successful business man, and very shocked that his son wished to study divinity. Capricorn smiled, thinking of that quiet, scholarly man and how lost he would have been in business, but he had been invaluable as the director of Capricorn's sporadic education. His final escape from the stage had come in the last year of the war when he got into the army and from there to M16. When he returned it was to the Metropolitan Police.

The first visit he had paid in England was to the Raintrees. With his different postings he had lost touch and was saddened to find the Vicar and his wife both dead. They had gone to London to serve on a committee helping war orphans and were killed by one of the last rockets. Rose had been left alone. He had thought a lot of Rose while he was away, and he was almost as shocked to find her married before she was eighteen as he had been at her parents' death.

Lavender was a rich, substantial man over twenty years her senior. Eventually Capricorn had come to understand the marriage. Rose's father—though he had seemed to the young Capricorn as merely an adult with other adults—had been almost old enough to be a grandfather at the time of Rose's birth. And Lavender had proved to be a good husband, and Rose had been happy, after all. From a shy girl she had become an assured, lovely matron enjoying a placid existence, and through the years of her marriage they had continued to be friends. Capricorn had visited her as his duties allowed, which was not often.

The signpost in front of him said 'Daines Barington 40 miles.' The last sign he had noticed had said 'Daines Barington 25 miles.' He pulled up and swore quietly to himself. He had missed the turn. A set of headlines projected themselves before his mental gaze:

'Scotland Yard detective misses signpost. Lost in country lane thirty miles from London. All hope abandoned.'

He turned, taking the road that would lead into town from the east, instead of, as he had intended, the west. Rose's house, she had explained, was one of the first in the town, on the westerly side, in the shadow of St. Cuthbert's. Now he would have to drive right through. He would stop and book a room at a hotel, then, and leave his gear. There was an old place that had looked pleasant, he remembered, for he had visited Daines Barington before while pursuing a large-scale embezzler whom he had tracked down in the taproom of Roseacre House. The man could have made good his escape by flying to the continent, but his liking for small English towns had been his undoing.

Looking around him at the new Daines Barington, Capricorn thought if the embezzler had seen this he would have moved right on and saved himself. He could hardly believe it was the same place. Almost opposite the small, modest Emanuel Church a loathesome-looking Moo-Cow milk bar, lurking behind some unconvincing Tudor beams, gleamed whitely into the street, sending forth an odour of burning fat and onions. Cramming the place, spilling out into the street, sitting on curbstones, munching and walking up and down with food and drink in their hands, were the scarlet-and-purple clad followers of Hightower.

Although it was broad daylight, each wore a helmet lit up by an electric light in the front rather like a miner's lamp. He recalled seeing something similar in London, but in certain parts of town eccentric dress is no novelty. Here they looked like the spotty symptoms of plague. Nor were their attentions confined to the Moo-Cow. A few yards further along a shop had been converted to a Siderea store. Purple and red banners decorated the front, the legend 'Siderea Saves' was written in a peculiarly glaring paint, and the window was full of emblems, books and placards, bearing Hightower's rubicund face.

Every street lamp had a placard attached——'Siderea Saves.' Many of the shops displayed Siderea products and emblems along with their other goods. Hand-made leather shoes in one window seemed to shrink uneasily from a rack of Siderea tights, and 'Fine Groceries' looked embarrassed by a display of books, the jackets all screaming 'Tell your ruin! Siderea Saves!'

Capricorn drew in his breath. How long had it taken this to happen? he wondered. Why did the shopkeepers cooperate? As he drove along slowly he saw that every shop that did not carry Siderea merchandise displayed a yellow notice. While he was watching, an indignant red-faced chemist in a white coat came out and tore the yellow notice down. As soon as he was back inside his shop, a Siderean approached, took out another yellow notice, and pinned it on the door post.

Curious, Capricorn parked his car and went to see what the notice was about. A crude drawing of a death's head sprawled across the cheap paper, and the words 'This shop is Anti-Siderea! Unhealthy for Sidereans! Do not trade here!' The lettering was awkward and apparently the first attempt had Anti spelled with an E, the ghost of which was still visible.

Boycott, Capricorn thought. He hadn't seen that for a long time. Was it a penalty, he wondered, for not displaying Siderea goods? He looked round. The local people in their subdued dress melted into the background and seemed to be outnumbered by Sidereans walking, Sidereans driving in every sort of conveyance from a sleek Mercedes Benz to a Mini-Minor that was almost falling apart, Sidereans hanging out of second story windows putting up flags, Sidereans on bicycles with trays, Sidereans with wheelbarrows, Sidereans picketing the bank waving yellow notices larger than all the rest.

As he entered Roseacre House, feeling rather grim, he saw that its windows displayed no Siderea goods and no yellow sheets either. As he signed the register he commented on this to the neat, middle-aged man wearing metal-rimmed spectacles, who stood behind the desk.

'We've been blessed,' the man said wryly. 'Hightower, in the days when he lived here, used to like to stop in at the tap for a drink now and again. He liked ginger beer with his whisky; the bar had to get a special stock.' The man's face was expressive; his lips curved into a quivering, upside-down U. 'Anyway, the disciples leave us alone. A holy spot, you might say.'

The two men looked out through the windows. The glass was old with a blue cast and slight distortion, and through that medium the scene outside looked even more strange and hectic. A band of Sidereans carrying banners marched five abreast down the street and the sound of their singing came, unwelcome, to Roseacre House.

'Hurrah! Hurrah! The Army of the Stars!

Hurrah! Hurrah! The Army of the Stars!

'We'll cleanse you and we'll take you

  from Earth right on to Mars

While we are cleansing the planet!'

'It's because it's Saturday,' the desk man said resignedly. He rang the bell for the porter. 'A lot of them are out of school. Not so bad in the week.'

'Siderea Saves!'

The yell was loud enough to make him start, although he was fifteen feet inside the hall of the solid old building. Capricorn shuddered as he went upstairs to a very pleasant bedroom with its own small sitting room. He stood for a while at the window, thoughtful, and contemplated the antics below.

The Superintendent, who appreciated tradition, beauty and dignity as much as any of the townspeople, sympathized with their feelings of outrage. It was easy to see why they felt, as his Chief had put it, that if there wasn't a law against this sort of thing, there should be. But he knew better than they the dangers of law based on sudden emotional response. Then he reproved himself for being patronizing: most of the thoughtful people probably did understand, or the outcry would have been greater. The common law was still respected in the country and small towns. In any event, he thought, with a sigh for a pretty town made ugly, making new laws was not his business. Not his pigeon at all.

three

'It seems to be hardly our pigeon, and you must think it pretty silly,
C₁ bursting in on you like this,' he apologized to the Superintendent
at the local station. 'But it's just an unofficial visit, you understand.'

The police station, a few doors down from the hotel, was pleasantly familiar in type and free from peculiar manifestations. The
worn linoleum, the battered desks might have been in any small station throughout the country. Only the excellent proportion of the
rooms and the mullioned window on the High Street reminded one
that this was Daines Barington, that the builder had known his business, and that this station had once been a private house.

Superintendent Griswald, a big, bluff man with an air more relaxed than his London counterpart would have, but with a quick, intelligent glance, did not look as though he proposed any annoyance
or indignation.

'We're very glad to have you, as it happens,' he said drily.

'You've seen the town for yourself, so you can imagine what we're up against. People expect us to do something, and there's damn-all we can do. But I suppose you know that.'

He shrugged his heavy shoulders impatiently.

'I daresay our CC, Colonel Farquar, has been in touch with London, because he gets pestered himself. But it's Immigration that gives them the permits; they're the only ones that can act. As far as we're concerned, the Sidereans are here legally and they don't break any laws.'

'There is this matter of the threatening letters to Brewster,' Capricorn mentioned. 'Although they're anonymous, there's no doubt, I take it, that Siderea is responsible?'

Griswald snorted.

'A lot of play-acting, if you'll take my opinion. They've been sending those letters all over the place for months to anyone they're annoyed with; there must be hundreds of 'em. They call 'em Warnings among themselves. Officially, they don't admit anything. Hard to prove in the courts.'

Capricorn nodded thoughtfully.

'You should see the things,' Griswald said in disgust. 'A rotten drawing of a skull and cross-bones. My young 'un of ten could do better. But that's as far as it goes. They never *do* anything. I've been up there and spoken to the people who run the place. There's a Mrs Portia Anthony, who has sense, and a kid called Frost, who hasn't. I told them there'd be trouble if any more got sent and Mrs Anthony—she didn't *admit* anything, of course—said she'd see into it. Told me she hadn't authorized any such thing, and I believe her. Like I said, it's a big act, anyway. Kids playing spacemen instead of cops and robbers.'

'They seem to have some sort of boycott going with the shopkeepers,' Capricorn pointed out.

'Mr Hartle—he's the lawyer for the town—is looking into that,' Griswald explained. 'But, like I tell 'em, it only means the Sidereans won't buy in the shops, and the shopkeepers say they don't want them anyway, so what's the fuss?'

'Our imperturbable British police,' Capricorn grinned.

Griswald looked reflective for a moment. He offered Capricorn a cigarette—who refused it with a feeling compounded of virtue and dejection—and lit one for himself.

'I was in Germany in '45,' he said. 'Opened up some of the

camps. Not the worst ones, they tell me. Not like Auschwitz. But still . . . little irritations like these young asses haven't seemed much, since.'

Capricorn regarded the country Super, pink-fleshed, with mild blue eyes, who looked as though he had been born to the placidity and gentleness of a little English country town and had never known anything else. He himself had seen some of those camps and knew what Griswald meant. Well, we're all world citizens now, he thought. No more island placidity.

'No,' Griswald went on, meditative. 'After you've seen the real thing you don't get excited about a lot of kid's stuff.'

The Nazis had been a pretty young group when they started, Capricorn remembered. Still, the Daines Barington Super had lived with the situation, and he looked like a man of sense whose opinion was worth weighing.

'No laws being broken?'

'I'll tell you the truth, they're more law-abiding than any group of youngsters I've ever seen,' Griswald said, almost irritably. 'Hightower left orders. No drinking, except on Saturday night. Drugs forbidden absolutely, all the way down to aspirin. No carrying on, and they don't, much. Pay their bills—sometimes not but that's when one of them gets over-enthusiastic and stays on after his money runs out. They take a lot of courses and the courses cost the earth. Mrs Anthony tries her best to collect for any landladies that get stuck. Keeps after the members of her flock from all over the world. Best collection agent I ever heard of. Daresay she'll follow them up when they go to the stars,' he grinned.

'Well, with all the fuss, we've gone after them for this, that and the other thing.' He didn't sound proud of it. 'Really, there's nothing. Summons 'em for not getting a car sticker. Or breach of the peace. We did that a few times. Then what d'you think they did?'

'I couldn't guess,' Capricorn said, truly.

'They paid the fines all right. But the next Monday they came into the station with a complaint. Said the bells of St Cuthbert's were disturbing *their* peace. They weren't Christians, they said, the saucy lot, and their Sunday was ruined by the clanking of those bells. Oh, you should've heard the Rector on that.'

His face lit up with a slow, very amused smile.

'I hadn't thought of it before,' he said with that detachment that had surprised Capricorn already, 'but you know those bells do make

55

the damnedest racket. Nobody in Daines Barington can have a sleep-in on Sunday and that's a fact.'

Capricorn thanked him for his help, and in turn was offered all the facilities Daines Barington could provide if he wished to stay. He explained he would be visiting Mrs Lavender and spending the night at Roseacre House, and would like to visit the Manor the next morning, if Griswald would be good enough to accompany him. He was about to take his leave when one more question occurred to him.

'So it's definitely your view there are no bad apples up at the manor? Or—' he hesitated, 'anyone who might be unbalanced enough for the play-acting to push over the line?'

Griswald paused for a moment, for the first time not quite sure.

'Well, about any of them being unbalanced, a bit of a crank I suppose you mean, of course, I wouldn't want to say. There's hundreds of 'em, and I'm no alienist. But I've met all their bigwigs, and there's only one I don't like the look of. That's the Jed Frost I mentioned. A bad type. Born troublemaker. He's been a regular nuisance. I think he's responsible for this Brewster business, the letters and damned silly threats. He's especially exercised right now,' Griswald said thoughtfully, 'because he's made a mess of the Manor. Hightower won't like that, and young Frost will lose his stripes, or whatever they call 'em.'

Capricorn looked curious.

'Well, you probably don't know but Hightower wanted planning permission to build on his pasture land. Town turned him down. Brewster did. A good thing too, the town couldn't soak up any more Sidereans than we've got—you ought to see the Three Feathers on Saturday night,' he said gloomily. 'You can't get a pint without seeing red in front of your eyes.

'Frost went ahead anyway; hired workmen, bought supplies, and started digging the foundation. The Court stopped all work, by order. So Frost is left with a big dirty hole, a lot of brick and stone, and a loss of several thousand pounds. So he's livid.

'For three months he's made a nuisance of himself. Demonstrating at the Town Hall. Yelling at Brewster in the streets. We're ready to pull *him* in on breach of the peace and it'll stick. Won't hurt him too much, though.'

He fumbled with a match to light a fresh cigarette. The flame spurted up and burned his fingers.

'Oh, blast,' he said, distracted for a moment.

'Frost is English, worse luck. Damned fool. His own worst enemy.'

'Does this Frost—what's his first name?'

'Jed. Jedediah, actually, I think,' the Super answered, stroking his burnt finger. 'He's from the North.'

'Does Mr Jedediah Frost have a record?'

The Super looked up, somewhat taken aback.

'I haven't checked,' he said, abashed. 'But I'll certainly do it.'

'Perhaps we can help,' Capricorn said, amiably.

'He did strike me as a bad lot,' the Super mused, 'but you said "unbalanced." I don't know I'd say that. Too sharp for his own good, that's all.'

'Jedediah Frost,' Capricorn repeated. 'We'll look him over. If he's writing those letters, maybe the Yard will frighten him off.'

'Good hunting,' the Super called as the London man took his leave, and Capricorn smiled, pleased to think that if he had any work to do here, he had a cooperative local Super to work with. Together they could deal with Jedediah Frost.

four

Hunting, however, was not uppermost in his mind as he went out into the High Street, where the bright clear light of the afternoon was turning golden just before the dusk. His professional instincts were only mildly aroused in a dispute that apparently belonged in the hands of lawyers and Other Departments. Still, he disliked anonymous letters and he loathed the kind of mind that sent them. In the morning he would go to the Manor, and he would call on the lawyer, Hartle. Now he would pay his expected visit to Rose.

He wondered how the last few years, and widowhood, had treated his lovely friend. Was her beauty beginning to fade? Approaching forty was she, like so many women, trying to ape the harsh modernity of girls half her age? His pleasant anticipation became tinged with reluctance. He would not like to see Rose changed. Then he laughed at himself for being a fool.

'You're too critical, Merle,' his aunts had said a thousand times, and they were right; no wonder he was a bachelor still. And in any case, was this the way a man thinks of a sister? He and Rose had been almost brother and sister for a long time. Surely old affection could brush over such infelicities. And what will Rose think of you, he mocked himself, no longer the youth who was the delight of the matinée ladies as they sighed over their clanking cups of tea. A Superintendent from the CID., moving up to middle age. And a good thing too, he thought with satisfaction, for he was, in truth, happy with his lot.

Her house lay, as she had explained, in the shadow of St

Cuthbert's, quite literally at this hour; the faint adumbration of its spires fell, as if protectively, over the small pretty house and garden. He smiled, for he would have guessed that this was Rose's house, almost without description. And yet, architecturally, it was nothing like the Chuffield vicarage; it was just the particular magic of the Raintree women that was so familiar, illuminating them both. He had been an adult and the Vicar and his wife dead before he ever realized that the old house was in itself hideous, and it had remained in his mind all his life as a picture of home.

What was it, he wondered, the care, the gleaming paint and glass, the light-coloured curtains, the fresh flowers on the sills, the neatness of the gardens, the atmosphere of calm? He remembered the frowsty lodging houses on the road, carpets never swept, fried fish and chips, jugs of beer on the washstand, Aunt Nelly or Dolly in a sleazy dressing gown, Aunt Tilly or Milly, her hair dyed mauve to look more silver-blond on stage, done up in a thousand curlers.

'No time for that,' his aunts would say indignantly when he proposed a general clean-up, a different regime. 'We're professionals. Not housewives, see.' And that was the truth. They had no time for housework, and not much time, over the long run, for their husbands or lovers either. Aunt Tilly, the one who had sawn her husband in half, was chiefly looked down upon afterwards for being unprofessional.

'Very bad for the act,' said Dolly and Milly and Nelly. They were, it was true, devoted to their craft, and it took their whole attention. And he was the same, he thought, resigned, no different really, after all. His flat was tidy—he had a good housekeeper—and he didn't have to dye his hair, but he was the same at heart. Only the profession was different.

He looked up and there was Rose smiling out at him from the shadow of the canopied doorway. How absurd he had been, he rejoiced, to think she could possibly have changed. She was, if anything, lovelier than ever. Her dress was of some light green stuff, summery, fluttering, with a skirt short enough to look modern, long enough for its length not to be noticeable; her hair was softly waved in a very becoming version of the loose new style. She looked perfect and young, one might have said, until one saw the girl on her right, and then it was apparent that Rose's look was not that of youth, but rather serene maturity without the lines, puffs and erosion of ill-health, temperament, anxiety or grief.

The girl—it must be Linda, whom he had last seen as a child in a gym slip—was of the new mode, straight-lined as though she were made with a clean steel superstructure. Her face might be as beautiful as her mother's, but without her enchanting prettiness. Linda, like so many young people, was grave, intent, a medieval page or an acolyte.

'I'm so silly,' Rose was laughing as she greeted him. 'I had almost given you up, and I had to come out and peep. I know that one can never rely on a policeman.'

He was reintroduced to the now grown-up Linda, seventeen, eighteen, he tried to remember the year of her birth. Three years, he thought, after the war.

The inside of the house, although obviously money had been spent, reminded him again of the Vicarage. Comfort and charm, Rose's favourite pastel colours, deep chairs, many cushions, a house run by a woman to suit a man. And the man was going to be this Richard Brewster.

Rose was smiling at him in the lamplight, saying how good it was to see him, how much she had to tell, asking if he would have recognized Linda, and it was for one moment like coming home. The gleam of her hair under the lamp, the soft swish of her skirt as she moved, were so familiar, as if no time had passed since last they met, that when he noticed the one small change it leapt to his policeman's eye like a clue in some major crime. On her left hand, where her plain wedding ring had been, she now wore a large, dome-shaped ruby surrounded by diamonds and set in heavy, twisted gold. He took a sharp dislike to that ring, though it was certainly a lovely piece, but it seemed to weigh down Rose's soft white hand, and the ruby was exactly the colour of fresh blood. As Rose's hand moved swiftly in her mild excitement, the ruby seemed to follow with a bright, crimson trail.

Four of them sat down to dinner in Rose's pretty dining room. Capricorn had to restrain his impatience to hear more about the threats: Rose had nothing further to tell him, and Brewster wasn't eager to discuss it at all. The dinner was good and varied, and Capricorn had time to study Rose's prospective husband. Well, he told himself, he could not be too chagrined about losing Rose again, or he most certainly would not like Brewster quite so much. And like him he certainly did.

Brewster had been a little late—his car had broken down and had had to be towed to the garage. After delivering himself of a few comments on so-called luxury cars in the age of mass production, he had shrugged philosophically and apologized to his hostess.

'Perhaps we should think of having a carriage and pair down here, eh, Rose? I think you would look charming up in a barouche.'

He had grinned at Rose, appreciating her beauty. Rose introduced the two men, and Brewster greeted her old friend with a sincere warmth. Capricorn, who remembered Sam Lavender, a kind man, obviously self-made and with few interests outside his business and his family, already middle-aged when he married the young Rose, was pleasantly surprised to meet the tall, soldierly-looking Brewster, still vigorous and very much in his prime, intelligent and well-informed; more than just a good citizen, he struck the Scotland Yard detective as certainly a leader of men.

Linda sat almost silent, leaving each tempting dish to be removed by the frowning parlourmaid, and gazed at nothing, looking moonstruck. Rose chatted and laughed. But the two men almost forgot these lovely women in the delight of finding they had both fought with the same regiment. Brewster had been a colonel, a veteran of many campaigns, Capricorn a young private just beginning his service, but differences of rank were as nothing as they re-fought battles and remembered England in her glory.

Capricorn had difficulty steering Brewster onto the subject of the threatening letters. He obviously preferred to expound his plan for breaking through Kesselring's Gothic Line after the fall of Rome, opening up the Po valley to the Allied troops and leaving their way clear to Vienna, perhaps, as early as the winter of 1944. Salt cellars, pepper pots, and spoons were drawn up to represent the Apennines, river valleys, and Kesselring's powerful forces; knives and forks indicated the Americans to the west and British, Polish, and South African forces on the Adriatic side, until the stern-featured parlourmaid removed them before serving the pudding.

No, Brewster said, he hadn't kept any of the letters. They'd gone straight into his waste-paper basket. 'Nonsensical stuff.' He dismissed the matter. 'Rose shouldn't have troubled you. I sincerely hope,' he said, sounding to the former private very much the colonel, 'I hope Rose didn't bring you here because of that.'

Rose crumbled a petit-four nervously, looking the picture of guilt.

'I came to see Rose and to congratulate you,' Capricorn said soothingly. It was difficult to offer protection, he thought, to a man who was known to have captured an enemy stronghold and taken two hundred prisoners with an advance party of only forty men.

Linda excused herself and seemed to melt away during the awkward moment. Rose shepherded the men into the drawing room for coffee and brandy.

'No formality here,' Brewster said, restored to gaiety. Capricorn tried to remember the last time he had been at a dinner where the women had obediently trotted off alone, but gave up.

'You're cold, Merle,' his aunts said, and they were right, for instead of wanting to knock Brewster down he would have preferred to be left alone with him at the table to finish off their army tales over the brandy bottle. Brewster's plan for piercing the Gothic line struck him as tactically sound, still there were one or two points he had wanted to bring up: the fatal thinning of troops along the Allied line to supply a force for the Riviera landing, for instance.

But Rose looked very lovely in the drawing room and he had a pang once more at seeing the heavy ring on her hand. She was glowing with unusual warmth and was obviously full of something she wanted to say. As soon as the men were comfortably ensconced in their chairs and properly provided with drinks and cigars, she rang the bell and asked the parlourmaid, who regarded her mistress with a more benign, indulgent air than she did the rest of the world, to bring in a package that had arrived that day.

'I shouldn't bore you with this, Merle,' Rose said, looking excited, 'but I couldn't wait another minute. Richard, do look at what just came!'

The maid brought in a wooden box, about two feet high and a foot square. Rose knelt down, her skirt falling around her like a pool of green water, and very carefully lifted a vase from its wrapping and held it up with both hands, a mermaid holding up a treasure from the sea.

Capricorn drew in his breath, and he saw that Brewster's eyes sharpened. What Rose was holding up to their gaze was a vase of jewelled Sèvres, its bright enamels gleaming in the lamplight, the burnished gold medallions shining richly. It was a piece of museum quality, and Capricorn, an art lover, took it, almost under compulsion, from Rose's outstretched hands and held it tenderly.

He often visited the salesrooms, rarely to buy, but to enjoy looking and observing. The habit was useful for his work, which he seldom forgot, for it gave him a good idea of who owned what at any particular time, and who was interested, and who might be tempted.

This particular vase he had seen and admired only recently. It had come on the market after being owned for about thirty years by a rich Yorkshire family. He had seen it before the auction, but it had been far beyond the purse of a policeman, even with the legacy he had received from his father. The day of the auction he had been busy on a case, and he hadn't known who bought the fine piece.

'Richard, you'll never guess who sent it!' Rose exclaimed.

Brewster took the vase from Capricorn and regarded it for a long thoughtful moment.

'Beatrice,' he said. His brow was knotted, and his usually sharp blue eyes were veiled and remote.

'But how could you have guessed?' Rose wailed.

Brewster came back from wherever, or whenever, he had been, staring a little.

He smiled at Rose, and turned to the Superintendent, bringing him back to the conversation.

'Beatrice is my stepsister,' he explained. 'She acts as housekeeper for me. It so happens that the family has wanted that vase for a long time. Beatrice's mother, my stepmother, chose it for a particular place in the front hall to finish off her decorating scheme. She had made up her mind to get that vase, and she was the sort of woman,' he smiled again, somewhat wryly, 'who, if she made up her mind to get something, usually got it. But this time, events miscarried. She was delayed in getting to the auction, and it went to a family in the north, I believe. And in spite of all the offers my father made, they declined reselling. Lucrezia, my stepmother, was so annoyed,' he smiled a little in recollection, 'that she would never put anything else in its place, and to this day that shelf is empty.'

He turned back to Rose.

'Beatrice must have heard of the sale, and gone up to buy it for us. I hadn't even realized she'd been to London. I must say, Rose, that was most kind of her. She's giving you the house, complete at last.'

'She's been so good,' Rose said earnestly. 'An angel, really. I felt quite an interloper at first, Merle, taking over a house that's almost a museum. And Beatrice has kept it all these years so well. She's amazing. I'd like you to meet her, Merle. We're having a little gathering tomorrow night at Brewster House. I know Beatrice will invite you if you're staying.

'You would think, Richard,' she spoke to him as if for a moment, she forgot the presence of a third person, 'you would think that Beatrice might have *minded* a little, you know. Giving up her brother and her house. And yet she doesn't turn a hair. Buys us this fantastic present and arranges to go on a world cruise.'

'As if anyone would mind you, my dear,' Brewster said, smiling—properly besotted, Capricorn considered. Rose was right—the sister must be unusual. A woman of character. But of all women to handle a sister who must be dispossessed, undoubtedly Rose was the one to do it most tactfully. Her charm would carry her through.

'Rose has been wonderful for Beatrice; she's made her into a new woman,' the lover said fondly. 'Beatrice has always been so housebound, and now look. Rose has taken her around and about, making her buy clothes for this trip.'

'Would you believe,' Rose said, wide-eyed. 'She was planning to go around the world in just what she said: two tweed suits and a black crêpe dinner dress.'

Capricorn was amused. Certainly, such a state of affairs would seem as criminal to Rose as, say, an axe murder to a police detective. He noticed that Brewster was looking at the vase with an air of satisfaction and—could it be a shade of relief? If he had been concerned about his sister's feelings on his marriage, perhaps this had settled it for him. That was as it should be. Brewster and Rose should be a happy couple, with no shadows to spoil the beginning. The thought brought him back to his work and the reason he was in Daines Barington, and he frowned a little. Richard Brewster had been threatened, and it was his job to find out who was making the threats and to stop them.

But before he could frame the questions that came to his mind, Rose, who was looking out of the window, turned round, laughing.

'Oh, do look at those two,' she said. 'Is it Romeo and Juliet, or The Babes in the Woods? They're not allowed to meet, you see,' she said to Capricorn mysteriously, 'but they manage to bump into each other somehow.'

Capricorn looked over her shoulder out to the shadowy garden. The moon was up and shed a fitful light through blowing cloud. Past the garden gate, up on the path, almost at the pale stones of St.

Cuthbert's, a man and girl stood hand in hand. They didn't seem to move or speak. Then the girl lifted her head—the man was much taller—and as the moonlight caught on her pale hair Capricorn recognized Linda, but the tall, lanky young man was someone he had never seen.

'This is silly, Rose,' Richard said, shortly. 'With your permission, I'll go out and bring them in. Linda will catch a cold; she has nothing round her shoulders.'

'Yes, do,' Rose said. 'The naughty child. It has to be accidental, you see.'

'What is this mystery?' Capricorn asked, guessing most of the answer.

'Silly Linda, who's in love,' Rose laughed. 'She's just as bad as I was.'

Had Rose really been in love with Sam Lavender, Capricorn wondered to himself as Rose went on.

'Only seventeen . . . But Hightower doesn't permit love affairs among the students. They can get *married,*' she said, looking puzzled, her smooth brow wrinkling attractively. 'But they mustn't court. It's all very difficult. And Linda is getting so *nervous.* I don't want to lose her,' she said plaintively. 'I did so want her to live here, I was going to give her this house when she married some nice English boy. But I'm beginning to wish he'd ask her. She'll be very shattered, I think,' she added, 'if he doesn't.'

Capricorn had no need to ask questions about the young man as, almost immediately, Brewster, who had taken on a no-nonsense, paternal air, brought in the two young people, who looked both happy and rather sheepish.

'This is Garry Wyatt, mother, Superintendent Capricorn,' Linda said, shyly. 'I had left one of my books. . . . and Garry was kind enough . . .''

'Hi,' the young man said in all all-inclusive American greeting.

Apart from his transatlantic informality he was a polite young man, and in spite of his somewhat embarrassing position he was gravely attentive to his hostess and courteous to Richard Brewster. The young people both had coffee—some of Linda's appetite was apparently restored and she nibbled on chocolate mints—and Garry had a glass of brandy with the other men.

Capricorn got the impression, as the young man looked about him, that this unexpected interlude of civilization did not come amiss. He must be a Siderean, from Rose's remarks, but he didn't wear the uniform; in his blue jeans, plaid shirt and leather jacket, he looked rather like a cowboy in an American film, he was appropriately long and lean, and his voice had a Western drawl. Siderean or not, he certainly showed no antagonism to Brewster, who was asking him searching questions. Capricorn felt for a moment that Brewster would demand to know the young man's intentions.

Linda glowed and more nearly resembled her mother than ever before. Her gaze hardly left Wyatt and she was most certainly very much in love. His manners were more controlled: he was older, definitely adult, but his feelings were apparent. Rose had a blazing love affair on her hands.

The conversation reverted to war, and it soon transpired that Wyatt was a veteran of Vietnam. One forgot, as Brewster remarked, that war had changed. Soldiers came and went while the war continued. Brewster obviously considered it a poor way of going on. Rose noticed his disapproval and in her gentle, absent-minded manner changed the conversation by asking the young man why he had come to England.

He thought a while before answering.

'Well, it's—it's something to do with what Mr Brewster said, I guess,' he answered slowly. 'There you are, over in Vietnam, in a war. Killing, and shooting, and all. Then your tour is up, and you're home. Home just like always. And that still going on.'

Capricorn and Brewster regarded him with sympathy. It was an old problem, that no civilian would ever understand: you were a soldier in a war and then you were home. Both men thought of their own homecomings and were silent.

But the American's problems weren't just the old ones. There were others, new, or at any rate, different.

'I wasn't a volunteer,' he said simply. 'I was drafted. I could've gotten out of it easy enough, staying at school, but it seemed right to go. The Chicanos went and a lot of guys from our ranch. So I got it over,' he said, looking up somewhat defiantly as if anyone might have accused him of right feeling or patriotism or some other unfashionable thing.

He frowned into the depths of the little fire in Rose's hearth, not exactly necessary but pleasant even on a summer's night in Daines Barington where the wind blew up chill and damp from the river.

'Well, when I first come out I tried going back to school. And to the kids it was like I'd done something terrible. I didn't think so,' he said. 'I was there. I saw what it was. I still think I was right to go. But you couldn't tell anybody. It got me, after a while,' he said. 'I went home and worked on the ranch. It's a good ranch and I like working on it. It'll be mine some day, if my old man doesn't get too bugged with me about something.' He smiled a little, reflectively. 'He's got a real blazing temper. Always threatening to leave the place to my cousin Richie, if I don't do what he says to do. And I don't, sometimes.'

The smile left, and his face went back to an expression both grim and rather too old for his young features.

'But right then I was no good for the ranch. I was kind of hung up on this thing. Remembering the kids at school, and then things people would say. Even Richie. And the newspaper and the TV. I started to feel like maybe I was crazy. Then I read some of Hightower's stuff, almost by accident. One of the hands gave me a book he'd picked up on a weekend in Dallas. It got me, and I went and saw some of his people. Then I tried some of his courses.'

He looked up from the fire, and now his face was quiet. A tormented young warrior, Capricorn thought; he's found himself a little peace. He felt a surge of compassion for all the young of this generation. For us, at least—he caught Brewster's eye and knew he was thinking the same—it was comparatively simple. We went, we fought, but we weren't worried whether we were doing the right thing; we were sure. And when we came home, we had the respect of our people. Our wounds were esteemed as honourable wounds.

'It's hard to explain what Hightower's method does,' the young man said. 'but, after a time, well, it's like—you know what you know. If you feel right, nobody is going to make you wrong. You can—hold your own place, if you get me.'

His long legs were stretched in front of him; his moccasined feet lay lightly on the rug, his arms rested on the chair, relaxed.

'People at home are all mixed up,' he said, 'but it won't bother me, now. Not about myself, I mean. I guess I'll be going home pretty soon.'

He smiled at them as if conscious of having talked more than his wont, and the smile was pleasant to see on that serious, candid face. Brewster looked satisfied with the young man, Rose covered his self-consciousness by refilling his cup, Linda looked alarmed, and Capricorn noted all their reactions rather absently as he took in the

67

significance of the young man's remarks. This youngster was no fool, he thought; perhaps this Hightower is a good psychologist after all. If he can heal those scars . . . After all, it's possible. The sun doesn't rise and set in Harley Street.

Rose, always interested in clothes, lightened the conversation.

'How is it, Mr Wyatt, that you don't wear the . . . the uniform?' she asked.

He laughed.

'I just can't stand dressing up. Never could, even when my mom liked to dress me up on Sundays for church. And one army is enough. Now don't you give me away,' he addressed Linda, who blushed. 'My excuse is it will frighten the horses. I look after the horses now that Hightower is away. Exercise them a bit.'

And the talk moved on to his father's ranch and cattle and horses, Capricorn was amused at Rose's wide-eyed wonder: he could see the old cowboy-and-Indian films rolling before her gaze while she looked on Garry as though he were a visitor from another planet. Linda was in a fair way to losing her admirer to her mother and looked just a trifle left out, as, he supposed, a girl must do in such a case. He looked at Brewster to see how he felt about the incorrigibly, the properly charming Rose.

Brewster was enjoying it. He liked to see the younger man fall a victim to his lady's charms. Brewster was too sure of himself to be jealous, too much of a man to be smallminded.

Rose had done well for herself, Capricorn decided, as the evening drew to a close, and he promised to try to be at Brewster House next evening for the small dinner. Garry left first and Linda was restored to happiness by walking with him down to the garden gate, properly dressed for out-of-doors on the orders of Brewster, who was obviously enjoying the paternal role.

Rose had done very well. Sam Lavender had been a good enough choice, a kind husband, a shrewd business man, a protector of a bewildered young girl, but Brewster was much more. Colonel Brewster had been a good soldier—he had received a decoration after Alamein, Capricorn remembered, from the talk of the men who had been with Brewster in the desert. He was a man of wide affairs, active in his town, and he had shown sensibility.

Yes, a fine man Capricorn thought, somewhat moodily, as he left the bright house and the glowing Rose and walked out alone into the cool, dark night. Just such a man as he himself would have liked to be were he a landowner instead of a mountebank's son turned sleuth. Then he laughed at himself, for he believed that a man's life was his choice, and as comfortable to him as an old shoe and that no matter how much he might admire more glittering models shown in the shops, nothing would fit all his corns and bumps as well as those wretched old objects he affected to despise.

Such philosophical thoughts occupied him as he walked by the tower of St Cuthbert's, the grey stone reflecting the dim moonlight, holding up the dark. Capricorn regarded the fine old church thoughtfully. Would a young soldier look for consolation there?

It was just as well, Capricorn considered, that it was Other Departments who had to decide on the authenticity of Hightower's doctrine, on his acceptability in Britain, his worth, or lack of it. Just as well he was a simple policeman, and his only job was to sniff after a crime. He himself was a man for St Cuthbert's, not the Moo-Cow Milk Bar, but he recognized his love for the old, the beautiful, the stable, and tried not to be bound by it. He knew that all virtue was not bound up in the established order, and he tried, conscientiously, to be fair.

Yes, he was glad it was not his problem. The night air smelt of damp grass and falling leaves, the path was soft under his feet, the branches of an ash tree made a delicate tracery against a patch of moonlit cloud. In the morning he would look into the matter of the letters, but if Garry Wyatt was what the Sidereans were producing, it didn't look as though there was going to be much to worry about.

Tranquil, he arrived at Roseacre House, quite ready for his bed. But a few hundred yards down the street flames leaped out of the darkness, shooting up into the sky. Capricorn paused, peering into the night. The fire seemed to be opposite the Moo-Cow, in the neighbourhood of the Emanuel Church. He moved quickly down the street to see what was going on.

The moon had hidden itself again, and at first he could only see a group of black-looking figures huddled round a huge bonfire. Excited voices came down the quiet High Street.

'But Jed, you can't!'

'Of course you can!'

'We're with you!'

'But don't you think . . .'

A wink of moonlight displayed them to be a large huddle of Sidereans on the path outside the Emanuel Church, where a bonfire of dead leaves had apparently attracted them, perhaps for warmth, perhaps for light. A few of them were adding sticks and twigs and paper cartons to the fire, while others were still streaming out of the confinement of the Moo-Cow to listen to the young man who was haranguing them from the top of the church steps.

He was not tall, but in the firelight he seemed lean, dark and commanding. His voice carried on the still air.

'We can't let him get away with it.'

'Right,' his followers screamed.

'He's kept our workmen off our own property over three months! Noah's property.'

'Yes!' the others chimed.

'After he promised Noah the new law would go through, he's squashed it! For good!'

'Yes, after he promised,' a heavy-set young woman shrieked in support.

'And today I got a letter,' the young man took an envelope from his short cloak and flourished it high, 'a letter from Noah himself. He's sending a special consultant to see our progress. Next week! We must get Brewster to move before that happens!'

'Ye-es,' the crowd screamed in one voice.

Capricorn frowned. He remembered Griswald talking about a trouble-maker, one Jed Frost. This was certainly he. His voice had the unmistakable note of the rabble-rouser, trouble in any place, at any time, more dangerous than ever with a crowd of excitable youth. He was angry, Griswald had said, because the courts had stopped his building plans. It was typical that he should blame Brewster personally. Such men liked to have one definite object for their rage.

'What, exactly, do you plan to do, Jed?' A calm, reasonable voice came from a plump matron in a voluminous cloak.

The dark figure at the top of the steps ignored her and spoke to the murmuring crowd.

'We'll destroy him if we have to! We'll sweep him out of the way like an insect!'

He snapped a branch from the nearest bush and held it in the fire until it burned brightly, then flourished the flaming brand in an arc around his head.

'We'll deal with him,' he screamed, passionately. 'We'll find a Path! There's a way to handle people like him, Hitlers, Stalins, all those who want to stop our advance to the stars!'

Without his saying another word his followers, except for the matron, each broke a long twig from a tree and lit it in the fire, then held the burning brands high in a many-circled belt of flame.

'Path 45!' Frost shrieked. 'Path 45!'

'Path 45!' the crowd roared, with one exception, 'Path 45!'

A small, nervous-looking man peeped out of the window of the house beside the church, a telephone receiver in his hand, and watched with relief as two large village constables converged upon the group.

The moment was over. At a word from the constables, Frost flung his brand onto the bonfire, leapt down the steps, and disappeared into the dark. The others followed more slowly, milling about and drifting off in twos and threes while the constables, bearing down massively, spoke in quiet but firm tones about breach of the peace, the breaking of ordinances and the necessity of moving along.

As the last of the Sidereans got into his car and roared away, one of the constables, recognizing Capricorn from his morning visit to the station, addressed him.

'Evening, sir.'

'Good evening,' Capricorn replied. 'That was well done.'

The constable smiled in pleasure but his face quickly darkened.

'The Super won't be pleased to hear of this.'

'That he won't,' his companion agreed.

'Super likes to think there's no harm in 'em,' the first constable said gloomily. 'But I don't like the sound of young Frost, and that's the truth. What's he working 'em up for, if not trouble,' he demanded.

'Superintendent Griswald agrees with you there, I think,' Capricorn said tactfully. 'I know he's keeping an eye on him.'

'Ought to be locked up—if you don't mind my saying so, sir.'

The constable, a tall man, looked up to the even taller Capricorn, apparently remembering that he was speaking to the Yard.

'But on what charge, you see, that's the problem,' Capricorn pointed out. He was wondering about that himself. The two constables hadn't heard as much as he had. Inciting to commit a crime? He would have a talk with Griswald as soon as possible. He instructed the two constables to make their report to the station straight away and bade the two unhappy-looking men goodnight, recognizing their dismay echoing in himself. The firelit scene had been unpleasant, at the least.

And what was Path 45? Was it the Wild West echo of Garry Wyatt in his mind that immediately made him think of a gun? Well, Hightower's Paths—he had seen the advertisements on hoardings all over London—were offered as man's release from his enslavement to his body and so from the earth to the stars. A large-calibre pistol would certainly take care of the body part. Was this just a grim Siderean joke or . . .

His uneasiness was great enough for him to telephone Superintendent Griswald at his home. He had to keep his voice low, as the telephone was at the reception desk and flurries of guests were passing through, laughing—the local cinema had just finished its performance of a comic film. Perhaps because of that, Griswald did not get the impact of the scene as he described it and did not seem disturbed.

'Young play-acting fool,' he said in disgust. Capricorn could hear a television set in the background piping forth some favourite Saturday night programme. A female voice was asking Griswald to 'talk quieter,' which to his credit, Capricorn thought, he ignored. He brooded, as he often did at such times, on the great advisability of the celibate state for policemen, or, he amended, the unmarried state. 'I wish Brewster would summons him. By the way, I heard that Hightower is coming back, or sending a deputy, to get rid of him. And not a moment too soon. Thanks for letting me know. We'll go up there and see him in the morning.'

Capricorn, unsatisfied, wishing he were there in his official capacity, went up to his pleasant room. The public uttering of threats—well, Griswald could deal with that. But those faces lifted into the circles of burning brands . . . Suddenly, Siderea seemed different from the benevolent helper of war veterans and asthmatic little girls.

His dreams were troubled and he woke in the night to rise and look out of his window onto the High Street of Daines Barington. He was no longer satisfied about the harmlessness of the threatening letters. Yes, he would go to that place first thing in the morning, as soon as he could dig out Griswald from connubial bliss. He went back to bed and slept lightly, uneasily, listening to the slow, steady thrum of rain on the window as it came down in the first storm of the season, heralding autumn, blowing from the West over the crown of Witch Hill, pouring into the streets and gardens of the sleeping town.

five

The morning, however, dawned bright, nightmares faded, and before Capricorn could speak to Griswald he received a call from London. His Chief was on the line.

'Sorry to break in on your bucolic Sunday,' he said jovially, 'I know you're supposed to be on leave, but can we have your presence for a couple of hours today anyway? Sergeant Copper brought home a good bag on the East Ham job. Pulled in a lot of barrow boys who carved up that pawnbroker. But when he searched the lodgings of one of them, Copper found some of the stuff from that Esso station hold-up tucked away in the garage. The money wasn't enough,' the Chief spoke with mild disdain at such clumsy amateurishness. 'They helped themselves to a few tyres and other bits and pieces. You and Copper must have been really dreaming not to catch them at it.'

Capricorn listened patiently. The Yard had had a tip on the possible hold-up, and he and Copper had gone to investigate, just in time, as Copper had said gloomily, 'to be too bleedin' late.' But Capricorn had caught a glimpse of one of the men as he sped away in a powerful car that managed to elude the police net, so carefully cast through four counties. Now the Chief wanted him for a positive identification.

'The station attendant, of course, isn't certain,' he said, with resignation at the apparent partial blindness and fragmentary memories of the general public.

Capricorn considered rapidly. The business of the Sidereans seemed less urgent in daylight. He promised to take the earliest train to town. Better to leave his car in the hotel garage than to get involved with returning weekenders later. If all went well he could take the evening train back.

He reached Griswald, who was in a benevolent Sunday mood, and changed the arrangement for their visit to the Manor to the next morning.

'Don't worry yourself,' Griswald said heartily. 'Last night, to be on the safe side, I sent a couple of men to watch Brewster House to see if any of those young sparks were up to mischief. On the quiet, of course. If he ever knew that I'd done it . . . He's a man that's used to handling things himself, you understand.' He chuckled. 'He's called me a frustrated nanny over this business already.'

'No results?' Capricorn asked.

'No Sidereans. One of my men got belly-ache from sampling Brewster's apples, I believe, while he lurked in the orchard.'

Capricorn laughed, and said he would keep in touch. He called Rose from the station, and apologized for not being able to join the party that night at Brewster House.

'Oh, Beatrice will be so disappointed,' her pretty voice was full of regret. 'She was going to call you at the hotel to make sure you came. Perhaps, if you do get back in time, you might come anyway? It's very informal. And there are some people I'd like you to meet, the Rector, and Dr Bailey.'

Capricorn promised he would if he possibly could, and caught the slow Sunday train to town. All went smoothly when he arrived. Sergeant Copper had indeed found the petrol-pump highwayman, and when they were finished the sergeant, his brush of dark red hair seemingly puffed up and gleaming with triumph and anticipation, prepared to go off merrily for the evening with his current girl friend.

'Where are you taking her?' Capricorn asked. He and Copper were on very amiable terms. The older man had not been certain that they would be when he had first met the slangy, rather brash and cynical young policeman, but he had found him to be, under his cockney intransigence, completely devoted to his job, and they had become friends.

'Oh, this one, she always wants to go to the pictures,' Copper replied, as he preened himself for the event. 'She's sort of old-fashioned, this bird.'

Interpreting correctly 'the pictures' as the cinema, Capricorn was faintly startled. So a liking for the cinema was already old-fashioned, was it? To aunts Tilly, Milly, Dolly and Nelly it had been a hated modern invention—probably to do with the devil, they had considered. It was a good thing to work with a young sergeant to keep one abreast of the times, Capricorn thought philosphically.

He took the slow local train down to Daines Barington in the warm, bright, late afternoon in a mildly sentimental and nostalgic mood. He would see the pretty Rose married again. Certainly, he had to admit, Colonel Brewster—it was like the man not to use his war-time title—Brewster and the small market town would be a better home for her than anything a peripatetic policeman could provide. The shadows around the empty station were blue, and he stood for a moment, enjoying the fading light while Rose's names sounded in his mind. Rose Raintree. Rose Lavender. Rose Brewster. But the last jolted a little, like a loose pebble, something to stumble over, not quite likely or right. Then he forgot his phonetic musing as a soberly dressed man, pale and with a rather formal air, approached him so quietly as to make Capricorn start a little when the man coughed apologetically and spoke.

'Superintendent Capricorn,' he inquired.

The detective's mind, from professional habit, jumped to conjectured disaster. A sudden anxiety kicked in the pit of his stomach. Had Brewster been attacked?

'I'm Purdy, sir, from Brewster House,' the man went on, his demeanour resolving itself into that of a well-trained servant. 'Miss Brewster told me to meet the 7:30, she thought you might be on it. Not much choice on Sunday,' he said with sympathy.

The Sunday service was snail-like, the Superintendent agreed. He looked at his watch, absently, catching his breath with the sudden relief and saw it was already 7:40. You're getting jumpy as an old woman, he told himself irritably. At the Yard it was often said that

75

Capricorn had an extra sense about the case he was working on, and his Chief sometimes teased, to Capricorn's inner fury, about the magic he had learned from the Great Capricornus. Sixth sense, he now reproached himself, more like the nerves of the classic old maid, sure of burglars under the bed.

The manservant indicated a small two-seater outside the station, in the area that should have been inhabited by taxis, all of which were having their day off.

'Miss Brewster apologizes for the runabout, sir,' he said as Cap-. ricorn hesitated. 'But the big car is in the garage for repairs. It often is,' he said, relapsing into a chronic grievance. 'And Mr Brewster just had to make two trips with this, to fetch Mrs Lavender and then all the way back for the Rector.'

Capricorn considered swiftly. He had been impatient to get up to the Manor, but Siderea, and possibly Griswald, would be off in Sunday pursuits. Yes, he could accept the invitation. Miss Brewster was gracious. Richard Brewster's guests might shed some light on the Manor's affairs that would help on his visit the next morning. With a word of thanks he got into the little car and enjoyed the winding road through the apple orchards heavy with fruit.

'A good apple harvest,' he remarked.

Purdy looked doubtful.

'Well, sir, I don't work out of doors, but Mr Brewster's been saying it's not as good as it looks. A big harvest, and our fruit is always a good fruit, but this year it's been touched with some new kind of blight, it seems. A lot of those apples are rotten inside.'

A countryman's lot is not so idyllic after all, Capricorn reminded himself. No thugs, no razor-carriers or skinheads, but there was always bad weather and blight. Then he saw Brewster House before him at the top of the drive and had to change his mind. For Brewster House it would be worth it, even to struggle with blight. It was not large, as the principal house of the neighbourhood might be, but its perfect proportion, harmony with its background, and Georgian elegance made it memorable. The evening light struck softly on the old stone walls and the front door stood hospitably open.

Capricorn left the car part way up the drive and walked the rest, the better to enjoy the aspect. It was a house meant to be approached slowly, he thought. One should not be decanted roughly from a two-seater into the very entrance. It must have been the pleasure of many

Brewsters and their friends, through the centuries, to ride up to that doorway on horseback or in a horse-drawn carriage and see the house, changing its aspect with the seasons, and yet unchanged.

His step was quiet for so tall a man and as he entered the fine hall he caught his two hostesses unaware. Rose, fluttering in a lace dress the colour of champagne, looking, as usual, calm and relaxed, was standing before an empty niche, measuring it with her graceful hands, apparently for the benefit of a small, dark, mannish-looking woman, carelessly dressed, with dust on her sensible shoes, who was approaching from the back of the house.

'There you are, Beatrice,' Rose was saying. 'I've been looking at this spot, and you're right: the vase will be perfect.'

'Lucrezia was right. She always was.' The dark woman took the compliment calmly. She caught sight of Capricorn and Rose followed her glance.

'Oh, Merle, you came, what luck!' she said happily and introduced him to Miss Brewster. The introduction over, she withdrew and left Miss Brewster to do the honors as hostess. Tactful Rose, Capricorn thought.

Miss Brewster explained that dinner would be late as her brother had had to go out unexpectedly on some urgent but, she hoped, brief business. In the meantime, if the Superintendent wished, she would show him the house. He accepted with pleasure and real interest, while his policeman's mind wondered what business would take a man like Brewster from his guests at dinner time.

His surprise and delight at Brewster House almost drowned out his mental questionings. As Rose had told him, the house was a museum. There were few places left in England, still private dwellings, that could match Brewster House in appointments. Richard Brewster was a man of sense and wealth, but whoever had decorated this house had been a connoisseur of a high order.

'I won't show you downstairs,' Miss Brewster chuckled. 'It's a secret sin. The servants complain. The house is built on a slope, you see, and the rooms under the drawing room are very dark. The only light comes from the side of the house. The Brewster who had the place re-built,' she explained, 'only did it for his wife. The story is that he preferred the dark old farmhouse, patched up as it was from Elizabeth's time; argued with the architect to try to keep some of its features, and when the new house was finished spent most of his time sulking in the servants' hall. He penny-pinched on the candles too, so the servants had to spend their few hours off in practically pitch darkness.'

She grinned, her dark, rather heavy features lightening into attractiveness, amused at the idea of the feudally arrogant Brewster ancestors. Her knowledge of the treasures of the house was extensive. Capricorn would have thought her a great lover of art except that her interest did not extend beyond the Brewster collection. She had no attention to spare for anything outside it. Miss Brewster was a curator, not a collector. He found the very self-possessed spinster with her rather sardonic wit entertaining: she was, as he had suspected, a woman of character.

They turned into the magnificent drawing room, still bathed in light—double summer-time, Capricorn noted half-consciously, the detective's mind recording time and variations from nature automatically while he took in more sharply the small group that was already assembled. Brewster was not among them. The feeling of uneasiness that had dogged him since the manservant met him at the station grew stronger. You're being foolish, he told himself again. You can't detain Brewster for his own protection. And you can't have all Siderea rounded up and deported: you're not in a totalitarian state. Still, he could find out where Brewster had gone. He looked round for his hostess but she had slipped away.

The wind was rising and from outside there came a rustle of leaves, swept too early from the branches, drifting still green and full along the colonnade. Standing in the window embrasure a slender man with a noble head and thick silver hair was reading in a sonorous voice from a manuscript against an obbligato of a linnet warbling in the garden.

'It hath been published to the town
That none shall entomb him or mourn
But leave unwept, unburied, a grisly feast for birds . . .'

Capricorn shivered involuntarily. Then he noticed Rose looking up from her chair with a deceptively attentive expression that he knew well enough to mean she was thinking of something quite different, probably her wardrobe for the next day, and a short, plump, balding man, regarding both Rose and the reader, looking sleepily amused.

'Oh, Merle,' Rose said, drawing him towards the silver-haired man, 'this is our Rector, Mr Theale from St Cuthbert's. He quite looks after Linda and me. He's been reading to us from this paper he's writing—too clever, really. Mr Theale, this is my old friend Superintendent Capricorn of Scotland Yard, but he's not at all frightening, so don't worry.'

At which, of course, the men laughed themselves into an instant sense of camaraderie, and Rose beamed and introduced the sleepy-looking man as Dr Bailey, who, she said plaintively, 'helped dear Linda so much, at least, as long as she was willing . . .'

'Now, don't worry,' Dr Bailey comforted her. 'You know Linda's doing well. This Siderea business has helped her. Taken her mind off her ailment. As a medical man,' he looked at Capricorn, his eyes twinkling, 'I ignore them, officially, but privately I can say—' Capricorn remembered Rose telling him with wide-eyed wonder that the town doctor was noted for his indiscretion—'privately I can say that I have seen many cures by Sidereans and many cases of varied ills lightened considerably, particularly those of nervous origin. And,' he added in some delight, 'they're far better than I am with the imaginary kind.'

'How would you account for that, doctor?' Capricorn asked, interested despite his mounting sense of uneasy impatience, irrational as that seemed in this quiet and civilized place.

'I don't,' Bailey said cheerfully, his plump, round face creased with amusement. 'Any more than I have to account for the cures at Lourdes, or other matters more in the province of the Rector here. His bailiwick I assure you.'

The Rector, to his obvious relief, was saved from having to comment by the appearance of Purdy with sherry and a tray of glasses, and by Rose, who took his manuscript from his hand, read a few lines, and looked discouraged.

'What a perfectly horrid idea,' she said. 'Can you imagine that nasty man, wanting to shut a girl up in a cave until she died.'

She trembled a little.

'And all for wanting to bury her own brother.'

'It was the law, my dear Mrs Lavender,' the Rector pointed out. 'That's what my book explains. Law and society against religion—'

She looked up thoughtfully.

'A very strange law,' she remarked. 'I'm quite sure now there's a law that you *have* to bury people. Rector, would there be a fine if you didn't?'

The Rector looked dismayed again. Capricorn was sure he had never been asked such a question before, and certainly did not know the answer. And neither do I, minion of the law that I am, he reflected. Rose!

She had not finished.

'Well, I still think it very horrid. Isn't it wonderful to be living now instead of all that time back when people were so impossible, shutting one another up in caves?'

Capricorn, who still had friends in MI6 and in the Special Branch, had opportunities to know more than the average citizen what was going on at that very moment in Arctic labour camps, African civil wars, and other haunts of misery around the world. It was England, he might have said, a country and her people, that gave Rose the quiet life she so appreciated: the civil order was of place, not of time; and its defence was active, not passive. But Rose was Rose, and a dinner party a party. No reason for him to disturb the comfortable group sipping Richard Brewster's excellent sherry. Where *was* Brewster?

And besides, he reflected, if he spoke the truth he would disturb Rose too much. For it was no longer true that England could protect her own: her defences were no longer adequate, her people divided into those who rested in the knowledge of the strength of her great ally, those who trusted to the goodwill of her enemies, those who vaguely did both, and those who were too vague to think at all. The thought was bitter to an old army man, and it spoiled the taste of sherry in his mouth. Brewster must feel the same, he thought, and missed him for a moment as one would an old and trusted comrade. Where could he be? He would find out from Miss Brewster.

At that moment the manservant, Purdy, opened the great double doors to the dining room and Capricorn saw his hostess. She was standing in the picture gallery that ran across the opposite wall, adjusting a portrait that seemed perfectly straight. Even in his impatience the Superintendent could not help noticing that the portrait was a Laszlo, and certainly one of his best works; the subject flashed from the frame with violent life; the vivid beauty of the woman, who seemed to lean back into the room, was an irresistible magnet to the eye. As he moved forward to approach his hostess, he caught the odd resemblance between the woman of the portrait and the dull, rough copy that was Miss Brewster. Poor creature, he thought, compassion flowing over his other concerns, what could be the life of a woman like that? Her brother.

Rose, wearying of the Antigone, anticipated him.

'Beatrice, shouldn't Richard be back by now? It's almost nine o'clock.'

'Goodness knows,' Miss Brewster said shortly. 'I think we'll have to go in to dinner. Cook tells me she can't hold it back any longer.'

She came down the graceful curving stair from the gallery with a heavy tread, moving awkwardly in delicate evening slippers. She had changed into the shoes that Rose had made her buy, Capricorn guessed, and she didn't like them.

Miss Brewster turned to the Superintendent.

'Perhaps you'll take Mrs Lavender in,' she suggested. 'Richard *would* go though I told him he'd be late. He said he would be back before Dr Bailey came. Dr Bailey is often delayed,' she said, as she helped herself to sherry and looked at the unfortunate doctor with disapproval.

'Only for births and deaths, my dear Beatrice,' he murmured. 'Always so untimely. Gertrude Hospeth's baby came at five o'clock this morning.'

Beatrice ignored these lights on medical life, and spoke to the Superintendent.

'He went to see those mad people at the Manor. One of them must have crept up to the house this evening, though nobody saw anything—the staff are always having a nice cup of tea in the back—and poked one of those letters under the door. He was furious and went off after them.'

'A threatening letter?' Capricorn asked, suddenly grim.

'Oh, another one of those grubby little things, all dirty thumbprints and death's heads.'

Miss Brewster dismissed the matter with the air of a woman whose dinner party has been spoiled.

In the silence that followed her remark, the sharp knocking at the front door was loud and clear. The door was opened and someone gave a little cough. To Capricorn the cough seemed to join the one he had heard at the station, and the same apprehension ground into him again, only much stronger.

You fool, Merle, he thought, you fool.

He was on his way to the door when the manservant stopped him at the entrance to the drawing room. Coldly, horribly, he was not surprised when the man whispered to him without looking at the mistress of the house.

'Superintendent Griswald is at the door, sir. When he heard you were here, and Dr Bailey, he asked to see you both. Perhaps you'd like to use the master's study.'

'Purdy, what are you whispering about?' Miss Brewster called. Capricorn was aware of her approach and spoke quickly to the Rector.

'Look after the ladies, will you, Theale? I'll be with you in a moment.'

The soft thud as he closed the door to the drawing room was followed by the muffled boom of the heavy front door of Brewster House. You're too late, roared in his head as he raced across the hall. You fool, you procrastinating fool, too late.

six

Griswald and a constable stood waiting, stiff and awkward, in Richard Brewster's private room; overflowing it seemed at that moment with images of Rose Lavender, photographs on desks and chairs and a large portrait glowing with colour behind the sombre policemen.

'Dead?' Capricorn asked.

Griswald nodded, catching his lower lip between his teeth.

'No chance of life. I sent up the ambulance but from what the man who found him said, Brewster's brains are spilled all over the Witch Hill Road. I just stopped in to warn the ladies on my way up and seeing you were here—the CC is asking to have you on the case,' he added. 'Too much for us, and that's a fact.'

'Of course,' Capricorn answered. He was already on the telephone, Richard Brewster's telephone that sat next to a photograph of Rose and Linda with Brewster in the centre, a laughing family group for a man who had no family. In a few moments all the arrangements were made. Sergeant Copper, at Capricorn's request, would come down on the first morning train.

He turned back to Griswald.

'A gunshot wound?'

'The postman, who found him, says it is,' Griswald answered. 'Two wounds, he says. He's an ex-service man.'

Capricorn spoke rapidly into the mouthpiece and hung up.

'Who's medical examiner down here, you, Bailey?'

Dr Bailey nodded, unable to talk. His sleepy look had gone and his soft, round face looked stiff and much older.

'All right then, let's get up there.'

'My car's outside,' Griswald said. There was sweat on his forehead and his eyes were oddly red as he looked straight at Capricorn.

'I was wrong.'

'We were both wrong,' Capricorn said shortly.

The Rector was waiting for them outside the drawing room.

'Is it . . . Is Richard. . . . ?'

'I'm afraid he's dead,' Capricorn said gently. The Rector is Richard's oldest friend, Rose had said.

'An accident?'

'He was shot.' Griswald's voice rasped, out of control.

The Rector flinched for a second, but recovered and spoke calmly.

'Don't worry, gentlemen. I know you have to go. I will take care of the ladies.'

Capricorn motioned to the constable.

'The Rector will help you. I want you to stay and get hold of the threatening letter. Don't get any more prints on it; and get it right down to the station. Then come on up to the Hill.'

The pale-faced constable—it was the one who had warned him against Jed Frost, Capricorn noticed, feeling as though he'd been kicked in the stomach—went with the Rector. Theale was acting like a man of sense in spite of his romantic looks, Capricorn thought, the thought itself a layer of coolness over the seething, acid self-reproach he would carry with him for a long time to come. He had enjoyed himself, relishing a man's treasures, while that man was being done to death.

In the car, shooting up the road towards Witch Hill, he asked questions, precisely, methodically. It was mere chance the body had been discovered so soon, Griswald said. The postman had a cable-gram for the Manor and its telephone line was damaged from the storm the night before. The postman had got on his bicycle and was puffing up the road with the message through the south pasture near the crown of Witch Hill when he had seen something lying on the road in front of him. He had dismounted; his first thought when he saw the body was that the man was a victim of a hit-and-run driver but as he got closer there could be no doubt about the gunshot wounds. He also, after a moment, recognized the dead man, although the head was badly shattered.

'A sensible fellow,' Griswald said, 'He turned round and stopped at the first house he came to and called the station. No word to the Manor.'

It was twilight when they came to the place in the road. Four con-stables were rigging up a tarpaulin—'I think it's about to rain,' Griswald said, and Capricorn nodded his approval. The ambulance sat on the side of the road; the emergency team stood by the hedge, smoking, obviously waiting to be dismissed. One of them came for-ward, spoke a few quiet words to Dr Bailey, and they piled back into their vehicle and made their way back down the hill. As they left, two of Griswald's men cordoned off the road and set up red lamps that glowed sulkily into the oncoming dusk. Except for the tramp of the constables' boots it was very quiet. A field mouse slipped through the hedge, stopped short at the body lying across its path, jumped and scuttled back. A mist was rising from the long grass.

Capricorn looked down at the corpse lying with the feet on the ex-treme edge of the road, the body at an angle of about forty-five de-grees. Brewster was dressed in the dark suit he had planned to wear for his dinner. It seemed oddly formal, lying in the road. Like all sudden death it looked wrong—out of place and time.

Dr Bailey was examining the body with the help of Griswald's torch. A shot in the back had entered the right side just below the shoulder blade; a shot to the head had shattered the whole left front. Blood and brains oozed on the tarred road. Capricorn, usually inured to violent death, felt sick in body and in mind. This was the man he had thought one of the finest types in the country. Whom he, Cap-ricorn, had been called upon to protect. And he had failed.

Well, no time for self-reproach. That could come later. Now he had another job. He had to find Richard Brewster's murderer.

The quiet was suddenly shattered by the noise of a motor-cycle.

The constable who had been left at Brewster House rushed panting up to Capricorn.

'P.C. Rummie reporting, sir. I thought I'd best let you know straight away. The lady, Miss Brewster, says the letter's not in the house, sir, that Mr Brewster took it with him. Rector and I looked about a bit to be sure, but there's no sign of it.'

'Did you check the waste paper baskets?'

'Yes, sir. No luck, sir.'

Capricorn frowned and glanced down at the body. Dr Bailey was still making his examination.

'Thank you, constable.'

Griswald came forward, rubbing his hands together against the chill.

'Ladies notified, Rummie?'

'Yes, sir. Mrs Lavender's not well, and the Rector is taking her home. Miss Brewster is very brave and like she always is. Says she'd like to see you, sir, about when she can have her brother's body.'

'I'll stop in on my way down,' Griswald said. 'Go back down to Brewster House, Rummie, and patrol the area. Watch for any intruders. Stable door,' he added with a sigh as P.C. Rummie roared off into the twilight.

Birds already roosting in the hedges twittered in reproach at the unaccustomed bustle. Dr Bailey had handled the body delicately, hardly touching it, his plump little hands surprisingly deft, and Capricorn watched with approval until the doctor nodded that he had finished.

'Nothing for me to tell you that you can't see yourself,' he said. 'Obvious enough.'

'He'd left the house about seven, according to Miss Brewster,' Capricorn replied. 'How close can you estimate the time of death?'

'Over an hour,' Bailey said, 'Could be two.'

He shrugged.

'Probably was killed when he first walked up here, but that's only a guess.'

Brewster's arm was stretched out in the road, his wrist watch still ticking, the luminous dial shining up eerily. Nine-fifteen. About twenty-five minutes since Rose had said, 'Shouldn't Richard be back?'

But Richard was already dead, his body lying in the ground mists.

The police van arrived with a photographer who took pictures of the body with a flashlight. While he worked, Capricorn took the torch over to the long grass. There was no sign of trampling, but it was lush and resilient. The murderer could have stood here, firing one shot, and then, approaching closer as Brewster fell, firing, close range and making sure . . .

'You'll keep your men away from here, of course,' he suggested and Griswald nodded.

'We'll take a look in the morning.'

He turned to Dr Bailey to discuss the post mortem and Miss Brewster's request.

When the photographer finished Capricorn examined the pockets of Brewster's suit and shirt, taking his wallet out and looking through every fold. Cigarette case, lighter, matches, change, money, cards. No letter of any kind. He nodded to Griswald, who had his men remove the body. Capricorn shone his torch on the road where Brewster's head had lain. His mouth twisting with distaste, he felt through the blood and fragments of bone. He took a small pick, dug out what he had been searching for and placed it on his handkerchief.

'A cartridge?' Griswald said, peering down. 'What is it?'

'A big one,' Capricorn answered thoughtfully. 'Looks to me like a .45.'

Griswald started. The two men looked at each other for a moment in silence. Then the rain started to come down.

seven

And so it was by night after all that Capricorn first saw Witch Hill Manor. Superintendent Griswald went back to town, leaving two constables on duty, driving Dr Bailey to Brewster House to see what could be done for the bereaved sister.

'What on earth are you going to do,' the doctor had asked, his usual light-hearted curiosity turned grim, 'with five hundred suspects?'

'Fortunately, it's not left to my personal brilliance,' Capricorn answered. 'We have our procedures.'

It was an official answer, he thought wryly, and about as meaningful as a doctor's reply to anxious relatives that a patient was comfortable. Standard procedures were efficient, but they had hardly been designed to cover a small army. However, there was going to be a great deal of donkey work and this was the time to begin. The gun had to be found. One bullet was still in the body; the other was already on its way to the police lab. The ghastly patch on the road would have to remain, until the morning brought the Yard technicians, under the canopy on the crown of the hill.

The words the Rector had quoted from the Antigone came shockingly to mind.

'. . . none shall entomb him or mourn
But leave unwept, unburied, a grisly feast for birds . . .'

The sister, he thought. Miss Brewster. Her loss was greater even than Rose's. What was the life of the plain woman, he had wondered earlier. Her brother.

With all its blinds drawn closely, Witch Hill Manor, a fantasy by Vanbrugh, was bleak, dark grey against a grey sky, under the pouring heavens. A huge cedar, black and still, guarded the barred door.

Capricorn had passed quickly through the gates, showing his credentials silently to the frightened-looking young Siderean in the gate house. The news had apparently preceded him. The great metal posts clanged at his back. Before him, to one side, an excavation—a large puddle now, littered with untidy piles of brick and stone—resembled bomb damage of the 1940s, an inelegant ruin, a monument to heedless impatience. The drive, which had not been widened since it was built for carriages, was overhung with trees whose branches interlaced to form a tunnel. Not a cheerful place to hunt for murderers on the loose.

One thing had already been done. Griswald would make sure that no foreign Siderean could leave before his statement was taken, checked, and he was cleared. British Sidereans would be requested to stay in the area. He could trust Griswald to be implacable; the easy tolerance of the small-town superintendent had been shattered by shock and replaced by a hard-eyed watchfulness.

As he approached, the great front door opened and a large woman, wrapped in a cloak which, drained of its garish colour, had a certain dignity, stepped forward to greet him.

'I am Superintendent Capricorn of Scotland Yard,' he said. 'I should like to see Jedediah Frost.'

'Mr Frost is away,' she answered. 'I'm Portia Anthony, in charge at the moment. Won't you come in?'

For a moment he was still.

'When did Frost leave?' he asked sharply.

'He took the 6.55 to London,' she replied. 'But please come in, Superintendent. I think I can reach him for you by telephone.'

Brewster had not left his house until seven o'clock. If this story was true, then Frost was clear, of the act itself, anyway.

'You're very wet,' the woman pointed out gently.

He was, he noticed. The downpour had been severe as it was sudden. There wouldn't be much left tomorrow in the way of tracks outside the canopied area by the time the men from London arrived. He wished, as he had wished before, foolishly, that murders took place at more convenient times.

'I've heard the dreadful news,' she said soberly. 'I was expecting you.'

He must have looked enquiring for she went on.

'Our telephone line had been out and the Daines Barington operator called through when it was repaired. She had just heard from one of the constables . . .'

He would have to speak to that constable, or Griswald would. Though perhaps the operator had been eavesdropping. Daines Barington was a small town. He followed Portia Anthony into the Great Hall, through a crowd of bustling, twittering Sidereans.

It must have been an impressive place before Siderea arrived. It was still possible to guess the original proportions and to glimpse part of the carved ceiling, three stories high. Siderea had converted it to a series of rabbit hutches, each with desk and two chairs, all occupied, and strung round with a complex of bare light bulbs. From above came the glare of strip neon. Notice boards were pinned on every available surface with multi-coloured papers fluttering all over them, and wire meshes were suspended from the ceiling to hold more and more notices, directives, orders of all kinds, giving the place the look of a military encampment.

The central aisles of cubicles were occupied by Sidereans scribbling furiously at huge piles of papers. Each aisle, Capricorn noticed, used a different colour. The cubicles by the walls, however, seemed to house some kind of inquisition. As Mrs Anthony stopped to answer a question he paused and overheard a solid young woman with stringy hair loudly questioning a frail, delicate beauty with great eyes and a profile like Nefertiti's.

'Did you have sexual intercourse since your last Confession?'

'Yes.'

'How many times?'

'Four.'

'Who with?'

At that point Mrs Anthony moved on and Capricorn, startled, went with her. To him, at that moment dark with death, the place was nightmarish, a vast humming hive of lunacy. He was relieved when she showed him into a smaller room—originally the pantry off the dining room, he conjectured—which was only divided into two, half of which appeared to be her office.

'I'm sure you will understand, Superintendent,' she said with composure, 'that in the circumstances I thought it better that staff and students continue their work.'

'I'm afraid you will have to ask them not to leave the buildings,' Capricorn said. 'Some constables will be here shortly.'

She nodded.

'I understand. They've already been told. No one will leave. Please sit down, Superintendent.'

She motioned him to a comfortable chair but he remained standing while she took her place at her desk.

'Where is Mr Frost?'

'He went up to London to meet Mr Hightower's personal representative who flew in today. They will be staying the night at the house of a Siderean in London. They're not in yet,' she said. 'I called immediately—' Her composure shook. 'Immediately. They're probably having a late dinner. I'll give you the address and the telephone number, but they will both be here tomorrow.'

'Did anyone go with Mr Frost to the station?'

She nodded.

'Noreen—General Stacy—drove him down.'

He made a note in his book.

'I'll take her statement first. You understand,' he said, 'that everyone will have to give a statement.'

If the Frost story held up, he thought unemotionally, we really do have four hundred and ninety-nine suspects. At least.

'We have just passed General Stacy,' Mrs Anthony hesitated, 'As you may have noticed, she was conducting a Confession. We never interrupt a Confession.'

'I noticed something,' he remarked drily. 'Rather public, isn't it?'

'We have so little space,' she sighed, and then, mindful of the implication of her words, became a little paler than she had been already. 'But it doesn't matter as much as you think,' she said. 'Our policy is to make people really face what they've done. When you do that, you don't care what other people hear or know.'

91

Capricorn was not in a mood to debate.

'Tell me first, how many Sidereans in the area are in the Manor tonight?'

'All of them,' she answered. 'We can have a roll call if you wish. Confession time is over in five minutes.'

'No absences?'

'Only Mr Frost. Oh, I forgot, Mr Wyatt. He has special hours; he looks after the horses. Once they're stabled for the night, he leaves. Otherwise the rule is very strict: hours are nine to twelve-fifteen, one to six, and when we have evening duty, seven until ten, or later.'

Capricorn remembered the tall Texan and also remembered the plague of Sidereans the previous evening in the town.

'How often do you have evening duty?'

'Whenever it's necessary. Most evenings.'

'You didn't have it yesterday,' he observed.

'Yesterday was a special mission ordered by Mr Frost. The whole group was ordered into town for a proselytizing mission,' she said evenly. 'It's called "Scattering The Seed." However, that was cancelled for today.'

'When was it cancelled?'

'At nine o'clock call. We were getting behind in our ordinary work.'

Her voice was calm. He watched her closely. If she was concealing something on that point, and he was sure she was, this was not the time to discover it. He made a mental note. It was convenient for the murderer that 'Scattering The Seed' had been cancelled and stray Sidereans kept off the Witch Hill road.

'Who gave the order?'

'I did. With the approval of the Commander-in-Chief.'

Her gaze met his watchfully. She was an open woman, he felt, who disliked holding back, though she was making a brave try. It was certainly difficult to believe that the excitable Mr Frost would have countermanded his own order—unless he had a good reason.

Mrs Anthony fidgeted through a crowded cupboard and produced a large, clean towel.

'You'd better dry off,' she said in a grandmotherly way, and he accepted, mopping his hands and face and hair. He caught her speculative look and guessed she was tempted to demand he remove his clothes and dry properly.

'Could I get you some hot coffee?'

92

Capricorn was used to missing his dinner, but was never inured to missing his coffee. However, though this woman seemed a pleasant and sensible creature—no one had given him that kind of look since Mrs Raintree had been concerned with the state of his underwear—he could not accept Siderean hospitality. Not more than a towel, anyway.

'Thank you, but I think we should get to that roll call. To your knowledge, Mrs Anthony, could any of the students or staff that are present have left the buildings after seven o'clock?'

'Not possibly. The only exit is through the gate-house and they would have been stopped to see if they had official permission to leave during working time. I would have to give that permission, and none was requested. And the students and staff work in groups; any absence would be noticed. Even a visit to the bathroom,' she looked at him under lowered lids, 'requires a pass. Bathroom passes are not easily obtained. When I heard about the death,' she said firmly, 'I checked the bathroom passes for the night. There were none. You see, Superintendent, it couldn't possibly have been any of our people, no matter what you might think.'

Superintendent Capricorn, who had known more murderers than he wanted to remember, considered that no matter what Mrs Anthony might think, or wish to think, it was certainly possible. As he came in himself he had noticed half a dozen ways in which someone might have slipped out of the Manor without going past the gatehouse.

'They are *good* people,' she said, 'in spite of what you might have been told.'

He looked at her directly.

'What is Path 45? Who are the Assassins?'

She seemed to shrink a little into the protection of her cloak.

'Path 45? Assassins?'

'Yes. What is it and who are they?'

'It was only a joke,' she said wearily. 'A silly joke of Mr Hightower's. And Siderea has many services, each with its own staff, but there is no such thing as an Assassin. We do have a Justice division that handles dismissals of staff and students when necessary or attacks from outside. They write letters or contact our solicitors in London. There is no physical violence. The term "Assassin" is a Siderea joke.'

'A joke someone took seriously,' he said. She might as well know.

'Exactly—how was Mr. Brewster killed?'

By now she was dead white. Suddenly she looked not like a portly British grandmother but a wrinkled crone.

'We don't have the ballistics report,' he said shortly. 'But I believe it was a pistol shot, a .45.'

The room had a feeling of complete silence although the noises from outside were clear enough. A voice, the one that had asked the very personal questions of the young beauty, was shouting:

'We don't have to answer anything we don't want to. We'll get our lawyer! We're star-born, what do we care about the Daines Barington police? This is our place and we can read the Riot Act and throw you out!'

'I don't think any of our people have one,' Mrs Anthony whispered. 'And I know them. None of them would . . .'

'We'll see,' he said. 'And now perhaps we can make sure everyone is here and begin taking the statements.'

They took the roll call in the glaring light of the Great Hall, Capricorn standing by Mrs Anthony, and watching everyone who answered. As she had said, everyone was present except Jed Frost and Garry Wyatt. With one exception. One name was not answered. The name was Linda Lavender.

eight

Superintendent Capricorn sat at the desk in his room at Roseacre House and regarded the neat piles of notes and statements that had been taken on the Brewster case, not with satisfaction from the amount of work that had been accomplished but with a look both puzzled and irritated.

Mechanically, all had gone well. Jedediah Frost had returned from London under the eye of a constable and accompanied by Hightower's representative, a stringy grey man who did not wear the uniform and looked more like an accountant than an apostle. Frost, who was already reduced to the ranks, looked like a rooster that had lost a battle as he sulked and snarled. But the story of his movements had been confirmed.

The Sidereans were as locked into Daines Barington as could be outside the totalitarian countries. The railway station was discreetly watched. The temporary drivers' licenses granted to foreigners had been picked up, and the Britishers, at Mrs Anthony's command, had given up the use of their cars.

That certainly couldn't have been done without Mrs Anthony's cooperation. As she was now in full charge Capricorn's job was made easier. He had had another short interview with her, this time in the office of the Commander-in-Chief, once the library of the master of the house. In the rather dark room of old books, leather chairs and smooth, dark tables, the bust of Hightower—plastic and wrought iron, with sheets of crumpled metal, poised in a tip-tilted, open-walled cube, the whole lit up by glaring neon—seemed to belong to a different world. But Mrs Anthony, sitting in a deep wing chair by the empty fireplace, belonged to both worlds. Her strange dress and the youthful eagerness of her expression belonged to the Sidereans, to Hightower, but the rest of that composed and capable person could have been part of the old Manor, as governess, housekeeper, or some odd member of the family who quietly ran the large estate while the master and mistress amused themselves.

She had looked at him with the gaze that in the young Sidereans was a comic eyes-on-stalks stare, but with her was merely a glance so direct that he felt no barriers, no social posturing, only an open communication.

'We are prepared to cooperate in any way you ask, Superintendent,' she had said in her level voice. 'Even if the request is, as you say, unusual. The Army of the Stars is used to following orders,' she added practically, 'and it won't be difficult at all to confine them to Daines Barington for a time. I'll collect all the British driving licenses. They can have an extra half hour on their dinner time so that they can walk to town when we have evening duty.'

It was amazing what people would put up with, Capricorn had noted, when it concerned the object of their religious fervour. But his mild amusement dissipated as he inevitably went on to question: had that same religious zeal driven one of them to murder? Mrs Anthony, at any rate, was convinced that all her charges were innocent. That was obvious.

'We're going to have regular evening duty,' she went on. 'I think it better to keep their minds occupied and their hands busy. No sense brooding over something not of our doing—directly,' she added, looking up at him with that surprising frankness. She was taking responsibility for the hate-crazed atmosphere, and Capricorn, sure that she personally had been against its creation, approved her attitude.

'I want you to find the murderer, because I want our people cleared. And I am sure they will be. Shouting and name calling is one thing, Superintendent, but murder is something else. There really was no motive. Mr Hightower's representative told me today that Mr Hightower was not very concerned about the building plans. His mind is full of other schemes in other parts of the planet . . . and elsewhere.' She smiled. 'It usually is.'

She had been pleasant, but very firm and assured, and she had shaken his hand, not in the double Siderea grip but in a plain, English handshake, and he had been convinced of her sincerity, at least.

As she had promised, there had been no outburst of indignation at the restrictive measures: no Britishers had called their members of Parliament or their friends of the press; no foreigners had called their consuls to bring pressure to bear. Siderea was on its best behaviour.

The lab confirmed that the murder weapon was a semi-automatic Colt .45, but the gun had not been found. Search warrants had been obtained from a reluctant magistrate who had made acid remarks about 'this wholesale business', and the appearance of the Chief Constable had been required to convince him of the necessity.

Griswald and his constables, as well as additional men who had been provided, had been over the Manor and the grounds and had even dragged the lake. The lodging houses where Sidereans stayed were still being searched, though Griswald was not optimistic about the outcome.

The post mortem had added nothing to what Capricorn had observed. The murdered man had been in excellent health. One bullet had lodged in the right shoulder, but death had been caused by the bullet that had entered the skull, piercing the right posterior lobe of the brain, and exiting through the left eye destroying the whole left anterior quarter of the skull. The time of death could not be narrowed down any further than the limits Dr Bailey had suggested, between about seven and eight.

But at seven o'clock Brewster had been just leaving his house, on foot, in the sight of the Rector, Rose and his sister. It would have taken him about half an hour, walking, to reach the point in the road where he was killed. At seven-thirty to eight o'clock, then or thereabouts. Capricorn wrote the time down, underlined it, and stared. There was still daylight at eight o'clock. And whoever had taken those shots had been standing there for anyone travelling the

Witch Hill road to see. The trajectory of the first bullet indicated a shot from about ten yards off, to the right, placing the killer on the open pasture. The second shot had been from above, again a little to the right, as the murderer had moved in closer to dispatch the recumbent victim.

Why that particular point, he fretted. It made no sense. Further on there were bushes and high hedges in plenty, trees to hide behind. But right there, at the very crown of the hill, the fence was low, too low to hide a child. The murderer had taken a chance on being seen by any passer-by.

In the town they were saying that all Siderea was in on the plot, but Capricorn dismissed that notion. No murderer would trust five hundred people with his secret. But why that completely open place? True, the road was used mostly by Sidereans, who were safely employed at the Manor at that time, but there was always the chance of someone slipping off, rules or no rules. And there had been the possibility of trespassers, who regularly cut across the land, jumping stiles, hedges, walls or any other obstruction, according to Griswald. If the cablegram had come a little earlier, the postman might have caught the murderer in the act.

Capricorn sighed. The rain had washed out any chance of finding an impression in the grass by the road. Nothing to indicate someone standing there, perhaps ignored by Brewster, perhaps hailing him, talking for a time, and pulling the weapon out as he was moving away. . .

Could the murderer have left the Manor at six, when the Sidereans went for their evening meal, clutching a .45 pistol without anyone noticing it, hung back from the rest without being missed, and sat calmly waiting on Witch Hill until Brewster arrived? How could he know that Brewster would come? Who had delivered the still-missing Warning? No Siderean had been seen round Brewster House that evening. Miss Brewster had discovered the envelope at about ten minutes to seven, she had said. Of course, she couldn't say how long it might have been lying there, but she conjectured not more than five minutes.

'I was going about the house,' she had said, 'and I certainly would have noticed such an object on the floor of the hall.'

The Rector, driven by Richard Brewster, had arrived about half past six. There had been no envelope on the floor then, he was sure.

'I might not notice such a thing at home,' he had said, his fine forehead wrinkled in the puzzlement that had afflicted him since the murder. 'I seem to have a lot of clutter, but in Brewster House anything out of place would leap to the eye.'

Capricorn turned to his notes on the inquest to see if any more could be dredged from them than he had found already. The Coroner, a firm and experienced man, had shepherded the jury to a verdict of 'Murder by person or persons unknown.' It was against their will and afterwards they were not quite sure how he had managed it. They had shown strong signs of wanting to name Siderea in a body as murderers until instructed that that was impossible. The townspeople in attendance were very much of the same point of view as the jury.

There had been murmurs of sympathy for Mrs Lavender, a pale, fragile and lovely witness—poor Rose, he thought, his mind dwelling for a moment on the personal tragedy of his friend—but most of the feeling of the town was obviously for Miss Brewster, still sallow, mannish and matter-of-fact. Dr Bailey, who had given his evidence first and waited with Capricorn, had remarked that Miss Brewster might have been too proud to call on anyone in the town but she had been there so long that her ways were accepted; her charities and hospital committee work had won respect, and her total self-abnegation in serving her brother made her situation peculiarly pathetic.

She had arrived late at the inquest and her entrance caused a stir, but she had been quiet and composed with no attempt to make any kind of effect. There was little she could add to what had already been said by Mrs Lavender and the Rector—the guests had been invited for seven o'clock although dinner was not to be served until eight. She allowed the extra time in case Dr Bailey was late. Dr Bailey looked somewhat abashed. Her brother had made two trips to fetch Mrs Lavender and the Rector as the big car was in the garage, arriving first at half past six with the Rector and at seven o'clock with Mrs Lavender. At about a quarter or ten minutes to seven she had found the letter, which had been pushed under the front door, and had been addressed to 'Richard Brewster.' The letter had turned out to be another 'Warning'—a skull and crossbones drawn on an odd sheet of paper.

Miss Brewster had not noticed what her brother had done with the letter. She expected he had thrown it away. But all four had examined it, and Richard had determined to go to the Manor to stop the nonsense. The Rector wanted to go with him, but her brother had insisted that he stay and entertain the ladies. Richard said that in all likelihood he would be back by half-past eight, and asked her to delay dinner half an hour.

Richard had decided to walk, Miss Brewster said, because he liked to walk, was a fast walker, and disliked her two-seater, which was the only car available. Besides that, he wanted the car to be at the station to meet the Superintendent if he came on the evening train. Capricorn had winced.

Sergeant Copper had taken Miss Brewster's original statement, and when the Superintendent had first read it the words had struck at him. Richard Brewster had thought of every courtesy for a man he had met the day before. If he had taken his sister's car himself, Capricorn thought savagely, perhaps the maniac with the gun would never have taken aim; the tempting target, alone, on foot at the road's edge, would never have appeared, and, the moment gone, the pressure, the insane urge, might have been dispersed.

'Had Mr Brewster been certain that the anonymous letter came from the Sidereans?' she was asked as the others had been, and her answer was the same.

'There was no question in his mind. My brother had no enemies. Except for these people, he was, all his life, a very popular man.'

And the long sigh that ran around the room said that the town agreed. There were many expressions of sympathy and kind wishes as Miss Brewster stepped from the witness stand. To all of them she responded silently, nodding her head in grave appreciation. But as she reached the door of the courthouse, a voice, louder than the rest called out:

'We're with you, Miss Brewster! Don't let them drive you away!'

At that she turned and looked up.

'Thank you,' she replied in her deep voice, 'I most certainly won't. You can be sure of that.'

She had given her small, rare smile, which seemed almost out of place on those sombre features, and she had left to the pleased hum of the crowd, whose members were agreeing, one with the other, that Miss Brewster was a brave woman and that Daines Barington should look after its own.

Mrs Anthony had been called, as the present chief of Siderea, and had testified that she had no knowledge of the anonymous letter, and that she had questioned each individual Siderean and was certain it didn't come from any one of them. She had been booed and heckled as she left the court and had to be escorted back to the Manor by two constables.

Capricorn sighed for the necessity, but that was not the reason for his present irritation. Taking the statements had been a Herculean job. Collating and sifting the relevant information had been much simpler than he might have supposed. Sidereans did everything in groups. They also wrote down everything they did, covering reams of paper daily that was split not only into hours, but minutes and seconds, with different coloured papers and inks to match the subject matter. Hightower, known as a prophet, a patriarch, and a pirate, as well as a psychologist and self-styled celestial navigator, was obviously also a bureaucrat to end all bureaucrats. An odd manifestation, but it certainly helped a police investigation. Or did it?

He frowned again. There were only two statements that were obviously, at first glance, unsatisfactory to use a polite term. And to his particular annoyance the two statements that did not check out and were full of inconsistencies and, probably, downright lies, were those of Garry Wyatt and Linda Lavender. It was absurd, but there it was.

He would have to see those two young people himself, that was certain. But he couldn't feel that he was on the track of anything there. Long, long ago he had taught himself not to draw any conclusions at the beginning of the case, but in this one—well, he would eat a constable's helmet if either of those two were a killer.

Then a nasty voice in his mind pointed out that Wyatt was a killer. He had been a combat soldier in Vietnam, an infantryman. He must have killed many men. Well, so have I, he argued with the nasty voice. If you look at things that way, half of the men in this country are killers. An interesting thought, the nasty voice answered and then shut up.

He looked at the statement of Jed Frost, which he had taken himself. Jed, diminished, sulky, apprehensive, would have been any policeman's pick for the role of suspect. True, Jed hadn't been in the army. That sort wouldn't, Capricorn thought, and then reprimanded himself for unfairness, Jed having grown up into a period of England at peace, of sorts. Yet the young man had all the earmarks of the criminal: an inflated opinion of his worth, a contempt for most of the human race, and no desire for any particular line of work. But Jed Frost also had a very good alibi.

No use jumping to conclusions. He had half suspected that Frost might have a record, but investigation had turned up nothing. The ticket seller at Daines Barington station had confirmed that he bought a ticket for the six fifty-five to London. The man had not seen Frost get on the train because he closed his office a few minutes before the train came in. The six fifty-five was the last train to town, very few people got on at Daines Barington—it was for the Brighton crowd, he explained—and anyway, anyone who wanted to could get a ticket on the train.

Noreen, or General, Stacy claimed she had seen him board the train, in a third class carriage. Inquiries were being made to find if any other passengers had seen him, but the train, apparently, had been almost empty, and he might have passed unnoticed, as he had gone to town in civilian clothes.

'We do that, sometimes,' Noreen had said, absently. 'Raw meat stares at us a lot, travelling.'

Raw meat, he had deduced, was, or were, non-Sidereans.

'People who don't know they're not just lumps of meat,' Noreen explained.

He had been moved to reply.

'There are other religions that believe in the existence of the soul,' he protested mildly.

'They don't know they *are* souls,' Noreen was earnest. He might have been learning his catechism. 'And they only believe it, maybe, once in a while, on Sundays. When you *know* you are a soul,' she went on, her stolid, plain face shining with an eagerness that made her, for the moment, attractive, 'it makes everything different. All the time.'

He was taken aback for a moment, although, with professional calm, he didn't show it. Any one of the disciples, he reflected, might have said the same thing. He wondered how the twelve would have fitted in Daines Barington—and then he closed his mind to speculation. He had a job of work.

Now, moodily, he looked over his notes on his interview with Noreen, and at her signed statement. She had seen Jed off on the six fifty-five and driven back very fast to the Manor in time for the seven o'clock taped lecture. Then she had sat in the back of the hall to listen and this was confirmed by one 'Colonel' Christopher Venable. Yet there was something about her statement that teased Capricorn's mind. Or was it hers? Something connected with another statement that did not quite jibe. He searched through every statement that seemed to have some bearing on 'General' Stacy's: Frost's, Venable's, Mrs Anthony's, but he could find nothing. Patient, he put the heaps aside. From experience he knew it was no use pushing at that any more for a time. Get on with other work and it would come.

He listed the questions that were the most vexing. Where was the gun? Where was the threatening letter? Why had no one seen the Siderean who delivered the letter? How had the murderer known that Brewster was coming up Witch Hill?

A chambermaid knocked at the door and made to enter, with a clank of dustpans and a flutter of dusters. Seeing him at work she excused herself and left, trying to muffle the sound of her tools. Someone had impressed her with the importance of Scotland Yard.

A maid. Any servant in the Brewster house. If one of them was a Siderean, or knew a Siderean . . . A telephone call, perhaps even an innocent call. 'Mr Brewster is on his way; he's very angry.'

No, that was no good. The Witch Hill Manor telephone line had been down. Down until nine o'clock; he had checked that. A call to somewhere else, to some missing Siderean ensconced in another house? Or some form of message to the Siderean, hidden, who had left the Warning? Merest conjecture, he thought in disgust. But he'd better question the servants at Brewster House. More urgently, though, he wanted to see Hartle, the lawyer, and the Rector. Tomorrow would be the funeral, so both of those calls should be made today.

On his way out he saw Sergeant Copper in the tap, eating what looked like a very good lunch and looking at a pile of newspapers. A waitress was fussing over him, giving him a great deal of attention, to the obvious annoyance of other customers whose knives and forks gleamed emptily in front of them. Copper's dark red hair glistened like a cockade, and he said something to the girl that made her giggle and flounce. When his sharp cockney gaze took in his chief, he motioned to him in humorous resignation.

'These country girls,' he said amiably, 'they won't leave you alone for a minute. You'd better sit down and 'ave something while you can. Close in twenty minutes and then you can starve until dinner. Shame they didn't do the old boy in in London. Save a lot of trouble. Go on, sit down,' he said, 'and I'll read you what they're saying about our wonderful Scotland Yard.'

Capricorn ordered a sandwich from the waitress when she returned with pudding for the sergeant, a portion that looked like enough for three and handsomely covered with cream. She took the Superintendent's order, sobered, and left with a more efficient and subdued air.

There was one paper from Daines Barington and two from London. Inevitably, the case had become the Witch Hill Murder, with overtones of mystery from the extra-terrestrial to the diabolic. 'Scotland Yard Bewitched,' was to have been expected. 'Five hundred Assasins loose?' was very bold, but the paper had covered itself by stating it was quoting an American weekly. Questions, it appeared, were being asked in the House about Siderea and its presence in the country. The Minister of Health was taking it under advisement.

Copper, amused by the press, from which he expected little but entertainment, chuckled.

'You'd better pull a rabbit out of the 'at for 'em, 'adn't you,' he said pointedly, knowing very well that a reference to his stage past caused his superior much mortification. For the most part, he was tactful enough, as he knew that Capricorn held a dreadful weapon over his own head. D.A. Copper, he liked to be listed in the records, and D.A. Copper he insisted was all of his name, but the Superintendent knew the naked truth. Copper's mother had been frightened by the German buzz-bombs, or doodlebugs as they were known in cockney London, and in some archaic sense of propitiating the gods she had christened her son, with the aid of a liberal-minded vicar, Doodlebug. The A was for Aloysius which she had 'thrown in' she said, 'not for anything special, but it sounded nice and posh.'

Capricorn eyed his subordinate with some severity.

'I should think there's more to do than sitting about taps, eating, wenching, and reading newspapers,' he replied.

''Aven't been here *all* morning,' Copper said, who had actually been there about twenty minutes. 'And I have a little something you might like to know.'

He smiled, a rather sweet smile that gave him for a moment the ingenuous look of a little boy.

'Dropped round at Brewster 'Ouse before,' he said. 'Back door. I had a nice chat with that manservant there, Purdy. Turned out he hates that big car he drives—always going wrong, he said. He's a motor-bike man. Owns a BSA himself. I was telling him about my Honda. Wish I had it here.'

Capricorn waited patiently.

'Said he used to take Gertie, the kitchenmaid, out on it. Went out quite a few times, they did, before she got all tied up with the Sidereans on her night off.'

Capricorn was still. The maid he had conjured up—she really existed. She could have heard Brewster's reaction to the letter. But then what? The telephone lines were down.

'Pretty good,' he said to Copper. 'Now all we have to find out is who she told that Brewster was on his way, in time for them to be at the top of the hill with the gun, waiting.'

He regarded his sergeant who was ordering 'tea, not coffee, darling,' from the blushing waitress, with every look of confident worth.

'Why is it you're not like these sergeants in mystery novels, placid, amiable, modest, just doing what you're told and letting me be the brilliant detective?'

Copper was sunny.

'Well, you see what it says 'ere, guv.'

He waved at the newspapers with the glaring headlines.

'Why no arrest in Witch Hill murder?' 'Are police seeing purple?' 'Is the Superintendent Star-Gazing?'

Capricorn paid the waitress, whose calm was shattering into giggles again. Had Copper actually smacked her backside? The elder man looked the other way.

'All right, I see I'll have to do without a Watson. I'll just go my dull way over to Hartle, the lawyer's. When you've quite finished what you're doing, and looked at your horoscope and studied the sports page, and indulged in any other amusements you have in mind, you might get back to Brewster House and take a statement from the kitchenmaid. Especially on whether she knew about the letter and if she mentioned it to anyone. Anyone at all.'

Capricorn was thoughtful as he went the short distance down the High Street towards Hartle's office. The High Street seemed oddly quiet today. There were far fewer Sidereans, the red and purple flashing only occasionally in and out of the Moo-Cow. Mrs Anthony was keeping them all busy up at the Manor.

All? How easily, and inaccurately, that word came to mind, he noticed.

'They're all here,' she had said that night, excepting Frost and Wyatt and, as it turned out, the love-struck Linda Lavender. But by 'all' she had meant her staff, or 'Army,' and students. There were left others like the kitchenmaid, occasional visitors, sympathizers.

He shook his head to clear from it the idea of the task being too great. Anyone who had gone to the Manor for a lecture or two would not get excited enough to kill a man. Not unless they were raving maniacs. But it was an insane murder. No really strong motive, or so it seemed. After his visit to Hartle, he would be certain.

nine

Hartle and Hartle occupied premises on the first floor of an incon-
spicuous building between a large shop displaying bathing suits and
summer dresses and the bank. The lettering on the window was old
and weatherbeaten, and no attempt had been made to keep it legible.
Daines Barington knew who Hartle and Hartle were and where they
were. No advertisement was necessary.

Capricorn walked up the narrow stairway to the door with the
brass plate and sign that said 'Walk In.' Inside there was just as little
desire to impress. Walls, rug, bookshelves, filing cabinets were all a
rather pale and dusty brown, and the little man sitting at the desk
with his back to the window was a rather pale and dusty brown himself.

Blinking, Hartle looked up. He had seen the Superintendent once
before, at the inquest, where he had appeared as a quietly dressed,
distinguished man. Now, as the door opened, the figure that moved

from the darkness seemed immoderately tall, surprisingly vivid despite his dark hair and clothes, filling the doorway and dominating the room.

'If I were a criminal, I would be very nervous at this moment, Superintendent,' he remarked.

Capricorn laughed.

'And I had hoped that "policeman" didn't stick out all over me.'

It didn't, Hartle reflected, as he pulled his most comfortable chair forward for this guest. What was it he looked like, a barrister, leading counsel for the Crown? A judge, perhaps?

'What can I do for you, Superintendent?'

'Just answer a few questions, if you will.'

'If I *may*,' Hartle corrected drily. 'I don't suppose it is personal information you want, but information about my late client.'

Capricorn nodded.

'We haven't taken a statement from you, as I don't think you saw Mr Brewster on the day of his death?'

'No,' Mr Hartle replied. 'Most unfortunate. Miss Brewster had telephoned me for an informal dinner, a spur-of-the-moment thing, but it was the night for the annual celebration of the Daines Barington Sheepherders' Society. Not an agricultural group—a historical association. The Hartles seem to have belonged to it forever. Dinner in Roseacre House. The service is not what it was,' he mourned, 'waitresses in the tap,' and then, with a little rap of his fingers on his desk, brought himself back to the matter in hand.

'Actually, I was to have seen Mr Brewster the next day. He had an appointment.'

'On the matter of the will,' Capricorn suggested, and Hartle sighed.

'Yes, I expected you would want to know about that. And I see no reason why I should not—' He paused as if he were searching for a reason, but gave it up. 'We don't have a formal reading of the will any more. I have already drafted some letters. I intend, of course, to speak to Miss Brewster tomorrow. But I am sure she knows the terms of her brother's will.'

'There was no change, then,' Capricorn asked, 'after his engagement to Mrs Lavender?'

'Well,' the lawyer still seemed reluctant. 'Well, I suppose I can tell you. The signing was arranged for the day of our appointment.'

'I see,' Capricorn said, and waited for him to continue.

'However,' Hartle went on, 'there wasn't as much of a change as you might suppose. Very little, really.'

'Perhaps you might tell me the terms of both wills,' the Superintendent suggested.

The lawyer took a deep breath.

'The fact is, Superintendent, that the late Mr Brewster—how dreadful,' he interjected with an unhappy look, 'to be calling my friend Richard the late Mr Brewster—was a very rich man. A very, very rich man. One of the great private fortunes of England,' he continued. 'You perhaps were misled by his holding the post of Town Clerk. But it is a Brewster tradition to hold some kind of civic post. John Brewster was a magistrate.'

The Superintendent was interested. Brewster had obviously been a man of means, but 'one of the great private fortunes of England' was unexpected. Or should it have been? He thought of the treasures of Brewster House, exquisite things that few men in the country could afford to keep in their homes.

'Most of the Brewster business affairs are handled by a firm of solicitors in London,' Hartle explained. "I handle their personal matters, as my family has always managed the Brewster affairs in Daines Barington itself. The Brewsters have been here a long time, a long time. Since before the Conquest.'

His fingers tapped sadly on the desk.

It was no use trying to hurry Mr Hartle, Capricorn thought resignedly. They were now back to the Conquest, and he would have to work his way up. Very different from the Sidereans, with their cry of 'Now, now.' Remarkably easy, they had been, as far as getting information. Once Mrs Anthony had told them to cooperate they had answered any question, immediately, in a more direct fashion than any other witnesses, or non-witnesses, in his experience. They actually knew what an answer was, without additions, explanations or justifications.

'Originally, the Brewsters were farmers, good yeoman farmers,' Hartle was on his way, 'and they made their land pay. Not like the Courtneys, and then the Gaylords, descendants on the distaff side, who had the Manor. Shooting and hunting. The Brewster land was orchard land. And they were merchants, with barges on the Baring and a business house in London. They picked up poor farmlands in the North in return for debt and they turned out to be sitting on coal, and the Brewsters built factories there. Everything that ruins other landowners the Brewsters turned to advantage.'

He smiled at the Superintendent, a little wintry smile.

'You think I'm wandering from the subject. But it seems necessary.'

'Not at all,' Capricorn said politely, and then wondered to which of the two sentences he was responding.

'So John Brewster, Richard's father, was a wealthy man when he married Richard's mother, Ann Venable. There was a lot of intermarriage between the Brewsters and the Venables,' Hartle added. 'Another tradition. But Ann Venable died young. It was his second wife, Lucrezia, that made the Brewsters the fortune that Richard inherited.'

'Miss Beatrice's mother was a rich woman?' the Superintendent asked.

'Lucrezia didn't have a penny. She was a very beautiful and aristocratic woman, and still young when she married John Brewster, who was already middle-aged. John had gone on a European tour and met her in Rome and brought her back with him. No, what enriched her husband was her tremendous flair for people, for social life, entertaining. . .'

He fell silent for a moment and then resumed tapping his fingers on his desk.

'We were all very entranced with Mrs Lucrezia,' he said. 'She filled Brewster House with the most important people in England and from the Continent. Not only society people but intellectuals, people in the arts and entertainment. Brilliant,' he sighed. 'Those days were brilliant. We won't see their like again. Well, it was some of these friends of Lucrezia's that started John's interest in broadcasting stations and record companies. It all seemed to make an enormous amount of money. Those affairs are handled by the London firm, of course. And then Richard, in his turn, became a part owner of a commercial television station, and in times when most old families are doing badly, the Brewsters are doing better than ever before.'

The Superintendent nodded and waited for him to get to the point.

'I tell you this, Superintendent, to explain to you that this fortune, although very large, is a living, working thing. It is not a matter that could be handed over to a home-loving woman like Miss Brewster to manage, or Mrs Lavender. John Brewster, in his time, had left everything to Richard, trusting him to take care of the girl. Richard had no son. He made the best arrangements he could, with certain enterprises to be sold; others, that did not need his personal management, to be placed in the hands of boards of directors. In the original will a sum was left to Miss Brewster for life, sufficient to the upkeep of herself in Brewster House, a very pleasant legacy. In the new will, if it had been signed, there was very little change except that she was to receive the White House, which has often been used as a dower house by the Brewsters, and Mrs Lavender, of course, would receive Brewster House and an income from the trust. The bulk of the property goes to the same beneficiary in *both* wills. That may have been changed later, of course, if there had been an heir, but until that time the original bequest remained.'

'And to which lucky person is this fortune to go?' Capricorn asked.

The lawyer was thoughtful.

'Brewster was something of a gambler, in a way. There is only one male relative, one young one, that is, and he not a Brewster but a Venable. So far he has shown no interest at all in business or the Brewsters, but he doesn't know about the will. I think Richard felt that inheriting the fortune might change all that. In any case, it's tied up well enough so that he cannot get full use of it until he's twenty-five, and he's only nineteen, as yet.'

'May I have his name and address?' Capricorn asked, getting his notebook ready.

'I have his family address, in London,' Hartle replied. 'But if you want to find him you don't have to go that far. He's right here.'

Capricorn, startled, looked sharply at the lawyer.

'That's correct,' Hartle said gravely. 'Christopher Venable is at Witch Hill Manor. He's a colonel, I believe, in Hightower's Army of the Stars.'

ten

Who benefits? rang through Capricorn's mind as he left Hartle's office. There were more questions he had to ask Richard Brewster's lawyer, but they could wait. This information had to be acted on. First he stopped at the police station and left word for Superintendent Griswald. The matter of the search for the gun had been complicated as well as tiresome. Even with all the extra men on the job, it seemed a task past the abilities of a squad of Herculeses. With the Manor itself so large and the Sidereans spread all over the town, the search seemed hardly worthwhile. As Griswald had said, there was nothing to stop the murderer from putting it into a place they had already searched.

But Capricorn knew that there was no point in worrying about the possible deviousness of the criminal. A routine search should be made, and it was being made. Then, if it wasn't found, the time would come to think about complications. 'But just so he doesn't get too sure of himself,' he advised Griswald, 'once or twice have the men go back to the same place.'

Griswald nodded.

'I'm glad you said "he," ' he observed. 'With this lot it might be he, she or it, as far as I can see.'

His attitude towards Siderea had changed, Capricorn noticed. The Daines Barington Superintendent felt that he had been fooled, his more humane feelings exploited. Although he was not in charge of the case, he was bitter about the press reports. It took Scotland Yard to be philosophic about pressmen, Capricorn thought. If you worried about them you had better resign and run a tea shop.

So he gave careful instructions for an immediate re-search of Venable's lodgings while he went over the young heir's statement. Motive was not as important to the Yard as people might think; it was evidence that counted, but certainly this Venable had a very strong motive, one of the greatest private fortunes in England. True, Brewster's marriage would not have changed his arrangements immediately, but Rose Lavender was not past childbearing and it had been possible that the boy would lose his inheritance. And he was a Siderean and probably loathed Brewster.

Capricorn shook off conjecture and returned to the facts. Sergeant Copper had taken the statement but Capricorn had talked to the boy himself, a serious, decent-seeming lad, obviously a product of a public school, and obviously enjoying his camaraderie with all sorts of human beings alien to him in many ways. He had not left with the rest at six o'clock; he had stayed to study for a test. After the tape-play, which was from seven to seven-thirty, he had taken the test in company with a dozen other Sidereans, until nine. After that he had been busy with administrative work in the company of Mrs Anthony. Every part of his statement was corroborated by at least one other person. Could all these people have been in collusion? Capricorn thought about it and decided he had better get up to the Manor straight away.

He put through a call to Mrs Anthony and asked that the test papers be sequestered, and that cooperative lady agreed. As soon as he had hung up, Griswald was on the line.

'Any luck?' Capricorn asked, suddenly eager.

'Nothing,' Griswald said gloomily. 'It didn't take long. He shares a room with three others. All they seem to have is a bedroll each and a change of clothes, and they share use of a kitchen with almost nothing in it. Whoever had that gun has probably buried it or posted it to Australia.'

'Well, just keep going.' Capricorn tried to sound encouraging. Weapons had been found before when the search had seemed hopeless. A murderer, as time passed, would feel confident, and grow careless, and that was the chance for the careful policeman. The murderer, or an accomplice.

He got his car, and drove through the High Street to its northern end, past the Emanuel Church. The sexton had been burning leaves again, as· he had on the day before Brewster's death. The smell of smoke filled the air until the road turned west, following the curve of the river. The Baring. Capricorn regarded the glint of water until it was out of sight. Centuries before, Griswald had told him, the river had wound round the foot of Witch Hill but it had been diverted to a wider loop. It was a mile now from the crown of Witch Hill to the Baring, yet it was possible, both policemen realized, that the gun that had killed Richard Brewster could be anywhere in the deep mud of the river bed. They had dragged the small ornamental lakes on the Manor grounds, but they could hardly drag the whole river. And the boathouse of the Manor had been well supplied with small craft.

As he passed the gate of Brewster House, Capricorn looked up the drive to see the house itself looking sombre now with the front door closed and all its blinds still drawn. The door would open tomorrow, and Richard Brewster would leave his house for the last time. Miss Brewster had asked for the body to be returned to Brewster House for the funeral. She and her brother would spend one last night together in their home.

Capricorn shivered although the sun shone bright and the afternoon was warm. All along the road, as far as he could see, the trees were heavy with fruit. The grass was full of windfalls—too many, even a townsman could see that. He remembered Purdy, Brewster's manservant, complaining about blight. Blight had fallen on the Brewster orchards, and on the Brewsters themselves. Richard had been the last.

As he began the climb through the pasture land up to Witch Hill he thought about Christopher Venable, who was to inherit the Brewster fortune, searching his memory for any further impressions he might have tucked away that now could be significant. How old was the boy, nineteen? Still apple-cheeked, voluble and stammering by turn, full of dog-like worship of Jed Frost, somewhat ambivalent about Noreen Stacy, as if loyalty combined with resentment.

Capricorn gained the place on the road nearest the crown of Witch Hill and stopped at the place where Brewster had fallen. The air was sweet with the scent of the clover that dotted the grass and thrumming with the sound of bees. Horses were drowsily cropping the grass in the shade of a clump of trees on the further slope. It was an innocent scene.

Capricorn looked about. Almost impossible to imagine the twilight night and the shattered body of a man lying in that very spot. Once more his gaze travelled to the field where the murderer must have stood, exposed for all to see, pistol in hand, waiting for the man he somehow knew enough to expect. The ground rose on that side to the peak of the hill. Even in twilight whoever stood there must have been clear in view. If he was lying down, the grass was hardly long enough for cover. Why there? It was one of the two great puzzles of the case. Why there? Why then?

Restless, Capricorn left the car and walked around, as he and Copper had done the day after the murder. The grass had been wet that morning and the ground soaked from the long rain. Now he noticed that on the north side of the hill the ground was less even. Ridges cut across the slope of the hill, and there were gullies and ditches where the grass grew long. About ten feet from the peak a deep gully ran for a few feet, overhung with long grass and briars. Squatting down, he examined the briar stems. They were bent and one or two were broken off. A passage had been made, perhaps by a burrowing animal or perhaps by a man seeking a place to lie flat until he heard the tread of feet at that lonely hour on the road. He could have bellied up from there, unseen, to the crest of the hill and as Brewster passed, raised his pistol and—

Here Capricorn stopped. The hill sloped down to the road, but very gently. Brewster was a tall man. If his assailant had been hiding in the grass, the trajectory of the first bullet would have been steeply upwards. As it was, the path was almost level. The killer had been standing upright, or almost upright. Had Brewster turned at the snapping of a twig in the grass, he could not have missed seeing him, gun in hand. Yes, the murderer had been very sure of his kill; very sure that Brewster was not accompanied; very sure he would be walking.

The detective sighed. He still had no answer to Why There? But he carefully marked the gully with two upright sticks that he ground deep into the soil. He would come back and examine it again. The

115

earth was dry and powdery on his hands, almost pure chalk under the top dirt, poor land, except for grazing. Not like the rich Brewster land, further down.

How had the murderer known Brewster was coming? Why Then? Could the kitchenmaid down at Brewster House have warned the Manor that he was on his way? Warned someone who just happened to have a pistol handy and who ran along to meet Brewster at the most exposed spot on the top of the hill? The idea seemed absurd.

Capricorn stood quite still while his mind raced round and round on a closed track. Catching himself, he shrugged and moved back to his car. When 'brilliance' fails, he told himself, get on with routine. A butterfly hovered close and a flock of swallows wheeled overhead as he started up. The migratory birds would soon be leaving. To humans it still looked like full summer, but the birds were readying for their winter flight. A winter that Richard Brewster would never see.

Sergeant Copper was interviewing the kitchenmaid. If she had warned the Manor, he would find out. The Superintendent smiled a little. Copper was noted for his success with the female young. They liked him, red hair, green eyes and all. And, it must be said, he liked them in return. His love affairs were frequent and much talked of in the Force, yet he remained blithely unattached. Capricorn's own love affairs had been much more discreet. In his young days, he reflected, they had had to be. He could not imagine, when he was a sergeant, confiding his amatory problems to a superior. Probably he would have been asked to resign. Conduct unbecoming. . .

Times had changed. Scanning the slopes on the way down to the Manor, he looked for young Wyatt, but he was not to be seen. He and Hightower's finest horses were out of sight, perhaps in the north pastures up near the woods. Capricorn had to talk to him after he talked to Venable. Wyatt had almost certainly been with Linda Lavender, 'spooning' as Capricorn's aunts used to call it, on the night of the murder, and probably hadn't observed much; still, a truthful statement should be made.

It was four o'clock when he drew up at the main block. Siderea was having its tea-time. Scarlet-clad figures were dotted all over the place, sunning themselves on the lawns, by the pond, sitting upon hedges and stiles, thronging round a drink dispenser, laughing and calling, all as happy as—

He tried to think of a comparison, and was surprised to find he could not. In truth, he couldn't remember a group that looked as open and high-spirited as all those young people, with a sprinkling of middle-aged and elders. Murder or not, as they sat and talked, laughed and ran, greeted each other with the peculiar Siderean double grasp, eyes shining and a healthy glow in their cheeks, they were the happiest-looking crowd he had ever seen. Sometimes a group of toddlers in a nursery, he thought, looked that bright but usually the brightness didn't last too long before at least one child would bump its knee or its head or in some other way collide with a hostile universe and be brought to tears. What did Hightower do to his disciples, Capricorn wondered, that removed the cares and greyness of ordinary life?

A group of girls ran by as he got out of his car, dressed only in the scarlet all-over tights, and very delightful they looked, he had to admit. They belonged to the new school of females, uncorseted, with not even a brassiere, he observed, and with such young and slender beauties, it made a very pretty sight indeed. He couldn't imagine what it would do to the rate of sex offenses, but that wasn't his worry at the moment.

Blond girls and brunettes, redheads, Scandinavians, and an oriental or two, freshfaced, with long, shining hair—no wonder the newspapers called it the home of orgies. It wasn't, but no doubt the pressmen would like to have it so.

Two girls swooped down on him and one grasped his hands.

'Tell me your ruin,' she demanded, 'Siderea saves!'

He looked into her laughing, freckled face.

'You are,' he said. 'I can tell already.'

The girls laughed.

'We have a Path for that,' the freckled one said. 'Sign up and see.'

'Are you sure that's a Ruin?' the other girl asked doubtfully, in a lisping American voice. She was the fair girl with the brown eyes and a head like Nefertiti's whom he had seen with Noreen Stacy on the night of the murder, confessing to her sexual crimes.

'A great theological puzzle,' he said gravely, and gently disengaged himself. As he stood by the front door, enjoying the scene almost against his will—Paradise Lost, he thought, a paradise appropriately full of houris, strange under an English sun—he could not help remembering the horror of that other night, in the rain, when this same place had been the scene of ugly nightmare. He had taken a statement from this girl sometime about four that morning.

And then, before anyone had answered his knock, the thing that had troubled him in all those statements came to mind. It was not Noreen Stacy's statement—not alone. It was this girl's. The words came back with startling clarity.

'After the tape I went over to wait for Confession. I had to wait a while because General Stacy puts the tape away and she was fussing around. She came over all red and puffing and got a demerit from the Confession Officer,' the beauty had said, her head leaning slightly towards him on that long and lovely neck, looking angelic, her American accent rather nasal, as she came, it appeared, from the Bronx.

As he waited in the reception room in the collection of rabbit hutches that was now the Manor, while a messenger searched for Christopher Venable, he realized what it was that had struck him as an anomaly and then been forgotten. A very small thing, really. Noreen Stacy had driven Jed Frost to the station for the 6.55, seen him off and then driven back fast, she had said, to be in time for the official evening session at seven o'clock, or just a few minutes late. She had listened to the tape for half an hour, seated, according to her statement, in the back of the hall, her usual place. Yet after putting the tape away, she was late and red in the face for the seven-thirty confession. Nefertiti added, perhaps in private revenge for her embarrassment, that General Stacy, when she began the Confession, was still breathing hard and her skin was blotchy. Nefertiti had the sort of skin that would never be blotchy.

Possibly it meant nothing. Filing a reel of tape was an effortless proceeding in most organizations, but in the warren before him, which looked like a fire waiting for the match, great exertion might be required for ordinary acts. The tapes could well be filed on wires from the ceiling. Still, he would check it. Noreen was obviously in love with Jed Frost. . .

The messenger returned with Mrs Anthony and Christopher Venable.

'Colonel Venable should be lecturing,' she explained to Capricorn, 'but I am excusing him for as long as you need him. Would you like to use the library, Superintendent?'

'Thank you.' He smiled at her. She was being as helpful as she could. The inside of the Manor depressed him, with the glaring neon even in daylight, the little hutches, the trailing wire, the dismal aspect of greatness come down in the world. The Sidereans were pouring in, their tea break over, the noise and laughter subduing itself in the presence of Authority—not his, Capricorn observed, Scotland Yard meant nothing to them, but Mrs Anthony's. Quiet, hardly glancing at her flock, she seemed to perceive them all at once, Argus-eyed.

'That big tree outside will do as our conference room,' he said.

And he and Venable went out to the pleasant shade of the huge cedar on the grassy bank opposite the house. Capricorn sat on the grass, his long legs drawn up comfortably. Venable looked for a moment as though he was going to be too dignified to sit; then changed his mind and plumped down on his haunches in an appealing, child-like way.

Nineteen, Capricorn thought, a difficult age. Not a man and not a child, sometimes one and sometimes the other. Now that he knew Venable was related to Brewster, the resemblance became obvious. He wondered that he hadn't noticed it before. It was a likeness of type more than feature or expression. A young Piers Plowman, flaxen-haired with staring blue eyes. Just about the age Richard Brewster must have been when his father brought home the dashing Lucrezia. What had she been then, twenty-four, twenty-six? Poor Richard.

'Mr Hartle just rang up,' Venable said importantly. 'He explained to me that he'd seen you, and told me about the will. I suppose,' he added grandly. 'that now I'm a suspect.'

'Don't be an ass,' Capricorn said, and caught him off guard. Venable blushed and was miserable at his blushing. Oh, damn, Capricorn thought, he was forgetting the awful tenderness of that age. He didn't want the boy upset and hostile.

'As long as you didn't know about the will—and Mr Hartle tells me you didn't—there would have been no reason for you to kill your cousin.'

'Second cousin,' Venable snapped. 'I'm a colonel in the Army of the Stars. I had as much reason as anybody.'

'Yes,' Capricorn said. 'But I have the statement here that you gave Sergeant Copper. From seven to half past you listened to a tape with the others; after that you took a test until nine, and then you worked with Mrs Anthony.'

'That's right,' Venable looked better. His colour returned to normal, and his expression was smug. 'That was the night I took the test.'

A moment before he had been annoyed at the idea he wouldn't be seriously considered as a suspect. But the mention of his alibi restored his good humour. Capricorn was puzzled. The boy looked pleased with himself. He had the unmistakable look of a youngster who had got away with something. But surely not murder.

Though Hartle could have been wrong. Brewster himself might have told the boy, perhaps in an effort to win him away from Siderea. And if he failed, he might have kept his efforts to himself. But this apple-cheeked lad a killer? The idea was incredible. And yet. . .

'Who are Jed Frost's particular friends?' he had asked Mrs Anthony, that first night.

She had considered.

'Friends . . . I don't know. You see, Superintendent,' she had explained, 'rank is as important here as it is in any other organization. Jed, as Commander-in-Chief, associates with other high-ranking officers, as they have the same privileges. General Stacy. Colonel Venable.'

And now here was Venable himself, flushed and a little silly from being thrust into prominence.

'I mayn't accept that fortune at all,' he told Capricorn, rather supercilious now. 'Or, very likely, I'll turn it over to Siderea for the good of the movement. I don't know that I have anything more to say.'

Capricorn, who had only one question left that he wanted to ask, watched the boy in some amusement. He looked so very young, with his bright eyes and firm clear flesh, effervescent with health, and now he was being made so rich, surely he was the darling of the gods. Or would be, once the horrible enigma of murder was solved and the aftermath cleared away.

A wind blew through the branches above them. It began to feel cool in the shade. It was time for Capricorn to move on. Venable tossed his Saxon shock of hair back from his face as they rose; drew himself up with military precision and looked the Superintendent firmly in the eye. Capricorn wanted to laugh again. Nineteen and a millionaire and very likely not as silly as he sounded.

'What did you have for dinner the night of the murder, before the tape play and your test?' he asked abruptly.

Venable's mouth opened a little in surprise.

'Why—I didn't go to dinner. I didn't take the time to eat anything. I studied for the test.'

'You didn't eat at all?' the Superintendent murmured, remembering Venable's statement, 'I had what was left of my sandwiches and cocoa from my thermos.'

'No, nothing,' Venable said, his blue eyes bulging slightly. Capricorn was certain he was trying to remember what he had said before, and failing.

'I see,' he replied. 'Well, I think that's all for now, Mr Venable. Enjoy your fortune.'

He meant it kindly, but it came out rather like Enjoy your cake.

Venable blushed again and rushed off to the Manor.

He was lying, Capricorn was sure. It was possible, of course, to forget that one had eaten a left-over sandwich on a busy evening, but at the hungry age of nineteen? And the boy's manner—he was hiding something. It was as strange as Noreen Stacy's huffing and puffing after a sedentary half hour. Two odd statements, both concerning friends of Jedediah Frost's. He found Mrs Anthony again, and together they took Venable's test papers and went over them in the library, as Hightower seemed to grin at them ghoulishly under his neon light.

Capricorn did not make much out of the test material. It was technical stuff in Hightower's peculiar jargon—long ago Capricorn had tried to read one of Hightower's books and given it up as unreadable, the matter wandering from pure science fiction to his own amalgam of Eastern philosophies written with intolerable repetitiousness in very bad English—but it seemed to be based on a set of instructions in applying Hightower's technique. The technique itself was a method of inducing recall of a very precise sort together with a lot of fantasy, but the instructions were as practical as an engineer's might be.

'It's all confidential,' Mrs Anthony sighed. 'Still, in this case. . .'

The test had been given from exactly 7:32 to nine. There was no supervision.

'Our students never cheat,' Mrs Anthony said proudly.

The honour system was much in use, apparently, at Witch Hill. The students had picked up the test papers from the desk and left their answers in a basket provided.

'Although there was no official supervision,' Mrs Anthony added,

'I did look in myself, twice, and observed them all, working away.'

Capricorn nodded.

'At 8:10, I remember from your statement,' he said, 'and again at 8:40.'

'Yes. After 8:40 I remained until they were finished, and we went in a group back to the main hall. Some of the failing students had questions to ask.'

Capricorn remarked that Venable had the highest score.

'The highest possible,' Mrs Anthony said proudly. 'He's a very brilliant young man. That's why he has risen to such high office. Mr Hightower doesn't care about experience,' she explained. 'To him, a person is able or not. If a child of three could handle a post, he would give it to him. We do have children of seven or eight on quite important work.'

He was taken aback for a moment with visions of child labour laws being flouted and Hightower as a latter-day Fagin. Well, that was not his business at the moment.

'Christopher's I.Q. is almost as high as Jed's,' she went on. 'Jed's is 200, you know. And I think that Colonel Venable is really more—' she hesitated.

'More stable?' Capricorn enquired.

She looked unhappy at the word.

'Let's say more matter of fact.'

She glossed it over. Capricorn supposed she had compunctions about passing judgement to the police on someone who had been, and might be again, her superior officer.

'And yet he appears to have lied on his statement,' Capricorn said, and watched her reaction.

She only looked a little puzzled.

'In what way, Superintendent?'

'On the statement he gave Sergeant Copper—a sworn statement,' he added, 'Venable said he studied for his test on his dinner hour, and finished some cocoa and sandwiches he had had for lunch. Now he apparently has forgotten that and says he didn't eat at all.'

'Oh, I don't suppose that has any significance, the eating,' she said, slowly and rather absently. 'He probably committed the Crime.'

'The crime?' Capricorn asked sharply.

'The Witch Hill Crime. Eating during working hours. So many of our people are young, you know, and always hungry, and eating facilities are very poor round here unless you have the time and money for Roseacre House, which no one has. Mr Hightower sets the basic schedule, an intensive one, and it can't be changed, but it's hard to get down to the Moo-Cow, be served and arrive back in an hour. When we have evening session, a lot of people don't get dinner. If they ate all their sandwiches earlier—and they usually do,' she said resignedly, 'they fortify themselves all evening with chocolate from the machine. Strictly forbidden, it's always coming up in Confession. I pretend not to see the bulging cheeks.'

He laughed.

'You sound like the headmistress of a school.'

'I was,' she said simply. 'Quite a large school, so not much surprises me here.'

He looked at the large, calm woman, who managed to have some dignity in her clown's dress, her neat and sensible person looking very civilized under Hightower's devilish grin. He believed her, but nevertheless noted that she had not seen the students at the test until 8:10. With the test wholly unsupervised, Venable could have slipped away long enough to get to the crown of Witch Hill and back. That he had completed the work and done well might suggest that he had used the full time; but as the other students had done so badly they must have been severely tried and not reliable witnesses of Venable's doings. From seven to 7:30 Stacy vouched for his being at the tape play. He asked Mrs Anthony to show him where that tape was stored.

It was not, as he had conjectured, on the ceiling, but it was possibly more inaccessible. A pantry by the former dining room was piled high with old campaign trunks that housed the tapes, and the reel in question was in a trunk all the way in the back of the pantry. To retrieve it involved climbing and exertion on the part of Mrs Anthony, and Capricorn apologized sincerely. He asked if it was usually General Stacy's job to put the tape away, and Mrs Anthony said thankfully that it was: also to get it out, but on the night in question, as the General had driven Jed Frost to the station, she had gone and dug it up herself.

Without knowing it, she had, apparently, cleared Stacy and Venable. Venable, Stacy and Frost. The names still rang together in his mind. He would like to talk to them all again.

But he could spare a moment for a question to satisfy a personal curiosity.

'How did you come here, if I might ask?' he said. 'If you'll forgive me, you seem rather different from the others.'

'Not so different,' she laughed. 'It's just that we older ones—and there are quite a lot of us—aren't as visible as the young people. We grub away behind the scenes.'

'I'm here,' she went on, 'because I truly believe in Hightower's work and want to help.'

Her sincerity was obvious, but he was still puzzled.

'How did you come to know him?'

'I met him when he first came to England. He was at a loose end, then, rather; he hadn't yet bought Witch Hill or started the Army of the Stars, and he had severed his connection with earlier organizations he had begun but found unsatisfactory. He lectured to schools, one of them mine. I was a widow with several children when I went back to teaching, Superintendent. Good, bright children, no trouble to me at all. Except for my youngest, who was my darling.' She sighed. 'A most beautiful child, a flower. But her mind. . .' She looked up at him, hesitating, searching for words.

'It was as though she moved in darkness. For a time she seemed normal enough, but then there were lapses into night and nightmare. Until she was eighteen it was one mental hospital after another. I can't tell you what that's like, Superintendent. There is no way to tell you, unless you've been through it yourself.'

She was quite right, he didn't know. There was Aunt Tilly in her home for the slightly dotty, but it seemed to suit her and had not caused him anguish. She enjoyed putting on shows for the other inmates and despised them no more than her audiences elsewhere.

'As I said, Hightower didn't have much to do at the time, and he met my daughter, who was having one of her short periods outside. The blessed man took an interest in her and worked with her himself for weeks. It took time,' she said earnestly, 'but, at the end, she was cured. Sane. Perfectly sane. That was over three years ago and she has never had an—an unhappy day since. She's with him now, on the Ark. And, Superintendent, the best psychiatrists in England had told me her case was hopeless. She would get worse and worse, they said, and soon she would have to be confined permanently. You should see her,' she said, her eyes blazing, 'a happy, healthy woman, glowing with life, like the girls you were watching outside.'

So she had observed him, Capricorn noted. Argus-eyed.

'I made up my mind then,' she said, 'that I would do anything I could to help Noah in his work. Even when he seems unreasonable or annoying,' she plucked at her garments with distaste, 'I always remember the enormous good of the work he's done, and the great potential for the future. Perhaps the only hope of the human race.'

He was touched by her story. Her devotion was understandable, even though his always doubting mind considered the Tsarina, the Tsarevitch and Rasputin.

'But what is it, exactly, that he does?' he asked.

'There are a lot of Paths, but in essence it's very simple,' she explained. 'He makes people see—he makes them realize that they are immortal souls.'

Outside the library windows the lawns and fields stretched westward to meet the sun, almost horizontal now, gold light blending with crimson, the long day of summer drawing slowly to its close. To the south the shadow of the cedar fell across the grass. Capricorn was shaken out of himself by her explanation. For a moment he had nothing to say. He didn't even wish to point out that every neighbourhood church has the same mission, and without scarlet tights. She would only reply, he was certain, that the churches were not as successful as Siderea.

He and Mrs Anthony regarded each other in a friendly communion that considering their short acquaintance was unusually close. How strange, his mind ticked over, for he was a reserved man, yet he and this portly grey-haired matron had the kind of intimacy more usually found in love, or after. And this wasn't love; certainly there was no touch of Eros.

But he had no further time to speculate, for at that moment the telephone rang and broke the bond.

'It's for you, Superintendent,' Mrs Anthony said composedly, as if for her the experience was not unusual.

Capricorn had not expected to hear such a jubilant voice on the other end of the line.

'We've all but got it,' Griswald said triumphantly. 'Only you're not going to like this.'

'All but. . .?'

'Our immigration people aren't nearly fussy enough,' Griswald went on. 'One young man came into the country with two rifles. We found them in his room, not hidden, right out in the corner of the room with ammunition in boxes. And we also found a box of .45 cartridges, though not the gun. So we waited for the young man to come in, and he admitted they were his, calm as you please. Yes, he had a Colt .45 pistol as well, he said. He'd brought his guns in case he got a chance to do some shooting. So we asked him, very nicely, if we could see the .45. And what d'you think?' Griswald asked triumphantly. 'When he went to his desk drawer, it seemed to have vanished. Quite upset he was, you'd think, to see him. "Oh," he says, "it's gone." We're still in the house, Capricorn. If you think we should get a warrant.—'

Capricorn knew without asking the question, but he asked it anyway.

'Which young man—?'

'It's your Yank friend,' Griswald told him. 'The horsy lad, Mr Garry Wyatt.'

eleven

Griswald lent Capricorn his private office in the police station to question Garry Wyatt. He left them alone, somewhat to Capricorn's relief, for he would not have wanted to go over Wyatt's statement in the country Super's presence. Certainly he would consider that Wyatt should have been under lock and key from the time he made it. The statement, like Linda Lavender's, was a glaring mass of contradictions and impossibilities.

Capricorn had not considered its unravelling a matter of first priority at the time. Linda had asked to be excused that evening from her studies to attend her mother's engagement party. But he knew that Beatrice Brewster, for whom young people did not exist, had not invited her. Rose had thought she was at the Manor. It seemed an obvious enough occasion for a lovers' tryst, and re-questioning the lovers had been put off for more urgent business.

But now the detective looked at the tall, lanky young man, hunched awkwardly in the small space between the chair and the Super's desk. Above him, in solitary splendour on the bare white wall, was a dark photograph of a former Superintendent with a Victorian grimness of aspect. Capricorn remembered the warnings he had received from his elders as a very young policeman about the dangers of ignoring the obvious, and sighed.

Garry was not clearing the matter up in a few words. No man-to-man confidence about a romantic evening was forthcoming. He was repeating the story of stabling his horses—he said seven o'clock now: it had been six-thirty before, Capricorn noted, and he had also at one point mentioned seven-thirty—then going straight to his lodgings, alone, without any dinner.

'Why didn't you eat dinner?' Capricorn asked.

'I just wasn't hungry, I guess,' the young man said, avoiding his eye.

He was an awfully bad liar. Surely he couldn't have had much practice. But murderers were not, of necessity, good liars. Capricorn thought of Venable. Another Siderean who had mysteriously lost his appetite on the night of the murder. After reading five hundred statements, as well as talking to Mrs Anthony, Capricorn believed that the last thing likely to happen. The Sidereans were always hungry, and their minds were constantly on food. Breakfast in their lodgings was often a problem, lunch, except for the small privileged group of high-ranking officers, meant the inevitable sandwiches, and by dinner time they would often eat three greasy hamburgers in the Moo-Cow with three helpings of chips. How they survived on such a diet was a miracle, but Hightower was perhaps miraculous because they were unusually healthy.

Capricorn quietly pointed out the variations in his statements.

'You've already been warned,' he reminded him.

'I know. Everything I say is being taken down and may be used as evidence.'

The young man ventured a smile. It was an attractive smile.

I'll be damned if he's the killer, Capricorn thought. What on earth would he want to kill Brewster for? But why won't he tell the truth about where he was? Surely he's not just shielding his lady's reputation? Reputations went out with the young twenty years ago.

'You admit to owning a semi-automatic Colt .45 pistol as well as the two rifles found on your premises?'

'Oh, yeah, I've got a Colt. Don't know where it could've got to; I really don't.'

He looked genuinely puzzled. He also sounded as though now he was telling the truth. Capricorn was exasperated. If the young American was the murderer, ·why would he have told Griswald and his men about the .45?

'You must realize that isn't very convincing.'

He thought a more pointed warning might be helpful.

'I think I should tell you that Superintendent Griswald is considering swearing out a warrant for your arrest.'

'For murder?'

Wyatt looked up. He had turned pale.

'A decision hasn't been taken.' Capricorn said, not adding that he had been against it, 'but you will be asked particularly not to leave the area, apart from the more general request that has been made of the Sidereans at the Manor. And now, if you please, I think you should stop playing games. I think you should tell me exactly where you were that evening and exactly what you were doing.'

But the young man looked down at his moccasins and did not reply and Capricorn, genuinely angry, realized that he was not going to tell the truth; nor did he, in spite of another hour of questioning.

'It's ridiculous,' he told Copper as they had a quick meal in the taproom. 'I've never seen anyone act more determinedly guilty. And I can't believe he's got anything to do with it. What's that you've got there?'

'Local dark ale,' Copper replied, drinking deep. 'Bloody good stuff.'

'The language of the Metropolitan Police is not what it was,' Capricorn remarked moodily, and called for the same.

Copper had his tankard refilled at the same time.

'Been enjoying yourself in here?' Capricorn asked with some sarcasm.

'Well, I've done better than waste time talking to a Yank who's just giving you a lot of chat,' Copper said, agreeably. 'That kitchen maid is out of it. Swears she was at the Emanuel Church fête that evening from six to nine, and about fifty people saw her. Saw a lot of her, seems like. She was an "attraction." A go-go girl, in gym shorts and the top of her bathing costume.' He shuddered. 'Thirty inch bust and forty hip if I'm any judge. And I am.'

Capricorn ignored this slur on bucolic beauty, his mind on another charmer, who was lovely, and a liar.

'I'll have to talk to Linda Lavender tonight,' he said in disgust. 'What a case. Frost makes the threats. Venable has the motive. And Wyatt is the only one with no alibi.'

'Alibis can be fudged,' Copper said cheerfully. 'And maybe Wyatt has a motive.'

Capricorn looked up from his vol-au-vent, which was all the Roseacre kitchen had left.

'And what have you found while you've been here at your ease, drinking this excellent ale?'

'Nothing like a tap for getting together,' Copper said. 'My old friend, the bike-fancier from Brewster House, came in for a quick one. All upset about the funeral tomorrow and the fuss they had bringing the coffin home. Stood him a couple of drinks and you'd be surprised some of the stuff he told me. First I gave 'im some tips on how to pull a likely bird and then he was eating out of my hand.'

Capricorn quickly translated 'pull a likely bird' to mean 'attract a probably willing female.'

'What did he tell you in return for this priceless information?'

'All about Brewster's women up in London. Had quite a few, over the years. Purdy—that's the bike bloke—was a bit on the jealous side. Sometimes, when he didn't take the train, Brewster had Purdy drive him to London and take him and his birds around. Not since your Mrs Lavender, though,' the sergeant added, kindly.

'And apart from this gossip--' Capricorn asked, while deciding that he should talk to Purdy himself, and consider the possibility of other suspects besides Sidereans. One of Brewster's former mistresses, angered by his prospective marriage . . . Yes, he would talk to Purdy. And also to the Rector, who was Brewster's oldest friend.

The waitress brought a dish of red currants covered with thick cream, and coffee. Both were good, and Capricorn's spirits rose a little in spite of his concerns.

'Kindly stop looking so pleased with yourself,' he adjured Copper, 'and tell me what little tit-bit you've been keeping for me.'

'I only wanted you to enjoy your dinner first,' Copper answered. 'I know that the Yank wasn't your fancy.'

'I don't think you can call Texans Yanks,' Capricorn replied, then asked with some foreboding. 'What is it?'

'They're all Yanks to me,' Copper said spiritedly. 'Texas is America, isn't it? This week, anyway? Well, that Yank has got a motive, all right. Purdy was telling me he and Brewster had a slap-up row the afternoon before the murder.'

He grinned.

'Griswald took his statement and never found out.'

Copper had the Londoner's relish of any hint of slowwittedness on the part of provincials.

'Said Griswald didn't ask about any quarrels so he felt it wasn't his place to say. But all the same, he'd heard Brewster hollering like mad in his study, and Purdy had let the Yank in.'

'What was the yelling about?' Capricorn asked crisply.

'Well, Purdy said he couldn't hear it all. The doors and walls in Brewster House are solid as the locals' heads. But I think he had an ear close to the keyhole because he says he heard Brewster warn him to keep clear of young Linda Lavender. They had some more arguing and then Brewster was yelling that if he didn't do as he was told, Brewster would have him thrown out of the country. It would be no trouble at all, the old man said. Someone up in the Home Office would take care of it. And all of Siderea had better watch out, because they all might get free transportation home. Stay away from the girl, or be deported. What d'you think of that for a motive?'

It didn't add up to anything that made sense, Capricorn thought, rather weary. And he had *liked* Garry Wyatt. But now everything was falling into place against him. Although the murder weapon had not been found, Wyatt had had the only .45 known to be in the area. And it was missing. Now it seemed there could also be a motive. Certainly he was the one person who had had the opportunity. He spent his days roaming the pasture where Brewster had been killed. There were all his lies about where he was at the time of the murder. Yes, he could have lingered on that pasture, with the gun concealed in any spot he liked to pick, and waited for Brewster to arrive. No need of telephone calls. He could just wait for his opportunity. No one would think anything of seeing him up on the hill; he was always there. Most likely if a dozen people saw him they would not remember if he was there at any particular time or not.

He would have to be questioned again. And so would Linda, who seemed to be mixed up in it. Linda. Oh, poor Rose. He hoped she was not going to be sorry she had asked her old friend, the CID Superintendent, to come down to Daines Barington.

Outside the leaded windows of Roseacre House, in the High Street, the lamps were going on. They glowed gold and comforting against the grey night, but Capricorn was not comforted. The world at that moment looked bleak and very sad.

twelve

The Superintendent was not, after all, to see Linda Lavender,. He called Rose from the tap to tell her he was on his way and found the household in chaos. Mrs Lavender had gone to the hospital, a flustered maid told him, with her daughter and Dr Bailey. Linda had had a bad attack of asthma, one of the worst she had ever suffered, and the doctor had removed her to the Daines Barington Infirmary.

Dr Bailey, from the hospital, assured the Superintendent that he could not see Linda that night.

'I've had to put her under a strong sedative,' he said. 'She must be absolutely quiet for at least twenty-four hours.'

'I'd heard she was cured,' Capricorn remarked.

'A remarkable improvement,' the doctor told him, 'until this flaring up. Quite unexpected.'

'I wonder what could have brought it on,' Capricorn ventured.

But the usually gossipy little doctor was oddly silent.

'You should be able to talk to her by tomorrow evening,' was all he said at last. 'I hope you won't upset her too much, Superintendent!'

'I hope I won't, too,' he answered, wryly.

The doctor had said goodnight in a rather flustered way, rather less friendly, Capricorn noticed, than when they had last spoken. Unfortunate to be a Superintendent of police, and have to question the statements of asthmatic girls, even when said frail young girls were lying their heads off.

Griswald had urged that they get the warrant for Garry Wyatt after the fiasco in the station, but Capricorn had let him go.

'Watch him,' he had instructed. 'We can wait a day or two. Perhaps the gun will turn up.'

But the Superintendent was not only looking for more evidence. He still felt obstinately convinced that Wyatt was not their man. In this day and age, he thought irritably, no young man would kill because an authoritative stepfather warned him away from a girl. He didn't have to. Girls took little notice of their own parents, let alone their mothers' future husbands. The youngsters go their own way, and older people have to put up with it. But why had Brewster taken a dislike to Garry Wyatt so suddenly? The ex-colonel had seemed to approve of the young veteran the night before.

Capricorn thought of the many hundreds of statements taken; not one had shown that Wyatt had been in Brewster House that day. He had concentrated too much on the Sidereans, he realized, soberly. His next stop would be St Cuthbert's. Brewster's oldest friend, the Rector, might have more to say. Later he would check on Purdy at Brewster House.

St Cuthbert's in the twilight looked like a monument to certainty, its spires pointing with confidence to the heavens, its massive doorway sheltering the late worshippers who were streaming out in surprising numbers. A large part of Daines Barington had attended, all townspeople with no hint of Siderea, the women hatted, gloved, wearing little pearl necklaces and shoes with heels, the men in dark suits. The Rector was on the steps, saying goodnight, and Capricorn waited until the last parishioner was gone.

'A little memorial for Richard,' the Rector explained. 'The funeral is tomorrow, but quite a lot of people asked for the extra service. Some can't get to the funeral, and others, I suspect, will attend both. Miss Brewster was here; she left a few minutes ago.'

'I did want to see you alone,' Capricorn said.

'Come to the Rectory,' Theale suggested.

They walked past the old churchyard.

'That's the Brewster plot.'

The Rector pointed out a corner shadowed by a black yew.

'They've always been buried here. We're getting crowded now,' he said meditatively. 'But there'll be room for Richard. And Miss Brewster could be buried here if she wished, but, of course, she's a Catholic. And not really a Brewster, perhaps you know. Never was.'

Capricorn followed him into the rambling, rather shabby, early-Victorian Rectory. The gardens were not too well kept and inside the house was bleak. The Superintendent, like everyone else in England, had read a good many racy stories in the daily press about the Rector's father, the rich and eccentric Sir Walter Theale, and he wondered a little.

The Rector was the baronet's only son. Perhaps Sir Walter's own interests took all the family funds, Capricorn speculated. Sir Walter, now in his eighties, was known for his socialist views, his protest marches and the unfortunate paternity suit brought against him without success by a young marcher.

'Theale admits intimacy but claims sterility,' the headlines had blazoned. Capricorn looked at the Rector with some sympathy. His problem parent must have given him some nightmares.

They sat in the rather cold drawing room on tapestry-backed chairs, once, probably, very fine, but now faded and patched. The Rector was the man who needed a woman like Rose, Capricorn thought absently, with his mind still fixed on the problem of his case.

'Theale,' he plunged in, 'would you have any ideas why Richard Brewster should have quarrelled with young Garry Wyatt on the day of his death?'

'Why, no,' the Rector said in some surprise. 'Did they quarrel? Richard said nothing about it that night, nor did Beatrice.'

'The servants say they did.'

'Purdy?'

Capricorn nodded.

'Well, I don't think Purdy would lie,' the Rector said thoughtfully. 'He would have no reason to do so. But I don't think it could be important to you, Superintendent.'

He coughed.

'Richard had taken to playing the Roman father to Linda, I fear. A new role for him; he was enjoying it. You don't suspect that young American, surely? He doesn't seem a criminal type.'

Murderers weren't always criminal types; that was the problem, Capricorn thought, but forbore to argue. He wanted to hear the Rector's view.

'He comes in quite often to St Cuthbert's,' Theale went on, obviously convinced that none of his flock would go so far astray.

Capricorn was surprised.

'But he's a Siderean. Isn't that heretical?'

'It's not a Christian heresy,' the Rector said, wrinkling his brow, 'Siderea is, as I understand it, pagan. His attendance is perhaps heretical to Siderea, but I believe Hightower doesn't care about that. He thinks traditional religion too unimportant to bother with.'

He looked downcast.

'Pagan?' Capricorn asked, guiltily aware that he was divagating. 'I know he teaches that they are immortal souls.'

'As I understand it,' the Rector said drily, 'he teaches them that they are gods. He goes far beyond Nietzsche—it's heady stuff for young people. Wyatt showed me some of their services. Very science fiction.'

'Did you tell Wyatt that?' Capricorn said, amused.

'Well, not exactly, you know,' the Rector said. 'But he got the idea. They are rather quick, I've found. He said it was pretty science fiction when Our Lord raised Lazarus from the dead. And he's quite right.' The Rector was trying very hard to be fair. 'To those simple people, hearing the story in those days—'

'Wouldn't it seem miraculous now?' Capricorn asked, 'even to our not-so-simple city people?'

'Oh, dear, no,' the Rector answered. 'Nowadays people would just think that Lazarus had been pickled or frozen or one of these modern things, or fitted with an artificial heart. Why, Dr Bailey was telling me the other day that it has become very difficult to say when a patient is dead. He said that they could be considered dead for some purposes but not for others.'

'Difficult for a clergyman,' Capricorn said gravely.

'It is, it is indeed,' Theale replied with fervour. 'And very disagreeable. What of the Resurrection? Some of my young people ask that question. And what can one answer? You can see that they imagine a lot of frozen assorted parts, like these new chickens in the grocers' shops.'

He shook his head and then smiled.

'But I'm boring you with my problems when you have come to ask questions. What can I tell you?'

'If I were sure of my questions, perhaps I wouldn't need the answers.' Capricorn smiled in return. 'But there were one or two things. . . Everyone is taking it for granted that the murderer was one of those Sidereans. But we have to cover all possibilities. I thought as Brewster's close friend you might be able to tell me if he had any other enemies. Someone that even Miss Brewster might not know about.'

The Rector was sitting with his long, slender legs crossed in front of him, leaning back in his chair, his profile a cameo against the dark tapestry. His brow furrowed at the question and he regarded Capricorn with something like dismay.

'Most certainly not,' he said, sounding like Miss Brewster. 'I testified at the inquest, if you remember, about that. I have never known a man so universally liked and admired.'

'I understand,' Capricorn said, encouraging, 'but sometimes these likes and dislikes are irrational, as indeed this one must have been. Even the Sidereans had no real reason to dislike him.'

'Oh,' the Rector said, in another tone, 'that was inevitable.'

Capricorn arched his eyebrows.

'I will explain that, if you wish. I trust I understand it,' Theale went on. 'But Richard certainly had no other enemies.'

'He was marrying,' Capricorn suggested, 'and he was fifty-five. One assumes there must have been other women, possibly not in Daines Barington—'

'Purdy has been gossiping,' the Rector said shortly. He looked annoyed and got up abruptly from his chair and went to the window, peering out onto his dismal stretch of lawn overlooking the churchyard.

'It's bad enough,' he said after a moment, 'that a man's life is destroyed by violence. Then his servants—remembered in his will, too—'

Capricorn guessed that the Rector was executor.

'His own servants gossip.'

Capricorn waited in silence.

'Richard has not been a celibate,' the Rector said at last. 'It is true, he has had women. We have talked about it, as friends, as well as parishioner and rector. But Richard always behaved very well. There was no bad feeling, no outcries at the parting. He chose well,' he said meditatively. 'Many fine women. He could have married any one of them with no disgrace. But he preferred to remain a bachelor until he met Mrs Lavender. And in any event, Superintendent,' Theale said briskly, 'I know that his last—affair—' he stumbled a little on the word, 'was more than three years ago. And the lady in question is now happily married.'

The darkening room was quiet. Capricorn stared through the window to the garden where the moon topped the trees, observing nothing. It would seem to be the end of that road. He was left with Siderea. 'And yet it's strange,' his voice was saying, springing from an uneasy feeling that here was the place that should be explored, an area that had been left untouched while he chased the excitable but really motiveless Sidereans, 'A man like that, who must have been pursued by many women, remaining a bachelor so long.'

The Rector moved away and walked round the room, lighting the lamps. The lamps were Victorian relics, heavily shaded in dark silks, somewhat faded, that cast small pools of light beneath them without adding much to the visibility of the room. From where he stood behind a particularly tall, draped monster, the Rector's voice came like a voice from the past.

'Not so strange, Superintendent. You never knew Mrs Lucrezia.'

Slowly the Rector went back to his chair and sat, perhaps intentionally, with his face in shadow.

'You've seen her portrait. Very like, but it can't really convey her quality, excitement.'

He fidgeted and Capricorn saw that his beautiful hands were tensely clasped.

'Richard was very young when Lucrezia came. What were we then, seventeen, eighteen? He looked like a Saxon page.'

Capricorn thought of Christopher Venable, who had seemed to him like a young Piers Plowman. Yes, at that age the resemblance would have been great.

'And Lucrezia was young. I've never known her age, exactly. She was not the sort of woman to tell.'

He smiled from the shadows.

'This is getting to be something in the nature of a confession.

Something I've never talked about, even with Richard. But if it saves you from looking in the wrong direction—I don't mind. It was all so long ago.'

Capricorn waited, silent.

'I myself am a clergyman, but not a professional celibate if you understand me, Superintendent.'

Capricorn nodded. 'You mean you could marry; it's not against your convictions, but you have chosen not to.'

'Chosen not to, yes, in a way. The truth is,' the Rector sighed, 'That Richard and I—like so many others—fell deeply in love with Mrs Lucrezia. So many men,' he went on thoughtfully, 'but we were boys. I don't think, looking back, that we ever recovered. Lucrezia died in 1944, but she remained with us in some way, to the detriment of other women. That was true of Richard, at any rate, until he met Mrs Lavender—so different,' he sighed again, 'and yet, equally charming. Strange,' he said, 'strange.'

He looked up and smiled at the Superintendent.

'You could say that was the excuse of two old bachelors, and I suppose a Freudian would have other ideas, but that's the way it always seemed to me.'

'Thank you for telling me,' Capricorn said sincerely. He was moved. It had probably not been easy for this dignified, patrician man to speak so freely of his inmost thoughts and feelings, and he had offered this to him, as help. 'You've certainly made things clear.'

Clear, but not helpfully clear, he realized. He was still trapped in the impasse of having Wyatt as chief suspect, Wyatt, whom he did not want to arrest.

'By the way,' he said. 'You mentioned that Miss Beatrice was not really a Brewster. You meant that she was adopted?'

'No,' Theale answered, hesitating. 'No, that is an odd thing. She has always been called Miss Brewster since she came to England, naturally, but there was never a legal adoption. Lucrezia,' he sighed, and moved his chair a little so that he sat in the light, 'Lucrezia was rather naughty there, I'm afraid.'

'You mean the late Mrs Brewster—'

'Women like Mrs Lucrezia prefer to be thought of as youthful, and Beatrice was quite a big child already when they came to Daines Barington. I had a feeling, from odd remarks that Lucrezia made, that children are much more *visible* here than they are in Rome. In her milieu, anyway. And, of course, Beatrice was not an appealing child. Plain, and she seemed very dull. Neglect, I suppose.'

The Rector's voice had been falling, steadily, until his last words were almost a whisper. Suddenly he shivered.

'It's cold in here,' he said, as if he had just noticed it, and he looked rueful, mindful of the comfort of his visitor.

'I'm afraid the housekeeping here is not what it is in Brewster House—or Mrs Lavender's establishment either. Let us have a little brandy, Superintendent. I don't know if you are still supposed to be on duty at this ungodly hour, but we could certainly consider it medicinal. I won't trouble my housekeeper, she retires early. If you will excuse me—'

He was back in a moment with a tray bearing two glasses and a bottle that he opened with some satisfaction.

'I think you'll enjoy this, Capricorn,' he said. 'From the cellar of Theale Towers.' Capricorn knew of the historic family home of the Theales. It had been mentioned in the newspapers lately as a disgrace, falling into dilapidation and decay as Sir Walter cared nothing for it and wanted to give it to the National Trust. Unfortunately the National Trust wasn't too eager to accept it in its present condition. In the meantime Sir Walter was happily living in King's Road.

'My father doesn't care for brandy.' The Rector was smiling. 'He's developed a fancy for cola drinks. It's the ''young thing'', he tells me.'

Capricorn, fervently glad he wasn't that young, savoured his cognac, *fine champagne*. He noticed the colour come back to the Rector's face, and watched him relax as he took his place again in the wing chair. Theale would become voluble now, the Superintendent thought, but he was no longer seized with impatience as he would have been years before. He had learned since then that the most valuable information came his way from such informal talks: things he could never have learned in the process of taking a statement, answers to questions he would never have thought to ask.

'I said I would tell you why I thought it inevitable there would be a major clash between Richard and the Sidereans,' the Rector said, 'though, of course, I didn't think it would end in such tragedy. Or perhaps I merely didn't wish to think it,' he added.

Capricorn noticed the Rector had veered away from the subject of Mrs Lucrezia's neglect of her daughter to a more general and probably less painful one. They would get back to it, he promised himself. Garry Wyatt was not yet under arrest. Something might yet come up in the Rector's rambling, some hint, some new aspect of the case, hitherto unexplored.

'You heard me reading from my little monograph on the Antigone,' he said, with a deprecating air. Rose had mentioned the Rector's articles and monographs. Highly thought of in literary circles.

'A snatch, only,' Capricorn apologized.

'Yes, well, my belief is that we have had a similar situation here in Daines Barington,' the Rector said gravely.

'As the Antigone?' Capricorn was puzzled.

'Except that this time it was Creon that died.'

The Rector was well launched now.

'The same pattern, an irrepressible religious impulse against a rigid social barrier. Richard was no Creon in our eyes, but certainly that's the way those young people saw him. He was the foundation of the opposition. They had to come into conflict. And it was he that lost.'

'But Rose told me Richard was not opposed to their plans; in fact, he was helping them.'

The Rector nodded. 'That was true, at first. But it could never have worked. They had to upset the town, if you know this town, and the town would want to cast them out. Richard was certainly the leader and that is why this hatred arose. Certainly, as time passed, when they annoyed Mrs Lavender and other townspeople and interfered with the running of the hospital—many of the younger nurses left to join Siderea, and the hospital was very much a Brewster gift to the town—he became as eager as anyone to see the last of them. The planning permission was definitely shelved as long as they were here, and it was in the Town Clerk's office that the plan was gathering dust.'

'You said, "a religious impulse," ' Capricorn reminded him.

'Oh, yes,' the Rector nodded, 'no doubt about that. They are in a fine fervour of proselytizing religious sentiment and sincerely believe that only they can save the souls of earth. Like nearly all fervent proselytizers,' he added ruefully, 'they believe, therefore, that it doesn't matter what they do to catch and save those souls, as nothing, nothing in this world or any other, is worse than being among the damned, cast out for eternity. The churchmen at the time of the Inquisition, after all, felt the same way.'

'This hardly seems the sort of town. . . .' Capricorn suggested, and the Rector laughed.

'My dear man! If Hightower had planned bloodshed,' he couldn't have picked better. You, of course, couldn't know Daines Barington as I do but. . . ! Of course he got Witch Hill at a great bargain. Prince Ranook was ready to give it away, I believe. He developed gout *and* rheumatism in both shoulders and fled to the south of France. But you must let me explain Daines Barington and you will understand.'

He leaned back in his chair with an expression on his fine distinguished features very similar to that worn by the harried little Hartle in his discursive mood. I'm going to get more history, Capricorn thought and resigned himself. It was true that history, English history especially, was one of his interests; it was also true that he had more work to do that night. But he would listen to the Rector until he finished.

'First let me give you a little more brandy,' Theale said. He poured a large glass, to last his story, Capricorn inferred, and then reproached himself for such unworthy thoughts, for his host was certainly giving of his best.

'In all its long and moderately distinguished history,' the Rector said, 'Daines Barington has never known commotion or upset. The Romans came across the small settlement halfway between the South Coast and Londinium. They did not find the natives hostile and passed them by. Waves of Danes, Vikings and other invaders lost their lust for battle by the time they reached the green and fertile valley, and those that stayed joined peacefully in farming and orchard keeping, leaving a legacy not of spilled blood but of golden-haired children with eyes the colour of periwinkle that grows on the banks of the Baring. The Normans parcelled out the town and surrounding country, according to the Domesday Book, to one of William's followers, but he, a man wise in his time, married the daughter of the man whose lands he had taken, so that the people felt no great change.'

The Rector looked happy now, the Superintendent noticed, launched on what sounded like another monograph, well away from unpleasant subjects to which they would have to return.

'The religious wars left the people almost undisturbed. Daines Barington turned Protestant under the Eighth Henry, returned to Catholicism under Mary Tudor, and, at Elizabeth's command, almost with a sigh of relief, they took the Anglican faith and clove to the Thirty-Nine Articles, which, I might say,' the Rector interrupted himself, 'are admirably suited to the spirit of the town. You saw the attendance tonight, Superintendent.

'At the time of the Revolution,' he took up the thread again, 'there were only three old Catholic women left in the town who were duly burned as witches in the market place. On the cobbles,' he murmured, 'where we still hold sheep auctions right up to today.'

'Were they connected with Witch Hill?' Capricorn asked. 'It's an odd name.'

'M'm. You touch on tender subjects, my dear Capricorn. The manor house of those days, a large place on the same site as the present one, was held by the Courtneys, ancestors of the Gaylords on the female side. The Courtneys had always been fervent Catholics. Under our good Protector, of course,' the Rector smiled, 'the Courtneys were known as good Protestants. But it was often rumoured in the town that the Courtneys secretly practiced Catholicism and that the manor was riddled with priests' holes that came out on Witch Hill. Strange how that kind of rumour will persist. The same rumour crops up in old parish records about the present Manor, though as it was built in the time of good Queen Anne, when the General Courtney who commissioned Vanbrugh was openly a practicing Catholic, the rumour seems absurd. But people love such tales.

'Yes, you're quite right, Capricorn, about the name of the hill. Mark Manor Mount it was called before, but the townspeople suspected that the Courtneys had taken the ashes of the three Catholic women and buried them, with a priest giving the sacrament, on the northerly slopes of the pasture, out of sight of anyone coming by from the town. That was probably true, as the Courtneys were a good Catholic family, as were the Gaylords, all the way to young Ron Gaylord, the last to live there.

'Religion made a bond between young Gaylord and Mrs Lucrezia, the only Catholics for miles around. Religion was the bond, and religion only,' the Rector repeated, the colour high in his cheeks, 'in spite of anything that you might hear elsewhere.'

Capricorn felt he wasn't likely to hear gossip about a woman who died a quarter-century ago, and he felt sorry for Theale, his hearth cold in front of him, still bearing a banner for the woman who had so carelessly beguiled him as well as Richard, and who had stunted the life of Beatrice. For all the Rector's enthusiasm, Capricorn didn't think he would have cared for Mrs Lucrezia. He thought of some of the flashing beauties he had known as a boy, actresses and performers of all sorts. But he had seen them too much when they were 'off' and had perhaps become cynical about those brilliant ladies.

'Stories that gossips tell,' the Rector still quietly burned, 'stories that Lucrezia slipped away under John's extremely jealous eye, meetings in secret passages, through those mythical priests' holes and the like.'

'Brewster House was built a little late for that,' Capricorn said, amused.

'Exactly,' the Rector said in triumph. 'There was nothing but a farmhouse in the time of religious persecutions, and in any event the Brewsters were always solidly Protestant. No, those stories were just spite, all because Mrs Lucrezia was, as well as beautiful and fascinating, of a different religion.

'Well, it goes to prove my point,' he sighed. 'Daines Barington does not like anything different from itself. Its soil is rich, the rainfall plentiful, the sunshine sufficient and its people think they are the blessed, if not the chosen.'

His tone lightened.

'After the episode of the three witches, Cromwell forgot the town; James the Second ignored it. William and Mary approved of it and how it flourished!'

'Later, it stoically bore the American occupation with little effect. An air squadron had its quarters ten miles away but Daines Barington was a wealthy town by then, the age of its inhabitants averaged over the middle mark, and the airmen mostly went to other towns in search of pubs and pubescent girls. When the war was over there had been no broken hearts that I know of,' he added, smiling, 'unless, of course, you count poor Beatrice.'

And so he had wound his way around to the story of Beatrice after all, the Antigone, for the moment, forgotten. Yet now it echoed in the Superintendent's mind, almost against his will.

'None shall entomb him or mourn. . .'

Tomorrow Brewster would be buried, he mentally assured the bereaved sister, and the insults to her brother's body smoothed over with the earth of Daines Barington, in the sanctity of St Cuthbert's, as he and his family would have wished. Or would this sister consider that unhallowed ground, he wondered, uneasy, and then listened determinedly to the Rector. The brandy is making me thick-headed, he thought, annoyed with himself.

'It's hard to believe now but Beatrice actually had a little

143

romance—though it wasn't very romantic,' the Rector mused.

'Life was very dull for Lucrezia once the war began, and, of course, painful, with Italy in the war. The people with whom she had filled Brewster House were scattered all over the world. Richard, of course, was in the army. Gaylord, her good friend, was killed almost immediately in the Battle of Britain. Lucrezia seemed to lose interest in life—she hated so to be bored. For a time some of the officers from the American air squadron were billeted at the Manor and although I don't think she cared much for any of them, Lucrezia would entertain them occasionally, as well as one could entertain then, to pass the time.'

'And one of the officers and Miss Brewster. . .' Capricorn asked.

'She was quite attractive, as young girls are. It's hard to believe now. The man was a major, not young, an eccentric, dry, old-maidish sort of man. He had a hobby of collecting odd things, nothing particularly valuable, or antique, just bits and pieces; a few books, weapons, some sticks of furniture that he intended, I suppose, to send to America after the war. He came from a place called Bridgeport, a backwater, he said. I don't know how much Beatrice really liked him, but he was the only man who ever paid her attention.'

Theale twisted his brandy glass, rolling it between his fingers thoughtfully.

'Lucrezia wasn't at all pleased when he proposed to Beatrice. Perhaps she didn't like the idea of having a daughter old enough to be married. And she felt it was an impertinence for such a dull, undistinguished man to raise his eyes to a Miss Brewster.'

'Though she wasn't really a Brewster, you said.'

'No, she wasn't. John had offered to adopt her, I believe, but Lucrezia had dampened the idea. Religious problems, she said, and other things. In truth, she didn't like the girl, and I believe at one time had thought of shipping her back to Italy, but the war stopped all that. Of course, in return, Beatrice adored her mother. She still keeps the place as a shrine. Nothing is ever changed there, you know, from the way it was in Lucrezia's day. I suppose some things must wear out, good as they were, but if so Beatrice replaces them with exactly the same stuffs and patterns. Amazing,' he sighed, looking round at his own dim drawing room, where the wallpaper was darkened with damp and the once fine rug showed patches largely bare.

'Anyway, Lucrezia laughed at the idea of the match. "A mangy old dog looking for a basket," was all she said of him.'

'Did Miss Brewster resent giving him up?' Capricorn asked with some interest.

'No, it didn't seem so. Lucrezia's word was law, and Beatrice didn't appear unhappy. She never wanted more than to be Miss Brewster of Brewster House. I had to intercede for her with the authorities at the beginning of the war because they wanted her real name on her ration book. Beatrice Marquisio. It was the first time I had ever heard it.

'But all the same, the major must have been fond of her, because when he was killed it was found he left all his bits and pieces to Beatrice, as well as a little life insurance. Which must be useful to her,' the Rector added thoughtfully, 'because although she's always been taken care of by the Brewsters, she has never had a penny piece to call her own. I suppose the major had no relatives; still, it was a gesture.'

Capricorn remembered Mr Hartle saying that all of John Brewster's estate had been left to Richard.

'Didn't Mrs Brewster leave her daughter anything?'

'No,' the Rector said, looking uncomfortable. 'I was her executor. Of course her personal possessions were not large, she died during the war before her husband, but she had some fine jewels and art objects, things of value. She left them all to Richard. "Let it all stay with Brewster House" she said, "I made it, and I like to think of it remaining complete." '

He was quiet for a moment, and then looked up.

'I'm keeping you, Superintendent, with my rambling. And I have no information to help you with in your search. Richard had no enemies, no ill-wishers, apart from Siderea, unless we could find perhaps a relative of someone he killed in the war.'

The Rector was smiling, as he escorted his guest to the door. But something in his words struck Capricorn, and he stood for a moment on the step, staring. He looked disturbed, relieved and perplexed in turn, until his features settled again into the usual CID expression of a guarded imperturbability.

'Not at all, Rector,' he murmured. 'You've been very instructive,' and he strode off briskly into the night, leaving the Rector looking puzzled and very much alone as he went back into his silent house.

thirteen

It already seemed like a long day, but it was by no means over.
Stopping in at the station to check on the progress of the search for
the gun, he found it humming with excitement. Copper was confer-
ring with Superintendent Griswald in his office and they both looked
relieved to see him.

'I, yi, just in time for a spot of bother,' Copper greeted him with
the exaggerated cockney that he affected when rather disturbed.

Griswald's eyebrows arched somewhat as if in comment that things
had changed since he was a young man on the Force.

'That young fool Frost has run off,' he said.

'Frost?' Capricorn asked, startled.

'P.C. Rummie here spotted him, he's sure, just a moment or two
ago, making for the London road in his own car.'

'Smart work,' Capricorn looked with appreciation on the constable who had deplored Jed's activity on the night of the bonfire.

'You're sure it was he?'

'Positive,' the constable said, looking happy. 'He was in that flashy red sports car of his, and I've given him warnings and summonses a half-dozen times. A reckless driver, that one.'

'We've notified the County, and London, to be on the safe side, so he'll be picked up,' Griswald explained. 'But I wonder what he did that for, the young fool. You had no evidence on him, did you, Superintendent?'

'Nothing.' Capricorn said. 'He was just about excluded. But—' he turned. 'Come on, Copper. Let's take a ride after Mr Frost and see where he's heading.

'Oh, Griswald,' he added, 'have the car watched but don't pick him up straight away.'

Griswald agreed, and Capricorn got his car quickly and he and Copper were soon heading for the London road at a rate of speed Constable Rummie would have thought excessive . The moon was up and the tree-shaded lanes had a fairy-tale quality as the car rushed on through the night.

Copper, who was not romantic, was wishing for this motor-bike. 'I could dodge around on that. D'you think we'll catch him, once he hits the main road?'

'With luck. Keep your eyes peeled. He'll be driving like a maiden aunt not to attract attention. Remember, he doesn't have a licence. If he hadn't had the bad luck to pass that bright young small town constable—so alert, Copper—he might have got away with it.'

They came out of the small winding lanes onto the main road, which was bearing little traffic at that hour: a few holiday-makers going home; lorries rumbling their ways up to town for night deliveries. Capricorn had been certain that London would be Jed's goal but as the fields and sheds of the local airport loomed up to their left, he and Copper gave each other a wondering glance. Could he—

'He has no passport; we checked on that,' Capricorn said thoughtfully, slowing down.

'And what would he bother with this place for?' Copper grumbled. 'Easier to get lost at London Airport. It's not much further.'

'A private 'plane,' Capricorn guessed, 'heading somewhere in this country.'

It was worth looking into, but if they were wrong they would certainly miss him on the road.

'Don't pick him up straight away,' Capricorn remembered telling Griswald. If they lost him, it was Capricorn who had made the blunder.

At that moment the beam from the rotating beacon swept the gate and lit up a vivid scarlet Alfa Romeo parked at an awkward angle just inside the gate. It looked as if it had been left by someone in a very great hurry indeed, and Capricorn was running towards it before Copper had pulled up. He checked the number plate. It was Frost's car. Capricorn considered fleetingly Jed's IQ of two hundred. It hadn't helped him much here. If he had taken a different car, he might have got away clean. But he would not lower himself by driving one of the battered old relics that most Sidereans owned. Vanity was his beginning and end, after all.

Capricorn peered round the field. The gate Jed had used was not the main gate of the airport. The white boundary lights illuminated a few small aircraft dotted about; the nearest hangar that he could make out by its winking red warnings was several thousand yards north. This was the private section of the airport. But where was Jed and whom had he come to meet?'

This was the employees' entrance, he guessed, some distance from the check-in centre. Frost would not have announced his presence if he came to meet someone, but the control tower would know what was coming in—or had already, perhaps, left.

'Over there,' he murmured to Copper. 'Get over and find out what's coming and going. I'll take a look around. I've got a hunch he's still here.'

Copper went back to the car and drove off to the public entrance, further north off the main road. The field was quiet, with no one interested in the comings and goings of the odd passer-by. Capricorn walked towards the landing fields, treading over grass and gravel. Filled-in ditches, he thought, it must have been marsh here once. The land inclined from the main road towards the cement strips, and between the light of the moon and the ceiling beams playing onto a patch of cloud, he had a good view. No one was visible waiting for an approaching 'plane.

He frowned in some perplexity. Perhaps Copper would find Jed, sitting quietly in the check-in hut, drinking a lemonade and watching the clock. But his mind refused to make the picture. Why would Jed, the vain, peacocking Jed, have left his car so unobtrusively all the way down here, and approached the hut on foot like a common mortal? It was hardly characteristic.

Yet if he was here, he was hiding. Capricorn imagined him crouching behind the fuselage of one of the 'planes, waiting for the approach of the expected aircraft, leaping out of his hiding place as it landed, pressing the pilot to leave without pause. But what purpose could he have? It would deceive no one who had followed him to the airport. The destination of a 'plane could hardly be kept a mystery from the control tower. He would have to know the police would be waiting for him at the other end. Like everything connected with this case, it made no sense. No sense at all.

Full moon, he thought, looking up. Maybe he should take to astrology. As one of Scotland Yard's most respected detectives, he wasn't doing too well. He walked about the apparently deserted field, peering under wings and into cockpits. The silence mocked him. Then he heard a faint rustle of gravel and spun around. There was quiet again, and then once more the faint sound.

In three long leaps and a run Capricorn was at the nose of a Piper Cub that rested, its wings tilted slightly with an abandoned air, towards the further edge of the field. His heart beating fast, he swung himself quickly round to the other side expecting to confront the fugitive, and wondered briefly if he were armed. But his outstretched hand fell to his side and his warning died on his lips when he saw, sitting on the down-tipped wing, not Frost, no human at all, in fact; only a large fat and lazy hare, washing its face in the moonlight, regarding him with mild astonishment at his unseemly antics.

'Damn,' he swore to himself. Could Frost have left the car there just to fox him and taken another car, by arrangement, and now be on the outskirts of London?

'Don't pick him up straight away, Griswald.'

Resigned, he looked about for Copper. Headquarters would have to be notified. He saw his car leave the check-in point and make its way through the airport lanes back towards him. One last look about—but no human form materialized. He was walking over to the lane when suddenly along the landing strip the green lights winked on, beckoning a safe approach to the 'plane that now Capricorn himself could hear humming towards him through the sky.

An excited Copper was at his side.

'It's a Cessna coming in,' he said. 'Pilot one Arthur Frost. Flight plan for return shows Chuffield airport as destination.'

'We'll be happy to meet Mr Frost,' Capricorn said, cheerfully, 'very happy indeed.'

And the 'plane glided in through the pale light to land smoothly and perfectly about a hundred yards from their feet. The pilot, a well-built, stocky man, jumped out and looked round him, as perplexed apparently as Capricorn had been at the absence of Frost the younger.

'Mr Frost?' Capricorn moved towards him.

'Who the devil are you?' the man asked angrily. 'What on earth is going on down here? And where is that confounded Jedediah?'

His accent was North Country—of course, Chuffield airport. Arthur Frost had a square jaw, a direct gaze and, Capricorn could see in the lights, a very annoyed flush. He moved with competence and assurance, a man of some authority.

'Superintendent Capricorn of Scotland Yard,' Capricorn murmured pleasantly, meanwhile watching the shadows for any approach of the young man who, he was sure, was still hiding in that field.

The man was visibly shocked.

'I'm sorry, Superintendent,' he said, embarrassed, and a look of worry replaced the anger in his face and manner.

'I really don't know what's happening. Is Jedediah in trouble with the law?' His tone was full of foreboding, as though he considered this possibility by no means unlikely. Capricorn turned to Copper and in an undertone asked him to continue the search.

'At the moment, for driving without a licence,' Capricorn said smoothly. 'I gather your son asked to meet you here—he is your son, I take it?'

'My only son,' Arthur Frost said gloomily, 'and often I wish I'd just had girls. He called me this afternoon—I hadn't heard from him for a year—with some hysterical rubbish about being threatened, and having to escape in secret. Couldn't go and buy a ticket like a normal human being. Had to bring me down here when I'm up to my eyes in business. Who the devil is threatening him, Superintendent, and since when,' he looked shrewdly at Capricorn and observed Copper hunting round the field. 'Since when does Scotland Yard chase after lads driving without their licences? I never knew he'd lost it,' he added, sounding depressed.

'Scotland Yard is interested in a murder,' Capricorn explained. 'Your son was asked to stay in the area as a possible witness. If he had said he wanted to visit his home, I've no doubt arrangements

could have been made. We have no evidence against him personally.'

'Then what is all this-cloak-and dagger nonsense?' Arthur Frost
wondered. 'Dragging us both out here. He told me to come after
dark, not to get out of the 'plane and be ready to take off straight
away. As if I didn't have to re-fuel.'

He beckoned to a mechanic who had drifted up slowly, mug of tea
steaming in his hand, and had stood patiently, entirely uninterested in
what was going on except for the appearance of the 'plane itself,
which he eyed with longing.

The elder Frost gave his instructions briskly and concisely, but
paused long enough to hear the mechanic's drawn-out questions with
politeness. How did such a man breed young Jed, the Superintendent
wondered, and shrugged. How had Mrs Lucrezia bred Beatrice? The
question that had stuck in his mind floated through the present business.

'I think he's gone, sir,' Copper came back to report, 'no sign—'

Just at that moment, from the other side of the landing strip, Capricorn heard a sound, a slight rustle that he was sure was not made
by another hare. Someone was moving on the other side of the field
near the longer landing strips for the large commercial 'planes. No
aircraft had provided cover on that side, and Capricorn had dismissed
it as a possible hiding place. Peering narrowly, he thought he saw
something dark moving on the other side of a wire fence.

He was a big man but he moved fast. Racing across the field, he
gained on the smaller, lighter figure that had broken cover now and
was running in plain view full tilt over the long landing field. The
approach lights were on and shouts and hollers from a ground crew
that was assembling indignantly warned him off and Jed swerved to
the fields on the other side. He's given up on the main road, Capricorn thought, but where is he headed for now?

On the other side of the airport, Capricorn recalled as he ran—
you're puffing, he thought in disgust, too much of the excellent beer
in the tap—on the other side was nothing but open country, fields
and hedges that turned into a stretch of woods running north of
Daines Barington. If Jed got that far they would need a whole search
party to find him.

Capricorn slipped on a stone in a gravelly ditch, swore, recovered
and when he looked up his bird had disappeared.

'That way,' Copper, not too far behind, pointed south, and Capricorn again picked up the dark figure moving with undiminished speed, darting from the shadow of the hedge into the light and back again. The line of woods to the southwest was black against the sky. Capricorn put on speed. No use trying to pace himself now, if Frost reached that wood he was lost.

Bracing himself, Capricorn leapt a three-foot hedge and almost tripped on the straggling branches on the far side, but he kept his man in sight. Sweat was salt in his mouth and his breath was beginning to catch. Too much desk work and contemplation—you're not Sherlock Holmes, he told himself, as annoyed with his complaining body as he would have been with a car that stalled.

The light from the airport didn't help now. Cloud drifted before the moon; the field darkened and he was running, running almost without seeing, following the faint sounds that he picked up from the fugitive ahead. Sickeningly, without warning, he was up to his waist in a ditch of cold and brackish water. It smelled foul and the surface was muddied with dead and floating things. Wading forward, he saw the flick of heels almost over his head, and he reached and grabbed the flying feet. He heard a cry and for a moment's triumph thought he had his man, but the shoes, unlaced in the modern style, came off in his cold wet hands. He grunted, leapt from the ditch and ran off again after the hastening figure, hampered now by the weight of his sodden clothes. The figure was almost at the line of woods and Capricorn's heart missed a beat. I've lost him, he thought, but at that moment the fugitive paused just one second to look round.

Capricorn was at the top of an incline, and without slowing down to break his momentum he hurled himself forward in one great leap and felt the other man beneath him. He had caught him only a glancing blow, and before he had his wind back Frost was struggling up and was almost away. With a last possible effort, breathless and half-stunned, Capricorn reached up and pinned the arms of the slighter man behind his back and brought him down again. The ground sloped away beneath them and they rolled about six feet, one body over the other, until they lay, finished, at the bottom with Capricorn sprawled over his captive.

Frost lay very quiet beneath him.

My God, I hope he isn't. . . but the Superintendent hardly had time to wonder about any possible bodily harm to his victim, and none to notice his own collection of bruises, scratches and other bodily mortifications which would call themselves to his attention very pointedly that night. He was much too surprised.

For Frost, after a groan and a feeble attempt to escape from Capricorn's firm grasp, finally, reluctantly, opened his frightened but apparently healthy eyes. There was no glaze of concussion, no flinch of pain, nothing but a vast, uncomprehending and then amused relief as he looked from Capricorn to the approaching Sergeant Copper, and back again.

'Well, I'll be—excommunicated,' he whispered, 'it's only you,' and he lay on his back, weak and limp, almost too tired to breathe, but painfully, slowly, and in spite of himself, laughing until the tears came.

fourteen

'Guv, you'd better stick with the Force,' Copper said meditatively. 'I don't see as how you'd fake it any more as a magician. Clumsy you've got, and that's the God's honest.'

He grinned at Capricorn's appearance: the purple bruise on the brow, the cut on the cheek, and the long scratches on the neck, all made from his tumble of the night before.

The injuries showed up bright and clear in the morning sunlight as the policemen had their breakfast in the coffee shop, once called the Hennery by Richard Brewster. But none of the town ladies were there at eight in the morning to hear the Sergeant's facetious remarks to his superior.

Copper buttered a bun, added marmalade, and drank some of the excellent coffee.

'Not bad, not bad at all,' he commented. 'What's the matter, Guv, aren't you hungry?' For Capricorn was eating little. 'P'raps you should leave this police work to younger men. Look at me, not a scratch, and a hearty appetite.'

'If you didn't eat so much you might be quicker on your feet,' Capricorn pointed out, 'and not have to leave all the rushing about to your superior officers.'

Copper smiled sweetly.

'Follow the officer, that's what we were taught in the army,' he said. 'No sense a lot of poor bloody non-coms rushing in, getting themselves killed for their ten bob a week. It's not,' he added, 'as if it did much good when you grabbed him.'

True enough, Capricorn thought, as he drank his coffee. His breakfast lay on his plate, well-cooked bacon and eggs, but he had no appetite. He was fed up, he might have said, with suspects. Frost was one more mystery. The story he had told last night had sounded like an attempt at melodrama by a six-year-old child. Yet his relief on seeing Capricorn had been real. He had been cheerful about returning to meet his father, not at all worried by the prospect of his arrest, and had listened quietly for a time to Capricorn and his father as they talked on the field.

Frost the elder had insisted on getting a lawyer for his son, whom he did not greet. His affection for the young man may have cooled over the years, but he behaved to the police as most parents would. Surely Jed did not have to be arrested for driving without a licence? If he returned to the Manor on his own volition, wouldn't a summons be enough?

Capricorn had hesitated, knowing his pretext for holding Frost was very flimsy, the slightest technicality. Frost's driving licence had not been suspended legally, after all. It was then that young Frost had become hysterical. To the astonishment of both his father and the Superintendent, it transpired that Jed would much rather be arrested on the spot than returned to Daines Barington, and the idea of being taken to the Manor filled him with frantic fear.

He had flung himself at Capricorn's feet.

'Don't send me there,' he had screamed. 'You don't know what'll happen. They'll get me away. *He*'s sent for me,' he ended with a whisper.

'Who sent for you? Who'll get you away?' his father asked with increasing annoyance.

But young Frost was practically gibbering.

'Hightower,' he said. His voice was very high-pitched. Capricorn remembered the resonant tones with which he had denounced Richard Brewster outside the Emanuel Church in the light of the blazing brands. What a distasteful young fellow Jed was, he thought. And now what was this?

'He's ordered me to the Ark,' Jed was babbling on. 'I won't go. I won't go. You don't know what they'll do to me there. You don't know. He'll keep me down in a chain locker, for as long as he likes. Months—years, if he wants. Bread and water. Punishments.'

'What is all this?' his father said angrily. 'Five minutes ago he was God and you had to devote your life to him and now he's the devil?'

'What's the difference?' Jed shivered in the cold night wind. 'He's angry with me, I tell you. You don't know what he's like.'

'What have you done?' Frost the elder looked as if he might like to keep his son on bread and water himself.

But Jed shivered more violently.

'A misunderstanding.' he muttered, 'Just bad timing, that's all, bad timing.' Jed's pupils were dilated with fear. 'But he won't give me a chance to explain. They'll drag me off.'

'How ridiculous,' his father scoffed. 'You mean kidnap?'

'Don't laugh,' Jed whispered nervously. 'They might be here, the Assassins. They have motor boats on the Baring. And a 'plane right here. You've no idea of the organization. It's hard to get away from them, I tell you.'

In the end, the elder Frost and Capricorn having conferred and agreed, Jed was taken to the nearest town of Redmond and left in the custody of the police there. Frost's lawyer, roused from his bed and told the circumstances, advised his client to agree to a charge of 'Breach of the peace.' Jed was willing to agree to anything—he would not have minded, Capricorn noted bitterly, being charged with the murder—as long as he was locked up and not in Daines Barington.

'You won't tell them where I am,' he pleaded.

'I don't know that the police exactly owe you any favours,' Capricorn had remarked, 'but, if you wish it, we won't.'

Which left them, as he told Copper, exactly where they were. They had no evidence against Jed and he didn't act like an apprehended murderer. A mere charge of murder, he implied, was as nothing to a Siderean. He had gabbled of excommunication, anathema, and other dreadful things which, he believed, could last through eternity. What would a mere fifteen or twenty years mean to someone like that? Capricorn brooded in disgust. Jed probably had worked it out that in a good modern prison time would pass pleasantly enough. Certainly better than dungeons and excoriations.

He might suggest to Frost senior that a doctor be consulted. Or would an ex-Siderean refuse a psychiatrist? Capricorn's bruises ached and he realized, in the bright light of morning, that he had chased Frost over the fields and ditches in the hope that he was pursuing a murderer, and that Garry Wyatt would be cleared.

His idea of the night before, born of the Rector's remarks and possibly the warmth of the brandy, seemed a little foolish this morning. It was as well he hadn't told Copper; he might think his superior, whom, contrary to appearances, he did respect, had lost his senses.

Just at the gloomy moment when it seemed that nothing in the case would ever resolve and joy in life was at an end, the door of the Coffee Shop opened with its little chime, and to his surprise Mrs Lavender entered. Rose had not been an early riser since her school days and Rose this morning was pale and tired. Her rather floating, full-skirted frock suggested afternoon or evening wear and, with compunction, Capricorn remembered Linda's illness. Rose had probably been up all night and just left the hospital. He stood quickly and escorted her to his table.

Charming as ever even in her weariness, she pleasantly greeted Sergeant Copper, who had taken her statement on the Brewster death, and who had compared trying to find facts in her answers to looking for a pin in a feather bed. Rose exclaimed mildly over Capricorn's appearance, but was satisfied with his story that he had slipped in a ditch without taking serious hurt.

'Nothing to eat for me, Merle,' she sighed. 'Just coffee. My poor women were up with me most of the night; I didn't have the heart to go home and wake them yet.'

Capricorn poured her coffee and ordered some of the sweet rolls he knew she liked, and had the satisfaction of seeing her eat and drink and look a little less exhausted.

'Linda is resting now,' she said. 'But, Merle, Dr Bailey asked me to say, perhaps you could put your questions off for another time? She's very tired, poor mite. It was a dreadful attack. There's always the problem, he says, of heart damage. If you could have seen her—'

She shuddered.

'Does the doctor have any idea of what brought it on?' Capricorn asked soberly. The name of Garry Wyatt seemed to hang almost palpably over the coffee cups, but Rose looked down and avoided his gaze.

'All the excitement,' she said vaguely. 'Merle, I must go home and get some rest before the funeral this afternoon, but if you can manage, I would like to see you today. Perhaps this evening?'

'Of course, Rose,' he answered. There were questions she had to answer. He suspected she knew the reason for Linda's illness perfectly well. Rose's fluffiness was partly a pose, and in matters relating to her family she was surprisingly shrewd and alert; beneath the sweetness and charm she was quite the hard-headed North-countrywoman. Chuffield's own. Which reminded him. Chuffield was not so large a town that the well-to-do families did not know each other.

'By the way,' he asked casually, 'did you know a family called Frost in Chuffield?'

'You mean that dreadful Jedediah? We knew his father very well.'

He stared at her for a moment. No use asking why she had never mentioned it before; she would only say he had never asked. And he hadn't.

She did not seem aware of any sin of omission now. Instead she was regarding her face in a little looking-glass.

'Oh, dear, I look such a mess,' she said regretfully.

In fact she looked remarkably lovely, and Capricorn wondered how many women of her age could keep their looks after a sleepless night. Then he reproached himself for the analytic thought.

'You're cold, Merle,' rang in his ears.

It came to him for the first time that now Mrs Lavender was free again, but he couldn't dwell on that realization as his mind was too busy on the Messrs Frost.

'What did you know about Jedediah in Chuffield, Rose?' he asked.

'Oh, he was always a most unpleasant boy,' she sighed. 'Of course, he was terribly brilliant as a child, and Arthur, his father, and poor Letitia who died, made such a fuss of him. They're nice people, but they'd never had a genius in the family before, and Jed was supposed to be a genius, though nobody knew quite what at.'

Rose, thoughtful, drank some more coffee.

'I don't think he did either. He was terribly spoiled. Nothing was ever good enough for him. I think it was at university he began to get in trouble. He'd always been so bright he'd never had to work, you see, but it was different there. Of course, there were other bright boys. He didn't like it. So he told his father he didn't want to waste his time; he wanted to go into business.'

'And did he?' Capricorn asked, as Rose seemed in danger of lapsing into reverie.

'His father took him into his business at first, but that didn't work out well.' Her brow wrinkled attractively. 'Dear Letitia didn't tell me what happened. She was so *loyal.*'

She stirred her coffee and looked down at the little vortex she had made.

'I don't think she'd like me to tell you now,' she said plaintively.

'Richard was murdered, Rose.' He hated to have to remind her but saw no other way.

'Yes,' she whispered, and the blue eyes filled with tears.

Capricorn felt like a fiend, but fortunately he had learned to separate his work from his emotions.

'Well, he set up in some sort of business. His father is something to do with steel, I think, and he went into the same line. I suppose his father helped, and I remember my husband saying that Jed used his father's credit a good deal. And he sold shares and did a lot of complicated things, I don't understand them all.'

'And then what happened?' Capricorn prodded gently.

'Well, it was all very strange.' She looked from him to Copper and back. 'When the trouble came, I don't know exactly what it was, but I do know it turned out that he had been stealing money from his own company. It seems you can do that,' she said, puzzled. 'Tens of thousands of pounds. It was an awful scandal at the time.'

Capricorn remembered he had searched the records and found nothing. 'But there was no prosecution.'

'No. I understand his father paid everything and it was sort of smoothed over. His father made a condition that Jed go to Australia, but I think he joined Siderea instead.'

Capricorn contemplated his ruined breakfast, thinking furiously.

Rose gathered her things and prepared to go.

'Rose,' he asked quietly, 'you don't happen to know what he did with the money, do you?'

Rose paused.

'Oh, yes, didn't I tell you? How silly of me! He's been like that for years. He *gambles,* you know. On horses. Roulette games if he can find them. Anything. He believes he's lucky, or that he has a special power, or something like that. Well he does win *sometimes* but of course he mostly loses and it was so dreadful for poor Letitia, she always had to give him her dress and housekeeping money. I believe he thought that Siderea would help him to win. It probably upset his wife, too,' she added.

'Wife?' Capricorn said, startled.

'Another Siderean. Very pretty, they say, but of course, she was gone when I came here.'

'Gone?'

'She ran off with Hightower when he went to his Ark. I suppose that's why he made Jedediah a field marshal or whatever it was. It *must* have been annoying when he was put back in the ranks. No wonder, really, that he was so angry with poor Richard.'

She sighed again, looked distracted, and with a sweet smile to Capricorn and Sergeant Copper she was gone. The two men, still standing, looked at each other.

'Whew,' Copper said. 'What a. . .'

'Don't say "bird" Copper, or any other term of disparagement,' Capricorn said severely. 'You might be dismissed from the Force. Mrs Lavender has been very helpful.'

'Um,' Copper, unabashed, resumed his seat and lit a cigarette. 'Might have been handy to know all that before.'

Capricorn paid his bill.

'I'm going to see the bank manager, Norris. It's a bit early,' he looked at his watch, 'but he might be in. In the meantime you might check at the station and see how Griswald is coming in the search for the gun. Perhaps you could give him a hand. I'll have to get up to the Manor later and find out about this Frost business. Dungeons,' he said, recalling Frost's terror, 'bread and water!'

It didn't seem to be possible, when he considered the sensible Mrs Anthony. He would have to talk to her again. But time was pressing. He had to come to a decision about Wyatt, to arrest him or not, and there seemed to be too much against him to let him go free. Yet Wyatt was a trained infantryman, fresh from Vietnam. Would he have needed two shots at that range? And any motive he might have was absurdly weak.

'Aren't you going to arrest that Yank?' Copper asked, his mind travelling on a parallel line.

Capricorn noticed the 'that Yank.' It was odd, he thought. To·his generation of Englishmen the Americans had been, for the most part, welcome allies, but with young men like Copper there was often this vein of hostility.

'Not yet,' he said. 'Aren't you afraid of cancer?' He watched Copper's deep inhalations with the interest of a man who had given up smoking—many times.

'No,' Copper said simply. 'Probably won't live that long anyway,' and he sniffed his cloud of blue smoke in great enjoyment.

Capricorn had had only three hours of sleep, but some of the jaded feeling ebbed away as he stepped out into the warm summer morning in the High Street. Wrens were calling to each other through the eaves, the air was soft, and the sky clear. Brewster had a good day for his funeral. Well.

Sidereans rushed along the street in cars and on foot, hurrying to be at the Manor before nine o'clock. Apart from their strange dress, they seemed much like any other group of students hurrying to class, a little bleary-eyed, carrying chocolate bars for quick energy and their lunches in satchels with the inevitable thermos sticking out of the top. A white-aproned boy stood in front of the Moo-Cow selling containers of steaming liquid to the late risers, probably in defiance of local ordinance.

Arriving at the bank, which might have been from a Cruikshank drawing in a novel of Dickens, he found he was in luck. Mr Norris was in and would see him, although the bank was not yet open for business. Capricorn followed a grave clerk dressed in a dark suit through the dim front room where another clerk was weighing copper coins on a scale and scooping them into canvas bags.

Norris's room behind his, was large and lighter, though the eight-foot dark oak desk could have been a museum piece. Norris himself, with a ruddy complexion and muscular body, looked more like a sportsman than a banker. A horse's head mounted on the panelled wall and a series of photographs of the Witch Hill hunt, confirmed the impression.

'Good morning, Superintendent,' Norris greeted him with a booming voice that seemed suitable for open-air sports. 'What can I do for you?' He followed Capricorn's gaze to a photograph of himself at the meet. 'I ought to take that down.' He laughed heartily. 'Gives the clients an idea my mind's not on my work. And on a day like this, it isn't.'

Capricorn guessed that this little joke had been made many times before, perhaps to put visitors at ease, perhaps to remind them that

Jasper Norris was not merely a banker but also belonged to an old county family. For some reason Capricorn's mind went to Beatrice Brewster, but he had no time to puzzle out the connection.

'I'm glad I caught you in so early; beforetimes, as it were. Your clients should be impressed by the hours you keep.'

Norris looked gratified.

'You'd be surprised, Capricorn, but in a town of this size, with one bank, a manager can have a lot more to do than in a branch up in London. But his work isn't recognized,' he said gloomily. 'A country manager, that's what people think. They forget about us, in the City.'

'I'm sure that recognition will come,' Capricorn said soothingly, wondering what post Norris had aspired to and failed. ''I have tried not to intrude and take up your time but I find I have one or two questions for you that might help clear up the Brewster case.'

'Shocking affair, shocking. Do sit down, Superintendent. Dreadful, dreadful. All those people should have been rounded up before this could happen—no criticism of the Yard, of course.' He interrupted what was probably a frequent speech with some embarrassment.

'I understand.' Capricorn took the proffered chair—intended for would-be borrowers and other suppliants, he supposed, as it was plain and not too comfortable, unlike the upholstered splendour of Norris's own chair, suitable for a man who had spent the previous day in the hunting field.

'I had hoped, Mr Norris, you might be able to enlighten me about some of the financial affairs of Siderea.'

'Then I must disappoint you,' Jasper Norris said with emphasis. 'Don't think,' he hastened to add, 'that this is on the grounds of professional discretion. No,' his manner was acerbic, 'No professional relations are involved between Mr Hightower and this bank, or any other English bank, as far as I have knowledge.'

Capricorn was taken aback.

'But surely,' he said, 'there are large sums of money involved in the Siderea operation? From what I've heard it's very far from charity.'

'Charity.' Norris made a short, explosive sound. 'As charitable as a gipsy who wants you to cross her palm with silver. I've said before, and I say it again now although it's too late, that miserable pack of thieves and swindlers should never have been allowed to settle in Daines Barington. Or in Great Britain, for that matter.'

'Quite so,' Capricorn said, it not seeming worth-while to argue. He imagined that Norris had been told the legal difficulties already. His fancy flickered for a moment over an England where strangers could be barred from any little community by law, and found himself back in the Middle Ages. Yes, certainly, in medieval England, Norris would have found no trouble at all. The Sidereans would have been branded, literally, rogues and vagabonds and cast out.

But it was hard to imagine Sidereans before the modern world. They were children of the age of space travel; post-atomic, certainly. Hightower made much of the scientific background of his discoveries, claiming his theory of time and space to be neo-Einsteinian, although also based on the Vedic hymns.

Norris, was, however, to shed a new light.

'I don't know what you'd call their manner of doing business: feudal, perhaps.'

Before this anomaly could be explained they were interrupted. A clerk was bowing in the doorway and ushering in a large, well-corseted lady with a purple suit and hat and a complexion to match.

'My dear,' Norris and the Superintendent rose. 'This is an unexpected pleasure.' His expression somewhat belied his words. 'Superintendent Capricorn of Scotland Yard, my wife.' He made the introductions while the clerk bustled in with a substantial-looking chair in which the lady seated herself.

'I hope I'm not interrupting?' she asked, rhetorically, smoothing out her long gloves.

'Nothing confidential, I believe?' Norris looked questioningly at the Superintendent, who replied, 'Certainly not as far as Mrs Norris is concerned. She may have something to add. You are one of the few people in town,' he addressed her, smiling, 'from whom we have not taken a statement. Above suspicion.'

His smile widened, as he deliberately used the charm that had delighted his female audiences so many years before. Mrs Norris seemed a formidable matron and, in the right mood, might have something of interest to report. Neither she nor her husband was afflicted with the reticent courtesy that had made other witnesses from the town rather less than useful to the police.

'I had to be above suspicion,' Mrs Norris said shortly, but with a certain unbending, what Capricorn's aunts would have called a bit of loosening of the stays, 'as I wasn't present that night. It's an accident that my husband wasn't there, he was invited but he was at the Sheepherders. A lot of nonsense, in my opinion, grown men gallivanting around in sheepskins.'

'Now, now, my dear,' Norris smiled in protest, 'A historic custom—'

His wife went on without pause.

'But it was no accident that *I* wasn't there because I've never been invited. Miss Beatrice Brewster,' she said forbiddingly, 'a foreign orphan as far as anyone knows, has never thought me good enough to ask to Brewster House.'

Norris looked embarrassed, his face turning a brick red, which his wife ignored. Dressed as she was in thick woollen cloth, she seemed to feel the heat and fanned her face vigorously with her large leather handbag.

'I was just answering a few questions for the Superintendent,' her husband ventured. 'Was there something in particular. . . ?'

'No,' she said with a suitable change of expression. 'You know the funeral is this afternoon, so I thought I would come into town early and do some shopping, have lunch and perhaps pay a condolence call on Beatrice, if she could stand my sullying her house. But with all this horror I couldn't sleep. I was up too early and now I'm here the shops aren't even open. I thought you might give me coffee, Jasper.'

'Certainly, certainly,' he said, jumping to his feet. He went to the door and gave orders to the clerk. 'Superintendent?'

'Not for me, thank you,' Capricorn said. 'But while you're waiting, perhaps you'll be kind enough to explain to me what I think you called Hightower's feudal banking practices?'

'Oh, yes,' he said in some relief, Mrs Norris having followed the clerk to give additional instructions, her voice coming clearly through the door although it had swung shut behind her.

'Well, the people in the town, Richard among them,' he said gloomily, 'they thought at first the Sidereans would bring business, shopkeepers, landladies and the like. But I told them then, and they're finding out, that it was a mistake from the beginning. If you knew how many of my clients who run businesses have been bilked by these people you would laugh at the idea of profit, Superintendent. And the cost to the town in services—the medical cost alone is staggering. Coming here from all parts of the world, needing teeth, eyeglasses, pre-natal care, delivery expenses, free milk for the children. . . It's true that Hightower pays his taxes,' he said angrily, 'but he only pays taxes for a private residence while he has run the place as a business from the start. The town has been very lax about it, very lax indeed. Particularly Richard. I don't like to speak ill of the dead, but there it is.'

'I can see it must be very annoying,' Capricorn said. 'And from what you said, Hightower didn't do his banking here?'

Norris leaned forward. His eyes were a little bloodshot—not from the hunting field at this time of year. Could Mrs Norris be driving him to drink? But perhaps it was just annoyance. He certainly sounded very angry.

'I've never seen a more crooked outfit except for a fun-fair,' he said positively. 'Hightower rakes in money by thousands of pounds daily—hundreds of thousands a week, sometimes, from what I can estimate. One person can go up there and spend two or three thousand pounds in a week easily. And this is just one of his operations. He has them all over the country and in almost any other country you can think of. Even behind the Iron Curtain, they say. But there are no books. Nothing is written down. No checks are ever used. If they get a check they'll cash it, at source if they can. Otherwise—'

'How do they manage?' Capricorn asked, puzzled. 'The Inland Revenue—'

'They let them get away with it!' Norris snapped. He had the expression of a man who had never got away with anything from the Inland Revenue. But perhaps he didn't want to, Capricorn considered. Old-fashioned, peppery, but probably an honest and scrupulous man.

'They pay for everything in cash. They get receipts. They pin the receipts to the bills and file them and that's their system. Every fee that comes in is supposed to be receipted and the receipt pinned to a duplicate of the invoice. The Revenue inspector told me about it,' he sniffed. 'He'd never seen anything like it.'

'And that's it?'

'That's it. Except for salaries, which he has to keep records of, under the law. But he pays those poor devils so little they'd all be eligible to apply for National Assistance if they took it into their heads.'

Capricorn noticed that for this purpose the evil Sidereans had become 'poor devils.' Well, the language was logical if the emotional sequence was not.

'Have they applied for assistance?'

'Not down here, it would be too easy to spot them,' Norris said in disgust. 'But you can bet, Superintendent, they're doing it up in London and the larger towns. That man has a gang of slave labour, that's what it comes to.'

He was certainly getting a lot of views on Hightower, Capricorn noted, for what good it would do him. From Garry Wyatt's philosopher and psychologist to Mrs Anthony's saviour, to Norris's superswindler. And then he remembered Frost the elder reminding Jed that one day he referred to Hightower as a god and the next as a devil. And Jed's startling answer had been, 'What's the difference?'

The coffee arrived and Mrs Norris back with it and Capricorn began to think of his next call. But he lingered a moment.

'What does Hightower do with his cash if he doesn't bank it?' he asked.

'That's what I meant when I said feudal,' Norris said, looking somewhat soothed at having told what he had so badly wanted to tell at the inquest where he had been firmly silenced by the Coroner. 'From what I hear—and I'm sure it's true—the money is packed up in a big satchel once a week and taken by a Siderean messenger to wherever Hightower happens to be. The Ark, right now. The way it was done before banking,' he said, 'except of course that now they fly. According to rumour, he transfers it all to gold bullion, but that's something we don't know.'

Mrs Norris clanked the cups busily. 'I would go to the bazaar at the Women's Guild this afternoon if it didn't seem disrespectful, just before the funeral,' she said. 'I don't think 'I'll venture to call on Miss Beatrice after all.'

'We're all invited to Brewster House after the funeral,' her husband said hastily. 'You can offer condolences then. No reason not to go to the bazaar if you would like to. Beatrice might be quite upset just now, in any case.'

'Pshaw!' Mrs Norris said superbly. 'The only thing that will upset Beatrice is having to watch the hoi polloi cluttering up that musuem she's running. And the only thing that will cheer her up is knowing it will be the last time.'

Capricorn had risen to take his leave but paused, interested in the exchange between husband and wife, obviously carrying on an old

166

argument—Beatrice only gave *bachelor* dinners, Rose had explained, quite odd—rather forgetting his presence.

'Really,' Norris protested, 'when you know how devoted Beatrice has been to Richard her whole life. Her feeling for her family—she even gave up the man she was engaged to because Lucrezia felt he would be an embarrassment as a Brewster relation.'

'Stuff and nonsense.' His wife banged her cup down on the saucer so that the spoon jumped. 'Beatrice didn't care anything about that man, and I don't think, whatever you say, that she cared much for Richard, either. She was insane when it came to that gadabout mother of hers, very unhealthy sort of business, and her mother wasn't all she should have been, by all accounts.'

Capricorn listened quietly.

'And she's just as insane about keeping everything the way it was, and being Miss Brewster of Brewster House. As long as she's not disturbed—which she won't be—she'll get over Richard's death very nicely indeed.'

She poured herself another large cup of coffee.

'Are you sure you won't change your mind, Superintendent? I will say, Jasper's staff make a good cup of coffee. Better than our Mrs Meeker does at home. I always say the men get the best of service. Men and Miss Brewster. Jasper's always happy to run over there at her beck and call, and it must be for the food as no man is going to be led astray by a woman looking like that. Just like the Daines Barington ice-cream man that used to come round on the tricycle, only without the moustache, or, at any rate, such a large, drooping one.'

She went on working herself up to a fine xenophobic frenzy.

'Now, if Richard had lived Mrs Lavender would have become the lady of Brewster House and Miss Beatrice would've been pushed off to the White House, and then she'd have been in a fine taking.'

'A very pleasant residence, the White House,' Norris remarked. 'Very desirable property. A woman of Miss Brewster's talent would have made something special from it.'

'Two decent bedrooms,' Mrs Norris retorted, 'Nowhere to put her servants. No need for servants, come to that. Well, we won't know what she thought about it, because she certainly will never say.'

Mrs. Norris went on, stirring and drinking her coffee and eating currant buns that the clerk somewhat belatedly had produced. The family discussion looked as though it might go on for a long time, until Mrs Norris chose to go to lunch, Capricorn suspected, and wondered how Norris did his work. Today, of course, was special. These incursions probably didn't come about very often. Today was the funeral.

He bade good-bye to the bank manager and his wife. Mrs. Norris was gracious and he was courteous in return, more than courteous, giving her once again his matinee-day smile. He was grateful to the sharp-tongued Mrs Norris. Odd, he considered, that he liked soft-voiced women who refrained from malicious gossip, yet they were no use at all to him in his profession . In this regard the vice was more helpful to the law than the virtue. Would Jed Frost say, 'What's the difference'?

It was past ten o'clock and customers were filling the front room of the—he almost thought of it as the counting house, so dim, so old-fashioned did it look, when he left the bank and made for the Infirmary. In spite of Dr Bailey, he had to talk to Linda Lavender, and clean up that much of his case.

He stopped in first at the station to see a rather downcast Gris-wald.

'Glad you got him,' he said, referring to the capture of young Jed. 'Heard from Redmond this morning. They say he's very quiet. No screaming for writs. Asked the Super if he'd like a game of chess.'

'Well, that shouldn't make you unhappy,' Capricorn smiled. 'unless the Super's a bad chess player.'

'Oh, it's not that, it's the damned gun. I'm going to have to call my men off. Not likely to turn up now. I hate to do it,' he said apologetically to Capricorn, who was officially in charge. 'but I don't see that I can justify any more time for Daines Barington men. There are other matters.'

Capricorn had to agree. The extra men who had been helping would probably be recalled also, now that the routine work on the case had been done. He couldn't justify more time either. He would have to confer with his Chief, he thought, and grimaced to himself. It would be nice if he had something to report other than a man with an alibi who was in gaol, a boy with a perfect motive who was excluded by the evidence, and a prime suspect whom Capricorn had failed to arrest.

fifteen

At the hospital, Dr Bailey still proved adamant. The little doctor in his starched white coat, pacing the grey corridors of the Infirmary, was no longer the friendly amused neighbour he had appeared to be at Brewster House. Authority hung about him along with the smell of antiseptic, and Scotland Yard could conjure up no matching powers to defeat him.

'I'm sorry, Superintendent,' he said, unpredictably grave. 'But I cannot allow you to see my patient yet.'

Young Linda had become 'my patient.' It was the other professions, more than the criminals, that made a policeman work for his money, Capricorn thought wryly. Between 'my patient' and 'my client' it was hard to get a moment of a witness's time.

'You understand, Doctor,' Capricorn found himself using the title although the man had been 'Bailey' up to the inquest, 'no one suspects Miss Lavender; there are just one or two points in her statement that are unclear. Nothing to excite her. Just three minutes—'

'Impossible at this juncture,' Bailey said, avoiding his gaze. 'I tell you, Superintendent, it's not that I don't want to cooperate with the police, but really, a human life is at stake.'

Capricorn was shocked.

'Surely Miss Lavender is not so seriously ill?' He tried to recall if he had ever heard of a death from asthma, but nothing came to mind. Heart failure, perhaps, in extreme cases.

'Is there a weakness of the heart?'

Dr. Bailey, the usually chatty Dr Bailey, still avoided his eye. 'I doubt if Linda could tell you anything about your case, Superintendent. I'm sure she couldn't.'

Disappointed, for this case was like walking through the Looking Glass; instead of getting ahead it seemed he had to run as fast as he could just to stay where he was, he answered more tartly than usual.

'I'm afraid that must be left for us to find out, Doctor.'

The doctor blushed a little.

'Superintendent, might I suggest you talk to Mrs Lavender? I believe she could tell you what you want to know.'

Capricorn stared. Had Linda confided to Bailey and her mother the reason for her absence from the Manor that night? Well, he would go and find out. Straight away. He would have to wake poor Rose but once this was cleared up she would rest better.

Bidding the doctor good day somewhat curtly, Capricorn found his own way out of the immaculate, shining modern wing. A small tablet close to the ground on the west wall bore the legnd 'Donated by John Brewster of this parish.'

Capricorn reflected on the service the Brewsters had given to the town in law, administration, medicine. And Rose had told him that the Brewsters still supported the old Gaylord almshouses. Families like that had done the work the whole nation was trying to equal now. Yet Richard Brewster had been barbarously murdered. His friends and family were getting ready for his burial, and the murderer was still at large. Scotland Yard had neither saved him nor avenged him.

Capricorn resolutely changed the direction of his thoughts. Self denigration was dangerously close to self pity. It was better to concentrate on his work; there was a lot to do before the day would be done.

His heart lightened a little on the way to Rose's house; Rose, at least, would tell him anything she knew. If he asked the questions, that is. He smiled to himself. Rose would not be obstructive.

St Cuthbert's, mellow in the morning sun, soothed his troubled spirit until he passed the old yew by the Rectory wall. The Brewster burial ground. Already two grave-diggers were at work, readying the grave for the coming interment. Capricorn hoped that Rose could not see it from her window.

The young maid who answered the door was flustered at his arrival. Madam was upstairs, resting.

'I would like to have a few words with her, if I may. It is urgent.' Capricorn said gently. 'Perhaps you will announce me.'

But the girl fetched Rose's stern-faced parlourmaid, and they consulted in whispers. Both women regarded Capricorn as if he were an SS guard come at night to make an arrest and drag Rose off to an unknown destination.

'It's with reference to Miss Linda,' he explained. 'It might be possible for Mrs Lavender to clear up something for us. Dr Bailey prefers that to Miss Linda being questioned in her present condition,' he added, not quite sure himself what Bailey had been talking about.

This seemed to hit the right note and the two females went into an advanced state of flutters. Rose has been giving them lessons, the Superintendent thought, resigned. But after a moment the elder woman drew herself up and addressed him like a conspirator.

'Well, in that case, we'll see what can be done, sir. I'll go up to Madam myself.'

He smiled at her encouragingly, and·she softened a little further.

'She had asked me to wake her with a cup of tea. I'll take a tray up now and see how she does.'

Her maids were treating Rose, in her bereavement, like a child with the chicken-pox, he thought, rather amused. He waited while the ceremonies were properly performed, and after about ten minutes the maid came down, with gentle tread, and told him he could go up to Madam's little sitting room, and showed him in.

It was a very small room and typical of Rose. For someone else it might have been a study, a small library, a storage room, but this could only be described as a boudoir. He supposed few modern women had such frippery. The walls were covered in pink silk, the light was soft rose-tone, and lace-covered blinds were drawn against the churchyard. The only furnishings were a little dressing table and a satin chaise lounge. It was very warm.

171

He could hear Rose padding about in the next room. Knowing her rather dilatory ways from a shared childhood, he called in brotherly fashion, 'Do hurry if you can, will you, Rose?'

But the woman who entered was somehow not the sisterly Rose, the fluffy but basically sensible old friend he had in mind. She had obviously been roused from bed and, unthinking, had drawn a film-thin wrap over her not-entirely opaque nightgown, a costume suitable for a honeymoon, bought with that in mind, the Superintendent's brain ticked off, adding up small facts whether he would or no.

Her hair was tumbled and her face flushed.

'Oh, Merle, what is it?' She looked distressed and almost beseeching, and then turned away, quickly, as if she did not, after all, want to know.

'Give me your coat, it's warm,' she said, rather vague, automatically the hostess, her attention wandering. 'Do sit down.'

He sat somewhat gingerly on the very feminine bit of furniture, it being the only place to sit, and Rose sat beside him. In the closeness and warmth of the room her scent, sweet and flowery, that he had always liked, took on a different note, more sensual and troubling.

'Rose,' he said firmly, 'Dr Bailey won't let me talk to Linda, but I must have certain information. Perhaps you can give it to me. The statement she made to the police as to where she was on the night of the murder was just a tissue of lies.'

Rose looked up at him helplessly.

'Does it really matter, Merle? It's naughty, I know, but you certainly don't suspect poor Linda?'

He looked at her, soft and warm and trembling—it was like trapping a bird, he felt, and he never had a taste for that—but he had to be brutal to shock her into frankness.

'I know how Linda feels about young Wyatt,' he said. 'Wyatt had a motive for the murder; he was almost certainly at the scene at the time it happened; he very likely owned the murder weapon. And he is lying his head off in a very stupid way.'

Rose looked as though she were about to burst into tears.

'But you can't suspect Garry!' she wailed. 'Oh, no, Merle, you mustn't!'

'If I could get the truth from anyone I might not,' he said shortly. 'Now, what do you know about all this?'

Instead of answering, she just stared blankly.

'And to think I brought you into this!' she said, with horror, speaking almost to herself.

'For goodness sake, don't be a fool!' He was almost shouting. It was like being smothered by a scented feather bed, he thought wearily, first Wyatt, then the doctor and now Rose.

It had never been the slightest use trying to provoke Rose, he recalled as she seemed to withdraw further and gazed down at her lovely hands.

'Is there any sense going on, asking all these questions, upsetting people,' she said slowly. 'So many of those Sidereans: you could never prove, could you, that it was any particular one of them. Isn't it all a terrible waste?'

'Rose,' he said, as he would to a child; troubled, for Rose was not a child. 'I'm a policeman. I have a job to do.'

She jumped up and swirled round the little room, wringing her hands distractedly.

'Richard's dead,' she said. 'Nothing will bring him back, and more lives will be ruined. Even if you find the murderer, and the jury convicts, he'll just sit in prison for a few years. What could that mean to Richard, or to anyone that loved him?'

Capricorn stood, grasped her hands, and spoke sternly.

'Richard was a man of the law, and he would want the law to function. What can you mean, Rose, and whom are you trying to protect?'

She didn't answer but stood stock still, her eyes downcast.

'Rose, where was Linda that night, and what is all this mystery?'

Without moving from the spot or trying to remove her hands, she very slowly raised her head. Her blue eyes, drenched with tears, were enormous; she was very close, and she spoke low, almost in a whisper.

'Merle, if I asked you to drop it, for my sake . . . I need you.' The words were hardly audible and yet the meaning very clear. She raised her hands and clasped them round his neck, and repeated softly, 'Merle, I do need you.'

The closeness and silence of the room, the warm, perfumed air, and the beautiful woman so close to him—a woman whom he had, in his way, loved for many years—flooded him with emotions and sensations for a moment out of control. In instinctive response his arms folded round her, and taking this as a sign of his relenting she looked

173

up at him and smiled, an uncertain and yet alluring, seductive smile.

He was almost mesmerized by the strange confusion. This was a Rose he had never seen. Rose, the cool beauty, almost untouched, he had always believed, by the passions of sex, who had certainly never sought to evoke any feeling stronger than chivalry in the male, that familiar friend was gone, and this was a woman of deeply erotic charm, from which, he realized almost helplessly, he seemed to have no defense.

It was as silent as if they were alone in the world. As she breathed softly her breast brushed against him and he bent towards her, the kiss forming on his lips, past restraint; still his mind coldly recorded what he was doing, what Rose was doing and how she looked, flushed, her eyes bright, her hair tumbled, just as she had looked, he recalled, in the lamplight the night he had met Brewster, when she had lifted up the vase of jewelled Sevres. And he remembered her exclamation.

Superintendent Capricorn looked at the woman in his arms, and released her gently.

'Rose, you're not yourself,' he said. 'I'm sorry I troubled you with this. Have your rest,' he turned to pick his coat up. 'I know the funeral is going to be an ordeal for you.'

She turned very white.

'What are you going to do?' she whispered.

He looked at her severely.

'You know, Rose,' he said, 'if people would tell the truth from the beginning, they would save themselves a lot of trouble and upset. It's when you try to protect the innocent that you confuse the case.'

'Then you don't think that Garry. . .' she was clutching her gown about her throat as if realizing for the first time her state of déshabillé, though the wisp thin garment did not do much for her purpose. What a very lovely woman she was, he thought, slipping back to his usual detached state.

'I have a strong belief about this murder,' he said gravely, 'but that isn't enough. We need evidence. I must get a straight story from young Wyatt, Rose. Just one thing before I go. You did see Richard that day before the evening party, didn't you?'

'Yes,' she said, surprised. 'How did you know?'

'And you told him something about young Wyatt and Linda that made him angry?'

She sat on the chaise-longue, looking small and crumpled.

'Yes,' she said, 'something, but please. . .'

'Who else was in the house, Rose?'

It was not the question she had expected, and she answered quickly, in surprise.

'Only Miss Brewster, I think. I—I wanted to be private, so I spoke to Richard in his study.'

He nodded.

'I see. And when you came back in the evening, who was there?'

She frowned.

'Well, Dr Bailey came later. Just the Rector, and Beatrice, of course. But why. . . ?'

His hand was on the door, but he turned back and spoke kindly.

'Rose, whatever is troubling you, you must be sensible. This is England. We don't leave murderers roaming about at will. I'm sure you'll be happier when it's all cleared up.'

He left his old friend looking lost and rather pitiful, her bare toes scrabbling in the carpet as if they were searching for the missing slippers that she had left, unknown to them, in the bedroom. His passion had swiftly cooled when his mind had grasped another missing piece in his puzzle, and as he left the house to find himself out in the lane in the glare of what was still early afternoon he thought for a moment of the amazing, complete transformation he had seen.

No, he decided, he had not misjudged Rose over so many years. The cool and rather placid beauty was her accustomed self. The sudden venture into the erotic was a role, not taken on for any of the usual reasons, not because she had fallen a victim at last to his masculine charm, but because she was deeply aroused by a feeling more natural to her. What was Rose's passion? He thought it over clinically. Not for men, but for her child. Yes, good, ordinary women like Rose—and she was ordinary enough except for her amazing looks—women like her could be aroused to all sorts of strange behaviour when a child was endangered. He was back with the problem of Garry and Linda. Perhaps he would arrest Garry, he thought, if only to get the truth out of him. There was nothing like a warrant to make a situation real to someone playing a game.

The grave-diggers had finished their work; the open trench was ready for Richard Brewster's coffin. Two robins hopped cheerily over the newly turned soil and a white butterfly hovered on the grass. Even here—His mind, and his body's memory, was carried back to the strange scene in the little pink room. Yes, Rose had acted for her child. Yet, for a moment—

He wasn't to continue that thought because the man he was planning to arrest came towards him, walking swiftly from the portico of St Cuthbert's. He hailed Capricorn energetically.

'Superintendent! I was just going to see you.'

In the bright sun Capricorn noticed that the young man was a little pale, but his face looked set and determined. He also looked peaceful, and the wariness that had sat so oddly on him in his interrogation had gone. Then Wyatt was directly before him, his face partly shadowed by a branch of the yew.

'I want to change my statement,' he said.

'I'm glad,' Capricorn said, 'but unfortunately I have a call to pay just now. Would you mind stopping in at the station and making your statement to Sergeant Copper?'

He saw the young man's face fall slightly, but Wyatt said instantly, 'Of course. I know you're busy. I've been seven kinds of a fool, Superintendent,' he added soberly, 'but wasting your time was probably one of the worst.'

Capricorn smiled.

'Oh, there are probably more heinous crimes than wasting the time of Scotland Yard, though I can't think of one off-hand. But you can give me just a minute and clear up one or two points before you go to the station. First, do you know what happened to your gun?'

The young man nodded.

'I've found out where it is, Superintendent. It hasn't been fired. There were no bullets in it when it was stolen and—you'll see it's not the gun.'

'I'm inclined to believe that,' Capricorn answered, 'but you will be a good soul and take it down to the station when you go, won't you?'

'Yes,' Wyatt said, 'it's at the Lavenders'. I'll get it right away.'

Capricorn kept his face expressionless only with a great deal of effort. On one pretext or another the police had looked over every house where a Siderean had stayed, with, he realized, one exception. No one was so crude as to search the house of the bereaved Mrs Lavender. Routine had been skipped. And with the usual result. He couldn't blame Griswald. He himself was in charge of the case.

'I was goin to see Mrs Lavender anyway,' Garry said. 'I was at the hospital this morning, and I've just been to see the Rector. He's a great guy,' he said with seeming inconsequence. 'He's marrying Linda and me next week. He's fixing up about the banns.'

'Congratulations,' Capricorn said, polite and amused. 'Mrs Lavender is resting, but I think you could wake her up to tell her that. I think she'll be quite pleased.'

So Rose's efforts had not been necessary after all. The young people were going to put their own affairs in order.

The tall, lanky Texan slouched against the fence of the churchyard, relaxed again now that the truth was out. All he needed to look like a cowboy in a Western film Capricorn thought, was the gun belt slung around the hips. A decent lad he had thought him, and events were proving he was right.

'Linda and I were on the hill that night,' he said.

'I had rather suspected as much,' Capricorn replied. 'What time did you leave?'

'That's the hell of it.' The young man looked worried. 'I'm not sure. I wasn't looking at my watch,' he explained.

'I understand,' Capricorn said gravely.

'And the evenings are long here. Linda left first—we never left together, and I hung around for a bit and then sloped off. I really didn't go to eat,' he added. 'I wasn't hungry. I was beginning to get worried about the whole thing. Me and Linda, I mean. Linda was nervous and jumpy and we almost had a fight. But I figure—and I've been thinking about it a lot—I figure Linda left maybe around ten after seven. I remember her saying it was ten minutes too late to make night duty. She just decided to take off home, being fussed and all. Her mom was over to the Brewsters, so there would've been no questions. I left just a little while later. Not more than five minutes; I smoked one cigarette.'

'And as you were leaving did you see someone? Someone who wasn't supposed to be there?' the Superintendent asked softly.

'I was afraid you'd ask that. Look, I did. He was hanging around waiting to talk to me when Linda went. But I'm sure he had nothing to do with the killing. I know Jed,' he said, 'and he's a nut, but not that much of a nut. His trouble was money. He came to see me because he thought I could maybe help him out. My father's rich,' he said, 'but I don't have much, just what I saved in the service. Nothing like what Jed needed to pull him out of this one.'

'How much did he ask for?'

'He said he might be able to cover with twenty thousand pounds for a while,' Garry said, 'but it was no use. I didn't have it, or anything like it. He was in a panic, you bet; he was terrified of being demoted, even just for a couple of weeks, because he knew someone would find he'd had his hands in the cash box. That's why I'm sure he didn't kill Brewster, because by that point it wouldn't have done him any good. Once he met Hightower's man it would be all over, and he had to go up that night.'

'In his statement he says he took the 6.55,' Capricorn replied. He didn't add that Noreen Stacy said she had seen him off.

'I think he meant to. But after he got to the station he must have thought of making one last try and came up to find me.'

'He couldn't have got there on foot from the station, even if he took the field path and ran all the way, in less than half an hour,' Capricorn pointed out.

Garry looked at him blankly.

'I don't think he came on foot.' He frowned. 'He didn't drive up the Witch Hill road or I'd have heard him. But we didn't stay and talk on the top of the hill; I went down the north slope to look in at the stables and Jed walked with me, talking a mile a minute. I had the idea he'd come that way; he probably looked in at the stables first. He didn't say, but I figured he'd come around by the north lane and left his car there. It winds around close to the hill and its not used much—a lot better than the Witch Hill road if you don't want to be seen.'

'Who left first?'

'I did. I left him sitting there by the stables looking miserable. I didn't figure he would go to London at all, I thought he would just take off and get lost. Maybe he thought he could try to talk the accountant around. Some chance. But I reckon Jed's too optimistic by nature to do a murder.'

'We'll have to discuss it with him,' Capricorn said drily. 'I suppose it was Miss Lavender who hid your gun after she'd heard about the shooting?'

'We don't have to go into that, do we?' Garry looked upset. 'You don't want to drag her into it.'

This case was full of people who wanted murders solved with no unpleasantness. Well, so were they all. The only difference this time was that he was personally involved. Perhaps someone else could have done better with this case. Very likely that involvement was causing the muddle in his mind. Each time he was almost certain of his case, something turned up that failed to fit into the pattern.

'You can also explain your compulsion to lie to the police,' Capricorn said sternly.

Garry shuffled his feet, looking for a moment very young.

'Well, at first, with Linda and me, we didn't want anyone to know because of the rules. I wanted to finish my advanced course, and I wanted Linda to finish her treatment—she was doing great before this,' he said dismally. 'But she'll pick up now, I'm sure.'

He looked at Capricorn with a shy smile.

'But then, well—Linda's my girl. We wanted to get married. But there was a hang-up.'

He kicked his foot on the grass, disturbing an ant colony and causing its members to run about frantically, believing, no doubt, that Doomsday had arrived. What was coming now, Capricorn wondered, surely not another wife, a divorce—no, the Rector wouldn't overlook a little thing like that. At that moment he saw the Rector himself, leaving the back door of his house to cut across the churchyard towards the Lavenders'. Garry was being forestalled. Theale would bring the good news. He would be the hero of Rose's day, after Capricorn had been the villain. He hoped Rose's mind would be at rest.

'When I went in the service,' Garry said ruminatively, 'my dad was pretty sore. I could've stayed on the ranch, like I told you, and he needed me, at that. He doesn't like foreigners, my pa,' he said simply, 'and, in one of his mads, he said if I came back with a foreign wife, he'd leave the place to my cousin Richie. Richie stayed home, and he never bugs the old man like me. Well, I wasn't about to worry. I didn't figure on getting married, and I didn't. Those days I didn't feel about the ranch the way I do now, anyway.'

'It's important to you,' Capricorn suggested.

Garry nodded, slowly.

'It always was, I just didn't know it,' he said. 'It's the only thing I was ever interested in, really. It's a great life.' His usually slow speech quickened as he spoke of his work. 'And people need good ranchers. After being in the East, you appreciate that.'

'What about Siderea?' Capricorn asked.

'It's Siderea that made me realize what I wanted. That's what it does, helps you to know yourself. And I know, now.'

'Is it really so terribly expensive?' Capricorn asked, remembering Norris, deflected for a moment from the Wyatt-Lavender drama.

'What's expensive?' Garry said. 'Sure, it costs money. But so does everything else. It's not subsidized by anybody. Hightower believes in making money, lots of it,' he said, 'and I don't see anything wrong with that. He uses most of it anyway in his research. You've never known a guy like him,' he said to Capricorn earnestly, who was sure the young man was right. 'Why, he could be a millionaire a hundred times over just on what he knew twenty years ago. But he keeps on researching, and as he finds better Paths out the old ones go, and everybody practicing has to learn all over. He doesn't hang on to anything because it's profitable. He's a real scientist,' he said with pride, 'not studying how to blow things apart, but how to put people back together.'

Hightower, benefactor and philanthropist. Another one for his collection.

'And then what happened with Miss Lavender?'

'Well, something happened, but I didn't know. That's why she was so jumpy,' Garry said, carefully examining a branch of the yew that seemed to have nothing special about it. 'She must have said something to her mother. Or Dr Bailey did. And Mrs Lavender must have told Brewster, because I got a message to go and see him at Brewster House. Well,' he looked very ashamed, 'that was some scene. You see, like I said, there were things I didn't know and he didn't tell me. I guess he thought I knew.' Wyatt looked uncomfortable and miserable at the idea. 'He asked a lot of questions about Linda and me—he was an old-fashioned sort of guy. Not that I mean he was wrong, at that,' he looked at Capricorn moodily. 'Guess I am really myself. Just this spring, sneaking around, things got kind of wild.'

His gaze went back to the yew branch as if he were determined to see nothing else. 'P'raps I sounded a bit off-hand. See, what I had wanted to do was to go home when I'd finished, and have Linda and Mrs Lavender come out and visit. I knew Dad couldn't resist 'em once they met. But I didn't want to write and say 'I'd gotten married and he could take it or leave it, because I was afraid he'd leave it.'

He seemed rather dismal at the thought.

'He could easy make the place over to Richie in one of his rages. And he's obstinate as the devil, once he's done something, good or bad. He might never change his mind. Brewster threw me out of his house,' he said, with a complete change of tone. 'He was damned well right.'

He sighed, turned, and looked straight at Capricorn.

'Linda and I just meant to keep things quiet for a bit,' he said. 'About a week before everything blew up I had written home and told the old man that I'd met someone I wanted to marry. I sent Linda's picture; I didn't see how he could get mad after that.'

He half-smiled and had a dreamy look. The Compleat Lover, Capricorn thought, but tolerantly.

'I hoped he might answer sort of friendly to the idea,' Wyatt went on, 'and I've been kind of stalling around. But when I heard this morning that Linda had been taken sick, I went up to the hospital. And Dr Bailey told me. So I fixed up with Linda and went straight to the Rector, and here I am.'

Somewhat sheepish, he stole a look at Capricorn from under his lowered eyelids.

'Better late than never,' Capricorn said, amused, 'in more ways than one.'

Garry actually blushed. There was hope for those young people even without the ranch, Capricorn judged. Poor Rose, the vicar's daughter. She must have been surprised and shaken, but she could cope with this. Murder was outside her comprehension, but a pregnant daughter was a phenomenon that did occur even in the North Country.

'It's all O.K., isn't it, Superintendent?' Wyatt said, a little anxiously. 'I mean, you get that I didn't do it?'

'I don't know about "all O.K." ' Capricorn smiled. 'Superintendent Griswald might want to summons you for causing the police so much trouble—that's officially known as breach of the peace. I think you just miss coming under the Sexual Offences Act, Linda's a little over the age, and you are getting married.'

Wyatt blushed again. 'But the murder—'

'If Frost changes his testimony and admits he saw you leave the hill, that helps to let you out. I didn't,' he said with a more friendly tone, 'believe you guilty anyway, you young ass. But among all you liars, you've made it much more difficult to get after the real murderer.'

He left Garry at the station to tell his story to the sardonic Sergeant Copper. Capricorn asked Copper privately to send the gun to the lab for ballistics tests and to verify Wyatt's story with Linda Lavender, who was certainly recovered by now, although he had no doubt that Wyatt was telling the truth at last. The young man would suffer for his sins. He, Capricorn, was no longer young, but he wouldn't care to have to tell a story like that to the cynical and somewhat ribald cockney sergeant, to read aloud and have to sign the statement under the gaze of his green eyes, at such times as full of common humanity as a cat's. Well, the young men would have to get through it together. He had problems of his own.

He remembered his earlier questions. Why there? Why then? He took out his notebook, where he had kept a summary of the whereabouts of the chief people involved at the time of the murder, and added: Linda Lavender on the Hill at about 7:10, Wyatt until about 7:20 and Jed Frost there from 7:20 to—? He also added a question mark by the name of Noreen Stacy. She had lied for Frost. Had she been the one who had driven him up the back lane? For all he had learned, he was no nearer finding out the answer to Why There and Why Then; in fact, he was further away. The Hill, that had seemed at least a rather deserted spot at that hour, now had people popping up all over like rabbits from a warren.

.He put the notebook away, reminding himself he had talk to Noreen Stacy. But not just then. He had more urgent business at Brewster House.

sixteen

To save time Capricorn took his car, but he parked it in a lane a few hundred yards from the approach. The ostensible reason for his visit was to be the questioning of Purdy, the manservant, but his main purpose was quite different and he wanted to give no warning of his arrival. Instead of walking up the drive with its handsome sweep to the front of the house, he took the northern slope of the gentle eminence on which the house was built and made his way through the gardens towards the servants' entrance.

In Georgian houses like Brewster House the back was often lovelier than the front. It was admirably planned: the gracious colonnade along the terrace that led into the drawing room, the dip of land below a riot of roses still although the summer was near its close; their blood-red profusion setting off admirably the grey stone figure, a squared, chunky, primitive Madonna that stood alone in the centre of the escarpment, crowning the more gentle fall of lawn and flower beds down to the river.

Making his way cautiously—he didn't want to be surprised by Beatrice Brewster, though she was most probably in her room preparing for the funeral—he slipped in through the open door on the side of the house that led to the kitchen quarters, below the level of the colonnade. The kitchen itself was empty except for a tortoise-shell cat that drowsed on the window, though trays were set out ready with cups, plates and glasses. The funeral feast was prepared, Capricorn noted sombrely.

He discovered Purdy in the stone-flagged pantry, already dressed in black, going over his supply of bottles and siphons. He jumped at seeing the Superintendent, who was quick to apologize.

'I wanted to see you without upsetting the house,' he explained. 'It seemed a pity to disturb Miss Brewster on police business today, so I just slipped in.'

Purdy nodded in approval.

'Very thoughtful of you, sir. I would be glad to help in any way. Are there—' he tried not to look too inquisitive—'any developments?'

'We're coming along,' Caprcorn said, more cheerfully than he felt. Too many developments, he might have said. 'Can we talk here? Or will we be disturbed?'

'This way, sir.' Purdy led him to a windowless room in back of the kitchen with a large fireplace, a few basket armchairs, a table and a sewing-machine. 'The staff sitting room,' he explained. 'But the women are all busy in the front of the house. We won't be disturbed.'

Sergeant Copper had done a good job when he took Purdy's statement, and the additional questions he had asked later had almost exhausted Purdy's knowledge of the incidents of that day. Capricorn had only a very few questions to ask, and he got the answers he expected. He was finished in twenty minutes and rose as if to leave, looking through the kitchen to the gravel path beyond, at the door to one side leading down to what appeared to be a basement laundry room, and the green baize door to the front of the house.

'Will you be attending the funeral, sir?' Purdy asked, after he had been duly thanked for his help.

'I doubt that I'll be finished in time,' Capricorn said with real regret. 'We still have some work to do.'

'Quite so, sir,' Purdy said, nodding. 'Miss Brewster asked me especially if I would forego the funeral, to make sure the preparations for the refreshments are all attended to. We have to show our respect for the dead,' he said, melancholy, 'in the way we know best.'

His sorrow at Brewster's death touched Capricorn for a moment.

The Superintendent murmured that he would let himself out and said good-bye as the man walked back to his pantry, obviously choked. It occurred to Capricorn as he waited quietly by the door that what he had just seen was the only unmixed expression of grief he had come across, though many people had been fond of Richard Brewster.

The tortoise-shell cat, more suspicious than Purdy, stalked in and sniffed carefully round the stranger's shoe. Richard Brewster's cat, Capricorn thought, as he rubbed its neck absent-mindedly. Did it miss its master? Rose must have suffered, but by the time he had talked to her, grief was alloyed with fear for her daughter. The Rector, Brewster's oldest friend, was sad but remote and contemplative. Hartle and Bailey both missed him but death was so much a part of their professional lives that it affected them as it did a policeman: a tragedy that would fade away in the press of everyday work. Then there was his stepsister, who had devoted her life to him, what of her?

He had lied to the admirable Purdy. He intended to see Miss Brewster but he wished to catch her unawares. If she was in her room dressing, or resting against the ordeal to come, he would be out of luck. He would discreetly look round and return another time. Stepping out on the other side of the baize door, he found himself at the foot of the service stairs that led to the back of the centre hall. From this point of vantage he had a clear view to the great front door, closed now, changed already from the open friendliness of Richard Brewster's time.

The door to his study was open. Capricorn could see, in the dim and glimmering light, the coffin resting on its bier. The clutter of Brewster's life was already cleared away. Only one candle burned, and the closed and draped coffin looked solitary and strange. Miss Brewster had insisted that the coffin be taken to the house before burial. It was her right, but the lonely grandeur seemed to Capricorn not suitable or fitting for such a warm and friendly man.

The Superintendent's luck was with him after all. As he stood, half hidden by the open study door, Miss Brewster came down the stairs with her firm, decided tread. She was wearing her usual country walking shoes, he noticed; nothing like the evening slippers she had frowned at on the night of the murder; the slippers that had hampered her customary confident stride; the slippers she had intended for her cruise.

There was a box in her arms and she held it as if it were a baby.

He could hardly have believed such a brusque woman to be capable of this tenderness. She stood by the niche in the wall that had stood empty for so many years, regarding it thoughtfully. Then she carefully withdrew from the box the glittering vase of jewelled Sevres and placed it at last in the place for which it had been intended.

Rose had returned her wedding gift, punctilious Rose; in the midst of her private confusion and upset, she had behaved correctly. Now Beatrice had the vase, and Brewster House, for her, was complete. She still stood, almost motionless, looking at the vase with a small, pleased smile.

'I hope I don't startle you, Miss Brewster,' Capricorn said, approaching.

She looked round, surprised, but showed no agitation.

'Why, Superintendent!'

'I hadn't meant to call on you today,' he lied. 'I was interviewing your manservant and came out through the wrong door, I see. I'm sorry to disturb you at such a time.'

'You don't disturb me,' she said, calmly. 'I've been seeing to the house. The maids, as you can imagine, are flustered and all thumbs. Dramatizing the situation.'

Her voice was deep for a woman and at the moment sounded rather tart. Miss Brewster, the Superintendent had noticed before, had the misfortune to have dark circles under her eyes ordinarily, and so it was difficult to tell at this time if she had been spending sleepless nights since her brother's death. Her bearing was almost military, her attitude to her servants that of annoyance with troops breaking down under fire. He shivered a little at that last word; his fancy was too close to the truth. A disciplined woman, certainly, she would never show her feelings to the world. He remembered the story of the unloved little foreigner, and the girl who had been ordered to give up her only lover.

'I wonder,' he said diffidently, 'if you do find you have a moment, as I am here, perhaps you might permit me to ask a question or two to clear up some points I'm still muddled about?'

'Certainly,' she said without hesitation. 'It's two hours until the funeral, and everything is well in hand. Won't you come and sit down?'

They went into the lovely, two-storied drawing room, and Miss Brewster waited for his questions. She was neither impatient nor inattentive but alert, squarely upright, looking efficient and managerial in her heavy tweed suit and country brogues, oddly at variance with the elegant *fauteuil* in which she sat. The doors to the dining room were partly open. Maids were setting a long buffet table with crystal and heavy silver dishes and, clad as they were in grey silk dresses and soft shoes they appeared more part of the place than its mistress. From overhead in the gallery, the portrait of Lucrezia seemed to look down mockingly at this odd-looking intruder in the room that was so much her own: all the stuffs in the two rooms, Capricorn noticed, from the rugs to the chair coverings and the brocade draperies at the windows, were of colours to blend with the portrait, but muted, so that the woman in the frame had to be the focal point of any gaze.

Beatrice herself seemed entirely unaware of her own incongruity, but for a moment Capricorn saw the room as Brewster must have envisaged it, with Rose Lavender in the chair that Beatrice now occupied—a startling change that would have been, with Rose as lovely as any of the treasures and the portrait fading into the background. Lucrezia would not have liked that, he thought fancifully, and then brought himself back to business.

'I know you've already given Sergeant Copper a very full and complete statement,' he apologized. 'But in the course of the investigation some things have come up that need to be checked, you understand.'

She nodded. A quiet woman, not given to chat. Brevity could be a useful trait in a witness; reticence was not.

'The threatening letter, I gather, has never been found?'

Beatrice shook her head.

'No. I conducted a thorough search of the house myself, with Purdy to help, and he went through the rubbish bins, but it definitely was not in the house. Richard must have taken it with him.'

'It was not on him when I arrived at the scene,' Capricorn murmured.

She shrugged.

'He wasn't likely to carry such a thing. He probably noticed he had it in his pocket, or maybe he left with it in his hand, and threw it away in a ditch.'

Capricorn didn't say that every ditch and lane in the area had been thoroughly searched while the police were looking for the gun. No such letter had turned up.

'You don't remember seeing him walk out with it?'

She considered.

'I didn't actually see Richard leave. It was a confusing evening, you understand. It was a very impromptu dinner party to begin with. Richard had only suggested it a day or two before—something of an engagement or pre-wedding dinner, I believe he had in mind, but he wished it to be very casual as he and Mrs Lavender weren't young people. As you know, some of the guests had already arrived. Dr Bailey was, as usual, late. When Richard saw the letter, he decided to rush out. It was an extraordinary thing to do,' she said, her voice level, as if she were speaking of a thoughtless guest rather than her murdered brother. Capricorn reflected that her composure was more extraordinary than Brewster's sudden determination to confront the Sidereans, but then he had always recognized her as a woman of strong character.

'I was going back and forth to the kitchen, making arrangements with the cook who was having hysterics about her soufflés.' Capricorn recalled that he himself had been an uncertain guest and must have added to her problems. 'I was in the back of the house for a moment when he actually left.'

Capricorn's gaze went to the portrait of Lucrezia as if searching for something, though he had no idea what. He felt vaguely perplexed. Then he realized what the puzzle was. 'The back of the house,' Miss Brewster had said. The kitchen quarters were in the back of the house, under the drawing room and the terraced colonnade, with the entrance on the west side, as he had found, to a semi-basement area. The dining room before him was in the front of the house. He remembered from his walk up the drive the even number of windows on both sides of the front, the symmetry being part of its charm. But where the windows ought to be was the panelled wall and the gallery where the portrait was hung.

He saw Miss Brewster's gaze upon him as he was craning his neck looking upwards. He laughed.

'I must look like a hypnotized turtle,' he apologized, 'but it is an amazing portrait. It's interfering with my concentration.'

Miss Brewster looked gratified.

'It's always said to have been one of Laszlo's best,' she said. 'Very like the original.'

'Your mother must have been a very lovely woman,' Capricorn said. 'And your father built that wall up, and the gallery, to display the portrait?'

'Oh, no,' she said, surprised. 'That has always been part of the room. A rather dreary colonel from Cromwell's army, a Brewster, of course, used to hang there. He was a relic of the old Brewster farmhouse, he frowned over the family dining table all through the generations, but Lucrezia said that so much militant Protestantism depressed her, and he was banished to the attic.'

She was smiling in recollection. The Superintendent conjectured that her mother's sayings had become treasured gems in her memory, to be taken out, breathed upon and brightened at frequent intervals.

'So you wouldn't know, really, once your brother had gone if any of the guests left the house, and then returned?'

Considering this she reflected for a moment, and then answered with decision.

'Well, no, but it would be most unlikely. There was only Mrs Lavender and the Rector, and the Rector was quite determined to read to us from the Antigone.' A faint smile lightened her heavy features. 'If you promise not to give me away, I'll confess that may have caused some of my trips to the kitchen. But he had Mrs Lavender firmly pinned down, and then Dr Bailey, when he finally arrived. I defy anyone,' she said cooly, 'to free themselves from the Rector once he has started on one of his papers. Only Lucrezia,' she looked upwards at the portrait, 'could do it. But Lucrezia never put up with anything she didn't like. Surely, Superintendent,' she turned to him in some surprise, 'you don't suspect any of my guests. It would seem . . . '

'Oh, no, certainly not,' he reassured her. 'It's just that we haven't progressed very far yet, and all that's left to us is to check and recheck on every aspect of the case. It would seem, you see,' he added carefully, 'that he was expected up on the hill. Yet only the people in this house could have known he had decided to go.'

'But that's nonsense,' she said in her decided manner. 'Surely it's obvious. Sending that letter at such a time, with Richard planning to be married in a few days, anyone might have assumed he would get angry enough to go up there.'

'It probably was something like that,' Capricorn admitted, and rose to take his leave. 'Oh, just one other thing. Did you know of your brother having some kind of quarrel with young Garry Wyatt that afternoon?'

'Garry Wyatt?' She looked blank, and Capricorn remembered Rose

189

telling him on his first night in Daines Barington, before Richard had arrived, that Beatrice Brewster refused to know people she considered not of her station, and never admitted to knowing the names of people whose acquaintance she didn't accept.

'She called me Mrs Lupin for a long time,' Rose had giggled, 'and Richard was *furious*.'

'The young man who is apparently courting Linda Lavender,' Capricorn explained. 'Perhaps you haven't met him. A tall young American.'

She looked vague.

'I don't seem to recall—My brother had a quarrel with him, you say?'

Capricorn didn't want to be the cause of Purdy losing his job.

'I have heard that Mr Brewster interviewed the young man here in his study, and that they had words.'

'It's possible,' she said, quite indifferent. 'Richard could have seen him without my knowing it. In the circumstances, he very likely would.'

Her manner implied there was something repugnant involved, with which naturally she would not wish to be associated.

'Can you think of any reason why your brother would have had harsh words with this young man?' he asked.

She thought for a moment.

'If the American was courting Linda Lavender—whatever people mean by that nowadays—that was probably why,' she said. 'My brother, as you know, had never married before and was childless. I had noticed that he was becoming rather heavily paternal to Linda. A Victorian parent.' She smiled, amused.

What a curious woman she was, Capricorn thought, with her detachment and flashes of humour, and her appreciation of her brother's attitude to the modern young. Her brother's murderer was still at large, and yet she had by no means jumped at the idea of the young foreigner's being involved, which would have been natural enough. No anti-Americanism here, he noted. Perhaps she was still kindly disposed to the United States because of the fond major who had left her all his bits and pieces.

'Miss Brewster,' he said, 'if you should be asked to conjecture, who would you think is most likely to be your brother's murderer?'

She walked with him to the front door. He remembered the house from his first visit. On the other side of the hail, past Brewster's study, was a family sitting room facing the east—the morning room, he supposed. In front there was a rather stiff, formal apartment, furnished in the French style, the kind of room where visitors might be asked to wait. And he noticed for the first time a similar but narrow room in front of the dining room. The maids were in there adjusting the blinds and the door was open. It was a small room with just space enough for a stiff Empire sofa, a fine chimney piece, and a table large enough for a hat and stick; a room where in the past unwanted suitors for Brewster ladies had been kept to cool their heels, no doubt, while the master of the house prepared harsh words for them in the comfort of his study.

'I hadn't realized,' Miss Brewster was saying, 'that there was any question. I was wondering why no arrest had been made. Surely it's quite obvious that it had to be that dreadful Mr —' Habit was too strong and she could not say the name. 'That awful person from that strange group who made all the threats.'

She closed the door on the maids in the front room and admired once again the adjacent ledge bearing the Sèvres vase, in the same attitude in which he had surprised her earlier. Instantly she seemed to have forgotten his presence in her rapt pleasure.

'You mean Jedediah Frost,' Capricorn said sombrely. 'He has accounted for his movements that evening, and his account has been substantiated.'

It was no longer true, of course, but he didn't need to explain to Miss Brewster as yet. Wyatt's testimony had left Frost alone on the hill with ample time to do the murder. And if he had no real motive, well, unreasoning hatred had proved motive enough in many other instances.

'Substantiated, I have no doubt, by another Siderean,' Miss Brewster said, as if that ended the matter. 'I hope you get the evidence, Superintendent.'

Courteously, she waited in the doorway as he took his leave. A most unusual woman, he thought. He walked this time down the driveway, in the open, admiring once more the graceful sweep to the gates. And as he opened the gate to leave, he heard behind him the heavy thud of the front door as he had heard it last the night Richard Brewster had been killed, a sound that presaged the end of a life, and perhaps an era. Brewster House was closed.

seventeen

In the sleepy little Redmond police station, Jedediah Frost had quite recovered. When Capricorn entered, Jed was sitting on the bed in his cell, playing chess with the sergeant who should have been on duty at the desk. He was obviously no match for Jed, who was crowing over him in very unsportsmanlike terms.

'Checkmate, you boneheaded minion of the law,' he laughed. His colour had quite returned to his cheeks, and his eyes once again were clear and glittering.

'And how is our prime suspect today?' Capricorn inquired of the sergeant who scrambled to his feet, somewhat abashed.

'Oh, come on, Supe,' Jed scoffed. 'You're really not trying to pin that murder on me, are you?'

'Supe' was not a form of address that Capricorn cared for, but he ignored it. 'You're going to have to answer some more questions,' he said with some pleasure. 'We would like to know the truth about

your movements that night, instead of the story you so carefully con-
cocted.'

He had the satisfaction of seeing Jed's composure shaken, but only
momentarily.

'Which one of them opened his trap?' he said, scowling. 'Not
Stacy already; I'll lay ten to one she's still sitting around heaving with
sex. Venable, I suppose. Now he's getting all the Brewster loot he
wants to be in with the law. Square at heart, I always figured it. A
Brewster like the old man.'

Jed had his revenge quickly, although he didn't know it. Capricorn, behind the carefully trained poker face of the CID man, was
decidedly shaken in turn. Venable! Well, he thought ruefully, he had
known the boy was lying when he interviewed him. It seems it
wasn't just a matter of forbidden chocolate bars.

'I don't care,' Jed went on blithely. 'I didn't shoot your chum. If
you had any sense,' his arrogance was back to normal, 'you'd see
there was no point in my killing him. My goose was cooked when
Hightower sent that fish-eyed accountant to look at the books.'

'I'm afraid,' Capricorn said with some restraint, 'that my sense has
little to do with it. Procedure requires that you make a full statement
and I would suggest that you tell *all* the truth. And I warn you again
that anything you say will be taken down and may be used as evidence.'

'Maybe I should have my lawyer,' Jed said sullenly. 'He's gone to
fix up about my passport. I don't have to say anything until he's
here, do I?'

'You can most certainly consult your solicitor,' Capricorn said
smoothly. 'However, I have to get back to Daines Barington. I'll just
take you down there, and your counsel can meet you.'

'I'll tell you now,' Jed snapped. 'I'm not going back there.'

He grinned, a cocky, insolent grin that gave Capricorn a strong
desire—unfortunately impossible of satisfaction for an English
policeman—to kick him in the seat, or at least to charge him with
something. He had to remind himself that unless he believed the
cunning Jed to have done a murder without possibility of gain, then
whatever sins against the English polity Jed had committed, they
were no worse than the sins of Linda Lavender, Garry Wyatt, and
rest of the false-statement brigade. Jed could hardly be treated as one
apart because of his general obnoxiousness.

'I did mean to catch that train. There was no way I could get out of it,' Jed said. 'I knew it was all up. But I got in a funk. I was in my office and I got the shakes. I couldn't seem to get on my feet and move. I wasn't sending you up the other night. I was *afraid*. Hightower's got his knife in me now.'

It sounded fascinating but there were more urgent matters.

'What did you actually do?'

'Noreen scared up Chris Venable, and they practically hauled me out of there. We all squeezed in my car—which wasn't easy, Noreen's as big as a cow—and Chris drove to the station. I bought my ticket. Then I saw a headline chalked up on a hoarding where an old geezer sells papers. Something about a stinking rich American oil man in England. And just as they were going, I got an idea. So I told them to leave the car and walk back.'

It was so like Jed it was probably true. Like him not to care that his friends would be late back to their duties, even later than they had expected, and have to suffer the consequences. Like him to leave them to cover his tracks when the murder had been discovered. Like him to carelessly give them away now, and leave them in trouble with the law.

'What time did they go, do you remember?' Capricorn asked, grim.

Jed shrugged.

'They'd bought my ticket, then the station closed. They argued till the train pulled out. It was on time. Then Venable sloped off. Stacy hung around, carrying on. I couldn't get rid of her until seven. When the clock struck, I remember, she got in hysterics about being late back and started running.'

'If you were going back to Witch Hill why didn't you take them in the car?' Capricorn asked.

'I wasn't sure what I was going to do. I didn't want them round my neck.'

Jed scowled, realizing the implications of what he'd said.

'Anyway, I drove round the back lanes; I didn't want to be spotted. I left the car in the old north lane and walked to Hightower's stables looking for Wyatt. The horses were there but he'd gone. I had an idea, though, so I went to the crown of the hill and there he was, just dragging himself out of a ditch with that Lavender bird. I'd seen them there before. I hung about until she took off. Could've fancied her myself,' he added, in parenthesis, 'but no chance with fat Stacy around.'

So far he'd confirmed Wyatt's statement, Capricorn noted. He was finally getting the truth, it seemed.

'If Stacy thought I gave one look at a girl,' Jed went on nastily, 'she'd get her into Confession to find out what was what. Trust the Yanks to move in on a good thing. Anyway, when she'd gone I walked with him back to the stables and I asked him for a loan. He's lousy with money,' Jed sounded bitter, 'like all the Yanks. But it was no go. Friends till you need 'em, but then they look out for themselves.'

Capricorn pondered these slurs on Great Britain's NATO ally, slightly uneasy, as anti-Americanism among the young always made him feel uneasy.

'They helped when we needed them in World Wars One and Two,' he remarked.

'Ancient history.' Jed tossed that aside.

The Superintendent decided that the clarification of Jed's mind would be too time-consuming a task, and he had to proceed with his case.

'Where did you go when you left the stables?'

'Back to my car in the north lane.'

'Which of you left first?'

Jed looked at him moodily, as if trying to decide whether it was worthwhile to lie.

'He did,' he said at last. 'I sat there trying to figure out what in hell to do.'

'How far did you see him go?'

'He walked down to the north lane. His lodgings are on the other side. Doesn't mean he couldn't have lain out and come back,' he added.

'Do you know what time it was when he left?'

'I didn't know you'd be interested; I didn't keep looking at my watch,' Jed said impatiently. 'I dunno. I do know, though,' he added, 'it didn't take long. Because I was in my car down the north lane practically back to the station when I heard that damn clock again, chiming half past.'

'Then where did you go?'

'To London, eventually. I didn't rush. I stopped at The Green Apple just before Redmond and had a few drinks. I didn't care if I ever met that bastard that Hightower sicked onto me. Going up to town, though, I figured maybe I could talk him round. But it was all for nothing. He sort of let me think it would be O.K. I had to go back anyway, since you put the police on me,' he grumbled. 'And when we got there it was all over. He'd just been stringing me along to get me back.'

Capricorn was taking down his words as he spoke. Jed was sprawling on his bed in a slouched, adolescent pose—twenty-six, the Superintendent reminded himself; Jed was stretching his youth and probably would continue to do so until he was forty. But however disagreeable he might be, this statement had the ring of truth. He could have killed Brewster—he was in the right place, and there was only his word that he was near the station at seven-thirty—but he had no motive at that point. His Nemesis was on the way, in either case. Unless he did it from opportunity and sheer bad temper.

'Does the north lane run behind Brewster House?' he asked.

Jed glanced up.

'Yes,' he said, sullen.

'And so you passed there shortly after seven, you say, and then on your way back, just before seven-thirty. On either occasion did you see anyone on the road or in the fields?'

'No,' Jed said. 'no one.'

'Think,' Capricorn urged. If what he had come to suspect was true, Jed must have seen someone.

'There wasn't anyone. It's not much more than a cow path; it's hell for driving, and it's out of the way except for a few houses north of the Manor. I didn't even notice any cows. If you think I met Brewster, I didn't. That pompous old sod wouldn't walk through the cow dung.'

He caught Capricorn's contemptuous glance.

'All right, I'm sorry. He's dead and all that and he was a pal of yours. But he must have driven somebody crazy for them to take a shot at him. Two shots, they made bloody well sure of it. I wasn't the only one couldn't stand him; there's proof of that. He was a—a murderee, that's what he was. An obstructive old sod that someone would have to get rid of.'

'I don't agree with your estimate of the late Mr Brewster,' Capricorn said tartly. 'But if there is such a thing as a murderee, don't you feel that your own existence is probably endangered?'

Jed, with one of his mercurial changes of mood, laughed.

'Oh, I'm a bastard, all right. It's a relief being out of Siderea in a way,' he added, meditatively. 'I can stop all that holier than thou.'

'I wonder that it attracted you in the first place,' Capricorn remarked.

Jed's eyes gleamed.

'Power,' he said, 'Hightower promises it, and he delivers. I was Commander-in-Chief in England. Not just five hundred at Witch Hill, but another fifteen hundred over the country, and growing every day. And not just that kind of power. Other power. He shows how to develop it, and it works.'

'Didn't work too well with the ponies,' Capricorn couldn't resist.

Jed flushed.

'It would've, if I'd had a bit more time. You wouldn't believe how much I'd made. I worked out this system where you're bound to win. I based it,' he explained, 'on a Recog. I had.'

'A recog?' Capricorn asked.

'Yes, Recog. Recognition. You see,' he said rather abstractedly, veering off into one of those capsule explanations of the universe to which Sidereans were prone—their delight in simplification and conciseness being at the other end of the human spectrum, Capricorn considered, from the Theales and Hartles of the world—'the human spirit knows everything because it is everything. We just agree to not-know a lot of stuff in order to have a game.'

'A game?'

'Yes, the physical universe, life, death and all that stuff. We had to agree to not-know, and to lose as well as win, or else it's no game, get it?'

He looked at Capricorn with a weary, patronizing expression as if to have to explain such basics left him in the position of an Einstein trying to explain his theories to a cretin. It sounded to Capricorn like the Indian concept of Lĩyā. Had he agreed to not-know the murderer of Richard Brewster? Philosophy or no philosophy, he was going to find out.

'You win some, you lose some,' Jed said with a shrug. 'But you can forget so much, you can forget how to win, and just be a victim. Well, I had this Recog. on the intergalactic principles of flow. The essence of the concept of number itself. Of course, there are cycles. Inflows and outflows. It just happened this Brewster business, which I was afraid would end up getting me demoted, came in a rather long period of outflow.'

'Stung Hightower for quite a packet, didn't you?' Capricorn retorted genially.

Jed tossed his head.

'It was nothing. Nothing to what I'd made for him. I came to Witch Hill when it opened with just a few hangers-on of his misfits, like Stacy who couldn't get a job in a good tea shop, and grandmothers like old Anthony. Just look what a business he has now! And I organized it. You didn't think it was that stodgy schoolmistress, did you? She's got as much fizz as last week-end's beer.'

Capricorn supposed Hightower must have had some reason for giving the rather shady young man such a high position. Rose thought the honour was a pacifier because Jed's wife had gone to the Ark, but Capricorn thought it likely that Jed had entrepreneurial qualities; his father was a successful man, after all.

'No, the trouble was, with a system like that you can't play it in pennies. You should,' and in the gleam of his eye Capricorn thought he saw the emptying of many more safes and cash registers to come, 'you should play it in millions. It's the rate of flow.' He had jumped to his feet and was walking up and down in his cell in his excitement. 'That's power. That's force. That's what'll move mountains. But if you gamble a few pennies and pounds here and there it's too weak; there'll be no impact. A baby dribbling its milk, that's all, don't you see?'

'I do indeed,' Capricorn said gravely. 'It's none of my business, and you don't have to answer this question if you don't want to, but exactly how much did you, er, borrow, from Mr Hightower?'

Jed looked unconcerned.

'I don't even know. Maybe forty thousand. Could be more. If it wasn't for that damned new wing, it would be back in the cash box pretty quick. I know I've got the winner of the St Leger. It came to me last night as I was dropping off to sleep. It's Falling Star, fifteen to one.'

'M'm,' Capricorn said. 'Thanks for the tip. Well, this is for you to read and sign, and I'll be seeing you again, I expect.'

Jed read the statement and signed it with his big, flamboyant signature.

'You can't keep me here much longer,' he said. 'My father's got me a passage on the *Queen of the East*. I'm going to Australia. There are no Sidereans in Australia,' he explained. 'Thank God I'll never have to see that crummy uniform again. I left 'em my old red combs,' he grinned. 'They'd already taken my gold bars. Plate,' he added, 'just junk. Hightower never gave much away.'

'I think we might be able to keep you for a few years,' Capricorn said. 'Let's see, unlawful flight to escape arrest. Assaulting a police officer. Hightower may charge you with theft.'

'He won't,' Jed answered confidently. 'He wouldn't get his money back that way. Besides,' he smiled a little, 'I know some of his business he might not want the world to know.'

He gazed, unseeing, through half-closed lids, and Capricorn wondered if a career as a blackmailer was being born.

'You don't want to keep me here, do you?' Jed added. 'You don't really suspect me, or is it you can't find anyone else and you're in trouble with the Yard?'

'Not quite yet,' Capricorn replied. 'But I think we'll keep you until the investigation is complete. And we have to untangle your new statement with Stacy and Venable.'

'Maybe they did it.' Jed laughed nastily. 'I got them good and worked up at Brewster. I think they would have, if I told them to. Venable thought Hightower was the Father and I was the Son.'

'And Miss Stacy was fond of you,' Capricorn suggested.

'Oh, that pig,' Jed sighed. 'It's worthwhile in a way, all this, to get rid of her. Wouldn't leave me alone. Sex-crazy, that's what she is. First she was after Hightower. Then she was spitting like a cat because he took Christine, my ex, to the Ark. Got into a fight with Chris, but she got more than she bargained for. A damned good-looking girl, Chris,' he said reflectively. 'But strong as a tiger. Noreen's all heft and no speed.'

He might have been discussing two prizefighters.

'You weren't disturbed when your wife left, then.'

It was hardly a question.

'No. We were divorcing anyway. I'm not meant to be a married man.'

He yawned.

'So Noreen came after me, but I hate those hefty women.'

'I thought you encouraged her affection,' the Superintendent murmured.

'Policy,' Jed said in gloom. 'I had some beautiful birds in London, but I had to stay on the good side of that pig, or she might have noticed more than was good for her. She's got a sharp eye when she's not drowning in her juices. But I had her and the kid well in hand, and between us we kept Portia A. well out of it. It's the old man's own fault,' he said. 'He set it up so it could be done, so it was done.' He smiled, a happy thought occurring to him. 'I've probably done him a favour; saved him from getting stung much worse. He ought to be grateful.'

Capricorn thought of the earnest-eyed if not overly attractive Noreen, perjuring herself for this young—words failed him, modern words, anyway. Cad, bounder, rotter—he must ask Sergeant Copper if there were any modern phrases to take their place, or perhaps the concept itself was old-fashioned. 'Maladjusted' was the cant of the time.

'I suppose there'll be some decent-looking birds in Australia.' Jed was surveying his future. 'Dad's always wanted me to go there. It might not be bad for a while.'

It seemed hardly fair to Australia, Capricorn judged, to loose this young monster upon them. But the Australians were a hardy and sensible breed, he hoped they could take care of themselves. Then his mind jumped to a picture of first Venable, then Stacy, toiling up Witch Hill, on foot, after seven o'clock. Both of them had to pass Richard Brewster, alive or dead. Neither of them could have reached the Manor before 7:40 at the earliest. Both must have missed the tape play.

Nerfertiti had said that Stacy came to 'Confession' red and out of breath at 7:40. She had probably just arrived, and she hadn't put the tape away at all until much later. Venable couldn't possibly have started that test at 7:30. Capricorn didn't feel particularly bitter that out of approximately five hundred Sidereans no one had noticed that Stacy and Venable were not in their accustomed places at the back of the room during the tape play, but only a half dozen students had taken that test. It was maddening that not one had observed Venable's partial absence. It was impossible to know when he had got back. Venable could easily have sent the letter; he could have met Brewster on the hill. But then Stacy came up after him.

Capricorn thought of all the forms that he had studied, together with Copper: Hightower's carefully planned forms that accounted for every minute of the day of his students and staff. As in every other tightly controlled bureaucracy, it seemed that the wily soon found ways to fudge. Venable had not seemed wily, but—And he had denied being away from the Manor at all; was that just youthful devilment, delight in foxing the police, or was it something more sinister?

Capricorn sighed and his head ached. Stacy and Venable—how could either of them have walked up the Witch Hill road clad in those scarlet tights, carrying a .45 pistol? Only Mrs Anthony was allowed to carry some kind of shoulder bag; the others had to stick their belongings in their boots. Could they have hidden the gun in advance? They couldn't be sure where they would meet Brewster. And then there was Capricorn's other idea, almost a certainty now. Somehow he couldn't believe Venable was a killer, any more than Garry Wyatt. And yet—it was a dilemma.

As he sat brooding, a constable came in with a cup of tea for Jed and a plate of digestive biscuits.

'Criminals fare better than Scotland Yard,' Capricorn said absently, reminded that he had had no lunch and almost certainly he would not have time for dinner. The constable blushed and invited the Superintendent to join him and the sergeant out front. Capricorn was happy to do so. The tea and biscuits were soothing; his head ceased to ache. The flavour of the digestives took him back to childhood, when his magician aunts would give him a plateful instead of a meal if they were rushed. He smiled, remembering the days when the night's performance was the great event and children were not coddled. He recalled once telling Aunt Dolly rather pompously, referring some trouble now forgotten, that he was on the horns of a dilemma. What was it she had said? 'Well, grab them both, luv, and get off.' Perhaps she had thought it was a mythical beast, part of a Christmas pantomime.

'Grab them both—'

'Oh, Lord,' he said aloud, suddenly, to the alarm of the constable who was refilling his cup.

'Yes, yes, thank you,' Capricorn said. 'The tea is very good.'

But he glared at it, the constable said later, commenting on the strangeness of people from Headquarters, as though it might sit up and drink him.

Capricorn finished, took out his notebook, stared at his notes and muttered. Then he thanked the local men, but before he left he went back again to the prisoner.

'By the way,' he remarked to Jed, who had apparently forgotten him and was watching a programme on a small television set with which he had somehow been provided, 'did you send that last letter?'

'Letter?' Jed looked around from the bunk in which he was reclining, annoyed at being interrupted in his diversion.

201

'The threatening letter that Brewster received that night somewhere between six-thirty and a quarter to seven. Did you arrange to have it delivered?'

'Look,' Jed retorted, slowly and patiently, as if he were trying to explain to a backward child. 'You probably won't believe this, but I *never* sent Brewster one of those letters. I didn't have to. All I had to do was to say he was a menace to Siderea in front of a bunch of the kids and sure as Falling Star is going to win that race, at least one of them would go off and write a scorcher. I never sent *anybody* a threatening letter. As a matter of fact,' he went on, 'I never write letters at all. I ring people up, it's quicker.'

He looked as if he was telling the truth, Capricorn thought, if any manifestation on the part of this natural criminal could be trusted.

'Do you have any idea who did?'

Jed shook his head, his attention now entirely absorbed in the television play.

'No idea,' he said absently. 'Could have been anyone. Probably Venable or Stacy. Silly sods.'

Capricorn left the station, grimly agreeing with Jed about the suggestibility of the young and the emotionally disturbed. He thought of the famous murder case of Thompson and Bywaters: both the wife and the lover had been hanged for the killing of the husband, though the wife had taken no part in it. But her letters to her lover had mentioned murder over and over again. Imagination, flights of fancy; her attempts at murder had proved to be mere literary art. Still the hardminded jury of those days had considered the letters inflammatory enough to make her a principal in the crime, and a harsh judge had given her the rope.

He sighed, for the puzzle was solved and he felt no joy at the solution. A policeman's fate. Even worse, he had no proof to stand up in court, and at this point it seemed unlikely he would ever get it. Resolutely he pushed such thoughts from his mind. From long experience he knew enough to get on with the next obvious step and leave worrying about the end of the case until he got there. He pushed his car almost to its limit to get the journey over.

eighteen

On either side of the road back to Daines Barington, the meadows
were rich with the golden sunshine of late summer afternoon.
Drowsy birds rested in the hedges, cows slept like portly but elegant
dowagers in the grass. To the west the Baring, tranquil, reflected the
deep blue sky that seemed to ripple through the long reeds. Capricorn
saw none of it; he was rushing along at fever pitch.

He had been only a half-mile from Redmond, passing Marlingly
station, when a headline chalked on a newsvendor's hoarding caught
his eye.

'Sidereans expelled from England.'

He had stopped, bought a paper, and noticed with discomfort the
same headline on a left-over copy of the morning edition. Scotland
Yard superintendents often were too busy to read newspapers, but
this time it looked like dereliction of duty. He scanned the article
quickly. The headline was substantiated by the text. A government

department had acted, and the Immigration people were authorized and ordered to revoke the permits for alien Sidereans to stay in the country.

He frowned, thinking quickly. It was hardly the best kind of coordination of activities. His request to Sidereans not to leave the Daines Barington area would have no force over this. If he wanted to keep any of the foreigners, he would have to make an arrest. Griswald was probably at the funeral. Well, his own best plan was to continue on to the Manor.

As the road swung round past the Brewster estate, he saw a small figure toiling up the road. Slowing down, he recognized the lawyer Hartle, dressed in black, blinking like a rabbit in the sun. His manner was distracted and his clothes, formal and almost Edwardian, were too warm for the weather and inappropriate for a country walk.

'Are you going to the Manor, Superintendent?' he asked. 'Can you give me a lift?'

Capricorn waited until the little man was settled in his seat, his gloves smoothed, his tall hat set neatly on his knees, and the car was in full motion again before he ventured an inquiring glance.

'Such an afternoon, such an afternoon,' Hartle whispered. His face was pale and his nose twitched. Definitely the White Rabbit, Capricorn thought, and reproved himself for frivolity. 'The funeral . . . my closest friend. . .missed the service . . . left my car . . . oh, dear, oh, dear.'

Hartle sighed, wriggled himself into some kind of composure, and spoke in a slightly stronger voice.

'You've heard this morning's news, of course, the Sidereans—very odd name. Very odd people. I had gone to Brewster House early. I was to accompany Miss Brewster with the—' he twitched unhappily, his lips shuttling between unhappy euphemisms for dead bodies— 'with poor Richard in a horse-drawn carriage—he would have liked that—to the cemetery. And after a most difficult time with Miss Brewster—most strange—most strange, my dear Superintendent—one of those dreadful people had the impudence to call at Brewster House—on such a day!—with a note from Mrs Anthony saying it is most *urgent* that I go up to the Manor. I can tell you Superintendent, I would have refused, except that Mrs Anthony has always proved herself a sensible, decent sort of woman—in her private capacity, she's a client of my firm.'

He added this as if it were a certificate of her acceptability. Capricorn remembered the Rector's certainty of Garry Wyatt's innocence: one of his parishioners.

'Bailey was there and took my place . . . ' He let his voice die away. 'Quite a sight, Capricorn. Black horses, very fine, the coachwork brilliant, something I haven't seen as well done for many years. Not since the Queen's coronation,' he said, and Capricorn felt it was a matter of grief that he hadn't ridden in the coach behind his old friend to his last place of rest.

'But duty . . . a client . . . Mrs Anthony said it was a matter of urgency for the town . . . '

'Well, with this news I can imagine they have urgent legal matters to be cleared away,' Capricorn said, as soothingly as he could. Were the Sidereans contemplating legal action, he wondered. It would mean a suit against the Crown. Surely they would not call on Hartle and Hartle for that.

'You say Miss Brewster was very distraught?' he inquired, hardly able to believe such a thing of the composed woman he had seen just a few hours earlier.

'Distraught is not the way I would describe her,' Hartle said, nettled. 'She has put me in a difficult position, a very difficult position indeed. For the first time in about forty years, Superintendent, I am not really sure of my client's rights in certain matters. I will have to consult other counsel.'

His voice trailed off, sounding fretful. Perhaps it was the heat. Mrs Anthony could have sent a car for him. Then the Superintendent thought of the driving licences that had been confiscated up at the Manor. They would have to be released. In the new circumstances, the Sidereans must be free to travel.

He was silent, thinking of all the implications, while the lawyer, in a series of sniffs and wiggles, prepared himself to speak. He pulled a glove off and without looking at it pulled it on again.

'You know, of course, Superintendent that we never divulge a client's affairs.'

Capricorn nodded, taking the 'we' to be editorial, or perhaps a gesture to that other Hartle of Hartle and Hartle, who was apparently no longer among the living.

'But I am faced with a problem, and it is not entirely legal. The interests of two of my clients conflict. And as you know one of the ladies concerned well, perhaps I might venture to sound your opinion. I would very much object,' he said strongly, 'to speaking to the lady herself in this matter. Legally and personally, I find it repugnant.'

Some conflict in Brewster's will, Capricorn imagined, between the dispositions for Miss Brewster and Mrs Lavender. He could probably put Hartle's mind at rest. Rose, he knew, would make no demands of any sort. She would probably accept no more from his estate than a keepsake, her engagement ring that was hers already.

As the lawyer fussed and explained over and over why it was perfectly correct for him to breach the client-solititor confidence and how immeasurably difficult the situation was, Capricorn listened with a fragment of attention, while his gaze took in the fields on Witch Hill, every bush and hedge and the wooden stile as they went up towards the peak. Here Richard Brewster had been killed.

He thought of the ditch he had marked, just out of sight on the other side of the hill. There someone had crouched, waiting. He believed he knew who that was, but where was the proof? Many people must have known about the convenient ditch. Jed had seen Garry and Linda coming from some hidden spot. Yet if they were there, or even close, it made his theory a nonsense. And viewed dispassionately, it was a most likely place for them to have spent their hours of love, out of sight of five hundred Sidereans, Wyatt's landlady, the gossiping townspeople and Rose, who in the matter of her own daughter would be hawk-eyed. Who knew that hill as well as Garry Wyatt, who covered every foot of it daily?

'I was alone with Miss Brewster, except for my niece who came from the Town Hall, until Bailey arrived,' Hartle was saying, 'but I was not expecting to talk business. I had come to comfort. . .'

He patted his pocket and Capricorn could almost see the two large white handkerchieves, starched and neatly folded, probably by his niece, the admirable Miss Hartle, once secretary to Richard Brewster.

'But instead, she was very calm and practical, and asked me to arrange for the return of the ring.'

Hartle's last words had been falling on Capricorn's ears not unpleasantly, rather like the droning of a blue-bottle. But suddenly the meaning of the last sentence struck him and he looked round, startled.

'Yes, you may well be surprised,' the lawyer said wretchedly. 'Most distressing. Nothing in the will to Mrs Lavender, in the circumstances, you understand. The new will was to have been signed the next day, as I told you. And Mrs Lavender, so correct . . . ' his voice returned to a whisper, 'returning all her wedding presents. A silver salver from my niece and myself. An old tapestry the Rector had sent. A breakfast set from the Norrises—modern stuff,' he said, deprecating as Miss Brewster would have been. Capricorn could see why they had always got on well. 'and that vase from Beatrice herself.'

He sighed.

'Women are extraordinary. Beatrice had spent most of her little principal on that vase.'

'The legacy from the major,' Capricorn remembered.

'Insurance,' Hartle nodded. 'And after such a gesture,' he went on, infinitely perplexed, 'to ask for the return of the ring! A lovely old piece, Superintendent, but hardly of a value—.'

'Did she say why she wanted it?' the Superintendent found himself interested.

'Well, it was her mother's, you see. John had bought it for Lucrezia in Rome before their marriage. Apparently it was a shock to Beatrice when Richard gave it to Mrs Lavender, although, fortunately, she said nothing at the time. She has some idea that it wasn't his to give. And legally,' his forehead wrinkled, 'it's a puzzle. The ring was Lucrezia's to dispose of as she chose. In her will she left her possessions to Richard, for the estate to remain intact, but she named each item specifically, all of her valuable pieces. She forgot to mention the ruby ring. My fault,' he sighed. 'I drew it up. It would have seemed insignificant. The jewels would normally have gone to Mrs Lavender on her marriage.'

He bit his lip in vexation.

'But if Miss Brewster insists, and she does—the ring not being mentioned in the will, and it was her mother's—'

He snuffled again.

'Most extraordinary. She had never shown any interest in the jewels over the years. Never wore a piece. You've seen her manner of dress. My niece,' he coughed, 'women notice these things; Vera says, not very feminine. The jewels were still in the safe in her mother's room, never opened, the room never used. All Lucrezia's gowns still in the wardrobe, I understand. Very odd.'

'I wouldn't worry,' the Superintendent said. The gates of Witch Hill loomed up before them. 'Mrs Lavender is an old friend of mine; I know her very well. You needn't say anything. I can put it to her in such a way that the ring will be returned to the estate without her even knowing it was asked for. Leave it to me.'

Mr Hartle sighed in profound relief.

The gate house was empty. Peering out, Capricorn saw that the gates were unlocked. A great bustle was taking place up and down the cool tunnel of a lane that led to the house. Cars were being driven—licences or no licences, he noted with resignation—lining up before the gates. Sidereans were running back and forth, bundles were thrown in the cars. Was that a fleet of trucks further down?

'Thank you,' the lawyer was breathing fervently in his ear. 'Oh, if you could do that, Superintendent—'

Hartle's cheeks were quite pink, Capricorn saw. Then his attention was caught up in negotiating the tunnel as he passed the waiting line of cars. From every building on the estate, large and small, packing cases were being hauled and stacked. Metal file cabinets tied with string stood around the grass like a strange new growth that had appeared overnight. Sidereans, moving very swiftly but still laughing and calling, were working like bees in the task of emptying Witch Hill Manor.

Inside the hall of the main block, under the fierce neon light, the place looked ravaged. The little hutments were ripped apart, the piles of papers gone, the notices torn from the wire. Odd stubs of pencils and rubber bands lay about the floor, and voices were yelling instructions to get a move on, and threats that people should shape up or ship out, which threats were greeted with loud laughter. Capricorn was irresistibly reminded of the evacuation of an army post, complete with litter and the resultant desolation.

'I suppose we *both* want to talk to Mrs Anthony.'

The lawyer looked at Capricorn apprehensively, obviously not wishing to claim precedence over Scotland Yard, but hoping very much to be able to attend some part of the funeral service for his closest friend.

'We can go in together,' Capricorn said, who was interested in what business Siderea had with the lawyer.

Mrs Anthony received them in the library. She was dressed in a dark coat and skirt suitable for travel, although she was still signing documents and sorting a pile of papers that seemed a yard high. The bust of Hightower and his neon light sat on the floor in a crate not yet nailed down. The library had already taken on, a more tranquil look.

She greeted them both with a smile and asked them to be seated.

Capricorn, however, remained standing while he attended to his more urgent business.

'You appear to be leaving us,' he said mildly.

'I was waiting to be in touch with you,' she said, still signing her papers as she spoke.

'You'll have to excuse me.' She indicated the mass of work. 'You understand this has to be done. I'm not breaking our agreement, Superintendent, but you see that the matter has been taken out of our hands. The action of the government was first made known to us, by the way, from the morning papers. And at exactly 10:30 a.m. I had orders from Mr Hightower to close our operation here. We leave at midnight to join him on the Ark.'

'The English also?' Capricorn asked.

'Yes,' she nodded. 'So I'm afraid it's up to you, Superintendent.'

Capricorn wasn't ready to ask for a warrant, though he would if he had to.

'At this moment,' he said slowly, 'I can't let Mr Venable, Mr Wyatt, Miss Stacy or Miss Lavender go. I have a lot more questions, and they might be needed as witnesses.'

She noted the names on a piece of paper.

'I see,' she said sardonically, 'you don't ask for Mr Frost. I gather you know of his whereabouts? We're interested.'

'We are not asking you for Mr Frost,' he hedged.

'May we ask you where he is?' she inquired. 'We have some questions we would like to ask him.'

'Perhaps we can discuss that a little later,' he said. 'In the meantime I must see Mr Wyatt, Miss Lavender if she's here, and the other two.'

'Certainly,' she said. 'Mr Venable had been waiting to see you, and I was going to take you to Mr Wyatt and Miss Lavender, who has quite recovered. You don't have to worry about Miss Stacy; she's still in the dungeon so she can't go anywhere. I'll have to release her now, and I'll take you along. I just need a few minutes for Mr Hartle, Superintendent, if you don't mind. Please wait here and we'll go down to the cells together.'

Capricorn, shocked at the mention of dungeons and cells from the prosaic Mrs Anthony, nodded. Jed, apparently, had not just been raving. What unsavoury business was all this? And how, he thought irritably, could Mrs Anthony be so calm about it?

She turned to the lawyer.

'As you see, Mr Hartle, this leaving is somewhat precipitous. It's also final. Mr Hightower, after the event of this morning, has decided that Great Britain is not worthy of the presence of Siderea; that is why we have to move so soon. He had been doubtful of England's future for some time, he told me, and this was the catalyst. And when Mr Hightower decides, he likes his decisions to be implemented immediately.

'As far as my personal affairs are concerned, Mr Hartle,' she said. 'I would like you to go on handling them for me. I will be in touch with you when I can.

'Now, on my recommendation of your firm, Mr Hightower has authorized me to engage you as our legal representative here to wind up any business left undone due to our sudden departure. I have here a signed power of attorney,' she passed a paper over to the startled lawyer, 'limited to these local matters, and I have a sum of money here for you to attend to any outstanding bills, et cetera, and to take care of the fees for any services you may render us. Mr Hightower wanted you to handle these things as he feels the townspeople will have confidence in you.'

She undid a metal box; took out piles of five pound notes, neatly wrapped in bundles of a thousand, and stacked them in front of him. 'If you will sign this receipt,' she said, handing him a sheet of paper, 'you will only have to take care of accounts payable. There are no accounts receivable, as we always get paid in advance. There are no wages due; that has all been settled.'

Hartle's mouth was opening and closing. Capricorn was not sure that the prim lawyer wanted to accept Hightower as a client, but he seemed mesmerized by the huge pile of crisp five-pound notes and Mrs Anthony's calm assumption that all was settled.

'There is one more thing,' she said, and took out another group of documents signed with her name as chief officer of Siderea, which she put on the pile in front of Hartle.

'Mr Hightower wished you to know that his displeasure at the action of the British government in no way affects his feelings of friendship for Daines Barington itself. He liked the town while he was here, and feels affection for it. He wanted you to know that he deplored the murder of Richard Brewster, whom he considered a personal friend, and he deeply regrets any actions of a certain irresponsible person, pretending to be a Siderean, that contributed to the unfortunate atmosphere between the Manor and the town before Mr Brewster's death.

'Sidereans accept responsibility for this, and according to our code, we make amends.'

She gave Capricorn a quick glance. It was different from her usual, open look; he felt it was somewhat guarded. Amends for exactly what, he wondered. Was she, after all, holding something back? Some suspicion, at least, that she had kept from him? Suddenly he wondered, if she knew the murderer to be a Siderean, would she turn him over to the police, or would she believe the crime better handled by Siderea itself?

'What Mr Hightower proposes, Mr Hartle, is this. Since he bought Witch Hill Manor, the price of landed property has steadily increased. Once Siderea has left, and the new law is passed—which we are sure will occur,' she said and smiled, 'Witch Hill Manor should sell for many times the price at which he bought it. But if the town wants the estate for any worthy project, to be leased as a school or nursing home, or hospital, whatever would be desired, Mr Hightower is prepared to sell to the town for the original price only.

'We leave it in your hands, Mr Hartle,' she said easily, rising and placing her hand on his shoulder for one second. 'And now, Superintendent, we'll go downstairs.'

And they were out of the library before Hartle had formulated either protest or gratitude or had even managed to think why the arrangment was impossible. Capricorn followed the robust form of Mrs. Anthony, for a moment distracted from his speculation by his respect for her handling of the lawyer. He suspected that the shock would force Hartle to do exactly what he was told and without one mention of the Norman conquest. Mrs Anthony had given him exactly seven and a half minutes. Capricorn decided he must study Siderea himself.

But—'Dungeons?' he inquired, as they went down the wide worn steps to what had been the servants' quarters below, and then two more flights to the old cellars.

Mrs Anthony laughed.

'You sound shocked, Superintendent.'

It was dark in the cellar—the old wine cellar? he wondered—and cavernous. His mind went back to the Rector's brandy-induced tales of rumoured secret meetings between Ron Gaylord and Lucrezia

Brewster: 'secret passages, priests' holes, and the like.' But Brewster House was built too late for that and so was this Vanbrugh mansion. Mrs Anthony had taken a torch from her handbag and lit the way.

'We have our own internal justice system in Siderea. Among ourselves. We never go to the courts, except when attacked by outsiders.'

She might have been answering his unstated question.

'It's not based on punishment or revenge,' she explained, as her sensible leather shoes—so much more becoming to her than high boots—squeaked on the damp stone flags. 'We just get people to acknowledge to themselves what they've done, see where they are in relation to others and their own goals, and put themselves in a better state.'

It sounded to Capricorn disagreeably like the Communist method of 'self-criticism' and he said so.

'Certainly not,' she said firmly. 'If there is one thing Mr Hightower dislikes more than anything else, it's Communism. A state suitable for ants or bees, but not for immortal spirits. No, our people aren't required to denigrate themselves. Merely to recognize their actions.'

Capricorn grimaced. 'Recognize' by whose standard? Hightower's? He himself preferred the idea of justice by an established code of law, where punishment was for acts committed, and not the thoughts and emotions which impelled them. This idea was not peculiar to Siderea, he mused; it was a distressing modern symptom. Were we on the way already to the Therapeutic State?

Philosophical speculation was pushed aside as Mrs Anthony opened a wooden door and Capricorn could make out, in the moving torchlight, a small space lined with wooden racks—he was right, he was in the old wine cellars—but all that it contained now was Noreen Stacy sitting on the floor and a china vessel in a corner that gave off a distressing olfactory advertisement of its purpose. Noreen's appearance shocked him. She wore a dirty, torn grey cotton shift, and her limp brown hair was covered in grey ash. At first sight she looked like a hag.

'All right, Noreen,' Mrs Anthony said, apparently unmoved. 'We're moving to the Ark. You may come up and help, but whether you can leave or not depends on the Superintendent. He has some questions to ask you.'

'Upstairs,' he said hastily. Scotland Yard was not going to question witnesses in dark cellars. He reflected it was certainly against the spirit of the Judges' Rules. Whatever Mrs Anthony might say about the internal system of justice in Siderea, he felt strongly, with Jedediah Frost, that they might do better to stick to Magna Carta, the common law, and the more usual system of jurisprudence.

Mrs Anthony also recalled Jed Frost, if she had for a moment forgotten him.

'I gather you don't intend to reveal Mr Frost's whereabouts?' she queried.

'I can give you the name and address of his solicitor,' he evaded her question. Really, he thought, he could hardly turn Frost over to something like this. Having witnessed Noreen's punishment for her minor lapse, what could they have in store for Frost? *Peine forte et dure?* The idea had its charms, but it could not be done.

'It doesn't matter,' Mrs Anthony said placidly. 'Mr Hightower won't trouble to prosecute. The money could not be recovered. Frost has already been excommunicated. There is no greater punishment.'

She left them at the top of the cellar stairs with a calm instruction 'Report to me in the library as soon as the Superintendent has finished with you, Private. You may change back to uniform, but hand in your gold bars.'

The Superintendent went to the window seat at one end of the passage and Noreen sat beside him, efficiently flicking the ashes from her hair. Seen in full daylight, she seemed none the worse for her experience. Her colour was still healthy and she was regarding him with her usual stalk-eyed stare and was not at all embarrassed or perturbed.

'What's all this?' he enquired. 'The penalty for lying to the police?'

'No,' she said, matter of fact. The former General was without a sense of humour, he saw. 'It was because I covered up for Jed. I don't mind. I did it and now I'll do something to make up.'

Capricorn wondered if she was expected to make up the forty thousand pounds or so that Frost had embezzled. From what Norris had said of the pay in the Army of the Stars, it could take several lifetimes.

'Does Siderean justice take account of crimes of passion?' he asked.

'I was a fool,' she said briskly. 'I was mad about Jed. But now I can see he's no good. He should have faced his trouble and gone through the States.'

'The States?' Capricorn, puzzled, envisioned Frost on a pilgrimage, perhaps on his knees, through North America.

'Yes, that's Siderea law. If you're court-martialled and found guilty of an offense, the Morale Officer will declare you in a State. I was put in Treason, second class,' she said seriously. 'If you agree with the designation you can stay in Siderea, and you work your way up through the States until you are in Normal, at least. Jed ran off,' she said with scorn, and Capricorn saw she would have forgiven him murder much more easily.

Capricorn wondered how serious she thought murder was. Siderean ethics, as far as he could see, related solely to the success of Siderea. The logic was simple: Siderea was the one and only method to save souls; therefore what helped Siderea was good, what hindered it was evil. Such dangerous notions were not too alarming when expressed by people who had taken traditional backgrounds into Siderea, like Mrs Anthony. They gave verbal allegiance to Hightower but conducted their lives according to voices heard in childhood: stealing, cruelty to others, killing are Bad. Kindness, forbearance, charity are Good. But what of those outcasts, misfits, who had never heard the voices, or never heeded them?

'I don't care about Jed any more,' Noreen continued. 'Fancy us going to the Ark,' she added, her native cockney more noticeable in her surprise. 'I bet I'll be able to work my way up to the State of Enemy in no time. I'll probably be in Doubt by the end of the week.'

Capricorn forced his mind from these intriguing sidelights on ecclesiastical justice back to the urgent case he was on.

'If you would care to give me a truthful version of your movements on the night of the murder, it would be helpful. I warn you again that anything you say will be taken down and may be used as evidence.'

'Oh,' she looked shocked, as if remembering there were other legal systems to be considered. 'I'd forgotten about that. Bother.'

'Your phrasing seems somewhat inadequate,' he murmured, 'but go on.'

He took her revised statement. It agreed with the one he had taken

214

from Jed Frost. She and Venable had dragged him forcibly into his car and driven him to the station.

'We didn't know then what he'd been up to,' she said gloomily. 'Though we could've, if we looked at the records. I suppose I didn't want to.' She sighed. 'Anyway, we bought his ticket, and then he got an idea and talked us into leaving the car. I didn't want to because we were late already and it meant running all the way, and I was halfway through my first Confession before I took a real breath.'

'Did Venable run with you?'

'Chris got tired of arguing. He left before I did. He had to take a test after tape-time.'

Capricorn recalled the tape.

'When did you put the reel of tape away?'

'Later on. While you were there, I think.'

'Your performance sheet shows you did that at 7:30,' he pointed out.

'We often make them up in the morning, to get beforehand,' she explained solemnly, without a twinkle.

Capricorn repressed his own, somewhat rueful amusement. Inconvenient as it had been for him, he was glad the iron bureaucracy had failed. He had a moment of anarchic joy for the wiliness of the human race.

'Do you know whom Frost intended to see?'

'No,' she said. 'Honestly, I thought he was going to drive towards London and see someone on the way before he picked up the Representative. So did Chris. We had no idea at all. Was it Wyatt?'

The Superintendent nodded.

'Did you see Frost on your way back?'

'No. He couldn't have used the Witch Hill road.'

'Did you see Venable ahead?'

'No, but he told me after he had come up across the fields.'

'Did you see Richard Brewster?'

'No.'

'But you must have done,' Capricorn said. 'He left Brewster House at seven and walked up the Witch Hill Road. You *must* have passed him.'

Noreen looked at him stolidly.

'Well, I didn't. Maybe he didn't walk up the road. He could have taken the field path and come to the top of the hill that way.'

'Then he would have arrived there faster. You would have certainly seen him.'

She shrugged.

'I don't know what he was doing. I didn't see him. Maybe he didn't leave when they told you, that lot in Brewster House.'

'Wait a minute. You know, I'd forgot. I did see someone, but I never thought of her as anyone, and I just didn't remember. She was running the other way, along the fields towards the town. I saw her cross the road; she was blubbering like a baby.'

She looked at him with a faint smile.

'Linda Lavender.'

Yes, of course. She would have seen her.

'But she couldn't have killed him,' Noreen said practically, 'or I'd have seen his body. He must've been killed after I'd gone. You could ask Chris.'

'Christopher Venable?' he asked, puzzled. 'But you said he left before you.'

She nodded.

'Yes. He was carrying on about his test. But Chris is always thinking of his belly. He dashed down to the Moo-Cow and got a bag of hamburgers to eat on the way back. I saw him sneak back in the Manor at a quarter to eight, while I was taking Confession from that American tart. He'd finished eating,' she said, recalling. 'He'd messed up the front of his tights. Gravy all over the "S",' she added with disapproval, as Capricorn's heart sank. 'Too young to be a colonel. Being quick at tests isn't everything. Too young to know what's what.'

Capricorn left instructions with Noreen to call in at the station the next morning and went somewhat grimly in search of Venable. He was loading a truck under the cedar in front of the main block. He was dressed only in a scarlet singlet and trunks—clean, Capricorn observed—the silver bars proclaiming him a colonel flashing on his shoulders. His face was flushed with effort till it matched his costume, and his straw-coloured hair was sprinkled with grey ash in some kind of penance.

Like Noreen Stacy he made no attempt to repeat their earlier story. They both knew Jed Frost well enough, apparently, to know he would give them away. Venable's new story confirmed Noreen Stacy's. He vacillated between embarrassment at being caught in a flagrant lie and pride at deceiving Mrs Anthony by completing his test and doing well although he had begun fifteen minutes late.

'The other kids weren't lying,' he said, referring to the statements of the other examinees that had seemed to corroborate his own false testimony. 'They were all slaving so hard they didn't notice I wasn't there in the beginning. They saw me in the back at the end, and it seemed like I was there all the time.'

'And how was it nobody noticed you two were not in the back while the tape was playing?'

Venable grinned in delight.

'Most people don't see much, ever. They think they see what they expect to see, unless something else comes up and eats them. The Venables have always been brainy, of course, like the Brewsters.'

Capricorn regarded the beaming youth gravely.

'What happened to the garment you were wearing that night?'

The round blue eyes popped at him.

'My uniform? It's in the wash. God knows what will happen to the wash now,' he said thoughtfully. 'Our stuff goes out all together. Grease dripped on it from the hamburgers while I was running back.'

'Where did you meet Brewster?' Capricorn asked.

'But I didn't! I told you the truth about that,' he said indignantly. 'After all, he was my cousin.'

And you are his heir, Capricorn could have added.

He explained, patiently.

'Mr Brewster left his house at seven o'clock. He walked up to the Hill, as far as we know, by the Witch Hill road. If you got to the Manor at a quarter to eight, you must have seen him.'

'No, I didn't,' Venable said triumphantly. 'The Moo-Cow is far south of the station, and if you cut across the fields to the Manor you don't come to the road until you're right in front of the door.'

He gave Capricorn a sidelong look and spoke again in quite a different voice, lower, penitent, the voice of a naughty child regretting his misdeeds.

'I think I heard it, though. The killing. I mean, the shots.'

'You heard?' Capricorn said. 'Where were you?'

'I was pretty far back in the south fields near the lake,' Venable said, frowning, 'the big lake, where the boat shed is. I heard a sound, but I didn't know what it was. It might have been a car backfiring.'

'Do you know what time that was?' Capricorn said.

'Well, I do,' Venable said, obviously ashamed, 'because I'd been looking at my watch as I went, checking the time. But I wasn't sure, you see, about the shots, and I'd promised not to tell on Jed, so I couldn't very well tell you before.'

His blue gaze fell on Capricorn expecting him to understand and accept his schoolboy code.

'So what time were the shots?' Capricorn said, expressionless.

'The first one was just at half past, because I was looking. And the next was about a minute after.'

'That long? Are you sure?' Capricorn said.

'It might have been longer,' Venable answered, 'because I was running, and I'd run quite a bit between the first report and the second. That's why at first I wasn't sure if the sound was a gun. It wasn't until the inquest I heard about the two shots and then I wondered.'

Capricorn regarded him for some time and sighed. He would have to find Mrs Anthony and see what he could do about getting Venable's soiled uniform. He started to warn him not to leave Daines Barington when the boy interrupted.

'I'm not going to the Ark,' he said, somewhat self-consciously. 'Actually, if you say it's all right, I would like to go up to London. I have some business matters to take care of.'

He looked important, young, and yet at the same time, Capricorn thought, the boy displayed something of the Venable-Brewster aura.

'There's a strike in one of the Brewster factories,' Venable explained, 'and I want to get those old trustees to let me help handle it. I've learned a lot in Siderea that'll be very useful in this sort of lark.'

Richard Brewster had guessed right, Capricorn thought. Whatever else the boy turned out to be, it was obvious he had the family sense for business. For him, Siderea could very easily move into the past.

He left with instructions to check with Superintendent Griswald later on, and found himself pleased, perhaps irrationally in the circumstances, to hear that Brewster's heir intended a condolence call that night at Brewster House.

'I was going to the funeral,' he explained, 'but I had to help with this move. My parents are there now. Superintendent,' there was a hesitation in his voice, but he went on, 'do you know who killed him?'

'In spite of the confusion you've caused,' Capricorn said with some asperity, 'the investigation is almost complete.'

'I hope you get the killer,' the young man said. He hoisted up another large crate onto the back of the lorry. 'I really hope you do.'

He sounded very much a member of the Venable-Brewster tribe. Richard Brewster, dead, had won over Hightower in that. From the west the rays of the sun struck across the lawns, blazing on the departing vehicles, almost horizontal now. I must get going, Capricorn thought, and quickened his pace. Somehow in that hectic removal he found the harried little woman who was in charge of the washing of uniforms. It wasn't too difficult, as she was standing on the lawn trying to stuff them into a hamper that was too small, hopping up and down with vexation and calling on the Almighty, in whom she was not supposed to believe, to give her patience.

Capricorn extricated her, and found with relief that all the garments were marked with name tapes and that the laundry had not been sent out since the night of the murder. Sometimes the police have a bit of luck, he reflected, though not often. He took the collection into the house and telephoned Sergeant Copper to come and sort the laundry, to the Sergeant's disgust.

'You are letting them go and we haven't found the gun?' he said, incredulous. 'Unless it turns out to be the Yank's.'

Capricorn sighed.

'It wasn't the decision of the lowly bods like us,' he said. 'But I'm holding those we need.'

'Hope you're hanging on to that Yank,' Copper said darkly, as he rang off. 'His bird backed up his tale, but what would you expect?'

Capricorn was, in fact, looking for Wyatt, and he didn't have far to go to find him. Among all the debris in the library, a small space had been cleared by the window. In the embrasure was Linda Lavender, magically recovered, dressed in rosebud-sprinkled organdy, with a circlet of flowers in her hair, and beside her was Garry Wyatt, dressed in his usual denims but very neat, with shining shoes and a rather pale face.

A few Sidereans stood about watching silently, while Mrs Anthony read from a black book with a cross on the front.

'Hold up the ring,' she was saying.

Garry Wyatt held the ring up to the light.

Oh, no, Capricorn thought and winced, poor Hartle, for the ring Wyatt was holding up was a ruby set in old gold, evidently donated by Mrs Lavender.

'Now, both of you, place a "C" inside the ring. Have you done

219

that?'

'Yes,' they said in unison, Linda's clipped English blending prettily with Garry's drawl.

'The "C" stands for cleansing,' Mrs Anthony said, 'and will remain there always to remind you that you have been cleansed, and you are making this agreement, to which you promise to be faithful. Do you, Linda, and you, Garry, wish to dwell with each other, to co-exist, two individuals, one partnership, down through the ages?'

'We do,' they said, confidently.

What a long time, Capricorn reflected, at least for one who had never quite been able to manage 'Till death do us part.'

'Place the ring on the bride's finger,' Mrs Anthony said, beaming. 'I pronounce you, by the laws of Siderea, husband and wife. And you may kiss the bride.'

There was laughter among the onlookers, and some of the girls threw flowers, roses, slightly tumbled, and their petals fluttered slowly over the bride and groom. From somewhere a large bottle of champagne was produced and poured into paper cups, and the health of the newly married pair was drunk. Mrs Anthony saw the Superintendent and came over.

'Is this legal?' he inquired.

Mrs. Anthony laughed.

'No, this is only a religious ceremony. I'm a minister of Siderea. They're being married by the Rector, but we did this so that their friends who are leaving tonight could wish them well. I hope you haven't come to arrest them, Superintendent. They look much too happy.'

Capricorn looked at the young couple by the window in a flurry of champagne, rose petals and good wishes.

'Not them,' he said, briefly.

She turned pale and he felt sorry for her. Whichever way the investigation ended, she would feel responsible for the tragedy. There was nothing to be done about that. Briefly he told her what was being done with the uniforms and why.

'It's the first time I've been glad that those wretched garments are so hard to wash,' she said. 'Your "evidence" will be intact, Superintendent, and will certainly clear Colonel Venable of everything except his foolish loyalty.'

'Linda and Garry are not going with you, I take it,' he said.

'No,' she answered, the strain leaving her features as she looked again at the young people. 'It's a pity, but Garry is taking Linda to Texas after the church wedding. His work here is finished.'

'Oh,' Capricorn said, 'that reminds me. I have something for them. It may be a wedding present.'

He went over to Wyatt and, detaching him firmly from his lady, asked him a question. The reply he received was what he had expected, but his heart beat faster and his blood raced in anticipation. It was all he could do not to go tearing off like a child after school, but he had a debt to pay.

'I've commited a crime against you,' he said cheerfully. 'I'm not sure what law I've broken, but it's quite serious.'

He fished from his pocket an envelope that Superintendent Griswald had given him.

'On the night of the murder,' he said, 'the postman was bringing up a cablegram for you. It was carried off with the exhibits and Superintendent Griswald asked me to return it, with his apologies. I'm afraid, ass that I am, I've been walking round with it in my pocket.'

Wyatt looked at it with wonder.

'It must be from my dad,' he said, and ripped it apart impatiently. After staring at it for a second he grinned broadly at Capricorn.

'Get that! Everything's O.K., after all. Listen to this: "Bring the bride. Cable and we'll get the cake. Your grandmother crazy over the picture you sent of that cute little girl. Give her our love."

'Hey honey,' he turned to his rose-covered bride. 'Everything's fine. Great! Let's have some more champagne.'

Capricorn had to leave them to their joy and rush away. He only paused, in the Great Hall, to say goodbye to Mrs Anthony.

'Are you planning on making an arrest?' she asked.

'Very soon.'

'You know—?'

'I'm almost certain,' he said, 'but we would have liked to find the gun.'

He looked at her troubled face.

'Is there anything you want to tell me?' he asked. 'Perhaps something you've learned since you gave your statement?'

'No, she answered. 'I've learned nothing.'

She seemed to hesitate, and for a moment he thought she might say more as she stared down at the floor. Then she shook her head impatiently as if to clear it, and when she spoke she was her usual brisk self.

'I'm going to call on Miss Brewster tonight, before I leave,' she said. 'I know the call might not be welcome, but I think I should. Perhaps I'll see you at Brewster House, Superintendent?'

'I'll be there if I can,' he said thoughtfully, 'but, should I not—'
He shook her hand.

'You've been helpful and I appreciate it,' he said.

'I was happy to help,' she said, with her great sincerity.

As he left her to hasten to his car, he found, to his surprise, that he was oddly sorry to see her go. A sensible woman. He wondered what she had thought of telling him and held back. A secret of the confessional? Those confessions hadn't seemed private, let alone secret, but perhaps there was some kind of obligation of silence involved. He forgot her as he turned towards the Hill.

nineteen

The top of Witch Hill was quiet in the still evening. As the last of
the sun's rays lingered on the grass, Capricorn felt the first faint
chill. Summer is over, he thought. The nights are drawing in.

He strode quickly to the place he had marked. One of his sticks
had already fallen into the long grass, but he found the ditch easily.
Its position was etched into his mind. Pushing the fronds and nettles
aside, he thrust his way through. It was as he had guessed and Wyatt
had confirmed. He was in a dark cave, almost completely hidden by
the overhanging lip at the entrance.

The torch he had brought with him was powerful and flashed a
bright beam of light round the cave. It was not as dismal as it had
first appeared. The walls were whitish, sand and chalk. The bottom
of the cave was dry; water would not settle here. Amazing, the way
it was hidden almost at the crown of the hill. He was a tall man, but
it was almost high enough, at the far end, for him to stand upright.

Lover's Lips, Garry had called it, laughing. No one else knew of it, he had said. He had discovered the place by accident one afternoon when he had dropped his cigarette lighter in the grass and gone groping after it. This was where Garry and Linda had spent their stolen hours, comfortable enough, no doubt, in summer weather.

Finding it, however, had not solved his problem after all. There was nowhere here that the murderer could have been hidden from the young lovers, even though they were interested only in each other. He felt a sharp stab of disappointment. The walls and roof were made of the same smooth chalk. He prowled round but there was nothing to see. Certainly not the gun, which he had suspected might still lie hidden here.

Yet the murderer must have come from the cave. It was the only answer to the puzzle. Why there, he had thought when he first saw the murdered man. The cave answered that question. Why then, had been the other. If someone had been waiting in the cave, the answer was simple. Brewster, leaving his house at seven, would have been expected just at that point by half past. The would-be killer had only to lie low in the ditch outside until Brewster passed by, shoot from behind him, and scuttle back into the cave. The exposure would have been very short.

Nevertheless, his theory must be wrong. Linda had left at about ten past; Wyatt had stood smoking just outside until at least seven fifteen. Then Jed had appeared and walked with him back to the stables. They had seen no one come up and hide in the cave. From the crown of the hill they would have seen for a considerable distance; if Brewster had left just a few minutes earlier they must have seen him.

Noreen Stacy had come shortly after Brewster. She had had to cover a greater distance, but she was running. And Venable had timed the shots at seven thirty. Alone in the cave with no one to watch, Capricorn allowed himself the luxury of a worried frown. If Griswald knew all of this, and that the nest of perjurers had not been taken into custody, he would be entitled to think Scotland Yard most careless. Had Venable lied?

Capricorn's mind raced, but he had come to an impasse. Theories were fine, he thought ruefully, but as far as any proof was concerned he was no further along than when the investigation had started. And now even the theory itself did not hold. Perhaps he should have called his Chief, he thought with sudden doubt, and tried to stop this wholesale exodus of Siderea, since he seemed to be back at the beginning.

Dejection came upon him until he took hold of himself. As an experienced detective he knew just what to do when his mind could go no further and emotion balked: he went back to work. Picking up the flashlight, he went around the cave again, but he saw nothing. Back at the entrance, he leaned out for a little air—only lovers could have found the cave pleasant for very long—his torch still in his hand. As the beam of light fell across the grass, about a foot from the corner of the lip something glistened.

Idly he stretched his hand out and picked it up. His casual glance grew keen and he shone the torch directly on it to make quite sure he was not mistaken, that wishful thinking was not deceiving him. It was a small object, two and a half inches long, less than half an inch across, with a pin attached. A piece of metal, thinly plated—the plate had worn off in spots. An emblem, nevertheless, of rank, of high rank, in the Army of the Stars.

Carefully he wrapped it in a handkerchief and wedged it firmly in an inside pocket. He found he felt no surprise. Part of his problem was solved, but what of the rest? Invigorated by success, he turned back to the cave. He had to be right. Someone with a gun had been in that cave and, unless that one could move round without a body, had been there while Garry and Linda were having their misunderstanding.

With the light touch he had learned long ago as a magician, Capricorn tapped over the walls and floor of the cave laboriously, inch by inch, but it was solid, with no gaps or cracks. Sighing, he worked his way to the very back of the cave and flashed his light methodically to and fro. Suddenly he exclaimed and stepped forward in excitement. The back wall was a slightly different colour from the rest; it was grey, and to his fingers' touch of a different texture, not powdery but rough and dense.

He moved his palm over it curiously. Yes, it was convex, and it did not seem to be part of the original structure of the cave. To one side there was a small space where it gaped away from the wall. He cast a beam of light through the aperture but he could only see the floor of the cave extending beyond, out of sight. He grinned to himself in triumph. There could have been another person in the cave besides Wyatt and Lavender. A small person could have got through that space, after hiding behind the rock until the lovers left. The murderer must have chafed at hearing the voices of Wyatt and Frost outside the cave so close to half past seven. Still, Capricorn had to make sure. He had to get round that rock.

'I hope you don't get too big,' his father, The Great Capricornus, had told him sternly, for he was already tall for his age at eleven years old. 'In our business it can be a nuisance.'

Well, he had. Six foot four, the pride of the Force. The rock, or boulder, for that was what it now appeared to be, slithered and shook a little as he squeezed his large frame somehow through the space, trying to collapse himself like a cat, wondering how on earth those fortunate felines did it with hardly a ruffling of fur. His sleeve was torn by the time he came out on the other side and he had a nasty graze on his neck. The boulder wobbled again.

Steady, he thought, and swore to himself. He didn't want that thing rolling after him. He flashed his light onto the back. It had fitted very well into the space, but on this side the ground sloped away under his feet and the rock, once dislodged, could well come thundering down. He looked round at the true back of the cave. There was a layer of blue flint here, occasionally yellowed with what might have been iron pyrite. Fools' gold.

Well, whatever it was, this wasn't a fool's errand after all, he rejoiced. His point was proven. Plenty of room for a killer to have waited here, perhaps spying on the lovers, enjoying who knows what kind of degraded pleasure, or perhaps merely fretting until they left, afraid that they would stay too long and Brewster pass by unharmed.

Capricorn pondered, the torch hanging slackly in his grasp. The letter had been delivered somewhere between half past six and a quarter to seven. Yet Garry and Linda had been in the cave since shortly after six. Capricorn had believed the person who delivered the letter and the armed killer to be the same. Physically, though, that was impossible. If the killer had hidden in the back of the cave, the hiding was done before six.

While he stood absorbed, puzzling over the discrepancy, he heard a footfall in the front of the cave. He looked through the crack to see who had followed him, but there wasn't enough light to make out more than a sturdy figure stooping. He lifted his torch and clicked it on but he saw only purple boots and red tights when the figure hurled itself forward, pushing at the stone. He reached out to catch whoever it was; his fingers grasped an arm, but the figure pulled

226

back sharply, the stone shifted, and the sleeve tore, leaving him grasping a piece of cloth while his assailant bolted. Capricorn made to lunge forward but the stone was dislodged and rolling and he jumped back in an awkward reflex. His groping feet stepped onto nothing and he felt himself falling, and the stone was falling, and he was hit a great crack on the head, and his feet stumbled onto something and then he fell further, the darkness moved eerily around him. He was very sick, he fell again, and then there was blackness and nothing at all.

Sometime later—he didn't know if it was minutes or hours—he came to, still sick and with a roaring headache, but as he found after a swift exploration, otherwise intact. He would have a large bump on his head where the boulder had struck him, but it didn't feel like anything more than that. Whatever he had hurtled down, the boulder hadn't followed him all the way. Somehow he had only received a glancing blow.

He looked about painfully as well as he could in the dark. His torch had fallen on the upper level. He found a match in his pocket and by its light he looked up into a neck-like passage stretching vertically overhead. About sixteen feet above him he could just make out the boulder, providentially wedged in a narrow spot that had most likely saved his life.

Whoever had pushed the stone had probably run off. Capricorn wondered if the intruder had known who was there, or if panic had followed discovery by anyone. His car was outside but it wasn't an official car. Yes, it might have been a moment's fear, and not necessarily murderous. He himself had not noticed the drop, he thought wryly. Damned fool. He looked for some kind of foothold on the walls above. On the right-hand side of the shaft he could make out small, worn ledges cut into the chalk. They were never meant for a man of his size; more for someone like Jed Frost, he thought. Determined, he bent down, which added to the excruciating pain in his head, and took his boots off. Carefully he moved from ledge to ledge, the cold chalk scraping unpleasantly against him. His loathing for dark, hidden places rose in him fiercely enough to cloud his brain but he pushed it aside. This was no time for neurotic whims, he told himself savagely, with a murderer out there ready to his hand.

From the top ledge he could reach the boulder easily. Digging his heels into the dirt, he reached out and with the full force of his powerful body pushed at the slab. It budged not a fraction of an inch. He pushed again, and then again. He began to sweat as he realized he could push no harder, and the monstrous stone was wedged solidly into the neck of the cave. And if he could lift it, he realized with horror, it would be no use. It was nowhere near the top of the neck; he remembered how far he had fallen before he was hit. He could only get up by carrying it Atlas-like on his back while his toes scrabbled for a foothold on the tiny ledges in the smooth sheer walls.

His whole body was slithery now with sweat. He wiped his hands and forehead and as he did his elbow brushed the chalk, making a whispering noise. At the same moment he fancied he heard another sound or did he? Was someone up there? He called, although the shouting hurt his head. He called again. There was no reply. Then he heard the sound again. Someone had approached and withdrawn; returned to see if he were still trapped, no doubt. Superintendent Capricorn, son of the Great Capricornus himself, had been buried.

In sudden rage he leaned forward and thrust against the maddening obstacle. He pushed again and again with both hands and all the strength of his muscles, pushed with all the power he could command. The stone stayed in place and he gave one last, furious thrust. Still the stone was unmoving but his toehold crumbled beneath him and he fell once more. he tried to protect his head, but it struck an abutting stone just before he reached the bottom of the pit. He rolled over a few times and then, once again, lay still.

When he recovered his rage had gone. He felt very ill indeed. The sound he had heard from above, the shuffling of booted feet, echoed in his mind; pictures of Garry and Linda drifted before him, jumbled together with the dank smell and rough surface of the floor of the cave under his hands. The cave. 'The caverned mansion of the Bride of Death.' Rose was quoting from the Antigone, and he was back in Brewster House and Richard Brewster was alive.

Coldly some governing part of his mind gathered up his scattered senses. There was no time for a wandering consciousness; a murderer was on the loose. Lifting his wrist, he checked the luminous dial of his watch. Unless it had broken in his fall—it still seemed to be ticking—not much time had elapsed. He had been lying unconscious this second time for about fifteen minutes, he judged.

Painfully, for his hands were badly scraped, he fumbled for his matches, lit one, and looked in front of him. His heart gave a great leap. Not a cave after all. The trapped man rejoiced; the policeman was more coolly pleased at the probable answer to a puzzle. What he saw showed that his guess had been right, though it had seemed a hundred-to-one chance—or five-hundred-to-one: longer odds than Frost's Falling Star. The floor and walls stretched before him without an end in sight. A passageway, perhaps an old water course.

There were only a few matches left and he needed to be sparing, but as he walked hunched over through the tunnel he lit another to be certain. Yes, a series of natural caves in the chalk had been connected and strengthened by man. Here and there an upright beam was set along the side, and split tree trunks mouldered overhead.

'Priests' holes,' the Rector had said, 'Underground passages. Absurd tales.'

But there had been a passage, possibly more than one. The chalk crumbled beneath his feet at a dip in the path, and he saw that someone had laid planking over the rough stretch. He expended another match, examining it. The planks were of a different era from the old uprights; boards cut by machine, modern in type though already rotting underneath. When had they been put there, he wondered, twenty, thirty years ago? Longer that that? The old Witch Hill Manor, with the religious troubles of its inhabitants, had been gone for centuries. He sighed, and his head ached sickeningly. If it hadn't been for that fall, he thought, vexed, as he groped his way along, at least he would know the direction he was going in. What a fool he would look if he came out into Mrs Anthony's private bath. He wondered if that would shake the lady's impregnable calm. Probably not.

He seemed to have been walking for a long time. He checked his watch: unless it was running slow, it had only been ten minutes. The air smelled like the earthen walls, as though it were the same substance, only less dense. He sneezed, shuddering, and the pain reverberated through his skull as though that skull were acres across instead of inches.

The passage narrowed again and his heart kicked against his chest as he thought he might be trapped again. He squeezed through, ripping his coat to tatters and scraping the skin of his cheek. How far had he walked? He tried to think, but it was hard to concentrate as the dark, the dust, and the oppressiveness of the tunnel caused the slow tide of fear to rise again.

Claustrophobia, he told himself firmly, was an infantile manifestation. He'd end up being treated by a doctor who'd ask him personal questions about his feeling for his mother. But his mother had died in childbirth and his father had wanted him to spend his life escaping from coffins buried underground.

He forced his mind to stop racing and concentrated on keeping his body moving forward at a steady pace. One match left. One match left. He must save it and go on walking. Carefully, steadily. Probably not far now, he consoled himself. He wondered where the tunnel came out and closed his mind against the possibility of coming up under the foundation of the present Witch Hill Manor. If it had been a water course, he told himself, it would run the other way down to the Baring.

He had left his boots back under the cave. His feet were sore from walking over pebbles and rough patches; his socks were in shreds. As something sharp bit into his bare heel he almost walked on, but it was too sharp for a pebble and he paused to pick it up. He was not going to use up his last match but he felt it carefully. It was metal, about an inch long, rolled, with one blunt end and the other torn and sharp. Wet, too; it had drawn his blood. He put it away in his pocket, next to the shiny bar he had found outside the cave. He realized he had dropped the piece of cloth he had pulled from the Siderean uniform—someone else could come back and find that.

The darkness was thick and seemed palpable. He walked on and on. His weakness was growing and his dizzy moments came more often. Fear came too, in the darkness, that he might walk into yet another pit, and he began feeling the walls beside him and kicking out in front before he stepped to test the safety of the passage. His arms and legs soon ached abominably. As he was wondering just how much further he could go, his foot struck wood in front of him. He reached forward and felt the smooth, polished surface: a door. He had come to the end of the passage.

Eagerly he felt around and found the latch. He tugged, but nothing happened. He struck his last match with care. A very solid-looking door barred the way. There was a heavy brass lock, turned dark green, under his hand. Whoever had mounted that lock had meant to keep intruders out. It was a sound piece of work still and quite obviously locked from the other side.

He called out without much hope, and his voice seemed to die around him. There would be no one on the other side of the door to hear, even should his voice penetrate. Passages like this would come out into a cellar or some out-of-the-way place. He didn't want to think it, but the thought came up and swallowed him. Whoever had pushed the boulder to the neck of the cave had done a thorough job of work. Whether Capricorn had found the passageway or not, he was trapped: a tight-wedged boulder on one end and a heavy locked door on the other. He was soundly and securely buried. His head buzzed, his nausea mounted, and Superintendent Capricorn was violently sick behind the tight-closed door.

In the dining room at Brewster House the mourners were assembled at the funeral feast. Beatrice Brewster, Dr Bailey, Mrs Lavender and the Rector, Mr and Mrs Norris—the last looking about with great interest—the Hartles, uncle and niece; Christopher Venable with his parents; a few other notables from the town and Mrs Anthony from the Manor.

Rose Lavender looked at her watch, set in a plain gold bracelet that glistened on her black chiffon sleeve. It was almost nine o'clock. It made no sense, she thought, but she felt just as she had done the night that Richard—she didn't want to think of that. Now, when she had expected to feel grief, what she felt again was—what? Apprehension. But why?

It's because Merle isn't here, she thought. He said he would try to come and I was sure he'd be here. Mrs Anthony said something about an arrest. It's almost nine. Why isn't Superintendent Capricorn here, she wanted to say aloud, but people would think it strange. Beatrice would be offended. And Beatrice herself was acting strangely enough; there was no sense adding to it.

It was the same as the day that Richard died. They had been very late then, waiting to start dinner. Today they had come back from the funeral, she and Beatrice and the Rector and Mr Hartle in the black, horse-drawn carriage that had come, so slowly, up the drive. Beatrice had seemed quite well then, but she herself had felt faint and had been glad of the Rector's arm to lean on.

But before all the guests had collected, Beatrice had suddenly announced that she felt ill and had to go to her room for a while. The mourners had gathered in the drawing room and wandered onto the terrace in the pleasant summer evening. It had been fully half-past eight before the big double doors to the dining room had been opened and the buffet dinner served to the guests, some of whom were hungry and all were thirsty and rather weary by then.

Beatrice had joined them, looked decidedly eccentric. She had taken off the plain, decent black coat and skirt that she had worn to the cemetery and, perhaps for comfort, had changed to a jacket and a pair of trousers. The costume might have been something left over from the war, but though the garments were curiously unfashionable Rose could see that they were new—bought, perhaps, for the occasion. For a moment Rose wondered if Beatrice had been drinking alone, as her cheeks had a high flush, but surely that was unthinkable. Grief, she mused, took different people in different ways.

To Rose's relief, Beatrice had been tolerable to Mrs Norris, and when the odd but quite pleasant Mrs Anthony from the Manor had called with her condolences and to say good-bye Beatrice had been unexpectedly genial, and invited her to stay to dinner. But to Christopher Venable who had come, in ordinary dress, with his parents to do honour to his kinsman and benefactor, Beatrice's behaviour could only be described as intolerably rude.

She had alternately ignored him and called him absurd names—Mr Beverage and Mr Fumble were only two—and generally behaved as if she considered him an outsider and an intruder. Perhaps she was thinking that Christopher would inherit Brewster House on her death. As if that could *matter*, Rose thought in dismay. His mother, a courteous, gentle woman had been disturbed, but Christopher himself had behaved with a surprising maturity, not reacting to Beatrice's hostile manner and continuing to treat her as his respected hostess and the bereaved sister of his cousin. Perhaps Siderea helped one to handle peculiar people.

Beatrice had been even stranger when dear Linda and Garry had stopped in for a moment to offer their condolences. She had stared at Linda's ring and rushed over to Mr Hartle and shouted into his ear, so that even in the general hum of talk people had looked round in surprise. Of course, if she had guessed about the little ceremony that afternoon, on the very day of the funeral, she would certainly consider it in very bad taste; as indeed it was, Rose admitted to herself, trying to be fair.

She watched Beatrice, still flushed, talking louder than usual, in a rather hectoring tone. Beatrice had taken an extra glass or two of wine with her dinner, Rose fancied, and it was not becoming. Standing by the open window now, talking with the Rector and Mr Norris, smoking a small cigar, she looked for all the world like the *man* of the house, small as she was. Rose dismissed the notion as absurd.

Three minutes to nine. The tragedy of the house was over; she couldn't understand why the feeling of apprehension grew so strong. No one would thunder on the door again to announce a death. Whomever Merle was going to arrest, and she could not imagine who it could possibly be unless it were that unpleasant Jedediah, it couldn't really affect this house. But why didn't Merle come?

Beatrice gestured with her small cigar towards the portrait and laughed that new, uncomfortable laugh. Some tale of her mother, whom Rose had often suspected of not being too nice. She had planned to take that portrait down in the days when—Really, if she didn't know how heart-broken Beatrice was, she would consider that she looked like a general after a successful battle. Where was Merle?

From the bottom of the gardens, towards the river, she could hear the song of a linnet rising sweet and pure above the muted chatter in the house. Soaring up, lilting and curiously sad, just as she had heard it on the night that Richard—Her palms were clammy, and yet she felt hot. She fumbled for her handkerchief and felt something strangely like panic rising.

Merle, she thought, Merle, wherever you are, please hurry. Come, Merle, come now.

Merle Capricorn, leaning half-conscious behind the tight-locked, bolted, heavy wooden door, raised his head slowly. He felt as though someone had poured a bucket of water over his head. He was a policeman with a job to do, and fortunately this time he was the one person who could handle this. He was not the son of the Great Capricornus for nothing.

The last match was burned out, but with the fear induced by claustrophobia mastered, he needed no light for what he had to do. His hands went to the lock and tapped round it. A heavy affair, not built in the twentieth century, but he had handled locks far more sturdy than that. His only problem would be if age and damp had warped the metal so that the mechanism jammed tight. But he doubted it. This door had been used recently; he would swear to it. He took his penknife and with the small pointed blade probed carefully. If anyone were to ask him how this was done, he reflected, he couldn't tell them. He had forgotten. But the memory was in his fingers and they moved as if by themselves, and his ear picked up the sound of the moving tumblers.

'You'll make a lot more money breaking out of prisons than putting people in them,' his father had said gloomily, when Capricorn first broached the subject of joining the police. His father had been right, of course, though Capricorn had not cared about that. His skill was still there, though. He would make a good cat burglar, he thought, his heart racing a little as he felt the pins give gently under his probe and the lock sprang free.

Free! He was exultant. In another moment he would be out of this pestilential grave that someone had planned for him: the murderer who had intended a double killing. The dank, fetid smell of burial would be out of his nostrils and the killer his for the taking. Joyous, he pushed the door, but to his surprise and growing dismay it did not give. It was still shut tight. His hands went back to the lock, but he had not been mistaken. The lock was open. The door had been bolted fast from the other side.

Some of the guests had already said good-bye. Mr and Mrs Venable had gone, though Christopher remained, the aura of the heir of the house already plain about him. Mr Norris had shown signs of wanting to leave, but Mrs Norris, resplendent in black and puce, looked as though wild horses—or Norris's car with its tamed power of a hundred horses—couldn't drag her from the drawing room.

'I won't be invited again,' she had said in a loud stage whisper. 'Not until young Christopher moves in.'

Beatrice must have heard, Rose thought uncomfortably, but she had made no sign. She stood still in the centre of a group of men, with Dr Bailey to one side and the Rector pinned to her left, still telling stories, not of her brother, as might have been supposed, but of Lucrezia, her adventures and her wit.

Rose's heart felt cold. Something had happened to Merle, she was sure, or he would have been there. He had gone to arrest a murderer. Could the same man have struck again, and Merle be lying somewhere as Richard had done? She shook herself, trying to get rid of such sick fancies. It would be better if she talked to the Rector, such a good, dear man, but Beatrice was not going to let her audience leave. She clutched him by the sleeve of his coat. Well, she was chief mourner.

If Merle would only come she would leave herself. The atmosphere of Brewster House, which she had always loved, tonight was sour and evil. It was only her imagination, but even the food and wine seemed tainted, and the air that flowed in so sweetly from the gardens was rank in her nostrils, sour with the smell of Beatrice's cigar.

Beatrice waved the cigar again in the direction of the portrait. She had the attention now of everyone in the room, and all the guests looked at the figure of Lucrezia: drawn towards it as if hypnotized by the enigmatic, smiling figure in the ornate gold frame, they gazed upward helplessly.

Capricorn had returned to work coldly and determinedly. The bolt would be a little harder, but no bolt had ever defeated his father, and this bolt would not defeat him. The image in his mind that he had been trying to hold back had forced itself forward, but he had conquered that wretched memory; he had a purpose and a plan.

It wasn't really a lock or bolt that had caused his father's entrapment and death. He had been doing his highest paid performance at a fairground: burial in a coffin sunk into a lake. For the Great Capricornus it was safe enough. The coffin was easy to unscrew, and a couple of pony tanks of compressed air with a regulator, all especially manufactured to fit into the space, were stowed away in a false bottom. To make it more impressive, the onlookers were kept standing about for fifteen minutes after the contraption was sunk, during which time his assistant would show great anxiety and build up tension, while the Great Capricornus leisurely released himself.

He had done the trick many times and complained that it was dull. The lake, pond, or river, whatever was being used, would be tested in advance to find a good solid bottom without too much mud; at the last minute a wire was attached by the assistant as the coffin was lowered, so that in case of any trouble as he got out he could pull the wire and be hauled up to the boat waiting above.

He had thought of everything, except what happened. The Great Capricornus, not yet fifty, had had a heart attack. The doctors said afterwards it must have come as soon as he hit bottom. He had never got to the air tank, never opened the screws or pulled the wire. He had suffocated.

Capricorn literally shook himself. No use thinking of that. He chipped away the wood of the door steadily, a little at a time. The wood had been thick and solid, but age and damp had done its work and he made good headway.

In a compartively short time he had whittled away enough to get his finger and thumb through. Squeezing on the metal rod he pushed it, little by little, towards the door's hinges. When it had moved, he began on the top bolt. It was a little more difficult, working from underneath, but the end was near, now, and his determination pushed him faster. At last he heard the final click as he pushed the last bolt free.

The door opened slowly, the hinges stiff with rust. There was still no light and he felt about cautiously. He was in a tiny chamber about three feet square. Three sides were smooth, but the fourth side—his excitement rose—the fourth side was a stairway. He felt the treads and risers cautiously. They were smooth, wooden, and in good condition. Carefully, quietly—easy in his stockinged feet—he groped his way up, round the closely twisting spiral. The staircase was high and steep; he seemed to have been climbing a long time, when with one last twist the stairway ended.

In front of him was a wall. At first it seemed smooth, but then his exploring hands found a panel that ran about seven feet high, he judged as he felt over his head, and about four or five feet wide. He could find no latch, but as he leaned against the door it gave a little with his weight. Exhilaration bubbled up inside him. Whoever had bolted the door below had been sure it would hold and had left the last exit unbarred. One strong push, he promised himself, and he would be free. He patted his pocket with the Siderean bar and the small metal cylinder that he'd found. Unless the gun was recovered, these might be his only proofs. He put his shoulder to the door, prepared for an effort, but it yielded at a touch.

Slowly at first, he pushed the panel forwards and sideways, lest the murderer be waiting ready to spring. The light came in, dazzling him for a moment. He saw the gleam of a fine wooden bannister and rail, a stretch of beautifully polished old wooden parquet, on which his feet looked grotesque, half naked in filthy, torn socks. Beyond the bannister, below the balcony was the Brewster dining room and the assembled guests, staring at him, mouths agape, as if he were Frankenstein's monster come to life.

Rose, who, like the others, had been staring up at the portrait, thought at first it was her dizziness and blurred vision that caused it to seem to move, and she had shaken her head to clear it. Stlll the portrait nightmarishly continued to swing forward and out, revealing a dark open space in the wall. I really am going quite mad, she thought, bewildered, and turned to Beatrice to relieve her heated fancy by the vision of someone solid and unfancial, but Beatrice at that moment was touching her wine goblet to Mrs Anthony's, smiling with a peculiarly Borgia-like expression, much too unapproachable for someone like herself. Just then Beatrice followed Mrs Anthony's gaze upwards to the moving portrait.

It really *was* moving. Beatrice's smile was frozen and her eyes grew enormous. Then, in a fraction of a second, from nowhere, Merle Capricorn stood in that very spot where the portrait had been; Merle, gazing down, looking ten feet tall, dark, dishevelled, with some controlled fire blazing, staring at Beatrice and her heavy shoes that were well cleaned but tied with old shoe laces that had one tab missing. How like his father he is! she thought, bemused, and later reproached herself, for she missed seeing Beatrice, who uttered an odd little cry, almost a whinny, like a startled mare. Suddenly she darted from the drawing room to the hall and in an instant, before Merle had jumped down from the balcony, she was back, holding the Sèvres vase in her arms like a baby.

Merle landed in the dining room lightly for such a big man, and surefooted as a cat. The crystal goblets on the sideboard only shivered and sighed. Beatrice's short hair stood on end. Her face was dead white and her eyes sank blackly into her head. With that same odd, whinnying sound she turned as Merle moved forwards; she was on the terrace, her voice rising horribly; she ran between the columns, seeming for a moment to fly over the escarpment; her trouser caught in the briers and she fell, head first, ten feet to the rose-covered soil below, with an odd, sickening low thud, a shriller scream was swallowed by a strange, gurgling sound, and then silence.

Merle was across the room and at her side before anyone else. How strange and fierce he looks! Rose thought and shivered, an avenging angel, or devil. No, not a spirit but a man, a terrifying man, and she held out her hand to the Rector who immediately was beside her, his arm encircling her waist. She stayed there, her face on his shoulder, not wanting to see or hear.

But some time later she had to hear. Dr Bailey's voice rose strong and clear from the garden.

'There's nothing I can do, Capricorn. Beatrice is dead.'

So I was right, Rose thought, dazed. Death had been waiting, but it was for Beatrice. It's presence had been so strong she had almost smelled it in the air, and she had thought that death had come for Merle.

'You must excuse me, my dear,' the Rector whispered. 'I must go for a moment.'

And the Rector went to join Bailey and the Superintendent while the other guests looked down in horror on the small smashed and broken figure at the foot of the grey stone Virgin, her blood running red over the dark red roses. Mrs Anthony, solemn, stretched out her hands and soundlessly uttered some words in benediction. The Rector looked where Capricorn was reaching into the shattered fragments of the Sèvres vase. The last of the daylight gleamed forlornly on the black metal object carefully held in a handkerchief by the Superintendent. Capricorn nodded to the watching Dr Bailey.

'The Colt .45,' Capricorn said slowly.

Mrs Anthony came down to join them and put both her hands lightly on the body and said a quiet prayer.

'Beatrice,' Dr Bailey said aghast, 'Beatrice.'

Christopher Venable was pale and still.

'Beatrice,' the Rector said sorrowfully, to his friend of over thirty years, 'Beatrice.'

And, taking charge from the policeman, who could do very little now, Geoffrey Theale, who had always, in spite of his profession, been squeamish about blood and death, put his hand on Beatrice's shoulder. Whatever sins she had committed, she was a Christian, and she had died unshriven.

'Send for a priest,' he said, his lips stiff.

And although they were of different faiths, and Beatrice had teased him about it all through their many years of friendship, there, in the garden, before her shocked and horrified friends and guests, he intoned his own prayer, and hoped it would help her soul, perhaps still fluttering close about them.

'Requiescat in Pace; Requiescat in Pace.' And, as there was no Catholic present to make the sign of the Cross, the stoutly Protestant Rector knelt close to the body and crossed himself.

'Go forth, O Christian soul, out of this world . . .'

Dr Bailey turned away and looked at Capricorn in disbelief.

'I can't believe it,' he said. 'I can't believe that Beatrice killed her brother.'

Capricorn was sombre.

'I was too late, once again,' he answered. 'It seems I always arrive too late at Brewster House. I could have told Beatrice, if only I could have stopped her. Miss Brewster did not kill her brother.'

Epilogue

Year 3, A.S.
Autumn

It was over three weeks before the inquest took place on Beatrice Marquisio, known as Beatrice Brewster. Capricorn, who was needed as a witness, travelled down alone. He and Sergeant Copper were already deep into another case, involving an international swindler who sold stolen stocks and bonds and annoyingly got himself murdered in a West End hotel. Copper was still shocked to discover that Beatrice had planned her brother's murder.

'The old girl with the garden,' he said in disbelief—he had had to take her statement while she was snipping dead heads off of her roses. 'Would've sworn it was the Yank. Just like them, getting girls in trouble,' he added unfairly, as Garry and Linda were by then properly married and, fast as these things were done nowadays, already safely ensconced in Texas. Capricorn piously hoped that Copper would behave as properly in like circumstance, but forbore to ask. 'The one bleeding place we didn't look for that gun,' Copper, who had done a good deal of the looking, said gloomily. 'Brewster 'ouse itself. In a flower pot in the garden,' for so he described the Sèvres vase.

'Most ballsed-up job I ever was on,' he nursed his grievance. 'Thought from the start there was more than one of 'em in it, but two different lots like that—and you don't think the old girl knew about the other one?'

'We'll never be sure,' Capricorn said slowly, 'but I don't think so. She went back for the gun, you see, and found it where she'd left it. If she hadn't been so certain of her guilt, I don't think she'd have made that frenzied dash at the last. She was too late arriving at the inquest to hear the medical evidence, and I don't suppose that anyone would have mentioned the two wounds in her presence. Everyone wanted to spare her feelings,' he added, with a shrug for the irony.

''Strewth.' Copper seemed unable to express his displeasure. It wasn't his moral sense that was outraged, his superior noted, but his sense of order. It had been an *untidy* case.

Copper's lower lip was pushed forward.

'You wouldn't have known Stacy'd killed him yourself if you hadn't found that bit of rubbish from the Barmy Army,' he judged.

'No,' Capricorn said, 'I was glad to find it, but Noreen had given herself away. She said nothing about hearing the shots, but she would have to have heard them on the Witch Hill road. She'd told so many lies, she just forgot to explain that.'

'Saw him wounded and finished him off,' Copper shook his head, 'like he was a rabbit or something.'

The Siderea habit of confession had proven fortunate for the Yard. When she was arrested, Noreen had made a very clear statement. She had heard the first shot, seen the injured man on the ground, and looked for the attacker, who had mysteriously disappeared. She had had a glimpse of a small figure in the ditch and followed. It wasn't until she found the gun Beatrice had dropped in front of the boulder that she had the idea of finishing the job on her imagined enemy.

'We might have screwed it down before,' Capricorn jibed mildly, 'if the search party hadn't been afraid of getting their little hands dirty.'

Noreen had told him that after spending precious time replacing the gun, she had panicked when she noticed the cartridge cases and just scooped them up and ran with them until she came to the excavation, which had proved a successful hiding place.

Copper made a noise indicating his disgust.

'We went all over that bloody 'ole. Dug the whole thing up—my back's still killing me from all that crawling around. A bad luck 'ole that was from the start.'

Jed Frost would have agreed with him.

'You'd have had to sieve for those shells,' Copper went on, aggrieved. 'We were looking for the gun. She might just as well left them where they were.'

Capricorn nodded.

'She wasn't thinking clearly. If we'd found them on the Manor grounds it would've implicated Siderea at once.'

'Her counsel will say there was no premeditation,' Copper brooded. 'You see. Even though she threatened Brewster for months.'

'She'll get a long prison term in any event,' Capricorn said soberly.

'Make no difference to her,' Copper was unappeased. 'She'll live better in prison than she did up there with that mob. You know what she's doing? Happy as a lark, she is. Organizing a new chapter of Siderea in prison. "Stars Behind Bars," she calls it. At least the old girl felt guilty.'

The inquest was sedately hurried through with as little sensation as possible. Accidental death had been the verdict, which was probably correct. Beatrice's part in her brother's death had had to be exposed, however, and the town was duly shocked. It was consoling itself by remembering that she had been a foreigner. Not really a Brewster at all. And it felt justified in its dislike of Siderea, for one of them had proved to be a killer as it had supposed.

Capricorn had spoken to Sir Harvey Read, the famous alienist, about that.

'Do you think that Siderea affected Stacy's mind? Or was she the type to commit murder anyway, when she was roused to such a passion and the opportunity so easy to hand?'

Sir Harvey had been professionally delighted with the Brewster case.

'The Witches of Witch Hill,' he murmured. 'Extremely interesting. Two cases of hysteria, quite distinct, bouncing off one another like that. As for Stacy being a type,' he shrugged, 'you did find some history there.'

For Capricorn had had a long letter of regret, after Noreen's confession, from Mrs Anthony. What she had been keeping back was her knowledge of an instability in Noreen, murderous rages she had had as a child, which had of course been revealed in Siderea's own Confessional.

'We were sure she had been cured,' Mrs Anthony had written, 'but some good has come of it all, after all,' she went on with the Siderean's incurable optimism. 'Noah has developed another Path, for her type of case, and such a thing will never happen again.'

He was glad that Mrs. Anthony was pleased. He hadn't added to her woe by telling her that Noreen had tried to immure him in another crime of opportunity, like the first. It would only end in Hightower developing another Path for that. As it was, Siderea was going to help Noreen with the new chapter. Capricorn could foresee her promotion to general again before she was convicted.

'A Nietzschean philosophy like that might provide a sanction,' Sir Harvey shrugged, 'but I would be inclined to blame the glands, not the Guru.'

He enjoyed his little witticism.

'Coming back from losing her lover, finding the other witch making the attempt, and then leaving the gun—ordinary enough, when you think of it. Emotionally that is. The truly interesting thing, of course, is that the Brewster woman, however she felt, would probably never have made the attempt except for the Sidereans threatening murder. It must have seemed the perfect cover. I wish I'd had a chance to see her. Emotionally infantile, I would venture to guess. Pre-puberty.'

'Pre-puberty?'

'Yes,' Sir Harvey nodded, stroking his chin in a manner so familiar from his many court appearances. 'Her attachment still to her mother, though the mother rejected her and died over twenty years ago. No involvement with the opposite sex—or even her own, in that way.'

He smiled, peering through his old-fashioned metal-rimmed spectacles that had suddenly become modern, like his Athenian attitude to sex.

'A curious attachment,' Sir Harvey went on, 'transferred to a house. As though she felt she somehow subsumed her mother, as long as she was the only female Brewster at Brewster House. A plain woman, you say. And the third witch that started it all, the Lavender, so beautiful.'

'Mrs. Lavender is hardly a witch,' Capricorn protested strongly.

'Isn't she?' Sir Harvey shrugged. 'Didn't she enchant a settled bachelor of fifty-five and begin the whole drama? A kindly witch, a beautiful witch, but a witch.'

Capricorn was rebellious. If there was a third, beautiful witch he would have named Lucrezia, who had stunted the lives of the young people in her care and caused the middle-aged explosions of passion and hate. His Chief had wondered about her.

'Fine old family, the Marquisios. Never knew Mrs Lucrezia, but I'd met a cousin of theirs, Guido Marquisio, in Rome. A little eccentric. Suppose there could have been insanity, somewhere, in the blood. . . .'

'A pathetic creature, Beatrice Brewster,' Sir Harvey had summed up from his height of omniscience, 'Pathetic.'

And she was, the policeman thought, remembering the crumpled figure with its brains stove in by Lucrezia's granite virgin. Then he remembered Richard Brewster, who had not been insane, or childish, and who had given much to his country, his family and his friends, and Capricorn thought of that life cut off; the body, in his mind still lying on the crown of Witch Hill, one eye staring sightlessly at the stars.

'. . . none shall entomb him or mourn
but leave unwept, unsepulchered, a grisly feast for birds . .'

Capricorn shivered a little as he walked through the High Street. His car was garaged in London, and he had come down by train. He had half intended to go and take a last look at Brewster House, shuttered and closed now, Hartle had told him, until the lawyers were finished and young Christopher decided what to do with it. But a cold wind had sprung up and the day seemed suddenly too dreary for so long a walk.

The last three weeks had made a great change in Daines Barington. Autumn had come swiftly; not the gentle golden autumn that sometimes graces England, but a grey forerunner of winter. The last summer flowers had withered and gone. Chrysanthemums died in bud from the sudden sharp frosts. All up and down the High Street not a flicker of colour was to be seen. The townspeople were already dressed in sober winter clothes. And the scarlet and purple of Siderea was on its way to being forgotten.

The wind blew and a few brown, dried leaves swept along in the gutter. Much had happened in three weeks. The Manor was empty. The town, as represented by Norris as acting head of the Council, was buying it for resale as a nursing home of a very superior kind.

The Superintendent paused outside the Emanuel Church. The Moo-Cow was already closed, the odour of frying fat quite gone, and a notice neatly placed over the window bore a sign 'For Rent.' He could have gone and looked once more at St Cuthbert's, but the Rector would not be there. The day after Brewster's funeral old Sir Walter Theale had died at last from an overdose of drugs, the picture papers had hinted. Theale was now Sir Geoffrey and a rich man, and as good fortune, like trouble, does not come singly, he had been offered a dean's hat and was already off to the lovely cathedral city of Cicester. And the third part of the former Rector's good fortune had become painfully apparent to Merle Capricorn.

With the Brewster murder solved he had some time for private thoughts and for fond recollections of the lovely Rose. The scene in her little room had come back to his mind insistently and he had wondered, and wondered . . . And he had rung Rose on the telephone from London. It had been Rose who had told him of the Rector's good fortune.

'Oh, he has been so *kind* to me Merle, since Richard—' she had sighed. 'I don't know what Linda and I would have done without him. I must tell you all about it when I see you.' She veered off to another subject. 'Such a pity you couldn't come to Linda's wedding. So beautiful, you know, St Cuthbert's, with the flowers. Linda wore pale yellow, so suitable for autumn,' she said, with relief at having solved a problem that had vexed her mind. 'The two darlings wanted me to go with them to Texas. I will visit, of course, but not quite yet. Perhaps when the baby—There's so much to do. I'm making changes. Mr Hartle is so clever; he's already got a buyer for this house.'

The Lavender house, too, was shuttered and empty. Rose was spending some time in London, buying clothes. She was not saying much about it, she had been fond of Richard Brewster and would show him due respect, but Rose, Capricorn realized ruefully, was a woman meant for marriage and she would be married to someone. He had lost again, before he had even begun his suit. At some time in the spring, he fancied, Rose Lavender, née Rose Raintree, would become Lady Theale. Lady Theale. It suited her, he thought. It had a nice ring to it.

A rotund, pink little man was hurrying by him, carrying a black bag.

'Dr Bailey,' the Superintendent said with pleasure. He had missed him at the inquest as Dr Bailey had testified early and then left.

'Capricorn,' the doctor beamed, their difference over Linda Lavender quite forgotten. 'Good to see you. I suppose this is your last visit to Daines Barington.'

'Unless you have an outbreak of villainy,' Capricorn said with something of a sigh. He had liked Daines Barington, but with Rose gone he would have no connection there.

'I'll walk with you to the station,' Bailey volunteered. 'I'm going down that way. Old Mrs Comfrey at the post office is complaining again of lumbago. You know, Capricorn, all the time the Sidereans were annoying her to distraction, she didn't call me once. Quite a lot of our boredom ailments, always big in a town like this, dropped off considerably. In a way, I'm going to miss them.'

The wind whistled down the street, empty now of all humans except themselves. A sparrow huddled on the cornice of an old grey shop-front, eying Capricorn moodily as if wondering why in creation sparrows didn't go south for the winter.

'And they really did cure some disabilities, I think you said,' the Superintendent remarked, remembering the conversation at Brewster House on the night of the murder.

'Oh, yes, no question, though I wouldn't want to swear to it in court,' Bailey grinned. 'Young Linda only relapsed under great pressure, and she recovered very quickly. And a lot of my own patients that I've never done much with showed remarkable improvement. Even a case of a broken leg that I set for a Siderean healed twice as fast as usual. I don't say it's consistent, and I don't know about a major disease, but Hightower has something, that's certain.'

'Norris seems to think he's gone off with the crown jewels, or the equivalent,' Capricorn replied.

Bailey chuckled.

'Hightower certainly snubbed his bank. But from what rumour tells me—' he looked slyly at Capricorn, 'after his adventures with one Jedediah Frost, the prophet may change his mind about banks.'

Capricorn had been very busy and had quite forgotten the Frosts, although Jed's father, who had proved to be a very decent sort of man, was paying the costs of Noreen Stacy's defense. Dr Bailey made him recall something.

'I've been so darned wrapped up—do you know who won the St Leger?' he asked.

Daines Barington station, empty, it seemed, of all life, was before them, the ticket office closed and shuttered.

'Did you have something on?' Bailey chuckled and Capricorn was resigned to all his patients hearing about the weakness for gambling at Scotland Yard. Capricorn hadn't, but he had mentioned Jed's prediction to Sergeant Copper, who had worn a certain air of satisfaction the last week or so.

'It was an outsider, twenty to one, Falling Star. Never heard of it,' Bailey said ruefully. 'I had a tenner on the favourite. But who can tell?'

Who indeed, Capricorn thought. Unless you have special Recognitions about inter-galactic flows.

'Hightower was generous to the town, after all,' he commented.

'A curious man,' Bailey nodded in agreement. 'Nobody wanted his people here, but—By the way, did that girl try to kill you, too? You never said much that night.'

'According to Miss Stacy, she did not,' Capricorn said, drily. 'She suddenly realized she had lost a shoulder bar and had gone to look for it. Pushing a large boulder at an intrusive representative of Scotland Yard was merely a panic-stricken reflex, she tells me.'

Dr Bailey shook his head.

'In some ways I'm glad they're gone, but it's as though their leaving has created a vacuum in their wake. With Brewster House closed, the Rectory unoccupied—there are rumours it might be secularized, I've heard, and the new Rector given a modern house on the Marlingly Road—that pretty Mrs Lavender gone, now Jasper Norris tells me he's been offered a London branch and Mrs Norris is wild to go—he's in no condition to ride any more so he might be off—the town seems rather lonely.'

His usually cheerful face was wistful.

Capricorn glanced up the track. The train was not in sight. The rails stretched as far as he could see through acres of mouldering, wind-swept leaves, while the trees poked skeletal branches towards a leaden sky. The waiting room was shut and bolted, and the two men propped themselves against the wall. Bailey, with a guilty look, produced a packet of cigarettes and Capricorn, with a shrug for good intentions, took one, and they smoked quietly for a few minutes.

'The worst of it is,' Bailey said, after a while, 'I really miss Beatrice, as well as Richard. I didn't realize it until she—she died—that for about twenty years dining at Brewster House had provided most of the amusement in my life. She was good company, and a wonderful hostess.'

'The Rector told me that,' Capricorn said. 'The same night he suggested that Brewster might have been killed by a relative of an enemy he had killed in the war. Far-fetched, but he so much wanted it to be a stranger. The juxtaposition of words made me think of Beatrice and her admirer, killed in the war. She had such an obvious motive, about to be replaced as she was by her brother's new wife. Yet having met her it was hard to believe that she had actually stood on Witch Hill and, in cold blood, shot her brother—even if he was only a stepbrother.'

'Are you sure it was in cold blood?' Bailey said. 'I don't know. And Richard was partly to blame, in a way.'

'Richard!' Capricorn said, stung, for he did not like to hear the man he thought of as a friend criticized, and so unfairly.

'Only in the way we all were,' Bailey brooded. 'I suppose we hadn't considered Beatrice enough, not realizing how much it meant to her to be Miss Brewster of Brewster House—Oh, I'm not excusing what she did, Superintendent,' he smiled. 'I know it must be the *bête noir* of the police, all crime being considered excusable.'

'It certainly makes life pleasant for criminals,' the Superintendent said drily. 'Or should we call them social allergics?'

'But you see,' Bailey went on earnestly, after a smile for the Newspeak, 'Richard had never shown any signs of even considering marriage until he was fifty-five. Naturally, Beatrice had felt secure in her own world. Daines Barington is known for its old bachelors and spinsters. She must have been sure that her life would always go on exactly as it had, with Richard, in all probability, dying first and leaving Brewster House to her. To be suddenly faced with the loss of everything—which is the way it must have seemed—was just too much. Her sense of reality,' he spoke slowly, 'couldn't take it in. When Richard gave her mother's ruby ring away, and she had to see it worn by another woman, a stranger she despised—I think it was then she lost her mental balance. I don't think she tried to kill Richard in cold blood. And in fact she didn't kill him. She didn't stop to make sure the wound was fatal.'

'She probably heard Noreen Stacy coming up the road,' Capricorn said, his face hard. 'She sent the last letter. She'd copied the Siderean ones but when we found it—still on her desk, by the way under the blotter: she didn't have much fear of the Metropolitan police—it was covered with her fingerprints and there were one or two attempts that she'd discarded, for good measure. And how artfully she managed the alibi: all of you there at the house, and while the Rector was reading she just slipped into the dining room, up the gallery stairs and through the portrait opening. Nobody would wonder where his hostess was just before a meal was to be served. You would naturally assume she was giving instructions in the kitchen. The staff thought she was upstairs. Only Purdy noticed she was missing, but he thought she was having a private drink in her room. She had taken to doing that, it seemed.'

Dr Bailey sighed, downcast.

'If you hurried,' Capricorn went on, 'and were familiar with that old water course, you could get to the Hill much quicker than anyone going by the road; it's more direct. Sergeant Copper timed it. She went and came back and none of you noticed. Later on she changed her shoes.'

'Changed her shoes?' Bailey said, puzzled.

'Her shoes got dusty in the tunnel. She'd also left behind a metal tab from her shoe lace, but I don't think she realized that. She did notice that she'd left the portrait crooked, though. Bailey, I saw her straightening it, and I noticed she had new slippers on, but I didn't add those things up until much later.'

'It was madness,' Bailey said with conviction. 'That covered way to the Hill—Hartle is having it looked into, the Archeological Society is interested, of course. They were talking about tributaries to the Baring, sewers from a manor house that once stood on the hill, old burial mounds, enjoying it enormously when I last looked in. Cursed thing,' he said in disgust, 'With that fantastic stairway—You know Capricorn, that connection must have been made originally with the old farmhouse. Nobody in these parts knew of any Brewster being a secret Catholic; it's amazing. Not mentioned in any of the parish histories. Not like the Manor. When the present Brewster House was built the owner must have had it copied, as some sort of joke, I expect. And then he put the portrait of Cromwell's colonel on the front. An expensive joke, but in those days that wouldn't have mattered.'

'A misfortune for the Brewsters,' Capricorn remarked.

Bailey nodded. The wind blew harder and he tightened his muffler round his neck.

'You think as I do, I see. If it wasn't for that damned passage, I don't think Beatrice would ever have thought of the murder, at least, not to get to the planning stage. It must have played on her imagination over the years. It's most unusual, with the entrance on the first floor. Unique, as far as I know. Damned clever. Soldiers could have poked around in the cellar forever and not found it. Made into the thickness of an inside wall. Amazing! And I know that Richard never suspected it, or old John either.'

'That was probably the point,' Capricorn said. 'I daresay Mrs Lucrezia found it when she took down the portrait of Cromwell's colonel.'

'And ran down the passage to meet young Ron Gaylord, a cosy tête-à-tête away from the eyes and ears of gossips. An attractive man he was. Very different from old John, who was certainly stodgy, though a good sort. They must have used that same cave where Wyatt and Linda—And little Beatrice found it, following her mother. She was always creeping about, watching her, but carefully, because Lucrezia would get furious. Well,' he said resignedly, 'it's all done. But it's given me a strong feeling against the single life, for some reason. And the Rector, you may have heard.'

Capricorn nodded ruefully.

'Yes, I've heard. Doctor, you mustn't wait with me any longer. You're very good but you'll catch a cold, and your patients have to rely on you alone now. No magical incantations from Hightower.'

Bailey laughed.

'Oh, I'm all right. But I will be getting along. As soon as I finish with Mrs Comfrey I'm going to meet a lady at the Town Hall.'

Capricorn looked inquiring.

'Miss Hartle, old Hartle's niece. She was Brewster's secretary. I treated her for shock. Deficient in iron. Badly nourished, too, like a lot of these women.' He blushed. 'I'm taking her to dinner at Roseacre House.'

The Superintendent smiled.

'Well, I hope you enjoy your evening,' he said.

He and Bailey shook hands, and the Superintendent watched the doctor walk back into town, a jaunty figure, and he wished him well. Perhaps some happiness might come from this, after all.

The train sighed its way into the station only ten minutes late and Capricorn jumped into an empty carriage. The line followed the Baring for a way. The river was pewter-coloured and the reeds looked black. It might have been November.

Just as the train, running north, diverged from the river and the road beside it that wound towards the west and Brewster House, a large, black Daimler drove up at a good pace, and Capricorn caught a glimpse of familiar faces--young Christopher and his parents. During the inquest Hartle had whispered that Christopher, to honour his benefactor, was changing his name to Brewster-Venable. And now he was coming to look over his house. It seemed that the Brewsters would continue, after all, in Daines Barington.

The line continued to run straight, by-passing Witch Hill, and the train moved swiftly on to London. Capricorn's mind went on to his new case, and he wondered how Sergeant Copper had fared with the swindler's young secretary. He ventured to suppose he had done well. He usually did. The young hound, he thought in amusement. Falling Star!

Up at Witch Hill Manor the wind blew hard and cold. Empty and boarded up, the main house sturdily withstood the blasts. Earth and dust were swept across the great hole left by Jedediah's builders, and stones and loose pieces of brick rattled across the grass. The birds were silent, hidden in the branches of the almost leafless trees. In the old greenhouse a pane of glass shook and snapped, the shards falling to the platform below where, three years before, Hightower had spoken, giving his long-remembered speech.

The wind howled down, startling a group of squirrels who had ventured through a hole in the boards searching for what might be found. They scattered for a time, and then ventured back cautiously. But there was nothing, nothing at all. The place had been swept clean. There was only the cold grey light, and the wind; and soon night fell, and there was only the wind, and the dark.